Angela Carter's

BOOK OF FAIRY
TALES

Angela Carter's

BOOK OF FAIRY TALES

Edited by Angela Carter

Illustrated by Corinna Sargood

virago

VIRAGO

This edition first published in Great Britain in 2005 by Virago Press
Reprinted 2005 (twice), 2006 (three times), 2007, 2008, 2009 (twice), 2010

First published in two editions as:

The Virago Book of Fairy Tales Collection, Introduction and Notes © Angela Carter 1990
Illustrations © Corinna Sargood 1990

The Second Virago Book of Fairytales Collection © The estate of Angela Carter 1992
Illustrations © Corinna Sargood 1992
Afterword © Marina Warner 1992

Copyright © The estate of Angela Carter 2005

A CIP catalogue record for this book
is available from the British Library.

ISBN 978-1-84408-173-8

Designed by Lore Morton

Typeset in Horley by M Rules
Printed and bound in Great Britain by
Clays Ltd, St Ives plc

Papers used by Virago are natural, renewable and
recyclable products sourced from well-managed forests and certified
in accordance with the rules of the Forest Stewardship Council.

 Mixed Sources
Product group from well-managed
forests and other controlled sources
FSC www.fsc.org Cert no. SGS-COC-004081
© 1996 Forest Stewardship Council

Virago Press
An imprint of
Little, Brown Book Group
100 Victoria Embankment
London EC4Y 0DY

An Hachette UK Company
www.hachette.co.uk

www.virago.co.uk

PUBLISHER'S NOTE

Angela Carter's Book of Fairy Tales brings together two collections of fairy tales that Angela Carter edited, which were published as *The Virago Book of Fairy Tales* (1990) and *The Second Virago Book of Fairy Tales* (1992).

About a month before she died in February 1992, Angela Carter was in the Brompton Hospital in London. The manuscript of the second collection lay on her bed. 'I'm just finishing this off for the girls,' she said. Her loyalty to us was boundless. When we first heard she was ill, we told her not to worry, we had published *The Virago Book of Fairy Tales*, that was enough. But no, Angela claimed it was just the project for an ailing writer to pursue. And so she worked on the book until a few weeks before her death. Though she had collected all the stories, and had grouped them under her chosen headings, she had not yet written an introduction and was unable to finish the notes. Shahrukh Husain, editor of *The Virago Book of Witches*, was able to draw on her own extensive knowledge of folklore and fairy tales to complete the notes including remarks and notes from Angela Carter's own files wherever they were left.

For this new edition we have printed the introduction Angela Carter provided for *The Virago Book of Fairy Tales*. Marina Warner wrote an appreciation of Angela Carter after she died. Published originally as the Introduction to the *The Second Virago Book of Fairy Tales*, it appears now as an Afterword.

Lennie Goodings
Publisher, Virago

CONTENTS

8. STRONG MINDS AND LOW CUNNING

9. UP TO SOMETHING – BLACK ARTS AND DIRTY TRICKS

10. BEAUTIFUL PEOPLE

INTRODUCTION

lthough this is called a book of fairy tales, you will find very few actual fairies within the following pages. Talking beasts, yes; beings that are, to a greater or lesser extent, supernatural; and many sequences of events that bend, somewhat, the laws of physics. But fairies, as such, are thin on the ground, for the term 'fairy tale' is a figure of speech and we use it loosely, to describe the great mass of infinitely various narrative that was, once upon a time and still is, sometimes, passed on and disseminated through the world by word of mouth – stories without known originators that can be remade again and again by every person who tells them, the perennially refreshed entertainment of the poor.

Until the middle of the nineteenth century, most poor Europeans were illiterate or semi-literate and most Europeans were poor. As recently as 1931, 20 per cent of Italian adults could neither read nor write; in the South, as many as 40 per cent. The affluence of the West has only recently been acquired. Much of Africa, Latin America and Asia remains poorer than ever, and there are still languages that do not yet exist in any written form or, like Somali, have acquired a written form only in the immediate past. Yet Somali possesses a literature no less glorious for having existed in the memory and the mouth for the greater part of its history, and its translation into written forms will inevitably change the whole nature of that literature, because speaking is public activity and reading is private activity. For most of human history, 'literature', both fiction and poetry, has been narrated, not written – heard, not read. So fairy tales, folk tales, stories from the oral tradition, are all of them the most vital connection we have with the imaginations of the ordinary men and women whose labour created our world.

For the last two or three hundred years, fairy stories and folk tales have been recorded for their own sakes, cherished for a wide variety of reasons, from antiquarianism to ideology. Writing them down – and especially printing them – both preserves, and also inexorably changes, these stories. I've gathered together some stories from published sources for this book. They are part of a continuity with a past that is in many respects now alien to us, and becoming more so day by day. 'Drive a horse and plough over the bones of the dead,' said William Blake. When I was a girl, I thought that everything Blake said was holy, but now I am older and have seen more of life, I treat his aphorisms with the affectionate scepticism appropriate to the exhortations of a man who claimed to have seen a fairy's funeral. The dead know something we don't, although they keep it to themselves. As the past becomes more and more unlike the present, and as it recedes even more quickly in developing countries than it does in the advanced, industrialized ones, more and more we need to know who we were in greater and greater detail in order to be able to surmise what we might be.

The history, sociology and psychology transmitted to us by fairy tales is unofficial – they pay even less attention to national and international affairs than do the novels of Jane Austen. They are also anonymous and genderless. We may know the name and gender of the particular individual who tells a particular story, just because the collector noted the name down, but we can never know the name of the person who invented that story in the first place. Ours is a highly individualized culture, with a great faith in the work of art as a unique one-off, and the artist as an original, a godlike and inspired creator of unique one-offs. But fairy tales are not like that, nor are their makers. Who first invented meatballs? In what country? Is there a definitive recipe for potato soup? Think in terms of the domestic arts. 'This is how *I* make potato soup.'

The chances are, the story was put together in the form we have it, more or less, out of all sorts of bits of other stories long ago and far away, and has been tinkered with, had bits added to it, lost other bits, got mixed up with other stories, until our informant herself has tailored the story personally, to suit an audience of, say, children, or drunks at a wedding, or bawdy old ladies, or mourners at a wake – or, simply, to suit herself.

I say 'she', because there exists a European convention of an archetypal female storyteller, 'Mother Goose' in English, 'Ma Mère l'Oie' in French, an old woman sitting by the fireside, spinning – literally 'spinning a yarn' as she is pictured in one of the first self-conscious collections of European fairy tales, that assembled by Charles Perrault and published in Paris in 1697 under the title *Histoires ou contes du temps passé*, translated into English in 1729 as *Histories or Tales of Past Times*. (Even in those days there was already a sense among the educated classes that popular culture belonged to the past – even, perhaps, that it *ought* to belong to the past, where it posed no threat, and I am saddened to discover that I subscribe to this feeling, too; but this time, it just might be true.)

Obviously, it was Mother Goose who invented all the 'old wives' tales', even if old wives of any sex can participate in this endless recycling process, when anyone can pick up a tale and make it over. Old wives' tales – that is, worthless stories, untruths, trivial gossip, a derisive label that allots the art of storytelling to women at the exact same time as it takes all value from it.

Nevertheless, it is certainly a characteristic of the fairy tale that it does not strive officiously after the willing suspension of disbelief in the manner of the nineteenth-century novel. 'In most languages, the word "tale" is a synonym for "lie" or "falsehood",' according to Vladimir Propp. '"The tale is over; I can't lie any more" – thus do Russian narrators conclude their stories.'

Other storytellers are less emphatic. The English gypsy who narrated 'Mossycoat' said he'd played the fiddle at Mossycoat's son's twenty-first birthday party. But this is not the creation of verisimilitude in the same way that George Eliot does it; it is a verbal flourish, a formula. Every person who tells that story probably added exactly the same little touch. At the end of 'The Armless Maiden' the narrator says: 'I was there and drank mead and wine; it ran down my mustache, but did not go into my mouth.' Very likely.

Although the content of the fairy tale may record the real lives of the anonymous poor with sometimes uncomfortable fidelity – the poverty, the hunger, the shaky family relationships, the all-pervasive cruelty and also, sometimes, the good humour, the vigour, the straightforward consolations of a warm fire and a full belly – the form of the fairy tale is not usually constructed so as to invite the audience to share a sense of lived experience. The 'old wives' tale' positively parades its lack of verisimilitude. 'There was and there was not, there was a boy,' is one of the formulaic beginnings favoured by Armenian storytellers. The Armenian variant of the enigmatic 'Once upon a time' of the English and French fairy tale is both utterly precise and absolutely mysterious: 'There was a time and no time . . .'

When we hear the formula 'Once upon a time', or any of its variants, we know in advance that what we are about to hear isn't going to pretend to be true. Mother Goose may tell lies, but she isn't going to deceive you in *that* way. She is going to entertain you, to help you pass the time pleasurably, one of the most ancient and honourable functions of art. At the end of the story, the Armenian storyteller says: 'From the sky fell three apples, one to me, one to the storyteller, and one to the person who entertained you.' Fairy tales are dedicated to the pleasure principle, although since there is no such thing as pure pleasure, there is always more going on than meets the eye.

We say to fibbing children: 'Don't tell fairy tales!' Yet children's fibs, like old wives' tales, tend to be over-generous with the truth rather than economical with it. Often, as with the untruths of children, we are invited to admire invention for its own sake. 'Chance is the mother of invention,' observed Lawrence Millman in the Arctic, surveying a roistering narrative inventiveness. 'Invention', he adds, 'is also the mother of invention.'

These stories are continually surprising:

> So one woman after another straightway brought forth her child.
> Soon there was a whole row of them.
>> Then the whole band departed, making a confused noise.
>> When the girl saw that, she said: 'There is no joke about it now.
> There comes a red army with the umbilical cords still hanging on.'

Like that.

> '"Little lady, little lady," said the boys, "little Alexandra, listen to the watch, tick tick tick: mother in the room all decked in gold."'

And that.

> *'The wind blew high, my heart did ache,*
> *To see the hole the fox did make.'*

And that.

This is a collection of old wives' tales, put together with the intention of giving pleasure, and with a good deal of pleasure on my own part. These stories have only one thing in common – they all centre around a female protagonist; be she clever, or brave, or good, or silly, or cruel, or sinister, or awesomely unfortunate, she is centre stage, as large as life – sometimes, like Sermerssuaq, larger.

Considering that, numerically, women have always existed in this world in at least as great numbers as men and bear at least an equal part in the transmission of oral culture, they occupy centre stage less often than you might think. Questions of the class and gender of the collector occur here; expectations, embarrassment, the desire to please. Even so, when women tell stories they do not always feel impelled to make themselves heroines and are also perfectly capable of telling tales that are downright unsisterly in their attitudes – for example, the little story about the old lady and the indifferent young man. The conspicuously vigorous heroines Lawrence Millman discovered in the Arctic are described by men as often as they are by women and their aggression, authority and sexual assertiveness probably have societal origins rather than the desire of an Arctic Mother Goose to give assertive role models.

Susie Hoogasian-Villa noted with surprise how her women informants among the Armenian community in Detroit, Michigan, USA, told stories about themselves that 'poke fun at women as being ridiculous and second-best'. These women originally came from resolutely patriarchal village communities and inevitably absorbed and recapitulated the values of those communities, where a new bride 'could speak to no one except the children in the absence of the men and elder women. She could speak to her husband in privacy.' Only the most profound social changes could alter the relations in these communities, and the stories women told could not in any way materially alter their conditions.

But one story in this book, 'How a Husband Weaned His Wife from Fairy Tales', shows just how much fairy stories could change a woman's desires, and how much a man might fear that change, would go to any lengths to keep her from pleasure, as if pleasure itself threatened his authority.

Which, of course, it did.

It still does.

The stories here come from Europe, Scandinavia, the Caribbean, the USA, the Arctic, Africa, the Middle East and Asia; the collection has been consciously modelled on those anthologies compiled by Andrew Lang at the turn of the century that once gave me so much joy – the Red, Blue, Violet, Green, Olive Fairy Books, and so on, through the spectrum, collections of tales from many lands.

I haven't put this collection together from such heterogeneous sources to show that we are all sisters under the skin, part of the same human family in spite of a few superficial differences. I don't believe that, anyway. Sisters under the skin we might be, but that doesn't mean we've got much in common. (See Part Six, 'Unhappy Families'.) Rather, I wanted to demonstrate the extraordinary richness and diversity of responses to the same common predicament – being alive – and the richness and diversity with which femininity, in practice, is represented in 'unofficial' culture: its strategies, its plots, its hard work.

Most of the stories here do not exist in only the one form but in many different versions, and different societies procure different meanings for what is essentially the same narrative. The fairy-tale wedding has a different significance in a polygamous society than it does in a monogamous one. Even a change of narrator can effect a transformation of meaning. The story 'The Furburger' was originally told by a twenty-nine-year-old Boy Scout executive to another young man; I haven't changed one single word, but its whole meaning is altered now that *I* am telling it to *you*.

The stories have seeded themselves all round the world, not because we all share the same imagination and experience but because stories are portable, part of the invisible luggage people take with them when they leave home. The Armenian story 'Nourie Hadig', with its resemblance to the 'Snow White' made famous via the Brothers Grimm and Walt Disney, was collected in Detroit, not far from the townships where Richard M. Dorson took down stories from African Americans that fuse African and European elements to make something new. Yet one of these stories, 'The Cat-Witch', has been current in Europe at least since the werewolf trials in France in the sixteenth century. But context changes everything; 'The Cat-Witch' acquires a whole new set of resonances in the context of slavery.

Village girls took stories to the city, to swap during endless kitchen chores or to entertain other people's children. Invading armies took storytellers home with them. Since the introduction of cheap printing processes in the seventeenth century, stories have moved in and out of the printed word. My grandmother told me the version of 'Red Riding Hood' she had from her own mother, and it followed almost word for word the text first printed in this country in 1729. The informants of the Brothers Grimm in Germany in the early nineteenth century often quoted Perrault's stories to them – to the irritation of the Grimms, since they were in pursuit of the authentic German *Geist*.

But there is a very specific selectivity at work. Some stories – ghost stories, funny stories, stories that already exist as folk tales – move through print into memory and speech. But although the novels of Dickens and other nineteenth-century bourgeois writers might be read aloud, as the novels of Gabriel Garcia Marquez are read aloud in Latin American villages today, stories about David Copperfield and Oliver Twist did not take on an independent life and survive as fairy tales – unless, as Mao Zedong said about the effects of the French Revolution, it is too soon to tell.

Although it is impossible to ascribe an original home for any individual story and the basic plot elements of the story we know as 'Cinderella' occur everywhere from China to Northern England (look at 'Beauty and Pock Face', then at 'Mossycoat'), the great impulse towards collecting oral material in the nineteenth century came out of the growth of nationalism and the concept of the nation-state with its own, exclusive culture; with its exclusive affinity to the people who dwelt therein. The word 'folklore' itself was not coined until 1846, when William J. Thomas invented the 'good Saxon compound' to replace imprecise and vague terms such as 'popular literature' and 'popular antiquities', and to do so without benefit of alien Greek or Latin roots. (Throughout the nineteenth century, the English believed themselves to be closer in spirit and racial identity to the Teutonic tribes of the North than to the swarthy Mediterranean types that started at Dunkirk; this conveniently left the Scots, the Welsh and the Irish out of the picture, too.)

Jacob Ludwig Grimm and his brother, Wilhelm Carl, philologists, antiquarians, medievalists, sought to establish the cultural unity of the German people via its common traditions and language; their 'Household Tales' became the second most popular and widely circulated book in Germany for over a century, dominated only by the Bible. Their work in collecting fairy tales was part of the nineteenth-century struggle for German unification, which didn't happen until 1871. Their project, which involved a certain degree of editorial censorship, envisaged popular culture as an untapped source of imaginative energy for the bourgeoisie; 'they [the Grimms] wanted the rich cultural tradition of the common people to be used and accepted by the rising middle class,' says Jack Zipes.

At roughly the same time, and inspired by the Grimms, Peter Christen Asbjørnsen and Jørgen Moe were collecting stories in Norway, publishing in 1841 a collection that 'helped free the Norwegian language from its Danish bondage, while forming and popularizing in literature the speech of the common people', according to John Gade. In the mid nineteenth century, J.F. Campbell went to the Highlands of Scotland to note down and preserve ancient stories in Scots Gaelic before the encroaching tide of the English language swept them away.

The events leading up to the Irish Revolution in 1916 precipitated a surge of passionate enthusiasm for native Irish poetry, music and story, leading eventually to the official adoption of Irish as the national language. (W.B. Yeats compiled a famous anthology of Irish fairy tales.) This process continues; there is at present a lively folklore department at the University of Bir Zeit: 'Interest in preserving the local culture is particularly strong on the West Bank as the status of Palestine continues to be the subject of international deliberation and the identity of a separate Palestinian Arab people is called into question,' says Inea Bushnaq.

That I and many other women should go looking through the books for fairy-tale heroines is a version of the same process – a wish to validate my claim to a fair share of the future by staking my claim to my share of the past.

Yet the tales themselves, evidence of the native genius of the people though they be, are not evidence of the genius of any one particular people over any other, nor of any one particular person; and though the stories in this book were, almost all of them, noted down from living mouths, collectors themselves can rarely refrain from tinkering with them, editing, collating, putting two texts together to make a better one. J.F. Campbell noted down in Scots Gaelic and translated verbatim; he believed that to tinker with the stories was, as he said, like putting tinsel on a dinosaur. But since the material is in the common domain, most collectors – and especially editors – cannot keep their hands off it.

Removing 'coarse' expressions was a common nineteenth-century pastime, part of the project of turning the universal entertainment of the poor into the refined pastime of the middle classes, and especially of the middle-class nursery. The excision of references to sexual and excremental functions, the toning down of sexual situations and the reluctance to include 'indelicate' material – that is, dirty jokes – helped to denaturize the fairy tale and, indeed, helped to denaturize its vision of everyday life.

Of course, questions not only of class, gender, but of personality entered into this from the start of the whole business of collecting. The ebullient and egalitarian Vance Randolph was abundantly entertained with 'indelicate' material in the heart of the Bible Belt of Arkansas and Missouri, often by women. It is difficult to imagine the scholarly and austere Grimm brothers establishing a similar rapport with their informants – or, indeed, wishing to do so.

Nevertheless, it is ironic that the fairy tale, if defined as orally transmitted narrative with a relaxed attitude to the reality principle and plots constantly refurbished in the retelling, has survived into the twentieth century in its most vigorous form as the dirty joke and, as such, shows every sign of continuing to flourish in an unofficial capacity on the margins of the twenty-first-century world of mass, universal communication and twenty-four-hour public entertainment.

I've tried, as far as possible, to avoid stories that have been conspicuously 'improved' by collectors, or rendered 'literary', and I haven't rewritten any myself, however great the temptation, or collated two versions, or even cut anything, because I wanted to keep a sense of many different voices. Of course, the personality of the collector, or of the translator, is bound to obtrude itself, often in unconscious ways; and the personality of the editor, too. The question of forgery also raises its head; a cuckoo in the nest, a story an editor, collector, or japester has made up from scratch according to folkloric formulae and inserted in a collection of traditional stories, perhaps in the pious hope that the story will escape from the cage of the text and live out an independent life of its own among the people. Or perhaps for some other reason. If I have inadvertently picked up any authored stories of this kind, may they fly away as freely as the bird at the end of 'The Wise Little Girl'.

This selection has also been mainly confined to material available in English, due to my shortcomings as a linguist. This exercises its own form of cultural imperialism upon the collection.

On the surface, these stories tend to perform a normative function – to reinforce the ties that bind people together, rather than to question them. Life on the economic edge is sufficiently precarious without continual existential struggle. But the qualities these stories recommend for the survival and prosperity of women are never those of passive subordination. Women are required to do the thinking in a family (see 'A Pottle o' Brains') and to undertake epic journeys ('East o' the Sun and West o' the Moon'). Please refer to the entire section titled: 'Clever Women, Resourceful Girls and Desperate Stratagems' to see how women contrived to get their own way.

Nevertheless, the solution adopted in 'The Two Women Who Found Freedom' is rare; most fairy tales and folk tales are structured around the relations between men and women, whether in terms of magical romance or of coarse domestic realism. The common, unspoken goal is fertility and continuance. In the context of societies from which most of these stories spring, their goal is not a conservative one but a Utopian one, indeed a form of heroic optimism – as if to say, one day, we might be happy, even if it won't last.

But if many stories end with a wedding, don't forget how many of them start with a death – of a father, or a mother, or both; events that plunge the survivors directly into catastrophe. The stories in Part Six, 'Unhappy Families', strike directly at the heart of human experience. Family life, in the traditional tale, no matter whence its provenance, is never more than one step away from disaster.

Fairy-tale families are, in the main, dysfunctional units in which parents and step-parents are neglectful to the point of murder and sibling rivalry to the point of murder is the norm. A profile of the typical European fairy-tale family reads like that of a 'family at risk' in a present-day inner-city social worker's casebook, and the African and Asian families represented here offer evidence that even widely different types of family structures still create unforgivable crimes between human beings too close together. And death causes more distress in a family than divorce.

The ever-recurring figure of the stepmother indicates how the households depicted in these stories are likely to be subject to enormous internal changes and reversals of role. Yet however ubiquitous the stepmother in times when the maternal mortality rates were high and a child might live with two, three or even more stepmothers before she herself embarked on the perilous career of motherhood, the 'cruelty' and indifference almost universally ascribed to her may also reflect our own ambivalences towards our natural mothers. Note that in 'Nourie Hadig' it is the child's real mother who desires her death.

For women, the ritual marriage at the story's ending may be no more than the prelude to the haunting dilemma in which the mother of the Grimms' Snow White found herself – she longed with all her heart for a child 'as white as snow, as red as blood, as black as ebony', and died when that child was born, as if the price of the daughter were the life of the mother. When we hear a story, we bring all our own experience to that story: 'They all lived happy and died happy, and never drank out of a dry cappy', says the ending of 'Kate Crackernuts'. Cross fingers, touch wood. The Arabian stories from Inea Bushnaq's anthology conclude with a stately dignity that undercuts the whole notion of a happy ending: '. . . they lived in happiness and contentment until death, the parter of the truest lovers, divided them' ('The Princess in the Suit of Leather').

'They' in the above story were a princess and a prince. Why does royalty feature so prominently in the recreational fiction of the ordinary people? For the same reason that the British royal family features so prominently in the pages of the tabloid press, I suppose – glamour. Kings and queens are always rich beyond imagining, princes handsome beyond belief, princesses lovely beyond words – yet they may live in a semi-detached palace, all the same, suggesting that the storyteller was not over-familiar with the lifestyle of real royalty. 'The palace had many rooms and one king occupied one half of it and the other the other half,' according to a Greek story not printed here. In 'The Three Measures of Salt', the narrator states grandly: 'in those days everyone was a king'.

Susie Hoogasian-Villa, whose stories came from Armenian immigrants in a heavily industrialized part of the (republican) USA, puts fairy-tale royalty into perspective: 'Frequently kings are only head men of their villages; princesses do the menial work.' Juleidah, the princess in the suit of leather, can bake a cake and clean a kitchen with democratic skill, yet when she dresses up she makes Princess Di look plain: 'Tall as a cypress, with a face like a rose and the silks and jewels of a king's bride, she seemed to fill the room with light.' We are dealing with imaginary royalty and an imaginary style, with creations of fantasy and wish-fulfilment, which is why the loose symbolic structure of fairy tales leaves them so open to psychoanalytic interpretation, as if they were not formal inventions but informal dreams dreamed in public.

This quality of the public dream is a characteristic of popular art, even when as mediated by commercial interests as it is today in its manifestations of horror movie, pulp novel, soap opera. The fairy tale, as narrative, has far less in common with the modern bourgeois forms of the novel and the feature film than it does with contemporary demotic forms, especially those 'female' forms of romance. Indeed, the elevated rank and excessive wealth of some of the characters, the absolute poverty of others, the excessive extremes of good luck and ugliness, of cleverness and stupidity, of vice and virtue, beauty, glamour and guile, the tumultuous plethora of events, the violent action, the intense and inharmonious personal relationships, the love of a row for its own sake, the invention of a mystery for its own sake – all these are characteristics of the fairy tale that link it directly to the contemporary television soap opera.

The now defunct US soap opera *Dynasty*, whose success was such a phenomenon of the early 1980s, utilized a cast list derived with almost contemptuous transparency from that of the Brothers Grimm – the wicked stepmother, the put-upon bride, the ever-obtuse husband and father. 'Dynasty's proliferating subplots featured abandoned children, arbitrary voyages, random misadventure – all characteristics of the genre. ('The Three Measures of Salt' is a story of this kind; R.M. Dawkins's marvellous collection of stories from Greece, most from as recently as the 1950s, frequently demonstrates Mother Goose at her most melodramatic.)

See also 'The Battle of the Birds' for the way in which one story can effortlessly segue into another, if there is time to spare and an enthusiastic audience, just as the narrative in soap opera surges ceaselessly back and forth like a tide – now striving towards some sort of satisfactory consummation, now reversing itself smartly as if it has been reminded that there are no endings, happy or otherwise, in real life: that 'The End' is only a formal device of high art.

The narrative drive is powered by the question: 'What happened then?' The fairy tale is user-friendly; it always comes up with an answer to that question. The fairy tale has needed to be user-friendly in order to survive. It survives today because it has transformed itself into a medium for gossip, anecdote, rumour; it remains hand-crafted, even in a period when television disseminates the mythologies of advanced industrialized countries throughout the world, wherever there are TV sets and the juice to make them flicker.

'The people of the North are losing their stories along with their identities,' says Lawrence Millman, echoing what J.F. Campbell said in the West Highlands a century and a half ago. But this time, Millman may be right: 'Near Gjoa Haven, Northwest Territories, I stayed in an Innuit tent which was unheated, but equipped with the latest in stereo and video gadgetry.'

Now we have machines to do our dreaming for us. But within that 'video gadgetry' might lie the source of a continuation, even a transformation, of storytelling and story-performance. The human imagination is infinitely resilient, surviving colonization, transportation, involuntary servitude, imprisonment, bans on language, the oppression of women. Nevertheless, this last century has seen the most fundamental change in human culture since the Iron Age – the final divorce from the land. (John Berger describes this in fictional terms with visionary splendour, in his trilogy *Into Their Labours*.)

It is a characteristic of every age to believe that it is unique, that our experience will obliterate everything that has gone before. Sometimes that belief is correct. When Thomas Hardy wrote *Tess of the d'Urbervilles* a century and a half ago, he described a country woman, Tess's mother, whose sensibility, sense of the world, aesthetic, had scarcely changed in two hundred years. In doing so, he – perfectly consciously – described a way of life at the very moment when profound change was about to begin. Tess and her sisters are themselves whirled away from that rural life deeply rooted in the past into an urban world of ceaseless and giddily accelerating change and innovation, where everything – including, or even especially, our notions of the nature of women and men – was in the melting pot, because the very idea of what constitutes 'human nature' was in the melting pot.

The stories in this book, with scarcely an exception, have their roots in the pre-industrialized past, and unreconstructed theories of human nature. In this world, milk comes from the cow, water from the well, and only the intervention of the supernatural can change the relations of women to men and, above all, of women to their own fertility. I don't offer these stories in a spirit of nostalgia; that past was hard, cruel and especially inimical to women, whatever desperate stratagems we employed to get a little bit of our own way. But I *do* offer them in a valedictory spirit, as a reminder of how wise, clever, perceptive, occasionally lyrical, eccentric, sometimes downright crazy our great-grandmothers were, and their great-grandmothers; and of the contributions to literature of Mother Goose and her goslings.

Years ago, the late A.L. Lloyd, ethnomusicologist, folklorist and singer, taught me that I needn't know an artist's name to recognize that one had been at work. This book is dedicated to that proposition and, therefore, to his memory.

Angela Carter, London, 1990

SERMERSSUAQ

(INNUIT)

Sermerssuaq was so powerful that she could lift a kayak on the tips of three fingers. She could kill a seal merely by drumming on its head with her fists. She could rip asunder a fox or hare. Once she arm-wrestled with Qasordlanguaq, another powerful woman, and beat her so easily that she said: 'Poor Qasordlanguaq could not even beat one of her own lice at armwrestling.' Most men she could beat and then she would tell them: 'Where were you when the testicles were given out?' Sometimes this Sermerssuaq would show off her clitoris. It was so big that the skin of a fox would not fully cover it. *Aja*, and she was the mother of nine children, too!

PART ONE

BRAVE, BOLD AND WILFUL

THE SEARCH FOR LUCK

(GREEK)

o go on and on with the story: there was an old woman and she had a hen. Like her the hen was well on in years and a good worker: every day she laid an egg. The old woman had a neighbour, an old man, a plague-stricken old fellow, and whenever the old woman went off anywhere he used to steal the egg. The poor old woman kept a lookout to catch the thief, but she could never succeed, nor did she want to make accusations against anyone, so she had the idea of going to ask the Undying Sun.

As she was on the way she met three sisters: all three of them were old maids. When they saw her they ran after her to find out where she was going. She told them what her trouble had been. 'And now,' said she, 'I am on my way to ask the Undying Sun and find out what son of a bitch this can be who steals my eggs and does such cruelty to a poor tired old woman.' When the girls heard this they threw themselves upon her shoulders:

'O Auntie, I beg you, ask him about us; what is the matter with us that we can't get married.' 'Very well,' said the old woman. 'I will ask him, and perhaps he may attend to what I say.'

So she went on and on and she met an old woman shivering with cold. When the old woman saw her and heard where she was going, she began to entreat her: 'I beg you, old woman, to question him about me too; what is the matter with me that I can never be warm although I wear three fur coats, all one on top of the other.' 'Very well,' said the old woman, 'I will ask him, but how can I help you?'

So she went on and on and she came to a river; it ran turbid and dark as blood. From a long way off she heard its rushing sound and her knees shook with fear. When the river saw her he too asked her in a savage and angry voice where she was going. She said to him what she had to say. The river said to her: 'If this is so, ask him about me too: what plague is this upon me that I can never flow at ease.' 'Very well, my dear river; very well,' said the old woman in such terror that she hardly knew how to go on.

So she went on and on, and came to a monstrous great rock; it had for very many years been hanging suspended and could neither fall nor not fall. The rock begged the old woman to ask what was oppressing it so that it could not fall and be at rest and passers-by be free from fear. 'Very well,' said the old woman, 'I will ask him; it is not much to ask and I will take it upon me.'

Talking in this way the old woman found it was very late and so she lifted up her feet and how she did run! When she came up to the crest of the mountain, there she saw the Undying Sun combing his beard with his golden comb. As soon as he saw her he bade her welcome and gave her a stool and then asked her why she had come. The old woman told him what she had suffered about the eggs laid by her hen: 'And I throw myself at your feet,' said she: 'tell me who the thief is. I wish I knew, for then I should not be cursing him so madly and laying a burden on my soul. Also, please see here: I have brought you a kerchief full of pears from my garden and a basket full of baked rolls.' Then the Undying Sun said to her: 'The man who steals your eggs is that neighbour of yours. Yet see that you say nothing to him; leave him to God and the man will come by his deserts.'

'As I was on my way,' said the old woman to the Undying Sun, 'I came upon three girls, unmarried, and how they did entreat me! "Ask about us; what is the matter with us that we get no husbands."' 'I know who you mean. They are not girls anyone will marry. They are like to be idle; they have no mother to guide them nor father either, and so it happens that every day they start and sweep the house out without sprinkling water and then use the broom and fill my eyes with dust and how sick I am of them! I can't bear them. Tell them that from henceforth they must rise before dawn and sprinkle the house and then sweep, and very soon they will get husbands. You need have no more thought about them as you go your way.'

'Then an old woman made a request of me: "Ask him on my behalf what is the matter with me that I cannot keep warm although I wear three fur coats one on top of the other."' 'You must tell her to give away two in charity for the sake of her soul and then she will keep warm.'

'Also I saw a river turbid and dark as blood; its flow entangled with eddies. The river requested me: "Ask him about me; what can I do to flow at ease?"' 'The river must drown a man and so it will be at ease. When you get there, first cross over the stream and then say what I have said to you; otherwise the river will take you as its prey.'

'Also I saw a rock: years and years have passed and all the time it has hung like this suspended and cannot fall.' 'This rock too must bring a man to death and thus it will be at ease. When you go there pass by the rock, and not till then, say what I have said to you.'

The old woman arose and kissed his hand and said Farewell and went down from the mountain. On her way she came to the rock, and the rock was waiting for her coming as it were with five eyes. She made haste and passed beyond and then she said what she had been told to say to the rock. When the rock heard how he must fall and that to the death of a man, he grew angry; what to do he knew not. 'Ah,' said he to the old woman: 'If you had told me that before, then I would have made you my prey.' 'May all my troubles be yours,' said the old woman and she – pray excuse me – slapped her behind.

On her way she came close to the river and from the roar it was making she saw how troubled it was and that it was just waiting for her to hear what the Undying Sun had said to her. She made haste and crossed over the stream, and then she said what he had told her. When the river heard this, it was enraged, and such was its evil mood that the water was more turbid than ever. 'Ah,' said the river, 'why did I not know this? Then I would have had your life, you who are an old woman whom nobody wants.' The old woman was so much frightened that she never turned round to look at the river.

Before she had gone much farther she could see the reek coming up from the roofs of the village and the savour of cooking came across to her. She made no delay but went to the old woman, she who could never keep warm, and said to her what she had been told to say. The table was set all fresh and she sat down and ate with them: they had fine lenten fare and you would have eaten and licked your fingers, so good it was.

Then she went to find the old maids. From the time the old woman had left them their minds had been on her; they were neither lighting the fire in their house nor putting it out: all the time they had their eyes on the road to see the old woman when she came by. As soon as the old woman saw them, she went and sat down and explained to them that they must do what the Undying Sun had told her to tell them. After this they rose up always when it was still night and sprinkled the floor and swept it, and then suitors began to come again, some from one place and some from another; all to ask them in marriage. So they got husbands and lived and were happy.

As for the old woman who could never keep warm, she gave away two of her fur coats for the good of her soul and at once found herself warm. The river and the rock each took a man's life and so they were at rest.

When the old woman came back home she found the old man at the very gate of death. When she had gone off to find the Undying Sun he was so much frightened that a terrible thing happened to him: the hen's feathers grew out of his face. No long time passed before he went off to that big village whence no man ever returns. After that the eggs were never missing and the old woman ate them until she died, and when she died the hen died too.

MR FOX

(ENGLISH)

ady Mary was young, and Lady Mary was fair. She had two brothers, and more lovers than she could count. But of them all, the bravest and most gallant, was a Mr Fox, whom she met when she was down at her father's country-house. No one knew who Mr Fox was; but he was certainly brave, and surely rich, and of all her lovers, Lady Mary cared for him alone. At last it was agreed upon between them that they should be married. Lady Mary asked Mr Fox where they should live, and he described to her his castle, and where it was; but, strange to say, did not ask her, or her brothers, to come and see it.

So one day, near the wedding-day, when her brothers were out, and Mr Fox was away for a day or two on business, as he said, Lady Mary set out for Mr Fox's castle. And after many searchings, she came at last to it, and a fine strong house it was, with high walls and a deep moat. And when she came up to the gateway she saw written on it:

Be bold, be bold.

But as the gate was open, she went through it, and found no one there. So she went up to the doorway, and over it she found written:

Be bold, be bold, but not too bold.

Still she went on, till she came into the hall, and went up the broad stairs till she came to a door in the gallery, over which was written:

Be bold, be bold, but not too bold,
Lest that your heart's blood should run cold.

But Lady Mary was a brave one, she was, and she opened the door, and what do you think she saw? Why, bodies and skeletons of beautiful young ladies all stained with blood. So Lady Mary thought it was high time to get out of that horrid place, and she closed the door, went through the gallery, and was just going down the stairs, and out of the hall, when who should she see through the window, but Mr Fox dragging a beautiful young lady along from the gateway to the door. Lady Mary rushed downstairs, and hid herself behind a cask, just in time, as Mr Fox came in with the poor young lady who seemed to have fainted. Just as he got near Lady Mary, Mr Fox saw a diamond ring glittering on the finger of the young lady he was dragging, and he tried to pull it off. But it was tightly fixed, and would not come off, so Mr Fox cursed and swore, and drew his sword, raised it, and brought it down upon the hand of the poor lady. The sword cut off the hand, which jumped up into the air, and fell of all places in the world into Lady Mary's lap. Mr Fox looked about a bit, but did not think of looking behind the cask, so at last he went on dragging the young lady up the stairs into the Bloody Chamber.

As soon as she heard him pass through the gallery, Lady Mary crept out of the door, down through the gateway, and ran home as fast as she could.

Now it happened that the very next day the marriage contract of Lady Mary and Mr Fox was to be signed, and there was a splendid breakfast before that. And when Mr Fox was seated at table opposite Lady Mary, he looked at her. 'How pale you are this morning, my dear.' 'Yes,' said she, 'I had a bad night's rest last night. I had horrible dreams.' 'Dreams go by contraries,' said Mr Fox; 'but tell us your dream, and your sweet voice will make the time pass till the happy hour comes.'

'I dreamed,' said Lady Mary, 'that I went yestermorn to your castle, and I found it in the woods, with high walls, and a deep moat, and over the gateway was written:

Be bold, be bold.'

'But it is not so, nor it was not so,' said Mr Fox.

'And when I came to the doorway over it was written:

Be bold, be bold, but not too bold.'

'It is not so, nor it was not so,' said Mr Fox.

'And then I went upstairs, and came to a gallery, at the end of which was a door, on which was written:

> *Be bold, be bold, but not too bold,*
> *Lest that your heart's blood should run cold.'*

'It is not so, nor it was not so,' said Mr Fox.

'And then – and then I opened the door, and the room was filled with bodies and skeletons of poor dead women, all stained with their blood.'

'It is not so, nor it was not so. And God forbid it should be so,' said Mr Fox.

'I then dreamed that I rushed down the gallery, and just as I was going down the stairs, I saw you, Mr Fox, coming up to the hall door, dragging after you a poor young lady, rich and beautiful.'

'It is not so, nor it was not so. And God forbid it should be so,' said Mr Fox.

'I rushed downstairs, just in time to hide myself behind a cask, when you, Mr Fox, came in dragging the young lady by the arm. And, as you passed me, Mr Fox, I thought I saw you try and get off her diamond ring, and when you could not, Mr Fox, it seemed to me in my dream, that you out with your sword and hacked off the poor lady's hand to get the ring.'

'It is not so, nor it was not so. And God forbid it should be so,' said Mr Fox, and was going to say something else as he rose from his seat, when Lady Mary cried out:

'But it is so, and it was so. Here's hand and ring I have to show,' and pulled out the lady's hand from her dress, and pointed it straight at Mr Fox.

At once her brothers and her friends drew their swords and cut Mr Fox into a thousand pieces.

KAKUARSHUK

(INNUIT)

ong ago women got their children by digging around in the earth. They would pry the children loose from the very ground itself. They would not have to travel far to find little girls, but boys were more difficult to locate – often they would have to dig extremely deep in the earth to get at the boys. Thus it was that strong women had many children and lazy women very few children or no children at all. Of course, there were barren women as well. And Kakuarshuk was one of these barren women. She would spend nearly all of her time digging up the ground. Half the earth she seemed to overturn, but still she could find no children. At last she went to an *angakok*, who told her, 'Go to such-and-such a place, dig there, and you will find a child . . .' Well, Kakuarshuk went to this place, which was quite a distance from her home, and there she dug. Deeper and deeper she dug, until she came out on the other side of the earth. On this other side, everything seemed to be in reverse. There was neither snow or ice and babies were much bigger than adults. Kakuarshuk was adopted by two of these babies, a girl-baby and a boy-baby. They took her around in an *amaut* sack and the girl-baby lent her her breast to suck. They seemed to be very fond of Kakuarshuk. Never was she without food or attention. One day her baby-mother said: 'Is there anything you want, Dear Little One?' 'Yes,' Kakuarshuk replied, 'I would like to have a baby of my own.' 'In that case,' her baby-mother replied, 'You must go to such-and-such a place high in the mountains and there you must start digging.' And so Kakuarshuk travelled to this place in the mountains. She dug. Deeper and deeper the hole went, until it joined many other holes. None of these holes appeared to have an exit anywhere. Nor did Kakuarshuk find any babies along the way. But still she walked on. At night she was visited by Claw-Trolls who tore at her flesh. Then there was a Scourge-Troll who slapped a live seal across her chest and groin. At last she could walk no further and now she lay down to die. Suddenly a little fox came up to her and said: 'I will save you, mother. Just follow me.' And the fox took her by the hand and led her through this network of holes to the daylight on the other side. Kakuarshuk could not remember a thing. *Aja*, not a thing. But when she woke up, she was resting in her own house and there was a little boy-child in her arms.

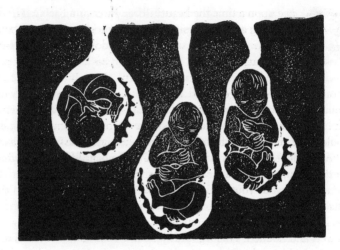

THE PROMISE

(BURMESE)

nce upon a time the beautiful daughter of a Rich Man was studying at a University. She was a most assiduous scholar and one day as she sat by the window of the classroom inscribing on a palm leaf with a stylus a valuable formula which the learned Teacher was reciting to the class, the stylus slipped through her tired fingers and fell through the window on to the ground. She thought that it would be disrespectful to the Teacher to ask him to pause, but if she left her seat to pick up the stylus, she would have missed the formula. While she was in that dilemma, a fellow-student passed by her window and she begged him in a whisper to pick up the stylus for her. Now the passer-by was a King's Son and a mischievous youth. In fun he replied, 'Promise me that you will offer me your First Flower on the First Night.' The Girl, engrossed in the Teacher's formula, comprehended at that moment only the word 'flower' and nodded. He forgot his joke in a short time, but thinking over the incident, the Girl comprehended later the full meaning of the Prince's words but thought no more of them and hoped that the words were said in fun.

At the end of their respective studies in the University, the Prince returned to his kingdom and soon after succeeded to his father's throne, and the Girl returned to her home in a neighbouring kingdom and soon after she married a Rich Man's Son. On the night of the wedding, her memory flew back to the incident of the stylus, and troubled by her conscience she confessed to her husband of her promise but expressed the belief that the young man was only joking. 'My dear,' replied the Husband, 'it is for him to say whether it was a joke or not. A promise made in honour must never be broken.' The Girl, after making obeisance to her husband, started at once on a journey to the neighbouring kingdom to fulfil her promise to the King if he should exact such fulfilment.

As she walked alone in the darkness, a Robber seized hold of her and said, 'What woman is this that walks in the night, bedecked with gold and jewels? Surrender me your jewels, and your silken dress.' 'Oh, Robber,' replied the Girl, 'take my jewels, but leave me my silken dress, as I cannot enter the King's palace, naked and ashamed.' 'No,' said the Robber, 'your silken dress is as precious as your jewels. Give me the dress also. The Girl then explained to the Robber the reason why she was travelling all alone in the dark. 'I am impressed with your sense of honour,' said the Robber, 'and if you will but promise to return here after giving the First Flower to the King, I shall let you go.' The Girl made the promise, and was allowed to continue her journey. She walked on until she passed under a banyan tree. 'What woman is this, that is so fresh and tender and yet walks alone at night?' said the Ogre of the tree. 'I will eat you up, as all those who pass under my tree during the hours of darkness belong to me.' 'Oh, Ogre,' pleaded the Girl, 'please spare me, for if you eat me now, my promise to the Prince will ever remain unkept.' After she had explained the purpose of her journey by night, the Ogre said, 'I am impressed by your sense of honour and if you will but promise to return here after you have met the King, I will let you go.' The Girl made the promise and she was allowed to continue her journey.

At last, without further adventure, she arrived at the city and was soon knocking at the gates of the King's palace. 'What manner of woman are you?' asked the palace guards. 'What mean you by coming to the palace and demanding entry at this hour of midnight?' 'It is a matter of honour,' replied the Girl. 'Please go and tell my lord the King that his fellow-student at the University has come to keep her promise.' The King, hearing the commotion, looked out of his bedroom window, and saw the Girl standing in the light of the torches of the guards, in the full bloom of her beauty. He recognized her and desired her, but when he had heard her tale he admired her for her loyalty to her oath, and her courage in facing all dangers and difficulties to keep her promise. 'My friend,' he said, 'you are a marvellous woman, for you prize your honour even above maidenly modesty. Your promise was demanded by me as a jest and I had forgotten it. So return you to your Husband.' So the Girl went back to the Ogre of the banyan tree, and said, 'Oh, Ogre, eat my body, but after eating, take my silken dress and my jewels, and give them to the Robber who is waiting for me only a few yards from here.' The Ogre said, 'Friend, you are a marvellous woman, for you prize your honour even above your life. You are free to go, as I absolve you from your promise.' The Girl went back to the Robber and said, 'Oh, Robber, take my jewels and my silken dress. Although I shall have to go back to my Husband naked and ashamed, the servants will let me in, for they will recognize me.' The Robber replied, 'Friend, you are a marvellous woman, for you prize your promise above jewels and fine dresses. You are free to go, as I absolve you from your promise.' So the Girl returned to her Husband, who received her with affection and regard, and they lived happily ever after.

KATE CRACKERNUTS

(ENGLISH)

nce upon a time there was a king and a queen, as in many lands have been. The king had a daughter, Anne, and the queen had one named Kate, but Anne was far bonnier than the queen's daughter, though they loved one another like real sisters. The queen was jealous of the king's daughter being bonnier than her own, and cast about to spoil her beauty. So she took counsel of the henwife, who told her to send the lassie to her next morning fasting.

So next morning early, the queen said to Anne, 'Go, my dear, to the henwife in the glen, and ask her for some eggs.' So Anne set out, but as she passed through the kitchen she saw a crust, and she took and munched it as she went along.

When she came to the henwife's she asked for eggs, as she had been told to do; the henwife said to her, 'Lift the lid off that pot there and see.' The lassie did so, but nothing happened. 'Go home to your minnie and tell her to keep her larder door better locked,' said the henwife. So she went home to the queen and told her what the henwife had said. The queen knew from this that the lassie had had something to eat, so watched the next morning and sent her away fasting; but the princess saw some country-folk picking peas by the roadside, and being very kind she spoke to them and took a handful of the peas, which she ate by the way.

When she came to the henwife's, she said, 'Lift the lid off the pot and you'll see.' So Anne lifted the lid, but nothing happened. Then the henwife was rare angry and said to Anne, 'Tell your minnie the pot won't boil if the fire's away.' So Anne went home and told the queen.

The third day the queen goes along with the girl herself to the henwife. Now, this time, when Anne lifted the lid off the pot, off falls her own pretty head, and on jumps a sheep's head.

So the queen was now quite satisfied, and went back home.

Her own daughter, Kate, however, took a fine linen cloth and wrapped it round her sister's head and took her by the hand and they both went out to seek their fortune. They went on, and they went on, and they went on, until they came to a castle. Kate knocked at the door and asked for a night's lodging for herself and a sick sister. They went in and found it was a king's castle, who had two sons, and one of them was sickening away to death and no one could find out what ailed him. And the curious thing was, that whoever watched him at night was never seen any more. So the king had offered a peck of silver to anyone who would stop up with him. Now Katie was a very brave girl, so she offered to sit up with him.

Till midnight all went well. As twelve o'clock rang, however, the sick prince rose, dressed himself, and slipped downstairs. Kate followed, but he didn't seem to notice her. The prince went to the stable, saddled his horse, called his hound, jumped into the saddle and Kate leapt lightly up behind him. Away rode the prince and Kate through the greenwood, Kate, as they passed, plucking nuts from the trees and filling her apron with them. They rode on and on till they came to a green hill. The prince here drew bridle and spoke: 'Open, open, green hill, and let the young prince in with his horse and his hound,' and Kate added, 'and his lady him behind.'

Immediately the green hill opened and they passed in. The prince entered a magnificent hall, brightly lighted up, and many beautiful fairies surrounded the prince and led him off to the dance. Meanwhile, Kate, without being noticed, hid herself behind the door. There she saw the prince dancing, and dancing, and dancing, till he could dance no longer and fell upon a couch. Then the fairies would fan him till he could rise again and go on dancing.

At last the cock crew, and the prince made all haste to get on horseback; Kate jumped up behind, and home they rode. When the morning sun rose they came in and found Kate sitting down by the fire and cracking her nuts. Kate said the prince had a good night; but she would not sit up another night unless she was to get a peck of gold. The second night passed as the first had done. The prince got up at midnight and rode away to the green hill and the fairy ball, and Kate went with him, gathering nuts as they rode through the forest.

This time she did not watch the prince, for she knew he would dance, and dance, and dance. But she saw a fairy baby playing with a wand and overheard one of the fairies say: 'Three strokes of that wand would make Kate's sick sister as bonny as ever she was.'

So Kate rolled nuts to the fairy baby, and rolled nuts till the baby toddled after the nuts and let fall the wand, and Kate took it up and put it in her apron. And at cockcrow they rode home as before, and the moment Kate got home to her room she rushed and touched Anne three times with her wand, and the nasty sheep's head fell off and she was her own pretty self again.

The third night Kate consented to watch, only if she should marry the sick prince. All went on as the first two nights. This time the fairy baby was playing with a birdie; Kate heard one of the fairies say: 'Three bites of that birdie would make the sick prince as well as ever he was.' Kate rolled all the nuts she had to the fairy baby until the birdie was dropped, and Kate put it in her apron.

At cockcrow they set off again, but instead of cracking her nuts as she used to do, this time Kate plucked the feathers off and cooked the birdie. Soon there arose a very savoury smell. 'Oh!' said the sick prince, 'I wish I had a bite of that birdie,' so Kate gave him a bite of the birdie, and he rose up on his elbow. By-and-by he cried out again: 'Oh, if I had another bite of that birdie!' so Kate gave him another bite, and he sat up on his bed. Then he said again: 'Oh! if I but had a third bite of that birdie!' So Kate gave him a third bite, and he rose hale and strong, dressed himself, and sat down by the fire, and when the folk came in next morning they found Kate and the young prince cracking nuts together. Meanwhile his brother had seen Annie and had fallen in love with her, as everybody did who saw her sweet pretty face. So the sick son married the well sister, and the well son married the sick sister, and they all lived happy and died happy, and never drank out of a dry cappy.

THE FISHER-GIRL AND THE CRAB

(INDIAN TRIBAL)

n old Kuruk and his wife had no children. The old man sowed rice in his field and, when after some days the rice had sprouted, he took his wife to the field to see it. On one side of the field was a gourd, and they took it home for food. But when the old man was about to cut it up, the gourd said, 'Cut me gently, gently, grandfather!' The old man was so frightened that he dropped it. He ran to his wife and said, 'This is a talking gourd.' 'Nonsense,' said the old woman and took the knife herself. But the gourd said, 'Cut me, gently, gently, old mother!'

So the old woman cut the gourd up carefully and slowly, and from inside there came out a crab. They got a new pot and put the crab

inside. The woman tied a basket to her belly and covered it with cloth. Then she went to the bazaar and told the neighbours, 'Look, in my old age Mahapurub has given me a son.'

After some time, she removed the basket and took the crab out of the pot and told everyone. 'Look, I have given birth to this crab.'

When the crab was grown up, they went to find him a wife. They got him a nice girl, but when she came to the house she was angry at finding herself married to such a creature. Every night she waited for him, but what could a crab do? Then the girl thought, 'I must find another man.' Whenever the crab spoke to the girl, she used to kick it away.

One day, the girl wanted to go to visit a man in another village. She let her parents-in-law and the crab go to sleep, and then crept out of the house. But the crab saw her go and he got out by another way and went ahead of her along the road. By the roadside there was a banyan tree; to this the crab said, 'Are you my tree, or whose tree are you?' The tree said, 'I am yours.' Then said the crab, 'Fall down.' The tree fell down. Now inside that tree there lived the shape of a youth. The crab took this on itself, and put its crab-shape into the tree instead. It went along the road a little and then told the tree to stand up again.

After a time, along came the girl. When she saw the beautiful youth under the tree, she was very pleased, and said, 'Where are you going?' He said, 'Nowhere, I am going home.' She said, 'Come and lie with me.' He said, 'No, I'm afraid. Your husband will beat me. But I'll come another day.'

Disappointed, the girl went on. She met a Chamar girl and two pretty Mahara girls. They too were looking for men. The Kuruk girl told them her story, and they took her with them to a dance, promising her a fine gallant. When they got there, they found that the crab-youth was there already. When they saw him, each girl longed to have him as a lover. He went to the Kuruk girl and she drew him aside. But he did nothing. She gave him her ornaments, and he went away.

When he reached the tree, he bade it fall down, and took his own crab-shape again, returning the shape of the youth to the tree. 'Stand up again,' he told the tree, and went home. After a little while the girl also came home. The crab asked her where she had been, but she was in a temper and kicked him out of bed. Then the crab gave her back her ornaments. The girl was frightened and declared that they were not hers.

The next day, the girl again gave everyone food and put them to sleep. This time she hid by the roadside, and watched to see what the crab would do. The crab came to the banyan tree and said, 'Are you my tree, or whose are you?' The tree said, 'I am your tree.' Then the crab said, 'If you are mine, then fall down.' The tree fell down, and the crab took the shape of the handsome youth, and let the tree stand up again.

The girl was watching all that happened. When the boy had gone on his way, she went to the tree and said, 'Are you my tree or whose are you?' The tree said, 'I am yours.' She said, 'If you are mine, then fall down.' The tree fell down, and the girl pulled out the crab-shape and killed it and threw it on a fire. Then she hid behind the tree and waited.

The youth went to the dance, but he could not find his girl, so he came back to the tree. The girl jumped out from behind the tree and caught him and took him home. After that they lived happily together.

PART TWO

CLEVER WOMEN, RESOURCEFUL GIRLS & DESPERATE STRATAGEMS

MAOL A CHLIOBAIN

(SCOTS GAELIC)

Once upon a time there was a widow, and she had three daughters; and they said to her that they would go to seek their fortune. She baked three bannocks. She said to the big one, 'Whether dost thou like best the little half and my blessing, or the big half and my curse?' 'I like best,' said she, 'the big half and thy curse.' She said to the middle one, 'Whether dost thou like best the big half and my curse, or the little half and my blessing?' 'I like best,' said she, 'the big half and thy curse.' She said to the little one, 'Whether dost thou like best the big half and my curse, or the little half and my blessing?' 'I like best the little half and thy blessing.' This pleased her mother, and she gave her the two other halves also. They went away, but the two eldest did not want the youngest to be with them, and they tied her to a rock of stone. They went on; but her mother's blessing came and freed her. And when they looked behind them, whom did they see but her with the rock on top of her. They let her alone a turn of a while, till they reached a peat stack, and they tied her to the peat stack. They went on a bit but her mother's blessing came and freed her, and they looked behind them, and whom did they see but her coming, and the peat stack on the top of her. They let her alone a turn of a while, till they reached a tree, and they tied her to the tree. They went on a bit but her mother's blessing came and freed her, and when they looked behind them, whom did they see but her, and the tree on top of her.

They saw it was no good to be at her; they loosed her, and let her come with them. They were going till night came on them. They saw a light a long way from them; and though a long way from them, it was not long that they were in reaching it. They went in. What was this but a giant's house! They asked to stop the night. They got that, and they were put to bed with the three daughters of the giant. The giant came home, and he said, 'The smell of the foreign girls is within.' There were twists of amber knobs about the necks of the giant's daughters, and strings of horse hair about their own necks. They all slept, but Maol a Chliobain did not sleep. Through the night a thirst came on the giant. He called to his bald, rough-skinned gillie to bring him water. The rough-skinned gillie said that there was not a drop within. 'Kill,' said he, 'one of the strange girls, and bring to me her blood.' 'How will I know them?' said the bald, rough-skinned gillie. 'There are twists of knobs of amber about the necks of my daughters, and twists of horse hair about the necks of the rest.'

Maol a Chliobain heard the giant, and as quick as she could she put the strings of horse hair that were about her own neck and about the necks of her sisters about the necks of the giant's daughters; and the knobs that were about the necks of the giant's daughters about her own neck and about the necks of her sisters; and she laid down *so* quietly. The bald, rough-skinned gillie came, and he killed one of the daughters of the giant, and he took the blood to him. He asked for MORE to be brought him. He killed the next. He asked for MORE ; and he killed the third one.

Maol a Chliobain awoke her sisters, and she took them with her on top of her, and she took to going. She took with her a golden cloth that was on the bed, and it called out.

The giant perceived her, and he followed her. The sparks of fire that she was putting out of the stones with her heels, they were striking the giant on the chin; and the sparks of fire that the giant was bringing out of the stones with the points of his feet, they were striking Maol a Chliobain in the back of the head. It is this was their going till they reached a river. She plucked a hair out of her head and made a bridge of it, and she run over the river, and the giant could not follow her. Maol a Chliobain leaped the river, but the river the giant could not leap.

'Thou art over there, Maol a Chliobain.' 'I am, though it is hard for thee.' 'Thou killedst my three bald brown daughters.' 'I killed them, though it is hard for thee.' 'And when wilt thou come again?' 'I will come when my business brings me.'

They went on forward till they reached the house of a farmer. The farmer had three sons. They told how it happened to them. Said the farmer to Maol a Chliobain, 'I will give my eldest son to thy eldest sister, and get for me the fine comb of gold, and the coarse comb of silver that the giant has.' 'It will cost thee no more,' said Maol a Chliobain.

She went away; she reached the house of the giant, she got in unknown; she took with her the combs, and out she went. The giant perceived her, and after her he was till they reached the river. She leaped the river, but the river the giant could not leap. 'Thou art over there, Maol a Chliobain.' 'I am, though it is hard for thee.' 'Thou killedst my three bald brown daughters.' 'I killed them, though it is hard for thee.' 'Thou stolest my fine comb of gold, and my coarse comb of silver.' 'I stole them, though it is hard for thee.' 'When wilt thou come again?' 'I will come when my business brings me.'

She gave the combs to the farmer, and her big sister and the farmer's big son married. 'I will give my middle son to thy middle sister, and get me the giant's sword of light.' 'It will cost thee no more,' said Maol a Chliobain. She went away, and she reached the giant's house; she went up to the top of a tree that was above the giant's well. In the night came the bald rough-skinned gillie with the sword of light to fetch water. When he bent to raise the water, Maol a Chliobain came down and she pushed him down in the well and she drowned him, and she took with her the sword of light.

The giant followed her till she reached the river; she leaped the river, and the giant could not follow her. 'Thou art over there, Maol a Chliobain.' 'I am, if it is hard for thee.' 'Thou killedst my three bald brown daughters.' 'I killed, though it is hard for thee.' 'Thou stolest my fine comb of gold, and my coarse comb of silver.' 'I stole, though it is hard for thee.' 'Thou killedst my bald rough-skinned gillie.' 'I killed, though it is hard for thee.' 'Thou stolest my sword of light.' 'I stole, though it is hard for thee.' 'When wilt though come again?' 'I will come when my business brings me.' She reached the house of the farmer with the sword of light; and her middle sister and the middle son of the farmer married. 'I will give thyself my youngest son,' said the farmer, 'and bring me a buck that the giant has.' 'It will cost thee no more,' said Maol a Chliobain. She went away, and she reached the house of the giant; but when she had hold of the buck, the giant caught her. 'What,' said the giant, 'wouldst thou do to me: if I had done as much harm to thee as thou hast done to me, I would make thee burst thyself with milk porridge; I would then put thee in a pock! I would hang thee to the roof-tree; I would set fire under thee; and I

would set on thee with clubs till thou shouldst fall as a faggot of withered sticks on the floor.' The giant made milk porridge, and he made
her drink it. She put the milk porridge about her mouth and face, and
she laid over as if she were dead. The giant put her in a pock, and he
hung her to the roof-tree; and he went away, himself and his men, to
get wood to the forest. The giant's mother was within. When the
giant was gone, Maol a Chliobain began – ' 'Tis I am in the light! 'Tis
I am in the city of gold!' 'Wilt thou let me in?' said the carlin. 'I will
not let thee in.' At last she let down the pock. She put in the carlin, cat,
and calf, and cream-dish. She took with her the buck and she went
away. When the giant came with his men, himself and his men began
at the bag with the clubs. The carlin was calling, ' 'Tis myself that's
in it.' 'I know that thyself is in it,' would the giant say, as he laid on to
the pock. The pock came down as a faggot of sticks, and what was in
it but his mother. When the giant saw how it was, he took after Maol
a Chliobain; he followed her till she reached the river. Maol a
Chliobain leaped the river, and the giant could not leap it. 'Thou art
over there, Maol a Chliobain.' 'I am, though it is hard for thee.' 'Thou
killedst my three bald brown daughters.' 'I killed, though it is hard for
thee.' 'Thou stolest my golden comb, and my silver comb.' 'I stole,
though it is hard for thee.' 'Thou killedst my bald rough-skinned
gillie.' 'I killed, though it is hard for thee.' 'Thou stolest my sword of
light.' 'I stole, though it is hard for thee.' 'Thou killedst my mother.'
'I killed, though it is hard for thee.' 'Thou stolest my buck.' 'I stole,
though it is hard for thee.' 'When wilt thou come again?' 'I will come
when my business brings me.' 'If thou wert over here, and I yonder,'
said the giant, 'what wouldst thou do to follow me?' 'I would stick
myself down, and I would drink till I should dry the river.' The giant
stuck himself down, and he drank till he burst. Maol a Chliobain and
the farmer's youngest son married.

THE WISE LITTLE GIRL

(RUSSIAN)

wo brothers were traveling together: one was poor and the other was rich, and each had a horse, the poor one a mare, and the rich one a gelding. They stopped for the night, one beside the other. The poor man's mare bore a foal during the night, and the foal rolled under the rich man's cart. In the morning the rich man roused his poor brother, saying: 'Get up, brother. During the night my cart bore a foal.' The brother rose and said: 'How is it possible for a cart to give birth to a foal? It was my mare who bore the foal!' The rich brother said: 'If your mare were his mother, he would have been found lying beside her.' To settle their quarrel they went to the authorities. The rich man gave the judges money and the poor man presented his case in words.

Finally word of this affair reached the tsar himself. He summoned both brothers before him and proposed to them four riddles: 'What is the strongest and swiftest thing in the world? What is the fattest thing in the world? What is the softest thing? And what is the loveliest thing?' He gave them three days' time and said: 'On the fourth day come back with your answers.'

The rich man thought and thought, remembered his godmother, and went to ask her advice. She bade him sit down to table, treated him to food and drink, and then asked: 'Why are you so sad, my godson?' 'The sovereign has proposed four riddles to me, and given me only three days to solve them.' 'What are the riddles? Tell me.' 'Well, godmother, this is the first riddle: "What is the strongest and swiftest thing in the world?"' 'That's not difficult! My husband has a bay mare; nothing in the world is swifter than she is; if you lash her with a whip she will overtake a hare.' 'The second riddle is: "What is the fattest thing in the world?"' 'We have been feeding a spotted boar

for the last two years; he has become so fat that he can barely stand on his legs.' 'The third riddle is: "What is the softest thing in the world?"' 'That's well known. Eider down – you cannot think of anything softer.' 'The fourth riddle is: "What is the loveliest thing in the world?"' 'The loveliest thing in the world is my grandson Ivanushka.' 'Thank you, godmother, you have advised me well. I shall be grateful to you for the rest of my life.'

As for the poor brother, he shed bitter tears and went home He was met by his seven-year-old daughter – she was his only child – who said: 'Why are you sighing and shedding tears, Father?' 'How can I help sighing and shedding tears? The tsar has proposed four riddles to me, and I shall never be able to solve them.' 'Tell me, what are these riddles?' 'Here they are, my little daughter: "What is the strongest and swiftest thing in the world? What is the fattest thing, what is the softest thing, and what is the loveliest thing?"' 'Father, go to the tsar and tell him that the strongest and fastest thing in the world is the wind, the fattest is the earth, for she feeds everything that grows and lives; the softest of all is the hand, for whatever a man may lie on, he puts his hand under his head; and there is nothing lovelier in the world than sleep.'

The two brothers, the poor one and the rich one, came to the tsar. The tsar heard their answers to the riddles, and asked the poor man: 'Did you solve these riddles yourself, or did someone solve them for you?' The poor man answered: 'Your Majesty, I have a seven-year-old daughter, and she gave me the answers.' 'If your daughter is so wise, here is a silken thread for her; let her weave an embroidered towel for me by tomorrow morning.' The peasant took the silken thread and came home sad and grieving. 'We are in trouble,' he said to his daughter. 'The tsar has ordered you to weave a towel from this thread.' 'Grieve not, Father,' said the little girl. She broke off a twig from a broom, gave it to her father, and told him: 'Go to the tsar and ask him to find a master who can make a loom from this twig; on it I will weave his towel.' The peasant did as his daughter told him. The tsar listened to him and gave him a hundred and fifty eggs, saying: 'Give these eggs to your daughter; let her hatch one hundred and fifty chicks by tomorrow.'

The peasant returned home, even more sad and grieving than the first time. 'Ah, my daughter,' he said, 'you are barely out of one trouble before another is upon you.' 'Grieve not, Father,' answered the seven-year-old girl. She baked the eggs for dinner and for supper and sent her father to the king. 'Tell him,' she said to her father, 'that one-day grain is needed to feed the chicks. In one day let a field be plowed and the millet sown, harvested, and threshed; our chickens refuse to peck any other grain.' The tsar listened to this and said: 'Since your daughter is so wise, let her appear before me tomorrow morning – and I want her to come neither on foot nor on horseback, neither naked nor dressed, neither with a present nor without a gift.' 'Now,' thought the peasant, 'even my daughter cannot solve such a difficult riddle; we are lost.' 'Grieve not,' his seven-year-old daughter said to him. 'Go to the hunters and buy me a live hare and a live quail.' The father bought her a hare and a quail.

Next morning the seven-year-old girl took off her clothes, donned a net, took the quail in her hand, sat upon the hare, and went to the palace. The tsar met her at the gate. She bowed to him, saying, 'Here is a little gift for you, Your Majesty,' and handed him the quail. The tsar stretched out his hand, but the quail shook her wings and – flap, flap! – was gone. 'Very well,' said the tsar, 'you have done as I ordered you to do. Now tell me – since your father is so poor, what do you live on?' 'My father catches fish on the shore, and he never puts bait in the water; and I make fish soup in my skirt.' 'You are stupid! Fish never live on the shore, fish live in the water.' 'And you – are you wise? Who ever saw a cart bear foals? Not a cart but a mare bears foals.'

The tsar awarded the foal to the poor peasant and took the daughter into his own palace; when she grew up he married her and she became the tsarina.

BLUBBER BOY

(INNUIT)

nce there was a girl whose boyfriend drowned in the sea. Her parents could do nothing to console her. Nor did any of the other suitors interest her – she wanted the fellow who drowned and no one else. Finally she took a chunk of blubber and carved it into the shape of her drowned boyfriend. Then she carved the boyfriend's face. It was a perfect likeness.

'Oh, if only he were real!' she thought.

She rubbed the blubber against her genitals, round and round, and suddenly it came alive. Her handsome boyfriend was standing in front of her. How delighted she was! She presented him to her parents, saying:

'As you can see, he didn't drown, after all . . .'

The girl's father gave his daughter permission to marry. Now she went with her blubber boy to a small hut just outside the village. Sometimes it would get very warm inside this hut. And then the blubber boy would start to get quite weary. At which point he would say: 'Rub me, dear.' And the girl would rub his entire body against her genitals. This would revive him.

One day the blubber boy was hunting harbor seals and the sun beat down on him harshly. As he paddled his kayak home, he started to sweat. And as he sweated, he got smaller. Half of him had melted away by the time he reached the shore. Then he stepped out of the kayak and fell to the ground, a mere pile of blubber.

'What a pity,' said the girl's parents. 'And he was such a nice young man, too . . .'

The girl buried the blubber beneath a pile of stones. Then she went into mourning. She plugged up her left nostril. She did not sew. She ate neither the eggs of sea-birds nor walrus meat. Each day she visited the blubber in its grave and talked to it and as she did so, walked around the grave three times in the direction of the sun.

After the period of mourning, the girl took another chunk of blubber and began carving again. Again she carved it into the shape of her drowned boyfriend and again rubbed the finished product against her genitals. Suddenly her boyfriend was standing beside her, saying, 'Rub me again, dear . . .'

The Girl Who Stayed
in the Fork of a Tree

(WEST AFRICAN)

his is what a woman did.

She was then living in the bush, never showing herself to anyone. She had living with her just one daughter, who used to pass the day in the fork of a tree making baskets.

One day there appeared a man just when the mother had gone to kill game. He found the girl making baskets as usual. 'Here now!' he said. 'There are people here in the bush! And that girl, what a beauty! Yet they leave her alone. If the king were to marry her, would not all the other queens leave the place?'

Going back to the town, he went straight to the king's house and said, 'Sire, I have discovered a woman of such beauty that, if you call her to this place, all the queens you have here will make haste to go away.'

The following morning people were called together and set to grind their axes. Then they started for the bush. As they came in view of the place, they found the mother had once more gone to hunt.

Before going, she had cooked porridge for her daughter and hung meat for her. Then only had she started on her expedition.

The people said, 'Let us cut down the tree on which the girl is.'

So they put the axes to it. The girl at once started this song:

> 'Mother, come back!
> Mother, here is a man cutting our shade tree.
> Mother, come back!
> Mother, here is a man cutting our shade tree.
> Cut! Here is the tree falling in which I eat.
> Here it is falling.'

The mother dropped there as if from the sky:

> *'Many as you are, I shall stitch you with the big needle.*
> *Stitch! Stitch!'*

They at once fell to the ground . . . The woman left just one to go back and report.

'Go,' she said, 'and tell the news.' He went . . .

When he came to the town the people asked, 'What has happened?'

'There,' he said, 'where we have been! Things are rather bad!'

Likewise, when he stood before the king, the king asked, 'What has happened?'

'Sire,' he said, 'we are all undone. I alone have come back.'

'*Bakoo!* You are all dead! If that is so, tomorrow go to the kraal over there and bring more people. Tomorrow morning let them go and bring me the woman.'

They slept their fill.

The next morning early, the men ground their axes and went to the place.

They, too, found the mother gone, while the porridge was ready there, and the meat was hanging on the tree . . .

'Bring the axes.' Forthwith they went at the shade tree. But the song had already started:

> *'Mother, come back!*
> *Mother, here is a man cutting our shade tree.*
> *Mother, come back!*
> *Mother, here is a man cutting our shade tree.*
> *Cut! Here is the tree falling in which I eat.*
> *Here it is falling.'*

The mother dropped down among them, singing in her turn:

> *'Many as you are, I shall stitch you with the big needle.*
> *Stitch! Stitch!'*

They were dead. The woman and her daughter picked up the axes . . .

'*Olo!*' said the king when he was told. 'Today let all those that are pregnant give birth to their children.'

So one woman after another straightway brought forth her child. Soon there was a whole row of them.

Then the whole band departed, making a confused noise.

When the girl saw that, she said, 'There is no joke about it now. There comes a red army with the umbilical cords still hanging on.'

They found her at her own place in the fork of the tree.

'Let us give them some porridge,' thought the girl.

She just plastered the porridge on their heads, but the children did not eat it.

The last-born then climbed up the shade tree, picked up the baskets which the girl was stitching, and said, 'Now bring me an axe.'

The girl shouted once more:

> '*Mother, come back!*
> *Mother, here is a man cutting our shade tree.*
> *Mother, come back!*
> *Mother, here is a man cutting our shade tree.*
> *Cut! Here is the tree falling in which I eat.*
> *Here it is falling.*'

The mother dropped down among the crowd:

> '*Many as you are, I shall stitch you with the big needle.*
> *Stitch! Stitch!*'

But there was the troop already dragging the girl. They had tied her with their umbilical cords, yes, with their umbilical cords. The mother went on with her incantation:

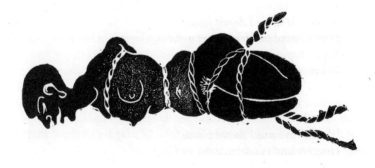

'Many as you are, I shall stitch you with the big needle.
Stitch! Stitch!'

In vain! The troop was already in the fields and the *ngururu* went up as far as God's abode, and soon the children were in the town.

As they reached it, the mother said, 'Since you have carried away my child, I must tell you something. She is not to pound in the mortar, nor to go to fetch water at night. If you send her to do one of these things, mind you! I shall know where to find you.'

Then the mother went back to her abode in the bush.

The following day the king said, 'Let us go hunting.' And to his mother he said, 'My wife must not pound in the mortar. All that she can do is to stitch baskets.'

While the husband was away there in the open flat, the other wives as well as the mother-in-law said, 'Why should not she also pound in the mortar?'

When the girl was told to pound in the mortar, she said, 'No.'

A basket of kafir corn was brought to her.

The mother-in-law herself took away the meal from the mortar, and then the other women in their turn brought corn and put it all there.

So the girl pounded, singing at the same time:

'Pound! At home I do not pound,
Here I pound to celebrate my wedding.
Yepu! Yepu!
If I pound, I go to God's.'

She began to sink into the ground but she went on singing:

'Pound! At home I do not pound,
Here I pound to celebrate my wedding.
Yepu! Yepu!
If I pound, I go to God's.'

She was now in the ground as far as her hips, then as far as her chest.

'Pound! At home I do not pound,
Here I pound to celebrate my wedding.

Yepu! Yepu!
If I pound, I go to God's.'

Soon she was down as far as her neck. Now the mortar went on by itself pounding the grain on the ground, pounding on the ground. Finally the girl disappeared altogether.

When nothing more was seen of her, the mortar still pounded as before on the ground.

The women then said, 'Now what shall we do?'

They went and called a crane, and said, 'Go and break the news to her mother. But, first, let us know, what will you say?'

The crane said, *'Wawani! Wawani!'*

They said, 'That has no meaning, go back. Let us send for the crow.'

The crow was called: 'Now what will you say?'

The crow said, *'Kwa! Kwa! Kwa!'*

'The crow does not know how to call. Go, quail. How will you do?'

The quail said, *'Kwalulu! Kwalulu!'*

'The quail does not know how to do it either. Let us call the doves.'

They said, 'Let us hear, doves, what will you call to her mother?'

Then they heard:

> 'Kuku! Ku!
> *She-who-nurses-the-sun is gone,*
> *She-who-nurses-the sun.*
> *You who dig,*
> *She-who-nurses-the-sun is gone,*
> *She-who-nurses-the-sun.'*

They said, 'Go, you know how to do it, you.'

The mother went when she heard the doves. There she was going toward the town. She carried medicines on a potsherd, also tails of animals with which she beat the air.

While she was on the road, she met a zebra:

> *'Zebra, what are you doing?*
> – Nsenkenene.
> *The wife of my father is dead.*
> – Nsenkenene.

O mother! You shall die.
– Nsenkenene.'

The zebra died. The woman went on, went on, went on, and then found people digging:

'You who dig, what are you doing?
– Nsenkenene.
The wife of my father is dead.
– Nsenkenene.
O mother! You shall die.
– Nsenkenene.'

They also died. The woman went on and went on, then she found a man beating a skin:

'You who beat, what are you doing?
– Nsenkenene.
The wife of my father is dead.
– Nsenkenene.
O mother! You shall die.
– Nsenkenene.'

When she reached the town there:

'Let me gather, let me gather
The herd of my mother.
Mwinsa, get up.
Let me gather the herd.

'Let me gather, let me gather
The herd of my father.
Mwinsa, get up.
Let me gather the herd.'

She then heard the mortar still sounding right above the child.

So she sprayed one medicine, then another.

There was the child already pounding from under the ground. Little by little the head came out. Then the neck, and the song was heard again:

'*Pound! At home I do not pound,*
Here I pound to celebrate my wedding.
Yepu! Yepu!
If I pound, I go to God's.'

The child was now in full view. Finally she stepped outside.
I have finished.

THE PRINCESS IN
THE SUIT OF LEATHER

(EGYPTIAN)

Neither here nor elsewhere lived a king who had a wife whom he loved with all his heart and a daughter who was the light of his eyes. The princess had hardly reached womanhood when the queen fell ill and died. For one whole year the king kept vigil, sitting with bowed head beside her tomb. Then he summoned the matchmakers, elderly women wise in the ways of living, and said, 'I wish to marry again. Here is my poor queen's anklet. Find me the girl, rich or poor, humble or well-born, whose foot this anklet will fit. For I promised the queen as she lay dying that I would marry that girl and no other.'

The matchmakers traveled up and down the kingdom looking for the king's new bride. But search and search as they would, they could not find a single girl around whose ankle the jewel would close. The queen had been such that there was no woman like her. Then one old woman said, 'We have entered the house of every maiden in the land except the house of the king's own daughter. Let us go to the palace.'

When they slipped the anklet on to the princess's foot, it suited as if it had been made to her measure. Out of the seraglio went the women at a run, straight into the king's presence, and said, 'We have visited every maiden in your kingdom, but none was able to squeeze her foot into the late queen's anklet. None, that is, except the princess your daughter. She wears it as easily as if it were her own.' A wrinkled matron spoke up: 'Why not marry the princess? Why give her to a stranger and deprive yourself?' The words were hardly spoken when the king summoned the *qadi* to pen the papers for the marriage. To the princess he made no mention of his plan.

Now there was a bustle in the palace as the jewelers, the clothiers, and the furnishers came to outfit the bride. The princess was pleased to know that she was to be wed. But who her husband was she had no inkling. As late as the 'night of the entering', when the groom first sees the bride, she remained in ignorance even though the servants with their whispers were busy around her, combing and pinning and making her beautiful. At last the minister's daughter, who had come to admire her in her finery, said, 'Why are you frowning? Were not women created for marriage with men? And is there any man whose standing is higher than the king's?'

'What is the meaning of such talk?' cried the princess. 'I won't tell you,' said the girl, 'unless you give me your golden bangle to keep.' The princess pulled off the bracelet, and the girl explained how everything had come about so that the bridegroom was no other than the princess's own father.

The princess turned whiter than the cloth on her head and trembled like one who is sick with the forty-day fever. She rose to her feet and sent away all who were with her. Then, knowing only that she must escape, she ran on to the terrace and leaped over the palace wall, landing in a tanner's yard which lay below. She pressed a handful of gold into the tanner's palm and said, 'Can you make me a suit of leather to hide me from head to heels, showing nothing but my eyes? I want it by tomorrow's dawn.'

The poor man was overjoyed to earn the coins. He set to work with his wife and children. Cutting and stitching through the night they had the suit ready, before it was light enough to know a white thread from a dark. Wait a little! and here comes our lady, the princess. She put on the suit – such a strange spectacle that anyone looking at her would think he was seeing nothing but a pile of hides. In this disguise she left the tanner and lay down beside the city gate, waiting for the day.

Now to return to my lord the king. When he entered the bridal chamber and found the princess gone, he sent his army into the city to search for her. Time and again a soldier would stumble upon the princess lying at the gate and ask, 'Have you seen the king's daughter?' And she would reply:

> *My name is Juleidah for my coat of skins,*
> *My eyes are weak, my sight is dim,*
> *My ears are deaf, I cannot hear.*
> *I care for no one far or near.*

When it was day and the city gate was unbarred, she shuffled out until she was beyond the walls. Then she turned her face away from her father's city and fled.

Walking and running, one foot lifting her and one foot setting her down, there was a day when, with the setting of the sun, the princess came to another city. Too weary to travel a step farther, she fell to the ground. Now her resting place was in the shadow of the wall of the women's quarters, the harem of the sultan's palace. A slave girl, leaning from the window to toss out the crumbs from the royal table, noticed the heap of skins on the ground and thought nothing of it. But when she saw two bright eyes staring out at her from the middle of the hides, she sprang back in terror and said to the queen, 'My lady, there is something monstrous crouching under our window. I have seen it, and it looks like nothing less than an Afreet!' 'Bring it up for me to see and judge,' said the queen.

The slave girl went down shivering with fear, not knowing which was the easier thing to face, the monster outside or her mistress's rage should she fail to do her bidding. But the princess in her suit made no sound when the slave girl tugged at a corner of the leather. The girl took courage and dragged her all the way into the presence of the sultan's wife.

Never had such an astonishing creature been seen in that country. Lifting both palms in amazement, the queen asked her servant, 'What is it?' and then turned to the monster and asked, 'Who are you?' When the heap of skins answered –

> My name is Juleidah for my coat of skins,
> My eyes are weak, my sight is dim,
> My ears are deaf, I cannot hear.
> I care for no one far or near.

– how the queen laughed at the quaint reply! 'Go bring food and drink for our guest,' she said, holding her side. 'We shall keep her to amuse us.' When Juleidah had eaten, the queen said, 'Tell us what you can do, so that we may put you to work about the palace.' 'Anything you ask me to do, I am ready to try,' said Juleidah. Then the queen called, 'Mistress cook! Take this broken-winged soul into your kitchen. Maybe for her sake God will reward us with His blessings.'

So now our fine princess was a kitchen skivvy, feeding the fires and raking out the ashes. And whenever the queen lacked company and felt bored, she called Juleidah and laughed at her prattle.

One day the *wazir* sent word that all the sultan's harem was invited to a night's entertainment in his house. All day long there was a stir of excitement in the women's quarters. As the queen prepared to set out in the evening, she stopped by Juleidah and said, 'Won't you come with us tonight? All the servants and slaves are invited. Aren't you afraid to stay alone?' But Juleidah only repeated her refrain:

> *My ears are deaf, I cannot hear.*
> *I care for no one far or near.*

One of the serving girls sniffed and said, 'What is there to make her afraid? She is blind and deaf and wouldn't notice an Afreet even if he were to jump on top of her in the dark!' So they left.

In the women's reception hall of the *wazir*'s house there was dining and feasting and music and much merriment. Suddenly, at the height of the talk and enjoyment, such a one entered that they all stopped in the middle of the word they were speaking. Tall as a cypress, with a face like a rose and the silks and jewels of a king's bride, she seemed to fill the room with light. Who was it? Juleidah, who had shaken off her coat of leather as soon as the sultan's harem had gone. She had followed them to the *wazir*'s, and now the ladies who had been so merry began to quarrel, each wanting to sit beside the newcomer.

When dawn was near, Juleidah took a handful of gold sequins from the fold of her sash and scattered them on the floor. The ladies scrambled to pick up the bright treasure. And while they were occupied, Juleidah left the hall. Quickly, quickly she raced back to the palace kitchen and put on the coat of leather. Soon the others returned. Seeing the heap of hides on the kitchen floor, the queen poked it with the toe of her red slipper and said, 'Truly, I wish you had been with us to admire the lady who was at the entertainment.' But Juleidah only mumbled, 'My eyes are weak, I cannot see . . .' and they all went to their own beds to sleep.

When the queen woke up next day, the sun was high in the sky. As was his habit, the sultan's son came in to kiss his mother's hand and bid her good morning. But she could talk only of the visitor at the *wazir*'s feast. 'O my son,' she sighed, 'it was a woman with such a face and such a neck and such a form that all who saw her said, "She is the

daughter of neither a king nor a sultan, but of someone greater yet!"'
On and on the queen poured out her praises of the woman, until the
prince's heart was on fire. Finally his mother concluded, 'I wish I had
asked her father's name so that I could engage her to be your bride.'
And the sultan's son replied, 'When you return tonight to continue
your entertainment, I shall stand outside the *wazir*'s door and wait
until she leaves. I'll ask her then about her father and her station.'

At sunset the women dressed themselves once more. With the folds of
their robes smelling of orange blossom and incense and their bracelets
chinking on their arms, they passed by Juleidah lying on the kitchen
floor and said, 'Will you come with us tonight?' But Juleidah only
turned her back on them. Then as soon as they were safely gone, she
threw off her suit of leather and hurried after them.

In the *wazir*'s hall the guests pressed close around Juleidah, wanting to see her and ask where she came from. But to all their questions
she gave no answer, whether yes or no, although she sat with them
until the dawning of the day. Then she threw a fistful of pearls on the
marble tiles, and while the women pushed one another to catch them,
she slipped away as easily as a hair is pulled out of the dough.

Now who was standing at the door? The prince, of course. He had
been waiting for this moment. Blocking her path, he grasped her arm
and asked who her father was and from what land she came. But the
princess had to be back in her kitchen or her secret would be known.
So she fought to get away, and in the scuffle, she pulled the prince's
ring clean off his hand. 'At least tell me where you come from!' he
shouted after her as she ran. 'By Allah, tell me where!' And she
replied, 'I live in a land of paddles and ladles.' Then she fled into the
palace and hid in her coat of hides.

In came the others, talking and laughing. The prince told his
mother what had taken place and announced that he intended to make
a journey. 'I must go to the land of the paddles and ladles,' he said. 'Be
patient, my son,' said the queen. 'Give me time to prepare your provisions.' Eager as he was, the prince agreed to delay his departure for
two days – 'But not one hour more!'

Now the kitchen became the busiest corner of the palace. The
grinding and sieving, the kneading and the baking began and Juleidah
stood watching. 'Away with you,' cried the cook, 'this is no work for
you!' 'I want to serve the prince our master like the rest!' said Juleidah.

Willing and not willing to let her help, the cook gave her a piece of dough to shape. Juleidah began to make a cake, and when no one was watching, she pushed the prince's ring inside it. And when the food was packed Juleidah placed her own little cake on top of the rest.

Early on the third morning the rations were strapped into the saddlebags, and the prince set off with his servants and his men. He rode without slackening until the sun grew hot. Then he said, 'Let us rest the horses while we ourselves eat a mouthful.' A servant, seeing Juleidah's tiny loaf lying on top of all the rest, flung it to one side. 'Why did you throw that one away?' asked the prince. 'It was the work of the creature Juleidah; I saw her make it,' said the servant. 'It is as misshapen as she is.' The prince felt pity for the strange half-wit and asked the servant to bring back her cake. When he tore open the loaf, look, his own ring was inside! The ring he lost the night of the *wazir*'s entertainment. Understanding now where lay the land of ladles and paddles, the prince gave orders to turn back.

When the king and queen had greeted him, the prince said, 'Mother, send me my supper with Juleidah.' 'She can barely see or even hear,' said the queen. 'How can she bring your supper to you?' 'I shall not eat unless Juleidah brings the food,' said the prince. So when the time came, the cooks arranged the dishes on a tray and helped Juleidah lift it on to her head. Up the stairs she went, but before she reached the prince's room she tipped the dishes and sent them crashing to the floor. 'I told you she cannot see,' the queen said to her son. 'And I will only eat what Juleidah brings,' said the prince.

The cooks prepared a second meal, and when they had balanced the loaded tray upon Juleidah's head, they sent two slave girls to hold her by either hand and guide her to the prince's door. 'Go,' said the prince to the two slaves, 'and you, Juleidah, come.' Juleidah began to say,

> My eyes are weak, my sight is dim,
> I'm called Juleidah for my coat of skins,
> My ears are deaf, I cannot hear,
> I care for no one far or near.

But the prince told her, 'Come and fill my cup.' As she approached, he drew the dagger that hung at his side and slashed her leather coat from collar to hem. It fell into a heap upon the floor – and there stood the maiden his mother had described, one who could say to the moon, 'Set that I may shine in your stead.'

Hiding Juleidah in a corner of the room, the prince sent for the queen. Our mistress cried out when she saw the pile of skins upon the floor. 'Why, my son, did you bring her death upon your neck? The poor thing deserved your pity more than your punishment!' 'Come in, Mother,' said the prince. 'Come and look at our Juleidah before you mourn her.' And he led his mother to where our fine princess sat revealed, her fairness filling the room like a ray of light. The queen threw herself upon the girl and kissed her on this side and on that, and bade her sit with the prince and eat. Then she summoned the *qadi* to write the paper that would bind our lord the prince to the fair princess, after which they lived together in the sweetest bliss.

Now we make our way back to the king, Juleidah's father. When he entered the bridal chamber to unveil his own daughter's face and found her gone, and when he had searched the city in vain for her, he called his minister and his servants and dressed himself for travel. From country to country he journeyed, entering one city and leaving the next, taking with him in chains the old woman who had first suggested to him that he marry his own daughter. At last he reached the city where Juleidah was living with her husband the prince.

Now, the princess was sitting in her window when they entered the gate, and she knew them as soon as she saw them. Straightway she

sent to her husband urging him to invite the strangers. Our lord went to meet them and succeeded in detaining them only after much pressing, for they were impatient to continue their quest. They dined in the prince's guest hall, then thanked their host and took leave with the words, 'The proverb says: "Have your fill to eat, but then up, on to your feet!"' – while he delayed them further with the proverb, 'Where you break your bread, there spread out your bed.'

In the end the prince's kindness forced the tired strangers to lie in his house as guests for the night. 'But why did you single out these strangers?' the prince asked Juleidah. 'Lend me your robes and headcloth and let me go to them,' she said. 'Soon you will know my reasons.'

Thus disguised, Juleidah sat with her guests. When the coffee cups had been filled and emptied, she said, 'Let us tell stories to pass the time. Will you speak first, or shall I?' 'Leave us to our sorrows, my son,' said the king her father. 'We have not the spirit to tell tales.' 'I'll entertain you, then, and distract your mind,' said Juleidah. 'There once was a king,' she began, and went on to tell the history of her own adventures from the beginning to the end. Every now and then the old woman would interrupt and say, 'Can you find no better story than this, my son?' But Juleidah kept right on, and when she had finished she said, 'I am your daughter the princess, upon whom all these troubles fell through the words of this old sinner and daughter of shame!'

In the morning they flung the old woman over a tall cliff into the *wadi*. Then the king gave half his kingdom to his daughter and the prince, and they lived in happiness and contentment until death, the parter of the truest lovers' divided them.

THE HARE

(SWAHILI)

ne day the hare went to the house of the hunter who was away hunting. He said to the hunter's wife: 'Come to my house and live with me; we have meat and vegetables every day.' The woman went with him, but when she saw the lair of the hare and had eaten grass with him and slept in the open with him, she was not satisfied. She said: 'I want to go back.' The hare said: 'You came here by your own choice.' The woman did not know the road in the bush, so she said: 'Come with me and I will cook a nice dinner.' The hare took her to her house. Then she said: 'Get me some firewood.'

The hare went to the forest and collected a load of firewood. The woman lit a fire and put a pot on it. When the water was boiling she put the hare into the pot. When the hunter came home she said: 'I caught a hare for dinner.' The hunter never knew what happened.

MOSSYCOAT

(ENGLISH GYPSY)

ere was once a poor ould widder-woman as lived in a little cottage. She'd two daughters; de younger on 'em was about nineteen or twenty, and she was very beautiful. Her mother was busy ivry day, a-spinning of a coat for her.

A hawker came courting dis girl; came reg'lar he did, and kept on a-bringing of her dis thing and dat. He was in love wid her, and badly wanted her to marry him. But she wasn't in love wid him; it didn't fall out like dat; and she was in a puzzlement what she'd best do about him. So one day she ext her mother. 'Let he come,' her mother telt her, 'and git what you can out'n him, while I finish dis coat, after when you won't have no need 'n him, nor his presents neether. So tell him, girl, as you won't marry him, unless he gits you a dress o' white satin with sprigs o' goold on it as big as a man's hand; and mind as you tells him it mus' fit exac'ly.'

Next time de hawker cam round, and ext her to wed him, de girl telt him just dis, de wery same as her mother'd said. He took stock 'n her size and build, de hawker did; and inside of a week he was back wid de dress. It answered de describance all right, an when de girl went upstairs wid her mother, and tried it on, it fit 'n exac'ly.

'What should I do now, Mother?' she ext.

'Tell him,' her mother says, 'as you won't marry him unless he gits you a dress med o' silk de color o' all de birds o' de air and as afore, it must fit you exac'ly.'

De girl telt de hawker dis, and in two or three days he was back at de cottage, wid dis colored silk dress de girl ed exted for; and being as he knowed de size from de t'other un, in course it fit her exac'ly.

'Now what should I do, Mother?' she ext.

'Tell him,' her mother says, 'as you won't marry him unless he gits you a pair o' silver slippers as fits you exac'ly.'

De girl telt de hawker so, and in a few days he called round wid 'em. Her feet was only about three inches long, but de slippers fit her exac'ly; dey was not too tight, neether was dey too loose. Agen de girl ext her mother what she should do now. 'I can finish de coat tonight,' her mother said, 'so you can tell de hawker as you'll marry him tomorrow, and he's to be here at 10 o'clock.' So de girl telt him dis. 'Think-on, my dear,' she says, '10 o'clock in de morning.' 'I'll be dere, my love,' he says, 'by God, I will.'

That night her mother was at work on de coat till late, but she finished it all right. Green moss and goold thread, dat's what it was med on; just dem two things. 'Mossycoat,' she called it, and give de name to de younger daughter, as she'd med it for. It was a magic coat, she said, a wishing coat, she telt her daughter; when she'd got it on, she telt her she'd only to wish to be somewhere, and she'd be dere dat wery instant, and de same if she wanted to change hersel' into summat else, like to be a swan or a bee.

Next morning de mother was up by it was light. She called her younger daughter, and telt her she mus' now go into de world and seek her fortune, and a handsome fortune it was to be. She was a foreseer, de owld mother was, and know'd what was a-coming. She give her daughter mossycoat to put on, and a goold crown to tek wid her, and she telt her to tek as well de two dresses and de silver slippers she'd had off'n de hawker. But she was to go in de clo'es as she wore ivery day, her working clo'es dat is. And now she's ready for to start, Mossycoat is. Her mother den tells her she is to wish herself a hundred miles away, and den walk on till she comes to a big hall, and dere she's to ext for a job. 'You won't hev far to walk, my blessed,' she says – dat's de mother. 'And dey'll be sure to find you work at dis big hall.'

Mossycoat did as her mother telt her, and soon she foun' herself in front of a big gentleman's house. She knocked at de front door and said as she was looking for work. Well, de long and de short of it was as de mistress hersel' come to see her; and she liked de look 'n her, de lady did.

'What work can you do?' she ext.

'I can cook, your ladyship,' said Mossycoat. 'In fact, I'm in de way o' being a wery good cook, from what peoples 'es remarked.'

'I can't give you a job as cook,' de lady tells her, 'being as I got one already; but I'd be willing to imploy you to help de cook, if so as you'd be satisfied wid dat.'

'Thank you, ma'am,' says Mossycoat. 'I s'd be real glad 'n de place.'

So it was settled as she was to be undercook. And after when de lady'd showed her up to her bedroom, she took her to de kitchen, and interdoosed her to de t'other sarvants.

'Dis is Mossycoat,' she tells 'em, 'and I've engaged her,' she says, 'to be undercook.'

She leaves 'em den, de mistress does; and Mossycoat she goes up to her bedroom agen, to unpack her things, and hide away her goold crown and silver slippers, and her silk and satin dresses.

It goes wi'out saying as de t'other kitchen girls was fair beside theirsels wid jealousy; and it didn't mend matters as de new girl was a dam' sight beautifuller nor what any of dem was. Here was dis wagrant i' rags put above dem, when all she was fit for at best was to be scullery girl. If anybody was to be undercook, it stands to sense it sud'er been one o' dem as really knowed about things, not dis girl i' rags and tatters, picked up off'n de roads. But dey'd put her in her place, dey would. So dey goes on and on, like what women will, till Mossycoat come down ready to start work. Den dey sets on her. 'Who de devil did she think she was, setting hersel' above dem? She'd be undercook, would she? No dam' fear . . . dey relow of dat. What she'd hev to do, and all she was fit for, was to scour de pans, clean de knives, do de grates and suchlike; and all she'd git was dis.' And down come de skimmer on top of her head pop, pop, pop. 'Dat's what you deserves,' dey tell her, 'and dat's what you can expect, my lady.'

And dat's how it was wid Mossycoat. She was put to do all de dirtiest work, and soon she was up to de ears in grease, and her face as black as soot. And ivery now and agen, first one and then another o' de sarvants, 'ld pop, pop, pop her a-top o' de head wid de skimmer, till de poor girls' head was dat sore, she couldn't hardly bide it.

Well, it got on, and it got on, and still Mossycoat was at her pans, and knives, and grates; and still de sarvants was pop, pop, popping her on de head wid de skimmer. Now dere was a big dance coming on, as was to last three nights, wid hunting and other sports in de daytime. All de headmost people for miles round was to be dere; and de master, and mistress, and de young master – dey'd niver had but one child –

in course dey was a-going. It was all de talk among de sarvants, dis dance was. One was wishing she could be dere; another'd like to dance wid some 'n de young lords; a third 'ld like to see de ladies' dresses, and so dey went on, all excepting Mossycoat. If only dey'd de clo'es, dey'd be al right, dey thought, as dey considered deirselves as good as high-titled ladies any day. 'And you, Mossycoat, you'd like to go, wouldn't you now?' dey says. 'A fit person you'd be to be dere in all your rags and dirt,' dey says, and down comes de skimmer on her head, pop, pop, pop. Den dey laughs at her; which goes to show what a low class o' people dey was.

Now Mossycoat, as I've said afore, was wery handsome, and rags and dirt couldn't hide dat. De t'other sarvants might think as it did, but de young master'd hed his eyes on her, and de master and mistress, dey'd al'ays taken partic'lar notice o' her, on account of her good looks. When de big dance was coming on, dey thought as it'd be nice to ex her to go to it; so dey sent for her to see if she'd like to. 'No, thank you,' she says, 'I'd niver think o' such a thing. I knows my place better'n dat,' she says. 'Besides, I'd greasy all de one side o' de coach,' she tells 'em, 'and anybody's clo'es as I comed up agen.' Dey make light on dat, and presses her to go, de master and mistress does. It's wery kind on 'em, Mossycoat says, but she's not for going, she says. And she sticks to dat. When she gets back into de kitchen, you may depend on it, de t'other sarvants wants to know why she'd bin sent for. Had she got notice, or what was it? So she telt 'em de master and mistress 'ed ext her would she like to go to the dance wid 'em. 'What? You?' dey says, 'it's unbelievable. If it had been one o' we, now, dat'd be different. But you! Why, you'd niver be relowed in, as you'd greasy all the gentlemen's clo'es, if dere were any as 'ed dance wid a scullery girl; and de ladies, dey'd be forced to howld dere noses w'en dey passed by you, to be sure dey would.' No, dey couldn't believe, dey said, as de master and mistress had iver ext *her* to go to de ball wid 'em. She must be lying, dey said, and down come de skimmer a-top of her head, pop, pop, pop.

Next night, de master and de mistress and dere son, dis time, ext her to go to de dance. It was a grand affair de night before, dey said, and she sud ev bin dere. It was going to be still grander tonight, dey said, and dey begged of her to come wid 'em, especially de young master. But no, she says, on account of her rags and her grease, and dirt, she couldn't and she wouldn't; and even de young master couldn't persuade her, though it wasn't for de want o' trying. The t'other sarvants just didn't believe her when she telt 'em about her being invited agen to de dance, and about de young master being wery pressing.

'Hark to her!' they says, 'What'll de upstart say next? And all dam' lies,' dey says. Den one o' dem, wid a mouth like a pig-trough, and legs like a cart horse, catches hold o' de skimmer, and down it comes, pop, pop, pop, on Mossycoat's head.

Dat night, Mossycoat decided as she'd go to de dance, in right proper style, all on her own, and wi'out nobody knowing it. De first thing she does is to put all de t'other sarvants into a trance; she just touches each on 'em, unnoticed, as she moves about, and dey all falls asleep under a spell as soon as she does, and can't wake up agen on deir own; de spell has to be broke by somebody wid de power, same as she has through her magic coat, or has got it some other way. Next Mossycoat has a real good wash: she'd niver been relowed to afore, sin' she'd bin at de hall as the other sarvants was retermined to mek and to keep her as greasy and dirty as dey could. Den she goes upstairs to her bedroom, throws off her working clo'es and shoes, and puts on her white satin dress wid de gowld sprigs, her silver slippers, and her gowld crown. In course, she had mossy coat on underneath. So as soon as she was ready, she jus' wished hersel' at de dance, and dere she was, wery near as soon as de wish was spoke. She did jus' feel hersel' rising up and flying through de elements but only for a moment. Den she was in de ballroom.

De young master sees her standing dere, and once he catched sight on her he can't tek his eyes off her; he'd niver seen anybody as han'some afore, or as beautifully dressed. 'Who is she?' he exes his mother; but she doesn't know, she tells him.

'Can't you find out, Mother?' he says. 'Can't you go and talk to her?' His mother sees as he'll niver rest till she does, so she goes and interdooses hersel' to de young lady, and exes her who she is, where she comes from, and such as dat; but all she could git out'n her was as she come from a place where dey hit her on de head wid de skimmer. Den presently, de young master he goes over and interdooses hissel', but she doesn't tell him her name nor nothing; and when he exes her to hev a dance wid him, she says no, she'd rather not. He stops aside of her though, and keeps exing her time and agen, and at de finish she says as she will, and links up wid him. Dey dances once, up and down de room; den she says she must go. He presses her to stop, but it's a waste o' breath; she's retermined to go, dere and den.

'All right,' he says – dere was nothing else he could say – 'I'll come and see you off.' But she jus' wished she was at home, and dere she was. No seeing of her off for de young master, dere warn't, she jus' went from his side in de twinkle of an eye, leaving him standing dere gaping wid wonderment. Thinking she might be in de hall, or de porch, a-waiting of her carriage, he goes to see, but dere's no sign on her anywheres inside or out, and nobody as he exed seen her go. He went back to de ballroom, but he can't think of nothing or nobody but her and all de time he's a-wanting to go home.

When Mossycoat gets back home, she meks sure as all de t'other sarvants is still in a trance. Den she goes up and changes into her working get-up; and after when she'd done dat, she come down into de kitchen agen, and touches each 'n de sarvants. Dat wakens 'em, as you might say; anyway, dey starts up, wondering whatever time o' day it is, and how long dey bin asleep. Mossycoat tells 'em, and drops a hint as she may have to let de mistress know. Dey begs on her not to let on about 'em, and most'n 'em thinks to give her things if she won't. Owld things, dey was, but wid a bit o' wear in 'em still – a skirt, a pair o' shoes, stockings, stays, and what not. So Mossycoat promises as she won't tell on 'em. An' dat night, dey don't hit her on de head wid de skimmer.

All next day de young master is unrestful. He can't settle his mind to nothing but de young lady as he'd fell in love wid last night at de wery first sight 'n her. He was wondering all de time would she be dere agen tonight, and would she vanish de same as she done last night; and thinking how he could stop her, or catch up wid her if she was for doing dis a second time. He must find out where she lives, he thinks, else how's he to go on after when de dance is over. He'd die, he tells his mother, if he can't git her for his wife; he's dat madly in love wid her. 'Well,' says his mother, 'I thought as she was a nice modest girl, but she wouldn't say who or what she was, or where she come from, except it was a place where dey hit her on de head wid de skimmer.'

'She's a bit of a mystery, I know,' says de young master, 'but dat don't signify as I want her any de less. I must hev her, Mother,' he says, 'whoiver and whativer she is; and dat's de dear God's truth, Mother, strike me dead if it ain't.'

Women sarvants 'es long ears, and big mouths, and you may be

sure as it wasn't long afore de young master and dis wonderful han'some
lady he'd fell in love wid was all de talk in de kitchen.

'And fancy you, Mossycoat, thinking as he specially wanted *you* to
go to de dance,' dey says, and starts in on her proper, meking all
manner o' nasty sarcastical remarks, and hitting her on de head wid de
skimmer, pop, pop, pop, for lying to 'em (as dey said). It was de same
agen later on, after when de master and mistress hed sent for her, and
exed her once more to go to de dance wid 'em, and once more she'd
defused. It was her last chance, dey said – dat was de sarvants – an' a
lot more besides, as ain't worth repeating. And down came de skimmer a-top of her head, pop, pop, pop. Den she put de whole devil's
breed 'n 'em into a trance like she done de night afore, and got hersel'
ready to go to de dance, de only difference being as dis time she put
her t'other dress on, de one med o' silk de color of all de birds o' de
air.

She's in de ballroom now, Mossycoat is. De young master, he's
waiting and watching for her. As soon as he sees her, he exes his
father to send for de fastest horse in his stable, and hev it kept standing ready saddled at de door. Den he exes his mother to go over and
talk to de young lady for a bit. She does dat, but can't larn no more
about her 'an she did the night afore. Den de young master hears as
his horse is ready at de door; so he goes over to de young lady, and
exes her for a dance. She says jus' de same as de night afore, 'No,' at
first, but 'Yes,' at de finish, and jus' as den, she says she mus' go
after when dey've danced only once de length o' de room an' back.
But dis time, he keeps howld 'n her till dey gets outside. Den she
wishes hersel' at home, and is dere nearly as soon as she's spoken. De
young master felt her rise into de air, but couldn't do nothing to stop
her. But p'raps he did jus' touch her foot, as she dropped one slipper;
I couldn't be sure as he did; it looks a bit like it though. He picks de
slipper up; but as for catching up wid her, it would be easier by far
to catch up wid de wind on a blowy night. As soon as she gits home,
Mossycoat changes back into her owld things; den she looses de
t'other sarvants from de spell she'd put on 'em. Dey've been asleep
agen, dey thinks, and offers her one a shilling, another a half a
crown, a third a week's wage, if she won't tell on 'em; and she promises as she won't.

De young master's in bed next day, a-dying for de love of de lady
as lost one 'n her silver slippers de night afore. De doctors can't do

him not de leastest good. So it was give out what his state was, and
as it was only de lady able to wear de slipper as could save his life;
and if she'd come forrad, he'd marry her. De slippers, as I said ear-
lier on, was only but three inches long, or dereabouts. Ladies came
from near and far, some wid big feet and some wid small, but none
small enough to git it on howiver much dey pinched and squeezed.
Poorer people came as well, but it was jus' de same wid dem. And in
course, all de sarvants tried, but dey was out'n altogether. De young
master was a-dying. Was dere nobody else, his mother exed, nobody
at all, rich or poor? 'No,' dey telt her, everybody'd tried it excepting
it was Mossycoat.

'Tell her to come at once,' says de mistress.

So dey fetched her.

'Try dis slipper on,' she says – dat's de mistress.

Mossycoat slips her foot into it easy enough; it fits her exac'ly. De
young master jumps out o' bed, and is jus' a-going to tek her in his
arms.

'Stop,' she says, and runs off; but afore long she's back agen in her
satin dress wid gowld sprigs, her gowld crown, and both her silver
slippers. De young master is jus' a-going to tek her in his arms.

'Stop,' she says, and agen she runs off. Dis time she comes back in
her silk dress de color of all de birds o' de air. She don't stop him dis
time, and as de saying used to be, he nearly eats her.

After when dey's all settled down agen, and is talking quiet-like,
dere's one or two things as de master and mistress and de young master'ld like to know. How did she get to dance, and back agen, in no
time, they exed her. 'Jus' wishing,' she says, and she tells 'em all as I've
telt you about the magic coat her mother 'ed med for her, and de
powers it give her if she cared to use 'em. 'Yes, dat explains everything,' dey says. Den dey bethinks theirselves of her saying as she
came from where dey hit her on de head wid de skimmer. What did
she mean by dat, dey wants to know. She meant jus' what she said, she
telt 'em; it was always coming down on her head, pop, pop, pop. They
were right angry when dey heard dat, and de whole of de kitchen sarvants was telt to go, and de dogs sent arter dem to drive de varmints
right away from de place.

As soon as dey could Mossycoat and de young master got married,
and she'd a coach and six to ride in, ai, ten if she liked, for you may be
sure as she'd everything as she fancied. Dey lived happy ever after, and

had a basketful o' children. I was dere when de owld son comed of age, a-playing de fiddle. But dat was many years back, and I shouldn't wonder if de owld master and mistress isn't dead by now, though I've niver heerd tell as dey was.

Vasilisa the Priest's Daughter

(RUSSIAN)

n a certain land, in a certain kingdom, there was a priest named
Vasily who had a daughter named Vasilisa Vasilyevna. She
wore man's clothes, rode horseback, was a good shot with the
rifle, and did everything in a quite unmaidenly way, so that
only very few people knew that she was a girl; most people thought
that she was a man and called her Vasily Vasilyevich, all the more so
because Vasilisa Vasilyevna was very fond of vodka, and this, as is well
known, is entirely unbecoming to a maiden. One day, King Barkhat
(for that was the name of the king of that country) went to hunt
game, and he met Vasilisa Vasilyevna. She was riding horseback in
man's clothes and was also hunting. When he saw her, King Barkhat
asked his servants: 'Who is that young man?' One servant answered
him: 'Your Majesty, that is not a man, but a girl; I know for a certainty
that she is the daughter of the priest Vasily and that her name is
Vasilisa Vasilyevna.'

As soon as the king returned home he wrote a letter to the priest
Vasily asking him to permit his son Vasily Vasilyevich to come to
visit him and eat at the king's table. Meanwhile he himself went to the
little old back yard witch and began to question her as to how he
could find out whether Vasily Vasilyevich was really a girl. The little
old witch said to him: 'On the right side of your chamber hang up an
embroidery frame, and on the left side a gun; if she is really Vasilisa
Vasilyevna, she will first notice the embroidery frame; if she is Vasily
Vasilyevich, she will notice the gun.' King Barkhat followed the little
old witch's advice and ordered his servants to hang up an embroidery
frame and a gun in his chamber.

As soon as the king's letter reached Father Vasily and he showed it to
his daughter, she went to the stable, saddled a gray horse with a gray

mane, and went straight to King Barkhat's palace. The king received her; she politely said her prayers, made the sign of the cross as is prescribed, bowed low to all four sides, graciously greeted King Barkhat, and entered the palace with him. They sat together at table and began to drink heady drinks and eat rich viands. After dinner, Vasilisa Vasilyevna walked with King Barkhat through the palace chambers; as soon as she saw the embroidery frame she began to reproach King Barkhat: 'What kind of junk do you have here, King Barkhat? In my father's house there is no trace of such womanish fiddle-faddle, but in King Barkhat's palace womanish fiddle-faddle hangs in the chambers!' Then she politely said farewell to King Barkhat and rode home. The king had not found out whether she was really a girl.

And so two days later – no more – King Barkhat again sent a letter to the priest Vasily, asking him to send his son Vasily Vasilyevich to the palace. As soon as Vasilisa Vasilyevna heard about this, she went to the stable, saddled a gray horse with a gray mane, and rode straight to King Barkhat's palace. The king received her. She graciously greeted him, politely said her prayers to God, made the sign of the cross as is prescribed, and bowed low to all four sides. King Barkhat had been advised by the little old back yard witch to order kasha cooked for supper and to have it stuffed with pearls. The little old witch had told him that if the youth was really Vasilisa Vasilyevna he would put the pearls in a pile, and if he was Vasily Vasilyevich he would throw them under the table.

Supper time came. The king sat at table and placed Vasilisa Vasilyevna on his right hand, and they began to drink heady drinks and eat rich viands. Kasha was served after all the other dishes, and as soon as Vasilisa Vasilyevna took a spoonful of it and discovered a pearl, she flung it under the table together with the kasha and began to reproach King Barkhat. 'What kind of trash do they put in your kasha?' she said. 'In my father's house there is no trace of such womanish fiddle-faddle, yet in King Barkhat's house womanish fiddle-faddle is put in the food!' Then she politely said farewell to King Barkhat and rode home. Again the king had not found out whether she was really a girl, although he badly wanted to know.

Two days later, upon the advice of the little old witch, King Barkhat ordered that his bath be heated; she had told him that if the youth really was Vasilisa Vasilyevna he would refuse to go to the bath with him. So the bath was heated.

Again King Barkhat wrote a letter to the priest Vasily, telling him to send his son Vasily Vasilyevich to the palace for a visit. As soon as Vasilisa Vasilyevna heard about it, she went to the stable, saddled her gray horse with the gray mane, and galloped straight to King Barkhat's palace. The king went out to receive her on the front porch. She greeted him civilly and entered the palace on a velvet rug; having come in, she politely said her prayers to God, made the sign of the cross as is prescribed, and bowed very low to all four sides. Then she sat at table with King Barkhat, and began to drink heady drinks and eat rich viands.

After dinner the king said: 'Would it not please you, Vasily Vasilyevich, to come with me to the bath?' 'Certainly, Your Majesty,' Vasilisa Vasilyevna answered, 'I have not had a bath for a long time and should like very much to steam myself.' So they went together to the bathhouse. While King Barkhat undressed in the anteroom, she took her bath and left. So the king did not catch her in the bath either. Having left the bathhouse, Vasilisa Vasilyevna wrote a note to the king and ordered the servants to hand it to him when he came out. And this note ran: 'Ah, King Barkhat, raven that you are, you could not surprise the falcon in the garden! For I am not Vasily Vasilyevich, but Vasilisa Vasilyevna.' And so King Barkhat got nothing for all his trouble; for Vasilisa Vasilyevna was a clever girl, and very pretty too!

THE PUPIL

(SWAHILI)

Sheikh Ali was an old teacher and Kibwana was his pupil. One day the teacher went out and the teacher's wife called Kibwana: 'You, young man, come quickly.' 'What for?' 'Stupid, you are hungry and you don't know how to eat!' 'All right,' said Kibwana when he at last understood. He went inside and lay with his teacher's wife. The teacher's wife taught him what the teacher did not teach him.

THE RICH FARMER'S WIFE

(NORWEGIAN)

here was once a rich farmer who owned big property; silver was stowed away in his chest, and he had money in the bank besides; but he felt something was wanting, for he was a widower. One day his neighbor's daughter was working for him, and he took a great fancy to her. As her parents were poor, he thought he had only to hint at marriage, and she would jump at the chance. So he told her he had really been thinking of getting married again.

'Oh, yes, one can think all kinds of things,' said the girl, chuckling to herself.

She thought the ugly old fellow might have thought of something that suited him better than getting married.

'Well, you see, I thought you might be my wife,' said the farmer.

'No, thank you,' said the girl, 'I can't see much in that.'

The farmer was not used to hearing 'No', and the less she wanted him, the crazier he was to have her.

As he did not get anywhere with the girl, he sent for her father and told him, if he could manage to make her consent, he need not pay back the money he had borrowed off the farmer and he might have the field that lay next to his meadow into the bargain.

Well, the father thought he would soon bring his daughter to her senses. 'She is only a child,' he said, 'and doesn't know what is best for her.'

But all his talking and coaxing did no good. She would not have the farmer, not even if he was plastered all over with gold right up to his ears.

The farmer waited day after day. Finally he grew so angry and impatient that he said to the girl's father, if he were going to keep his promise, matters would have to be fixed at once, for he would not wait any longer.

The father saw no way out of it except for the rich farmer to get everything ready for the wedding, and, when the parson and the wedding guests were there, to send for the girl just as if she were wanted for some work on the farm. When she came, he would have to marry her in a hurry, so she would have no chance to change her mind.

The rich farmer thought this was all right, so he set to brewing and baking and getting ready for the wedding in grand style. When the guests had come, the rich farmer called one of his boys and told him to run down to the neighbor's and ask him to send what he had promised.

'But if you're not back right away,' he said, shaking his fist at the boy, 'I'll . . .' he didn't have a chance to say more, for the boy was off like a flash.

'My boss wants you to send what you've promised him,' said the boy when he got to the neighbor's, 'but you've got to hustle, for he's in an awful hurry today.'

'All right, run down to the meadow and take her along, for there you'll find her,' said the neighbor.

The boy hurried off, and when he got to the meadow, he found the daughter raking.

'I came to fetch what your father has promised my boss,' he said.

'Ah, ha, is that the way you're going to fool me?' thought the girl.

'Is that what you're after?' she said. 'I suppose it is that little bay mare of ours. You must go over and get her; she's tethered on the other side of the peas.'

The boy jumped on the back of the little bay mare and rode her home at full gallop.

'Have you got her with you?' said the rich farmer.

'She's down at the door,' said the boy.

'Take her up to my mother's room,' said the farmer.

'Goodness gracious, how are you going to manage that?' said the boy.

'You just do as I tell you,' said the farmer. 'If you can't manage it alone, get the others to help you.' He thought the girl might make trouble.

When the boy saw his master's face, he knew there was no use arguing. So he got all the help and hurried down. Some tugged at the head, and some pushed behind, and at last they got the mare upstairs and into the bedroom. There lay the wedding finery all ready.

'Well, I've finished the job, boss,' said the boy, 'but it was no easy matter, the very worst I've ever had to do on this farm.'

'All right, you shan't have done it for nothing,' said the farmer. 'Now send the women folk up to dress her.'

'But, my goodness gracious!' said the boy.

'No nonsense,' said the farmer; 'tell them to dress her and to forget neither wreath nor crown.'

The boy hurried down into the kitchen.

'Now, listen, girls,' he said, 'hurry upstairs and dress the little bay mare as a bride. I guess the boss wants to make the wedding guests snicker.'

Well, the girls dressed the little bay mare in everything that was there. Then the boy went down and said she was ready, with wreath and crown and all.

'All right, bring her down,' said the rich farmer. 'I'll receive her myself at the door.'

There was a terrible clatter on the stairs, for this bride did not come down in satin slippers. But when the door was opened, and the rich farmer's bride came into the parlor, there was plenty of giggling and snickering.

And as for the rich farmer, he was so pleased with his bride that he did not go courting again.

KEEP YOUR SECRETS

(WEST AFRICAN)

certain girl was given by her parents to a young man in marriage. She did not care for the youth, so she refused and said that she would choose a husband for herself. Shortly after there came to the village a fine young man of great strength and beauty. The girl fell in love with him at first sight and told her parents that she had found the man she wished to marry, and as the latter was not unwilling the marriage soon took place.

Now it happened that the young man was not a man at all, but a hyena, for although as a rule women change into hyenas and men into hawks, the hyena can change itself into either man or woman as it may please.

During the first night the two newly married ones were sleeping together the husband said: 'Supposing that when we go to my town we chance to quarrel on the road, what would you do?' The wife answered that she would change herself into a tree. The man said that he would be able to catch her even then.

She said that if that was the case she would turn into a pool of water. 'Oh! that would not trouble me,' said the hyena man, 'I should catch you all the same.'

'Why, then I should turn into a stone,' replied his spouse. 'Still I should catch you,' remarked the man.

Just at that moment the girl's mother shouted from her room, for she had heard the conversation: 'Keep quiet, my daughter; is it thus that a woman tells all her secrets to her man?' So the girl said no more.

Next morning, when the day was breaking, the husband told his wife to rise up as he was returning to his home. He bade her make ready to accompany him a short way down the road to see him off. She did as he told her, and as soon as ever the couple were out of sight of the village the husband turned himself into a hyena and tried to catch the girl, who changed herself into a tree, then into a pool of water, then into a stone but the hyena almost tore the tree down, nearly drank all the water and half swallowed the stone.

Then the girl changed herself into that thing which the night before her mother had managed to stop her from betraying. The hyena looked and looked everywhere and at last, fearing the villagers would come and kill him, made off.

At once the girl changed into her own proper form and ran back to the village.

THE THREE MEASURES OF SALT

(GREEK)

here was once a king with nine sons; he was faced by another king with nine daughters: in those days everyone was a king. Every morning each king used to go out to his frontier to greet the other. Once as they met at the frontier and greeted one another the king with the nine daughters said to the other: 'Good day, my lord king, you with your nine boys, and may you never get a wife for any of them!' When the other heard this he was smitten to the heart, and sat in a corner of his palace deep in thought. One of his sons came up: 'What is the matter, Father, that you are so sorrowful?' 'Nothing, my son.' The next brother asked him: 'Nothing, my son; I have a headache.' The third one came: 'But why won't you tell us what is the matter?' The king said not a word. Not to make too long a story, they all asked him and to none of them would he say what was the matter. The boys left him. Midday came and the king had no appetite to eat. God brought the day to its evening; then the dawn; but the king was still wrapt in thought. The eldest son came to him again: 'But, Father, this cannot be endured; a day and a night you are here fasting and sorrowful, and yet you won't tell us what is the matter.' He said: 'But what can I say, my son?' He told him what had happened between him and the other king: 'When he saw me yesterday morning he said to me: "Good day, king, with your nine sons, and may you never get a wife for any of them!"' 'And is it this that has filled you with such great bitterness, Father? Tomorrow when you meet, you must say to him: "Good morning, my lord king, with your nine daughters, and may you never get a husband for any of them."' Next day very early the king went out to his frontier and when he saw the other king he said: 'Good day, my lord king, with your nine daughters, and may you never get a husband for any of them.' When the other king heard this, how vexed he was! He too went and sat in a corner of his palace all full of trouble.

One of his daughters came and said: 'What is the matter, Father?' 'Nothing, my daughter.' Then the next daughter asked him: 'Nothing at all but a headache.' Then came the third. The king said: 'I told you there is nothing the matter.' Thus not to make a long story, all the nine came and asked him and he would tell none of them. Then his daughters left him. Midday came, but he would not eat. God brought the day to its evening; then the dawn; still he was wrapt in care. Then at last his daughters said: 'But this cannot be endured: for him to sit all by himself a day and a night; to put not even a crumb of church bread in his mouth, and to refuse to breathe a word of what is the matter, but just to put us off with stories!' The eldest went again to her father: 'Dear Father, why please won't you tell us what is the matter?' 'If you want to know, my daughter, the king over the way said to me: "Good day, my lord king, with your nine daughters, and a husband for none of them may you never have!"' She was a clever girl and said: 'Are you grieved for that, Father? Tomorrow you must answer him and say: "Since I have no husband for my girls, why, give me one of your sons: my eldest daughter can very easily rub three measures of salt on his face and he be none the wiser."' As the girl had told him, so he did.

Next day when they greeted one another very early, he said to the other king: 'Since I have no husband for any of my girls, give me one of your sons; my eldest daughter is a match for him; very easily can she rub three measures of salt on his face and he be none the wiser.' So they made the match and married the eldest son with the eldest daughter. When they lay down in bed the first evening the prince said to his newly wed princess: 'You have managed it very well, you clever girl, and now we are married; but tell me what are these three measures of salt which you would rub on my head and I be none the wiser?' She said: 'I won't tell you.' 'Tell me or I will go away and leave you.' 'Go then; only let me know where you are going so that I can send you a letter sometimes.' 'I am going to Salonika.' So the youth made all ready. She too went off in a ship and reached that same place before him.

By the shore she met an old woman who said to her: 'You must be newly come here. If you like, I have a house I can let you have near the sea, a house for a king's daughter.' The girl went up into the house and then she said to the old woman: 'A prince will be coming here in a day

or two and you must bring him here.' 'At your orders, my lady,' said
the old woman. Next day the prince arrived. The old woman went
down to the shore and said to him: 'I can bring you to a house fit for
a prince; you will also have there a girl to kiss.' He went up into the
house and saw the princess. 'Good day, and you are very much like my
wife: what am I to think of it?' 'Well, well, my good Christian,' says
she: 'Man to man and thing to thing, likenesses there are everywhere.'
But of course the woman was the wife herself. All day they talked and
in the evening they lay down together. She became with child and had
a boy baby: when he was born the room was full of light, for on his
brow was the star of morning. Within the year the prince wanted to go
away, and she said: 'And won't you leave some present for your child?'
Then he took out his gold watch and hung it on the baby, and to the
old woman he gave a present of a thousand gold pieces. When he had
gone, his wife embarked in a ship and came to her country before him.
The boy she handed over to a nurse and he was brought up in a
golden room below the earth which she had constructed in her father's
palace. She warned all the maidservants that they must say nothing to
the prince when he came back about her being away; only that she had
had a cold and been ill all the year. Next day the prince arrived; he
asked how his wife was. They said: 'As I could wish your ill-wishers
were, and this all because of your absence.' Then he came to find her
and they kissed one another, and he said: 'I am told that you have been
ill because of our separation, but it was all your fault because you
would not tell me about those three measures of salt which you said
you would rub on me and I be none the wiser. Now tell me,' said he.
'No, I won't tell you.' 'Obstinate are you? Well, so am I. Either you
will tell me or I shall go away and leave you.' 'Go then; only tell me
where you will be that I may be able some time to send you a letter.'
'In Aigina,' said he.

When he went off, she too went by another way and took ship and
came to Aigina before him. There on the shore she found the same old
woman – it was really her Fate – and again she went with her to a
house on the shore. Next day the prince also arrived and the old
woman took him to the same house and left him there and then went
off. As soon as the prince saw the woman in the house he ran and
kissed her. She said: 'And what makes you so passionate just from
seeing me?' 'I have a wife just like you and she came to my mind.'
'Man to man and thing to thing, likenesses there are everywhere.' All

day they were there talking and in the evening they lay down together and so every evening, until she was with child and had a boy baby; when he was born the room was full of light, for on his brow was the shining moon. Before a year was over he gave the boy his gold walking-stick for a remembrance: he kissed him; gave the old woman another thousand gold pieces as a present and went away. Thus he went off and his wife after him. She came first to her house and handed over this second child to the same nurse and gave the servants a present not to tell that she had been away; in the palace she again played the part of the sorrowful woman. When her husband came next day, he questioned the servants about his wife, and they told him that all the year she had shut herself up in sorrow. The servants went back again and the prince came to his wife and said: 'Whatever you may have suffered, it is all the fault of your ladyship. But now do tell me what are those three measures of salt you would rub on my face and I be none the wiser: if you won't, I shall be off again.' 'And a good journey to you; only tell me where you are going and I shall know if at any time I want to send you any news.' 'I'm going to Venice.'

Again he took ship and she followed, arriving before him. The same old woman appeared and took her to a great big palace on the shore. In two or three days the prince arrived. The old woman said to him: 'You are welcome, prince. Pray be so good as to come to my house and stay there as long as you please, because I have a girl there for you.' 'Wonderful,' said he. Then he went and again he saw the woman; he said: 'Oh, how like you are to my wife!' 'Man to man and thing to thing, likenesses there are everywhere.' Not to make a long story, she became with child and bore a daughter; the room was full of light, for on her forehead was the shining of the sun. They christened the child and called her Alexandra. Before the year was out the prince wanted to go away and the princess said to him: 'Won't you at least make the baby some present for her to remember you?' Says he: 'Of course. Even without you telling me I had been thinking of it.' He went to the shops and bought a string of precious stones of all sorts, a thing beyond price – when you say from Venice, you can imagine what it was – and he hung it on the baby's neck; also he bought a dress all of gold, and he took off his ring and gave it to her. Then he kissed the baby and gave the old woman a thousand gold pieces as a present and went off. The princess starting after him arrived at her house before him; she handed the child over to the nurse with money for her trouble and made a present to the women servants not to tell of her. Again she shut herself up in the palace pretending to be full of grief. In two or three days her husband came and asked the servants: 'How is my wife?' said he. 'As I would wish your ill-wishers were, and all for your absence.' He went and found her in a sad state. He said: 'And whom can you blame? You have asked for what has happened to you. Why wouldn't you tell me what are those three measures of salt which you would smear over my face and I be none the wiser? But tell me now.' 'I won't tell you.' 'This cannot be endured. Tell me or I will leave you and take another wife.' 'Well, go and marry again and I will come and give you my blessing.' Then he made up a match with another princess nearby and fixed say next Sunday for the wedding.

All the world went to give them their blessing and the instruments of music were playing. Then his first wife dressed herself in her best and fitted out her three children finely; to the eldest she gave the watch, to the second the walking-stick, and the youngest she adorned with the string of jewels and the ring. The nurse brought them and they all went to join in the blessings at the marriage service. All the women danced in the hall and their eyes were upon the children and the mother because all the room was bright as lightning from the morning star and the sun and the moon, all on the children's foreheads. All said: 'Joy and delight to the mother who bore them!' The prince too left the girl whom he was going to marry and stared at the children; the young bride was full of jealousy. Then the two boys were heard talking to their sister, who was not yet I suppose a year old and was being carried by the nurse, the boys being in front of her: 'Little lady, little lady,' said the boys, 'little Alexandra, listen to the watch, tick tick tick: mother in the room all decked with gold.' When the prince heard this he could endure no longer and right in the middle of the marriage service he left his new bride and ran up to the children. He looked at them and saw the string of jewels and the watch and the ring, and so he recognized them.

His former wife was standing by and he asked whose children these were. 'Yours and mine; one of them we had at Salonika, the second at Aigina, and the youngest at Venice. The woman whom you met in all those three places, each of them was I, and when I left the place I always got ahead of you. And to think that you should not know your own children! These were the three measures of salt which I was to smear on your face and you be none the wiser.' He lifted up the children and in his delight kissed them all. He took them to his former house and their mother too with them. And so the new bride was left there with the bath grown cold and she half-married.

THE RESOURCEFUL WIFE

(INDIAN TRIBAL)

woman was so mad with love for her lover that she gave him all the rice in the bin, and had to fill it with chaff so that her husband would not notice what she had done. By and by the days for sowing came round, and the woman knew she could no more deceive her husband.

One day her husband went to plough his field which lay near a tank. The next morning his wife went very early to the tank, made herself naked and smeared mud all over her body. She sat down in the grass waiting for him. When he came, she suddenly stood up and in a loud voice cried, 'I am going to take away your two bullocks. But if you need them you can give me the grain in your bin and I will fill it with chaff instead. But one or the other I must have, for I am hungry.'

The man at once said that the Goddess – for so he thought her – should take the grain, for he knew he would be ruined if he lost his bullocks. 'Very well,' said the wife. 'Go back now to your house, and you will find that I have taken your grain, but I have put chaff in its place.' So saying she disappeared into the tank.

The man ran home and found in fact that all the grain was gone and his bin was full of chaff. His wife quickly bathed and changed her clothes, and came home by way of the well where she told the other women the story with great pride.

AUNT KATE'S GOOMER-DUST

(NORTH AMERICAN: OZARKS)

ne time there was a farm boy named Jack and he wanted to marry a rich girl that lived in town, but her pappy was against it. 'Listen, Minnie,' says the old man, 'this feller ain't house-broke, scarcely! He's got cowdung on his boots! He cain't even write his own name!' Minnie didn't turn no answer, but she knowed what Jack could do, and it suited her fine. Booklearning is all right, but it ain't got nothing to do with picking out a good husband. Minnie had done made up her mind to marry Jack, no matter what anybody said.

Jack wanted to run off and get married regardless, but Minnie says no, because she don't figure on being poor all her life. She says we got to make Pappy give us a big farm with a good house on it. Jack he just laughed, and they didn't do no more talking for awhile. Finally he says well, I'll go out to Honey Mountain tomorrow, and see what Aunt Kate thinks.

Aunt Kate knowed a lot of things that most folks never heard tell of. Jack told her what a fix him and Minnie was in, but Aunt Kate says she can't do nothing without silver. So Jack gave her two dollars, and it was all the money he had. Then she fetched him a little box like a pepper-duster, with some yellow powder in it. 'That's goomer-dust,' she says. 'Don't get it on you, and be careful not to get none on Minnie. But you tell her to sprinkle a little on her pappy's pants.'

Late that night Minnie dusted some powder on the old man's britches, where he had hung 'em on the bedpost. Next morning he broke wind right at breakfast, so loud it rattled the pictures on the wall and scared the cat plumb out of the kitchen. The old man thought it must be something he et. But pretty soon he ripped out another one, and it wasn't no time at all till he was making so much noise that

Minnie shut the windows for fear the neighbours would hear it. 'Ain't you goin' down to the office, Pappy?' says she. But just then the old man turned loose the awfullest blow-out a body ever heard, and he says, 'No, Minnie. I'm going to bed. And I want you should fetch Doc Holton right away.'

When Doc got there Pappy was feeling better, but pretty white and shaky. 'Soon as I got in bed the wind died down,' he says, 'but it was terrible while it lasted,' and he told Doc all about what happened. Doc examined Pappy a long time and give him some medicine to make him sleep. Minnie follered Doc out on the porch, and Doc says, 'Did you hear them loud noises he keeps talkin' about, like somebody breakin' wind?' Minnie says no, she didn't hear nothing like that. 'Just as I thought,' says Doc. 'He just imagined the whole thing. There ain't nothing wrong with your pappy, only his nerves.'

Pappy slept pretty good, on account of the medicine Doc give him. But next morning, soon as he got up and put his clothes on, he begun to break wind worse than ever. Finally he fired off a blast that sounded like a ten-bore shotgun, so Minnie helped him back in bed and sent for the doctor. Doc give him a shot in the arm this time. 'Keep that man in bed,' says he, 'till I get Doctor Culberson to come over and look at him.' Both of them doctors examined Pappy from head to foot, but they couldn't find nothing wrong with him. They just shuck their heads, and give him some more sleeping medicine.

Things went along like that for three days a-running, and finally Doc says Pappy better stay in bed all the time for awhile, and take medicine every four hours, and maybe he would be happier in a institution. 'Put me in the asylum, just because I got wind on the guts?' yelled Pappy. And with that he begun to raise such a row the doctor had to give him another shot in the arm.

Next morning Pappy set up in bed a-hollering how the doctors are all damn fools, and Minnie says she knows a fellow that can cure him in five minutes. Pretty soon Jack come a-walking in. 'Yes, I can cure you easy,' he says, 'but you got to let me and Minnie get married, and give us one of them big farms.' Pappy wouldn't even speak to Jack. 'If this halfwit cures me,' he says to Minnie, 'you can have any goddam thing you want.' Minnie walked over and stirred up the coals in the fireplace. Soon as it got to burning good, Jack took the tongs and throwed Pappy's britches right in the fire.

When Pappy seen them pants a-burning he was plumb speechless.

He just laid there weak as a cat, and Jack marched out like a regular doctor. But after while the old man got up and put on his Sunday clothes. He never broke wind, neither. Minnie fixed him a fine breakfast, and he et every bite of it and never even belched. Then he walked round the house three times, without feeling no gas on his innards. 'Well, by God,' he says, 'I believe to my soul that damn fool did cure me!' On the way down town he stopped in to see Doc Holton. 'I finally got well, without no thanks to you,' says he. 'If you had your way, I'd be in the crazy-house this minute!'

Soon as he got Doc told, Pappy went over to the bank and deeded his best farm to Minnie. He give her some money to buy horses and cows and machinery. And so her and Jack got married, and they done all right. Some folks say they lived happy ever after.

The Battle of the Birds

(SCOTS GAELIC)

here was once a time when every creature and bird was gathering to battle. The son of the king of Tethertown said, that he would go to see the battle, and that he would bring sure word home to his father the king, who would be king of the creatures this year. The battle was over before he arrived all but one fight, between a great black raven and a snake, and it seemed as if the snake would get the victory over the raven. When the king's son saw this, he helped the raven, and with one blow takes the head off the snake. When the raven had taken breath, and saw that the snake was dead, he said, 'For thy kindness to me this day, I will give thee a sight. Come up now on the root of my two wings.' The king's son mounted upon the raven, and, before he stopped, he took him over seven Bens, and seven Glens, and seven Mountain Moors.

'Now,' said the raven, 'seest thou that house yonder? Go now to it. It is a sister of mine that makes her dwelling in it; and I will go bail that thou art welcome. And if she asks thee, Wert thou at the battle of the birds? say thou that thou wert. And if she asks, Didst thou see my likeness? say that thou sawest it. But be sure that thou meetest me tomorrow morning here, in this place.' The king's son got good and right good treatment this night. Meat of each meat, drink of each drink, warm water to his feet, and a soft bed for his limbs.

On the next day the raven gave him the same sight over seven Bens, and seven Glens, and seven Mountain Moors. They saw a bothy far off, but, though far off, they were soon there. He got good treatment this night, as before – plenty of meat and drink, and warm water to his feet, and a soft bed to his limbs – and on the next day it was the same thing.

On the third morning, instead of seeing the raven as at the other times, who should meet him but the handsomest lad he ever saw, with a bundle in his hand. The king's son asked this lad if he had seen a big black raven. Said the lad to him, 'Thou wilt never see the raven again, for I am that raven. I was put under spells; it was meeting thee that loosed me, and for that thou art getting this bundle. Now,' said the lad, 'thou wilt turn back on the self-same steps, and thou wilt lie a night in each house, as thou wert before; but thy lot is not to lose the bundle which I gave thee, till thou art in the place where thou wouldst most wish to dwell.'

The king's son turned his back to the lad, and his face to his father's house; and he got lodging from the raven's sisters, just as he got it when going forward. When he was nearing his father's house he was going through a close wood. It seemed to him that the bundle was growing heavy, and he thought he would look what was in it.

When he loosed the bundle, it was not without astonishing himself. In a twinkling he sees the very grandest place he ever saw. A great castle, and an orchard about the castle, in which was every kind of fruit and herb. He stood full of wonder and regret for having loosed the bundle – it was not in his power to put it back again – and he would have wished this pretty place to be in the pretty little green hollow that was opposite his father's house; but, at one glance, he sees a great giant coming towards him.

'Bad's the place where thou hast built thy house, king's son,' says the giant. 'Yes, but it is not here I would wish it to be, though it happened to be here by mishap,' says the king's son. 'What's the reward thou wouldst give me for putting it back in the bundle as it was before?' 'What's the reward thou wouldst ask?' says the king's son. 'If thou wilt give me the first son thou hast when he is seven years of age,' says the giant. 'Thou wilt get that if I have a son,' said the king's son.

In a twinkling the giant put each garden, and orchard, and castle in the bundle as they were before. 'Now,' says the giant, 'take thou thine own road, and I will take my road; but mind thy promise, and though thou shouldst forget, I will remember.'

The king's son took to the road, and at the end of a few days he reached the place he was fondest of. He loosed the bundle, and the same place was just as it was before. And when he opened the castle-door he sees the handsomest maiden he ever cast eye upon. 'Advance, king's son,' said the pretty maid; 'everything is in order for thee, if thou wilt marry me this very night.' 'It's I am the man that is willing,' said the king's son. And on the same night they married.

But at the end of a day and seven years, what great man is seen coming to the castle but the giant. The king's son minded his promise to the giant, and till now he had not told his promise to the queen. 'Leave thou the matter between me and the giant,' says the queen.

'Turn out thy son,' says the giant; 'mind your promise.' 'Thou wilt get that,' says the king, 'when his mother puts him in order for his journey.' The queen arrayed the cook's son, and she gave him to the giant by the hand. The giant went away with him; but he had not gone far when he put a rod in the hand of the little laddie. The giant asked him – 'If thy father had that rod what would he do with it?' 'If father had that rod he would beat the dogs and the cats, if they would be going near the king's meat,' said the little laddie. 'Thou'rt the cook's son,' said the giant. He catches him by the two small ankles and knocks him – 'Sgleog' – against the stone that was beside him. The giant turned back to the castle in rage and madness, and he said that if they did not turn out the king's son to him, the highest stone in the castle would be the lowest. Said the queen to the king, 'we'll try it yet; the butler's son is of the same age as our son.' She arrayed the butler's son, and she gives him to the giant by the hand. The giant had not gone far when he put the rod in his hand. 'If thy father had that rod,' says the giant, 'what would he do with it?' 'He would beat the dogs and the cats when they would be coming near the king's bottles and glasses.' 'Thou art the son of the butler,' says the giant, and dashed his brains out too. The giant returned in very great rage and anger. The earth shook under the soles of his feet, and the castle shook and all that was in it. 'OUT HERE THY SON,' says the giant, 'or in a twinkling the stone that is highest in the dwelling will be the lowest.' So needs must they had to give the king's son to the giant.

The giant took him to his own house, and he reared him as his own son. On a day of days when the giant was from home, the lad heard the sweetest music he ever heard in a room at the top of the giant's house. At a glance he saw the finest face he had ever seen. She beckoned to him to come a bit nearer to her, and she told him to go this time, but to be sure to be at the same place about that dead midnight.

And as he promised he did. The giant's daughter was at his side in a twinkling, and she said, 'Tomorrow thou wilt get the choice of my two sisters to marry; but say thou that thou wilt not take either, but me. My father wants me to marry the son of the king of the Green City, but I don't like him.' On the morrow the giant took out his three daughters, and he said, 'Now son of the king of Tethertown, thou hast not lost by living with me so long. Thou wilt get to wife one of the two eldest of my daughters, and with her leave to go home with her the day after the wedding.' 'If thou wilt give me this pretty little one,' says the king's son, 'I will take thee at thy word.'

The giant's wrath kindled, and he said, 'Before thou gett'st her thou must do the three things that I ask thee to do.' 'Say on,' says the king's son. The giant took him to the byre. 'Now,' says the giant, 'the dung of a hundred cattle is here, and it has not been cleansed for seven years. I am going from home today, and if this byre is not cleaned before night comes, so clean that a golden apple will run from end to end of it, not only thou shalt not get my daughter, but 'tis a drink of thy blood that will quench my thirst this night.' He begins cleaning the byre, but it was just as well to keep baling the great ocean. After midday, when sweat was blinding him, the giant's young daughter came where he was, and she said to him, 'Thou art being punished, king's son.' 'I am that,' says the king's son. 'Come over,' says she, 'and lay down thy weariness.' 'I will do that,' says he, 'there is but death awaiting me, at any rate.' He sat down near her. He was so tired that he fell asleep beside her. When he awoke, the giant's daughter was not to be seen, but the byre was so well cleaned that a golden apple would run from end to end of it. In comes the giant, and he said, 'Thou hast cleaned the byre, king's son?' 'I have cleaned it,' says he. 'Somebody cleaned it,' says the giant. 'Thou didst not clean it, at all events,' said the king's son. 'Yes, yes!' says the giant, 'since thou wert so active today, thou wilt get to this time tomorrow to thatch this byre with birds' down – birds with no two feathers of one colour.' The king's son was on foot before the sun; he caught up his bow and his quiver of arrows to kill the birds. He took to the moors, but if he did, the birds were not so easy to take. He was running after them till the sweat was blinding him. About midday who should come but the giant's daughter. 'Thou art exhausting thyself, king's son,' says she. 'I am,' said he. 'There fell but these two blackbirds, and both of one colour.' 'Come over and lay down thy weariness on this pretty hillock,' says the giant's daughter. 'It's I am willing,' said he. He thought she would aid him this time, too, and he sat down near her, and he was not long there till he fell asleep.

When he awoke, the giant's daughter was gone. He thought he would go back to the house, and he sees the byre thatched with the feathers. When the giant came home, he said, 'Thou hast thatched the byre, king's son?' 'I thatched it,' says he. 'Somebody thatched it,' says the giant. 'Thou didst not thatch it,' says the king's son. 'Yes, yes!' says the giant. 'Now,' says the giant, 'there is a fir-tree beside that loch down there, and there is a magpie's nest in its top. The eggs thou wilt find in the nest. I must have them for my first meal. Not one must be burst or broken, and there are five in the nest.' Early in the morning the king's son went where the tree was, and that tree was not hard to hit upon. Its match was not in the whole wood. From the foot to the first branch was five hundred feet. The king's son was going all round the tree. She came who was always bringing help to him. 'Thou art losing the skin of thy hands and feet.' 'Ach! I am,' says he. 'I am no sooner up than down.' 'This is no time for stopping,' says the giant's daughter. She thrust finger after finger into the tree, till she made a ladder for the king's son to go up to the magpie's nest. When he was at the nest, she said, 'Make haste now with the eggs, for my father's breath is burning my back.' In his hurry she left her little finger in the top of the tree. 'Now,' says she, 'thou wilt go home with the eggs quickly, and thou wilt get me to marry tonight if thou canst know me. I and my two sisters will be arrayed in the same garments, and made like each other, but look at me when my father says, go to thy wife, king's son; and thou wilt see a hand without a little finger.' He gave the eggs to the giant. 'Yes, yes!' says the giant, 'be making ready for thy marriage.'

Then indeed there was a wedding, and it *was* a wedding! Giants and gentlemen, and the son of the king of the Green City was in the midst of them. They were married, and the dancing began, and that was a dance? The giant's house was shaking from top to bottom. But bed time came, and the giant said, 'It is time for thee to go to rest, son of the king of Tethertown; take thy bride with thee from amidst those.'

She put out the hand off which the little finger was, and he caught her by the hand.

'Thou hast aimed well this time too; but there is no knowing but we may meet thee another way,' said the giant.

But to rest they went. 'Now,' says she, 'sleep not, or else thou diest. We must fly quick, quick, or for certain my father will kill thee.'

Out they went, and on the blue gray filly in the stable they mounted. 'Stop a while,' says she, 'and I will play a trick to the old hero.' She jumped in, and cut an apple into nine shares, and she put two shares at the head of the bed, and two shares at the foot of the bed, and two shares at the door of the kitchen, and two shares at the big door, and one outside the house.

The giant awoke and called, 'Are you asleep?' 'We are not yet,' said the apple that was at the head of the bed. At the end of a while he called again. 'We are not yet,' said the apple that was at the foot of the bed. A while after this he called again. 'We are not yet,' said the apple at the kitchen door. The giant called again. The apple that was at the big door answered. 'You are now going far from me,' says the giant. 'We are not yet,' says the apple that was outside the house. 'You are flying,' says the giant. The giant jumped on his feet, and to the bed he went, but it was cold – empty.

'My own daughter's tricks are trying me,' said the giant. 'Here's after them,' says he.

In the mouth of day, the giant's daughter said that her father's breath was burning her back. 'Put thy hand, quick,' said she, 'in the ear of the gray filly, and whatever thou findest in it, throw it behind thee.' 'There is a twig of sloe tree,' said he. 'Throw it behind thee,' said she.

No sooner did he that, than there were twenty miles of black thorn wood, so thick that scarce a weasel could go through it. The giant came headlong, and there he is fleecing his head and neck in the thorns.

'My own daughter's tricks are here as before,' said the giant; 'but if I had my own big axe and wood knife here, I would not be long making a way through this.' He went home for the big axe and the wood knife, and sure he was not long on his journey, and he was the boy behind the big axe. He was not long making a way through the black thorn. 'I will leave the axe and the wood knife here till I return,' says he. 'If thou leave them,' said a hoodie that was in a tree, 'we will steal them.'

'You will do that same,' says the giant, 'but I will get them home.' He returned and left them at the house. At the heat of day the giant's daughter felt her father's breath burning her back.

'Put thy finger in the filly's ear, and throw behind thee whatever thou findest in it.' He got a splinter of gray stone, and in a twinkling there were twenty miles, by breadth and height, of great gray rock behind them. The giant came full pelt, but past the rock he could not go.

'The tricks of my own daughter are the hardest things that ever met me,' says the giant; 'but if I had my lever and my mighty mattock, I would not be long making my way through this rock also.' There was no help for it, but to turn the chase for them; and he was the boy to split the stones. He was not long making a road through the rock. 'I will leave the tools here, and I will return no more.' 'If thou leave them,' says the hoodie, 'we will steal them.' 'Do that if thou wilt; there is no time to go back.' At the time of breaking the watch, the giant's daughter said that she was feeling her father's breath burning her back. 'Look in the filly's ear, king's son, or else we are lost. He did so, and it was a bladder of water that was in her ear this time. He threw it behind him and there was a fresh-water loch, twenty miles in length and breadth, behind them.

The giant came on, but with the speed he had on him, he was in the middle of the loch, and he went under, and he rose no more.

On the next day the young companions were come in sight of his father's house. 'Now,' said she, 'my father is drowned, and he won't trouble us any more; but before we go further,' says she, 'go thou to thy father's house, and tell that thou hast the like of me; but this is thy lot, let neither man nor creature kiss thee, for if thou dost thou wilt not remember that thou hast ever seen me.' Everyone he met was giving him welcome and luck, and he charged his father and mother not to kiss him; but as mishap was to be, an old greyhound was in and she knew him, and jumped up to his mouth, and after that he did not remember the giant's daughter.

She was sitting at the well's side as he left her, but the king's son was not coming. In the mouth of night she climbed up into a tree of oak that was beside the well, and she lay in the fork of the tree all that night. A shoemaker had a house near the well, and about midday on the morrow, the shoemaker asked his wife to go for a drink for him out of the well. When the shoemaker's wife reached the well, and when she saw the shadow of her that was in the tree, thinking of it that it was her own shadow – and she never thought till now that she was so handsome – she gave a cast to the dish that was in her hand, and it was broken on the ground, and she took herself to the house without vessel or water.

'Where is the water, wife?' said the shoemaker. 'Thou shambling, contemptible old carle, without grace, I have stayed too long thy water and wood slave.' 'I am thinking, wife, that thou has turned crazy. Go thou, daughter, quickly, and fetch a drink for thy father.' His daughter went, and in the same way so it happened to her. She never thought till now that she was so loveable, and she took herself home. 'Up with the drink,' said her father. 'Thou home-spun shoe carle, dost thou think that I am fit to be thy slave.' The poor shoemaker thought that they had taken a turn in their understandings, and he went himself to the well. He saw the shadow of the maiden in the well, and he looked up to the tree, and he sees the finest woman he ever saw. 'Thy seat is wavering, but thy face is fair,' said the shoemaker. 'Come down, for there is need of thee for a short while at my house.' The shoemaker understood that this was the shadow that had driven his people mad. The shoemaker took her to his house, and he said that he had but a poor bothy, but that she should get a share of all that was in it. At the end of a day or two came a leash of gentlemen lads to the shoemaker's house for shoes to be made them, for the king had come home, and he was going to marry. The lads saw the giant's daughter, and they never saw one so pretty as she. ' 'Tis thou hast the pretty daughter, here,' said the lads to the shoemaker. 'She is pretty, indeed,' says the shoemaker, 'but she is no daughter of mine.' 'St Nail!' said one of them, 'I would give a hundred pounds to marry her.' The two others said the very same. The poor shoemaker said that he had nothing to do with her. 'But,' said they, 'ask her tonight, and send us word tomorrow.' When the gentles went away, she asked the shoemaker – 'What's that they were saying about me?' The shoemaker told her. 'Go thou after them,' said she; 'I will marry one of them, and let him bring his purse with him.' The youth returned, and he gave the shoemaker a hundred pounds for tocher. They went to rest, and when she had laid down, she asked the lad for a drink of water from a tumbler that was on the board on the further side of the chamber. He went; but out of that he could not come, as he held the vessel of water the length of the night. 'Thou lad,' said she, 'why wilt thou not lie down?' but out of that he could not drag till the bright morrow's day was. The shoemaker came to the door of the chamber, and she asked him to take away that lubberly boy. This wooer went and betook himself to his home, but he did not tell the other two how it happened to him. Next came the second chap, and in the same way, when she had gone to rest – 'Look,' she said, 'if the latch is on the door.' The latch laid hold of his hands, and out of that he could not come the length of the night, and out of that he did not come till the morrow's day was bright. He went, under shame and disgrace. No matter, he did not tell the other chap how it had happened, and on the third night he came. As it happened to the two others, so it happened to him. One foot stuck to the floor; he could neither come nor go, but so he was the length of the night. On the morrow, he took his soles out of that, and he was not seen looking behind him. 'Now,' said the girl to the shoemaker, 'thine is the sporran of gold; I have no need of it. It will better thee, and I am no worse for thy kindness to me.' The shoemaker had the shoes ready, and on that very day the king was to be married. The shoemaker was going to the castle with the shoes of the young people, and the girl said to the shoe-maker, 'I would like to get a sight of the king's son before he marries.' 'Come with me,' says the shoemaker, 'I am well acquainted with the servants at the castle, and thou shalt get a sight of the king's son and all the company.' And when the gentles saw the pretty woman that was here they took her to the wedding-room, and they filled for her a glass of wine. When she was going to drink what is in it, a flame went up out of the glass, and a golden pigeon and a silver pigeon sprung out of it. They were flying about when three grains of barley fell on the floor. The silver pigeon sprang, and he eats that. Said the golden pigeon to him, 'If thou hadst mind when I cleared the byre, thou

wouldst not eat that without giving me a share.' Again fell three other grains of barley, and the silver pigeon sprang, and he eats that, as before. 'If thou hadst mind when I thatched the byre, thou wouldst not eat that without giving me my share,' says the golden pigeon. Three other grains fell, and the silver pigeon sprang, and he eats that. 'If thou hadst mind when I harried the magpie's nest, thou wouldst not eat that without giving me my share,' says the golden pigeon; 'I lost my little finger bringing it down, and I want it still.' The king's son minded, and he knew who it was he had got. He sprang where she was, and kissed her from hand to mouth. And when the priest came they married a second time. And there I left them.

Parsley-girl

(ITALIAN)

nce upon a time, when it was winter, a woman said: 'I've a real craving for some parsley. There's lots of parsley in the Holy Sisters' garden. I'll go and get some.'

The first time, she took one sprig of parsley and she didn't spy a soul. The second time, she took two sprigs and nobody spotted her. But the third time, just as she was picking herself a whole bunch, a hand fell on her shoulder and there was a great big nun.

'What are you doing?' asked the nun.

'Picking some parsley. I've a real craving for some parsley because I'm going to have a baby.'

'Take all the parsley you want, but when you've had your baby you must call him Parsley-boy if he's a boy or Parsley-girl if she's a girl, and when the baby grows up you must give it to us. That is the price of your parsley.'

Although she laughed it off at the time, when the woman's little girl was born she called her Parsley-girl. Sometimes Parsley-girl went to play beside the convent wall. One day one of the nuns called out to her: 'Parsley-girl! Ask your mother when she's going to give it to us.'

'All right,' said Parsley-girl.

She went home and said to her mother: 'The nun was asking me, when are you going to give it to them?'

Her mother laughed and said: 'Tell them to come and take it themselves.'

When Parsley-girl went back to play beside the convent wall, the nun said: 'Parsley-girl, did you ask your mother?'

'Yes,' said Parsley-girl. 'And she said you must take it yourself.'

So the nun stretched out her long arm and picked Parsley-girl up by the scruff.

'Not me!'

'Yes, you!'

And the nun told Parsley-girl about the parsley and the promise. Parsley-girl burst out crying. 'Naughty Mummy! She never said a thing!' When they went inside the convent, the nun said: 'Put a big pot of water on the fire, Parsley-girl, and when it comes to the boil, in you go! You'll make us a nice little supper.

Parsley-girl burst out crying all over again. Up popped a little old man out of a casserole.

'Why are you crying, Parsley-girl?'

'I'm crying because the nuns are going to eat me for supper.'

'They're not nuns, they're mean old witches. Put the pot of water on the fire and stop crying.'

'Why should I stop crying? The nuns are going to eat me.'

'Oh, no, they're not. Take this magic wand. When they come to see if the pot is boiling, give them a little tap with it and they'll all jump in like frogs into a pond.'

Although she thought: 'The little old man only said that to stop me crying,' she felt a bit better. When the pot boiled, she called out: 'Sisters! Sisters! The pot is boiling!'

They all came to see, crying: 'Oh, what a lovely supper we're going to have!' Parsley-girl was scared stiff so she picked up the magic wand and hit them all on their big, fat bottoms and, yes! they all jumped, splash, into the pot.

'Take the pot off the fire, Parsley-girl! We were only joking!'

'Oh, no, you weren't! You're not nuns at all, you're witches! You stay there until you're good and done, but don't think I'm going to do you the honour of eating you, you're much too old and tough. I'll look on the stove to see what else you've got.'

She went to the stove and there, in a casserole, she found a fine young man.

'Hello, fine young man. I'm hungry.'

'Don't make fun of me. I'm not young at all, I'm old and ugly.'

'Oh, no, you're not.' And she showed him his fine reflection in the washing-up bowl. 'But as for me, I'm just a little girl, worse luck.'

'You're not a little girl at all,' he said. 'I'll show you.'

And he measured her up against the wall to show her how tall she'd grown. Then Parsley-girl said: 'I'm going to make you a proposition.'

'Whatever can it be?'

'Let's get married.'

'But you're so pretty and I'm so plain.'

'I think you're very good-looking, personally.'

'All right. If you want to get married, I'll marry you.'

'Then let's have some supper and go to bed. We can find a priest tomorrow.'

'But don't let's stay in the convent, because the nuns put the devil in the place where Jesus ought to be.'

They went to look for the devil but he had turned back into Jesus because of the magic wand. Parsley-girl said: 'You do realize I've killed all the witches, don't you?'

They looked inside the pot. It was full of corpses.

'Let's dig a hole and bury them and then let's get out of here.'

They had supper, then they went to bed. They went to the priest in the morning and got married.

CLEVER GRETEL

(GERMAN)

here was once a cook named Gretel, who wore shoes with red heels, and when she went out in them, she whirled this way and that way and was as happy as a lark. 'You really are quite pretty!' she would say to herself. And when she returned home, she would drink some wine out of sheer delight. Since the wine would whet her appetite, she would take the best things she was cooking and taste them until she was content. Then she would say, 'The cook must know what the food tastes like!'

One day her master happened to say to her, 'Gretel, tonight I'm having a guest for dinner. Prepare two chickens for me and make them as tasty as possible.'

'I'll take care of it, sir,' Gretel responded. So she killed two chickens, scalded them, plucked them, stuck them on a spit, and toward evening placed them over a fire to roast. The chickens began to turn brown and were almost ready, but the guest did not make his appearance. So Gretel called to her master, 'If the guest doesn't come soon, I'll have to take the chickens off the fire. It would be a great shame if they weren't eaten now, while they're still at their juiciest.'

'Then I'll run and fetch the guest myself,' said the master.

When the master had left the house, Gretel laid the spit with the chickens to one side and thought, if I keep standing by the fire, I'll just sweat and get thirsty. Who knows when they'll come? Meanwhile, I'll hop down into the cellar and take a drink.

She ran downstairs, filled a jug with wine, and said, 'May God bless it for you, Gretel!' and she took a healthy swig. 'The wine flows nicely,' she continued talking, 'and it's not good to interrupt the flow.' So she took another long swig. Then she went upstairs and placed the chickens back over the fire, basted them with butter, and merrily

turned the spit. Since the roast chickens smelled so good, Gretel
thought, perhaps something's missing. I'd better taste them to see
how they are. She touched one of them with her finger and said,
'Goodness! The chickens are really good! It's a crying shame not to eat
them all at once!' She ran to the window to see if her master was on his
way with the guest, but when she saw no one coming, she returned to
the chickens and thought. That one wing is burning. I'd better eat it
up.

So she cut if off, ate it, and enjoyed it. When she had finished, she
thought, I'd better eat the other wing or else my master will notice that
something's missing. After she had consumed the two wings, she
returned to the window, looked for her master, but was unable to see
him. Who knows, it suddenly occurred to her, perhaps they've
decided not to come and have stopped somewhere along the way.
Then she said to herself, 'Hey, Gretel, cheer up! You've already taken
a nice chunk. Have another drink and eat it all up! When it's gone,
there'll be no reason for you to feel guilty. Why should God's good
gifts go to waste?'

Once again she ran down into the cellar, took a good honest drink,
and then went back to eat up the chicken with relish. When the one
chicken had been eaten and her master still had not returned, Gretel
looked at the other bird and said, 'Where one is, the other should be
too. The two of them belong together: whatever's right for one is
right for the other. I think if I have another drink, it won't do me any
harm.' Therefore she took another healthy swig and let the second
chicken run to join the other.

Just as she was in the midst of enjoying her meal, her master came
back and called, 'Hurry, Gretel, the guest will soon be here!'

'Yes, sir, I'll get everything ready,' answered Gretel.

Meanwhile, the master checked to see if the table was properly set
and took out the large knife with which he wanted to carve the chickens and began sharpening it on the steps in the hallway. As he was
doing that the guest came and knocked nicely and politely at the door.
Gretel ran and looked to see who was there, and when she saw the
guest, she put her finger to her lips and whispered, 'Shhh, be quiet!
Get out of here as quick as you can! If my master catches you, you'll
be done for. It's true he invited you to dinner, but he really wants to
cut off both your ears. Listen to him sharpening his knife!'

The guest heard the sharpening and hurried back down the steps as fast as he could. Gretel wasted no time and ran screaming to her master. 'What kind of guest did you invite!' she cried.

'Goodness gracious, Gretel! Why do you ask? What do you mean?'

'Well,' she said, 'he snatched both chickens just as I was about to bring them to the table, and he's run away with them!'

'That's not at all a nice way to behave!' said her master, and he was disappointed by the loss of the fine chickens. 'At least he could have left me one of them so I'd have something to eat.'

He then shouted after the guest to stop running, but the guest pretended not to hear. So the master ran after him, with the knife still in his hand, and screamed, 'Just one, just one!' merely meaning that the guest should at least leave him one of the chickens and not take both. But the guest thought that his host was after just one of his ears, and to make sure that he would reach home safely with both his ears, he ran as if someone had lit a fire under his feet.

THE FURBURGER

(NORTH AMERICAN)

lady went into a pet shop to buy a rare exotic animal, one that no one else had. When she told the storekeeper what she wanted, he proceeded to show her everything that he had in the line of rare and exotic animals. After much distress, the lady hadn't found anything quite unusual enough to suit her taste. She made one last plea to the storekeeper. Out of desperation, the storekeeper said, 'I do have one animal left that you haven't seen yet; however, I am somewhat reluctant to show it to you.' 'Oh, please do,' cried the lady.

So the storekeeper went back into the backroom of the store, and after a little bit returned with a cage. Putting the cage on the counter, the storekeeper proceeded to open the cage and take out the animal and set it on the counter. The lady looked, but all she saw was a piece of fur, not a head or a tail, no eyes, nothing. 'What in the world is that thing?' said the lady. 'It's a furburger,' said the storekeeper very nonchalantly. 'But what does it do?' asked the lady. 'Watch very carefully, madam,' said the storekeeper. Then the storekeeper looked down at the furburger and said, 'Furburger, the wall!' And immediately the animal flew over and hit the wall like a ton of bricks, completely destroying the wall and leaving nothing but dust. Then, just as swiftly as before, the furburger flew back and sat on the counter again. Then the storekeeper said, 'Furburger, the door!' And immediately the animal flew over and hit the door like a ton of bricks, completely demolishing the entire door and doorframe. Then, just as quickly as before, the furburger flew back and sat on the counter.

'I'll take it,' said the lady. 'All right, if you really want it,' said the storekeeper. And so, as the lady was leaving the store with her furburger, the storekeeper said, 'Pardon me, ma'am, but what are you going to do with your furburger?' And the lady looked back and said, 'Well, I've been having trouble with my husband lately, and so tonight when I get home, I'm going to put the furburger in the middle of the kitchen floor. And when my husband comes home from work, he will come in the door and look down and say to me, "What in the hell is that?" and I'm going to say, "Why, dear, that's a furburger." And my husband will look at me and say, "Furburger, my ass!"'

PART THREE

SILLIES

A Pottle o' Brains

(ENGLISH)

nce in these parts, and not so long gone neither, there was a fool that wanted to buy a pottle o' brains, for he was ever getting into scrapes through his foolishness, and being laughed at by everyone. Folk told him that he could get everything he liked from the wise woman that lived on the top o' the hill, and dealt in potions and herbs and spells and things, and could tell thee all as'd come to thee or thy folk. So he told his mother, and asked her if he could seek the wise woman and buy a pottle o' brains.

'That ye should,' says she: 'thou'st sore need o' them, my son; and if I should die, who'd take care o' a poor fool such's thou, no more fit to look after thyself than an unborn baby? but mind thy manners, and speak her pretty, my lad; for they wise folk are gey and light mispleased.'

So off he went after his tea, and there she was, sitting by the fire, and stirring a big pot.

'Good e'en, missis,' says he, 'it's a fine night.'

'Aye,' says she, and went on stirring.

'It'll maybe rain,' says he, and fidgeted from one foot to t'other.

'Maybe,' says she.

'And m'appen it won't,' says he, and looked out o' the window.

'M'appen,' says she.

And he scratched his head and twisted his hat.

'Well,' says he, 'I can't mind nothing else about the weather, but let me see; the crops are getting on fine.'

'Fine,' says she.

'And – and – the beasts is fattening,' says he.

'They are,' says she.

'And – and – says he, and comes to a stop – 'I reckon we'll tackle business now, having done the polite like. Have you any brains for to sell?'

'That depends,' says she, 'if thou wants king's brains, or soldier's brains, or schoolmaster's brains, I dinna keep 'em.'

'Hout no,' says he, 'jist ordinary brains – fit for any fool – same as everyone has about here; something clean commonlike.'

'Aye so,' says the wise woman, 'I might manage that, if so be thou'lt help thyself.'

'How's that for, missis?' says he.

'Jest so,' says she, looking in the pot; 'bring me the heart of the thing thou likest best of all, and I'll tell thee where to get thy pottle o' brains.'

'But,' says he, scratching his head, 'how can I do that?'

'That's no for me to say,' says she, 'find out for thyself, my lad! if thou doesn't want to be a fool all thy days. But thou'll have to read me a riddle so as I can see thou'st brought the right thing, and if thy brains is about thee. And I've something else to see to,' says she, 'so gode'en to thee,' and she carried the pot away with her into the back place.

So off went the fool to his mother, and told her what the wise woman said.

'And I reckon I'll have to kill that pig,' says he, 'for I like fat bacon better than anything.'

'Then do it, my lad,' said his mother, 'for certain 'twill be a strange and good thing fur thee, if thou canst buy a pottle o' brains, and be able to look after thy own self.'

So he killed his pig, and next day off he went to the wise woman's cottage, and there she sat, reading in a great book.

'Gode'en, missis,' says he, 'I've brought thee the heart o' the thing I like best of all; and I put it hapt in paper on the table.'

'Aye so?' says she, and looked at him through her spectacles. 'Tell me this then, what runs without feet?'

He scratched his head, and thought, and thought, but he couldn't tell.

'Go thy ways,' says she, 'thou'st not fetched me the right thing yet. I've no brains for thee today.' And she clapt the book together, and turned her back.

So off the fool went to tell his mother.

But as he got nigh the house, out came folk running to tell him that his mother was dying.

And when he got in, his mother only looked at him and smiled as if to say she could leave him with a quiet mind since he had got brains enough now to look after himself – and then she died.

So down he sat and the more he thought about it the badder he felt. He minded how she'd nursed him when he was a tiddy brat, and helped him with his lessons, and cooked his dinners, and mended his clouts, and bore with his foolishness; and he felt sorrier and sorrier, while he began to sob and greet.

'Oh, Mother, Mother!' says he, 'who'll take care of me now! Thou shouldn't have left me alone, for I liked thee better than everything!'

And as he said that, he thought of the words of the wise woman. 'Hi, yi!' says he, 'must I take Mother's heart to her?'

'No! I can't do that,' says he. 'What'll I do! What'll I do to get that pottle of brains, now I'm alone in the world?' So he thought and thought and thought, and next day he went and borrowed a sack, and bundled his mother in, and carried it on his shoulder up to the wise woman's cottage.

'Gode'en, missis,' says he, 'I reckon I've fetched thee the right thing this time, surely,' and he plumped the sack down kerflap! in the doorsill.

'Maybe,' says the wise woman, 'but read me this, now, what's yellow and shining but isn't gold?'

And he scratched his head, and thought, and thought, but he couldn't tell.

'Thou'st not hit the right thing, my lad,' says she. 'I doubt thou'rt a bigger fool than I thought!' and shut the door in his face.

'See there!' says he, and set down by the road side and greets.

'I've lost the only two things as I cared for, and what else can I find to buy a pottle of brains with!' and he fair howled, till the tears ran down into his mouth. And up came a lass that lived near at hand, and looked at him.

'What's up with thee, fool?' says she.

'Oo, I've killed my pig, and lost my mother, and I'm nobbut a fool myself,' says he, sobbing.

'That's bad,' says she; 'and haven't thee anybody to look after thee?'

'No,' says he, 'and I canna buy my pottle of brains, for there's nothing I like best left!'

'What art talking about!' says she.

And down she sets by him, and he told her all about the wise woman and the pig, and his mother and the riddles, and that he was alone in the world.

'Well,' says she, 'I wouldn't mind looking after thee myself.'

'Could thee do it?' says he.

'Ou, ay!' says she; 'folk says as fools make good husbands, and I reckon I'll have thee, if thou'rt willing.'

'Can'st cook?' says he.

'Ay, I can,' says she.

'And scrub?' says he.

'Surely,' says she.

'And mend my clouts?' says he.

'I can that,' says she.

'I reckon thou'lt do then as well as anybody,' says he; 'but what'll I do about this wise woman?'

'Oh, wait a bit,' says she, 'something may turn up, and it'll not matter if thou'rt a fool, so long's thou'st got me to look after thee.'

'That's true,' says he, and off they went and got married. And she kept his house so clean and neat, and cooked his dinner so fine, that one night he says to her: 'Lass, I'm thinking I like thee best of everything after all.'

'That's good hearing,' says she, 'and what then?'

'Have I got to kill thee, dost think, and take thy heart up to the wise woman for that pottle o' brains?'

'Law, no!' says she, looking skeered, 'I winna have that. But see here; thou didn't cut out thy mother's heart, did thou?'

'No; but if I had, maybe I'd have got my pottle o' brains,' says he.

'Not a bit of it,' says she; 'just thou take me as I be, heart and all, and I'll wager I'll help thee read the riddles.'

'Can thee so?' says he, doubtful like, 'I reckon they're too hard for women folk.'

'Well,' says she, 'let's see now. Tell me the first.'

'What runs without feet?' says he.

'Why, water!' says she.

'It do,' says he, and scratched his head.

'And what's yellow and shining but isn't gold?'

'Why, the sun!' says she.

'Faith, it be!' says he. 'Come, we'll go up to the wise woman at once,' and off they went. And as they came up the pad, she was sitting at the door, twining straws.

'Gode'en, missis,' says he.

'Gode'en, fool,' says she.

'I reckon I've fetched thee the right thing at last,' says he.

The wise woman looked at them both, and wiped her spectacles.

'Canst tell me what that is as has first no legs, and then two legs, and ends with four legs?'

And the fool scratched his head, and thought and thought, but he couldn't tell.

And the lass whispered in his ear:

'It's a tadpole.'

'M'appen,' says he then, 'it may be a tadpole, missis.'

The wise woman nodded her head.

'That's right,' says she, 'and thou'st got thy pottle o' brains already.'

'Where be they?' says he, looking about and feeling in his pockets.

'In thy wife's head,' says she. 'The only cure for a fool is a good wife to look after him, and that thou'st got, so gode'en to thee!' And with that she nodded to them, and up and into the house.

So they went home together, and he never wanted to buy a pottle o' brains again, for his wife had enough for both.

Young Man in the Morning

(African American)

An old lady lived in the country was anxious to get married, but was too old, like me. And there was a young man come through the yard mornings, who she wanted to marry. So he told her, 'If you wet your sheet and wrap it around you, and stay on the roof all night tonight, I'll marry you in the morning.'

And she was fool enough to try it. She wrapped the wet sheet around her and went upon the roof, and sat there and shivered. The young man stayed in the house to make sure she stayed on the roof. Through the night he could hear her shivering and saying:

> *Oooooh, oooooh,*
> *Young man in the morning.*

She meant she'd just make it till morning, if she didn't freeze. (She sure was dumb.) Every time she said it she'd get weaker. So about three o'clock in the morning the sheet was ice, and the young man heard her rolling off the roof of the house and hit the ground in the yard, froze stiff. And when she landed he says, 'What a blessing. No old woman for me.'

NOW I SHOULD LAUGH,
IF I WERE NOT DEAD

(ICELANDIC)

nce two married women had a dispute about which of their husbands was the biggest fool. At last they agreed to try if they were as foolish as they seemed to be. One of the women then played this trick. When her husband came home from his work, she took a spinning-wheel and carders, and sitting down, began to card and spin, but neither the farmer nor anyone else saw any wool in her hands. Her husband, observing this, asked if she was mad to scrape the teazles together and spin the wheel, without having the wool, and prayed her to tell what this meant. She said it was scarcely to be expected that he should see what she was doing, for it was a kind of linen too fine to be seen with the eye. Of this she was going to make him clothes. He thought this a very good explanation, and wondered much at how clever his good wife was, and was not a little glad in looking forward to the joy and pride he would feel in having on these marvellous clothes. When his wife had spun, as she said, enough for the clothes, she set up the loom, and wove the stuff. Her husband used, now and then, to visit her, wondering at the skill of his good lady. She was much amused at all this, and made haste to carry out the trick well. She took the cloth from the loom, when it was finished, and first washed and fulled it, and last, sat down to work, cutting it and sewing the clothes out of it. When she had finished all this, she bade her husband come and try the clothes on, but did not dare let him put them on alone, wherefore she would help him. So she made believe to dress him in his fine clothes, and although the poor man was in reality naked, yet he firmly believed that it was all his own mistake, and thought his clever wife had made him these wondrous-fine clothes, and so glad he was at this, that he could not help jumping about for joy.

Now we turn to the other wife. When her husband came home from his work, she asked him why in the world he was up, and going about upon his feet. The man was startled at this question, and said: 'Why on earth do you ask this?' She persuaded him that he was very ill, and told him he had better go to bed. He believed this, and went to bed as soon as he could. When some time had passed, the wife said she would do the last services for him. He asked why, and prayed her by all means not to do so. She said: 'Why do you behave like a fool; don't you know that you died this morning? I am going, at once, to have your coffin made.' Now the poor man, believing this to be true, rested thus till he was put into his coffin. His wife then appointed a day for the burial, and hired six coffin-carriers, and asked the other couple to follow her dear husband to his grave. She had a window made in one side of the coffin, so that her husband might see all that passed round him. When the hour came for removing the coffin, the naked man came there, thinking that everybody would admire his delicate clothes. But far from it; although the coffin-bearers were in a sad mood, yet nobody could help laughing when they saw this naked fool. And when the man in the coffin caught a glance of him, he cried out as loud as he could: 'Now I should laugh, if I were not dead!' The burial was put off, and the man let out of the coffin.

THE THREE SILLIES

(ENGLISH)

nce upon a time there was a farmer and his wife who had one daughter, and she was courted by a gentleman. Every evening he used to come and see her, and stop to supper at the farmhouse, and the daughter used to be sent down into the cellar to draw the beer for supper. So one evening she had gone down to draw the beer, and she happened to look up at the ceiling while she was drawing, and she saw a mallet stuck in one of the beams. It must have been there a long, long time, but somehow or other she had never noticed it before, and she began a-thinking. And she thought it was very dangerous to have that mallet there, for she said to herself: 'Suppose him and me was to be married, and we was to have a son, and he was to grow up to be a man, and come down into the cellar to draw the beer, like I'm doing now, and the mallet was to fall on his head and kill him, what a dreadful thing it would be!' And she put down the candle and the jug, and sat herself down and began a-crying.

Well, they began to wonder upstairs how it was that she was so long drawing the beer, and her mother went down to see after her, and she found her sitting on the settle crying, and the beer running over the floor. 'Why, whatever is the matter?' said her mother. 'Oh, Mother!' says she, 'look at that horrid mallet! Suppose we was to be married, and was to have a son, and he was to grow up, and was to come down into the cellar to draw the beer, and the mallet was to fall on his head and kill him, what a dreadful thing it would be.'

'Dear, dear! what a dreadful thing it would be!' said the mother, and she sat down aside of the daughter, and started a-crying too. Then after a bit the father began to wonder that they didn't come back, and he went down into the cellar to look after them himself, and there they two sat a-crying, and the beer running all over the floor. 'Whatever is the matter?' says he. 'Why,' says the mother, 'look at that horrid mallet. Just suppose, if our daughter and her sweetheart was to be married, and was to have a son, and he was to grow up, and was to come down into the cellar to draw the beer, and the mallet was to fall on his head and kill him, what a dreadful thing it would be!'

'Dear, dear, dear! so it would!' said the father, and he sat himself down aside of the other two, and started a-crying.

Now the gentleman got tired of stopping up in the kitchen by himself, and at last he went down into the cellar too, to see what they were after; and there they three sat a-crying side by side, and the beer running all over the floor.

And he ran straight and turned the tap. Then he said: 'Whatever are you three doing, sitting there crying, and letting the beer run all over the floor?'

'Oh,' says the father, 'look at that horrid mallet! Suppose you and our daughter was to be married, and was to have a son, and he was to grow up, and was to come down into the cellar to draw the beer, and the mallet was to fall on his head and kill him!' And then they all started a-crying worse than before.

But the gentleman burst out a-laughing, and reached up and pulled out the mallet, and then he said: 'I've travelled many miles, and I never met three such big sillies as you three before; and now I shall start out on my travels again, and when I can find three bigger sillies than you three, then I'll come back and marry your daughter.' So he wished them goodbye, and started off on his travels, and left them all crying because the girl had lost her sweetheart.

Well, he set out, and he travelled a long way, and at last he came to a woman's cottage that had some grass growing on the roof. And the woman was trying to get her cow to go up a ladder to the grass, and the poor thing durst not go. So the gentleman asked the woman what she was doing. 'Why, lookye,' she said, 'look at all that beautiful grass. I'm going to get the cow on to the roof to eat it. She'll be quite safe, for I shall tie a string round her neck and pass it down the chimney, and tie it to my wrist as I go about the house, so she can't fall off without my knowing it.' 'Oh, you poor silly!' said the gentleman, 'you should cut the grass and throw it down to the cow!' But the woman thought it was easier to get the cow up the ladder than to get the grass down, so she pushed her and coaxed her and got her up, and tied a string round her neck, and passed it down the chimney, and fastened it to her own wrist. And the gentleman went on his way, but he hadn't gone far when the cow tumbled off the roof, and hung by the string tied round her neck, and it strangled her. And the weight of the cow tied to her wrist pulled the woman up the chimney, and she stuck fast halfway, and was smothered in the soot.

Well, that was one big silly.

And the gentleman went on and on, and he went to an inn to stop the night, and they were so full at the inn that they had to put him in a double-bedded room, and another traveller was to sleep in the other bed. The other man was a very pleasant fellow, and they got very friendly together; but in the morning, when they were both getting up, the gentleman was surprised to see the other hang his trousers on the knobs of the chest of drawers and run across the room and try to jump into them, and he tried over and over again, and he couldn't manage it; and the gentleman wondered whatever he was doing it for. At last he stopped and wiped his face with his handkerchief. 'Oh dear,' he says, 'I do think trousers are the most awkwardest kind of clothes that ever were. I can't think who could have invented such things. It takes me the best part of an hour to get into mine every morning, and I get

so hot! How do you manage yours?' So the gentleman burst out a-laughing, and showed him how to put them on; and he was very much obliged to him, and said he should never have thought of doing it that way.

So that was another big silly.

Then the gentleman went on his travels again; and he came to a village, and outside the village there was a pond, and round the pond was a crowd of people. And they had got rakes, and brooms, and pitch-forks, reaching into the pond; and the gentleman asked what was the matter. 'Why,' they say, 'matter enough! Moon's tumbled into the pond, and we can't rake her out anyhow!' So the gentleman burst out a-laughing, and told them to look up into the sky, and that it was only the shadow in the water. But they wouldn't listen to him, and abused him shamefully, and he got away as quick as he could.

So there was a whole lot of sillies bigger than them three sillies at home.

So the gentleman turned back home again, and married the farmer's daughter, and if they don't live happy for ever after, that's nothing to do with you or me.

THE BOY WHO HAD
NEVER SEEN WOMEN

(AFRICAN AMERICAN)

here was a boy in Alabama, I think, they raised never to see a girl till he was twenty-one – they was kind of 'sperimenting. He was raised by mens. So when he was twenty-one his daddy carried him to where the high school children would pass by when they came home for dinner at noon. And he seen them from the windows coming along so pretty, with their ribbons and long hair ('cause they had long hair in those days), and smiling and playing. And he said, 'Daddy, Daddy, come here. Looky looky, what are those?' 'Those are ducks.' 'Give me one, Daddy.' 'Which one do you want?' 'It don't make no difference, Daddy, any one.'

So it's better to let them grow up with each other, so they can pick a little.

The Old Woman Who
Lived in a Vinegar Bottle

(ENGLISH)

nce upon a time there was an old woman who lived in a vinegar bottle. One day a fairy was passing that way, and she heard the old woman talking to herself.

'It is a shame, it is a shame, it is a shame,' said the old woman. 'I didn't ought to live in a vinegar bottle. I ought to live in a nice little cottage with a thatched roof, and roses growing all up the wall, that I ought.'

So the fairy said, 'Very well, when you go to bed tonight you turn round three times, and shut your eyes, and in the morning you'll see what you will see.'

So the old woman went to bed, and turned round three times, and shut her eyes, and in the morning there she was, in a pretty little cottage with a thatched roof, and roses growing up the walls. And she was very surprised, and very pleased, but she quite forgot to thank the fairy.

And the fairy went north, and she went south, and she went east, and she went west, all about the business she had to do. And presently she thought, 'I'll go and see how that old woman is getting on. She must be very happy in her little cottage.'

And as she got up to the front door, she heard the old woman talking to herself.

'It is a shame, it is a shame, it is a shame,' said the old woman. 'I didn't ought to live in a little cottage like this, all by myself. I ought to live in a nice little house in a row of houses, with lace curtains at the windows, and a brass knocker on the door, and people calling mussels and cockles outside, all merry and cheerful.'

The fairy was rather surprised; but she said: 'Very well. You go to bed tonight, and turn round three times, and shut your eyes, and in the morning you shall see what you shall see.'

So the old woman went to bed, and turned round three times, and shut her eyes, and in the morning there she was in a nice little house, in a row of little houses, with lace curtains at the windows, and a brass knocker on the door, and people calling mussels and cockles outside, all merry and cheerful. And she was very much surprised, and very much pleased. But she quite forgot to thank the fairy.

And the fairy went north, and she went south, and she went east, and she went west, all about the business she had to do; and after a time she thought to herself, 'I'll go and see how that old woman is getting on. Surely she must be happy now.'

And when she got to the little row of houses, she heard the old woman talking to herself. 'It is a shame, it is a shame, it is a shame,' said the old woman. 'I didn't ought to live in a row of houses like this, with common people on each side of me. I ought to live in a great mansion in the country, with a big garden all round it, and servants to answer the bell.'

And the fairy was very surprised, and rather annoyed, but she said: 'Very well, go to bed and turn round three times, and shut your eyes, and in the morning you will see what you will see.'

And the old woman went to bed, and turned round three times, and shut her eyes, and in the morning there she was, in a great mansion in the country, surrounded by a fine garden, and servants to answer the bell. And she was very pleased and very surprised, and she learned how to speak genteelly, but she quite forgot to thank the fairy.

And the fairy went north, and she went south, and she went east, and she went west, all about the business she had to do; and after a time she thought to herself, 'I'll go and see how that old woman is getting on. Surely she must be happy now.'

But no sooner had she got near the old woman's drawing-room window than she heard the old woman talking to herself in a genteel voice.

'It certainly is a very great shame,' said the old woman, 'that I should be living alone here, where there is no society. I ought to be a duchess, driving in my own coach to wait on the Queen, with footmen running beside me.'

The fairy was very much surprised, and very much disappointed, but she said: 'Very well. Go to bed tonight, and turn round three times, and shut your eyes; and in the morning you shall see what you shall see.'

So the old woman went to bed, and turned round three times, and shut her eyes; and in the morning, there she was, a duchess with a coach of her own, to wait on the Queen, and footmen running beside her. And she was very much surprised, and very much pleased. BUT she quite forgot to thank the fairy.

And the fairy went north, and she went south, and she went east, and she went west, all about the business she had to do; and after a while she thought to herself: 'I'd better go and see how that old woman is getting on. Surely she is happy, now she's a duchess.'

But no sooner had she come to the window of the old woman's great town mansion, than she heard her saying in a more genteel tone than ever: 'It is indeed a very great shame that I should be a mere Duchess, and have to curtsey to the Queen. Why can't I be a queen myself, and sit on a golden throne, with a golden crown on my head, and courtiers all around me.'

The fairy was very much disappointed and very angry, but she said: 'Very well. Go to bed and turn round three times, and shut your eyes, and in the morning you shall see what you shall see.'

So the old woman went to bed, and turned round three times, and

shut her eyes; and in the morning there she was in a royal palace, a queen in her own right, sitting on a golden throne, with a golden crown on her head, and her courtiers all around her. And she was highly delighted, and ordered them right and left. BUT she quite forgot to thank the fairy.

And the fairy went north, and she went south, and she went east, and she went west, all about the business she had to do; and after a while she thought to herself: 'I'll go and see how that old woman is getting on. Surely she must be satisfied now!'

But as soon as she got near the Throne Room, she heard the old woman talking.

'It is a great shame, a very great shame,' she said, 'that I should be Queen of a paltry little country like this instead of ruling the whole round world. What I am really fitted for is to be *Pope*, to govern the minds of everyone on Earth.'

'Very well,' said the fairy. 'Go to bed. Turn round three times, and shut your eyes, and in the morning you shall see what you shall see.'

So the old woman went to bed, full of proud thoughts. She turned round three times, and shut her eyes. And in the morning she was back in her vinegar bottle.

TOM TIT TOT

(ENGLISH)

nce upon a time there was a woman, and she baked five pies. And when they came out of the oven, they were that over-baked the crusts were too hard to eat. So she says to her daughter:

'Darter,' says she, 'put you them there pies on the shelf, and leave 'em there a little, and they'll come again.' She meant, you know, the crust would get soft.

But the girl, she says to herself: 'Well, if they'll come again, I'll eat 'em now.' And she set to work and ate 'em all, first and last.

Well, come supper-time the woman said: 'Go you, and get one o' them there pies. I dare say they've come again now.'

The girl went and she looked, and there was nothing but the dishes. So back she came and says she: 'Noo, they ain't come again.'

'Not one of 'em?' says the mother.

'Not one of 'em,' says she.

'Well, come again, or not come again,' said the woman, 'I'll have one for supper.'

'But you can't, if they ain't come,' said the girl.

'But I can,' says she. 'Go you, and bring the best of 'em.'

'Best or worst,' says the girl, 'I've ate 'em all, and you can't have one till that's come again.'

Well, the woman she was done, and she took her spinning to the door to spin, and as she span she sang:

> 'My darter ha' ate five, five pies today.
> My darter ha' ate five, five pies today.'

The king was coming down the street, and he heard her sing, but what she sang he couldn't hear, so he stopped and said:

'What was that you were singing, my good woman?'

The woman was ashamed to let him hear what her daughter had been doing, so she sang, instead of that:

> *'My darter ha' spun five, five skeins today.*
> *My darter ha' spun five, five skeins today.'*

'Stars o' mine!' said the king, 'I never heard tell of anyone that could do that.'

Then he said: 'Look you here, I want a wife, and I'll marry your daughter. But look you here,' says he, 'eleven months out of the year she shall have all she likes to eat, and all the gowns she likes to get, and all the company she likes to keep; but the last month of the year she'll have to spin five skeins every day, and if she don't I shall kill her.'

'All right,' says the woman; for she thought what a grand marriage that was. And as for the five skeins, when the time came, there'd be plenty of ways of getting out of it, and likeliest, he'd have forgotten all about it.

Well, so they were married. And for eleven months the girl had all she liked to eat, and all the gowns she liked to get, and all the company she liked to keep.

But when the time was getting over, she began to think about the skeins and to wonder if he had 'em in mind. But not one word did he say about 'em, and she thought he'd wholly forgotten 'em.

However, the last day of the last month he takes her to a room she'd never set eyes on before. There was nothing in it but a spinning-wheel and a stool. And says he: 'Now, my dear, here you'll be shut in tomorrow with some victuals and some flax, and if you haven't spun five skeins by the night, your head'll go off.'

And away he went about his business.

Well, she was that frightened, she'd always been such a gatless girl, that she didn't so much as know how to spin, and what was she to do tomorrow with no one to come nigh her to help her? She sat down on a stool in the kitchen, and law! how she did cry!

However, all of a sudden she heard a sort of knocking low down on the door. She upped and oped it, and what should she see but a small little black thing with a long tail. That looked up at her right curious, and that said:

'What are you a-crying for?'

'What's that to you?' says she.

'Never you mind,' that said, 'but tell me what you're a-crying for.'

'That won't do me no good if I do,' says she.

'You don't know that,' that said, and twirled that's tail round.

'Well,' says she, 'that won't do no harm, if that don't do no good,' and she upped and told about the pies, and the skeins and everything.

'This is what I'll do,' says the little black thing, 'I'll come to your window every morning and take the flax and bring it spun at night.'

'What's your pay?' says she.

That looked out of the corner of that's eyes, and that said: 'I'll give you three guesses every night to guess my name, and if you haven't guessed it before the month's up you shall be mine.'

Well, she thought she'd be sure to guess that's name before the month was up. 'All right,' says she, 'I agree.'

'All right,' that says, and law! how that twirled that's tail.

Well, the next day, her husband took her into the room, and there was the flax and the day's food.

'Now there's the flax,' says he, 'and if that ain't spun up this night, off goes your head.' And then he went out and locked the door.

He'd hardly gone, when there was a knocking against the window.

She upped and she oped it, and there sure enough was the little old thing sitting on the ledge.

'Where's the flax?' says he.

'Here it be,' says she. And she gave it to him.

Well, come the evening a knocking came again to the window. She upped and she oped it, and there was the little old thing with five skeins of flax on his arm.

'Here it be,' says he, and he gave it to her.

'Now, what's my name?' says he.

'What, is that Bill?' says she.

'Noo, that ain't,' says he, and he twirled his tail.

'Is that Ned?' says she.

'Noo, that ain't,' says he, and he twirled his tail.

'Well, is that Mark?' says she.

'Noo, that ain't,' says he, and he twirled his tail harder, and away he flew.

Well, when her husband came in, there were the five skeins ready for him. 'I see I shan't have to kill you tonight, my dear,' says he; 'you'll have your food and your flax in the morning,' says he, and away he goes.

Well, every day the flax and the food were brought, and every day that there little black impet used to come mornings and evenings. And all the day the girl sat trying to think of names to say to it when it came at night. But she never hit on the right one. And as it got towards the end of the month, the impet began to look so maliceful, and that twirled that's tail faster and faster each time she gave a guess.

At last it came to the last day but one. The impet came at night along with the five skeins, and that said:

'What, ain't you got my name yet?'

'Is that Nicodemus?' says she.

'Noo, t'ain't,' that says.

'Is that Sammle?' says she.

'Noo, t'ain't,' that says.

'A-well, is that Methusaleh?' says she.

'Noo, t'ain't that neither,' that says.

Then that looks at her with that's eyes like a coal o' fire and that says: 'Woman, there's only tomorrow night, and then you'll be mine!' And away it flew.

Well, she felt that horrid. However, she heard the king coming along the passage. In he came, and when he sees the five skeins, he says, says he:

'Well, my dear,' says he. 'I don't see but what you'll have your skeins ready tomorrow night as well, and as I reckon I shan't have to kill you, I'll have supper in here tonight.' So they brought supper, and another stool for him and down the two sat.

Well, he hadn't eaten but a mouthful or so, when he stops and begins to laugh.

'What is it?' says she.

'A-why,' says he, 'I was out a-hunting today and I got away to a place in the wood I'd never seen before. And there was an old chalk-pit. And I heard a kind of a sort of a humming. So I got off my hobby, and I went right quiet to the pit, and I looked down. Well, what should there be but the funniest little black thing you ever set eyes on. And what was that doing, but that had a little spinning-wheel, and that was spinning wonderful fast, and twirling that's tail. And as that span that sang:

> *"Nimmy nimmy not*
> *My name's Tom Tit Tot."'*

Well, when the girl heard this, she felt as if she could have jumped out of her skin for joy, but she didn't say a word.

Next day that there little thing looked so maliceful when he came for the flax. And when night came, she heard that knocking against the window-panes. She oped the window and that come right in on the ledge. That was grinning from ear to ear, and Oo! that's tail was twirling round so fast.

'What's my name?' that says, as that gave her the skeins.

'Is that Solomon?' she says, pretending to be afeard.

'Noo, t'ain't,' that says, and that came further into the room.

'Well, is that Zebedee?' says she again.

'Noo, t'ain't,' says the impet. And then that laughed and twirled that's tail till you couldn't hardly see it.

'Take time, woman,' that says; 'next guess, and you're mine.' And that stretched out that's black hands at her.

Well, she backed a step or two, and she looked at it, and then she laughed out, and says she, pointing her finger at it:

> 'Nimmy nimmy not
> Your name's Tom Tit Tot!'

Well, when that heard her, that gave an awful shriek and away that flew into the dark, and she never saw it any more.

The Husband Who Was
to Mind the House

(NORWEGIAN)

here was once a man so surly and cross that he never thought his wife did anything right in the house. So one evening, in hay-making time, he came home, scolding and swearing, and showing his teeth and making a dust.

'Dear love, don't be so angry, there's a good man,' said his goody; 'tomorrow let's change our work. I'll go out with the mowers and mow, and you shall mind the house at home.'

Yes, the husband thought that would do very well. He was quite willing, he said.

So, early next morning, his goody took a scythe over her neck, and went out into the hay-field with the mowers and began to mow; but the man was to mind the house, and do the work at home.

First of all he wanted to churn the butter; but when he had churned a while, he got thirsty, and went down to the cellar to tap a barrel of ale. So, just when he had knocked in the bung, and was putting the tap into the cask, he heard overhead the pig come into the kitchen. Then off he ran up the cellar steps, with the tap in his hand, as fast as he could, to look after the pig, lest it should upset the churn; but when he got up, and saw the pig had already knocked the churn over, and stood there, routing and grunting amongst the cream which was running all over the floor, he got so wild with rage that he quite forgot the ale-barrel, and ran at the pig as hard as he could. He caught it, too, just as it ran out of doors, and gave it such a kick that piggy lay for dead on the spot. Then all at once he remembered he had the tap in his hand; but when he got down to the cellar, every drop of ale had run out of the cask.

Then he went into the dairy and found enough cream left to fill the churn again, and so he began to churn, for butter they must have at dinner. When he had churned a bit, he remembered that their milking cow was still shut up in the byre, and hadn't had a bit to eat or a drop to drink all the morning, though the sun was high. Then all at once he thought 'twas too far to take her down to the meadow, so he'd just get her up on the house-top – for the house, you must know, was thatched with sods, and a fine crop of grass was growing there. Now their house lay close up against a steep down, and he thought if he laid a plank across to the thatch at the back he'd easily get the cow up.

But still he couldn't leave the churn, for there was his little babe crawling about on the floor, and 'if I leave it,' he thought, 'the child is safe to upset it.' So he took the churn on his back, and went out with it, but then he thought he'd better first water the cow before he turned her out on the thatch, so he took up a bucket to draw water out of the well; but, as he stooped down at the well's brink, all the cream ran out of the churn over his shoulders, and so down into the well.

Now it was near dinner-time, and he hadn't even got the butter yet; so he thought he'd best boil the porridge, and filled the pot with water, and hung it over the fire. When he had done that, he thought the cow might perhaps fall off the thatch and break her legs or her neck. So he got up on the house to tie her up. One end of the rope he made fast to the cow's neck, and the other he slipped down the chimney and tied round his own thigh, and he had to make haste, for the water now began to boil in the pot, and he had still to grind the oatmeal.

So he began to grind away; but while he was hard at it, down fell the cow off the house-top after all, and as she fell, she dragged the man up the chimney by the rope. There he stuck fast; and as for the cow, she hung halfway down the wall, swinging between heaven and earth, for she could neither get down nor up.

And now the goody had waited seven lengths and seven breadths for her husband to come and call them home to dinner; but never a call they had. At last she thought she'd waited long enough, and went home. But when she got there and saw the cow hanging in such an ugly place, she ran up and cut the rope in two with her scythe. But as she did this, down came her husband out of the chimney; and so when his old dame came inside the kitchen, there she found him standing on his head in the porridge pot.

PART FOUR

GOOD GIRLS AND
WHERE IT GETS THEM

East o' the Sun and
West o' the Moon

(NORWEGIAN)

nce on a time there was a poor husbandman who had so
many children that he hadn't much of either food or clothing to give them. Pretty children they all were, but the
prettiest was the youngest daughter, who was so lovely
there was no end to her loveliness.

So one day, 'twas on a Thursday evening late at the fall of the year,
the weather was so wild and rough outside, and it was so cruelly dark,
and rain fell and wind blew, till the walls of the cottage shook again.
There they all sat round the fire busy with this thing and that. But just
then, all at once something gave three taps on the window-pane. Then
the father went out to see what was the matter; and, when he got out
of doors, what should he see but a great big White Bear.

'Good evening to you,' said the White Bear.

'The same to you,' said the man.

'Will you give me your youngest daughter? If you will, I'll make
you as rich as you are now poor,' said the Bear.

Well, the man would not be at all sorry to be so rich; but still he
thought he must have a bit of a talk with his daughter first; so he went
in and told them how there was a great White Bear waiting outside,
who had given his word to make them so rich if he could only have the
youngest daughter.

The lassie said 'No!' outright. Nothing could get her to say anything else; so the man went out and settled it with the White Bear, that
he should come again the next Thursday evening and get an answer.
Meantime he talked his daughter over, and kept on telling her of all
the riches they would get, and how well off she would be herself; and
so at last she thought better of it, and washed and mended her rags,

made herself as smart as she could, and was ready to start. I can't say her packing gave her much trouble.

Next Thursday evening came the White Bear to fetch her, and she got upon his back with her bundle, and off they went. So, when they had gone a bit of the way, the White Bear said –

'Are you afraid?'

'No! she wasn't.'

'Well! mind and hold tight by my shaggy coat, and then there's nothing to fear,' said the Bear.

So she rode a long, long way, till they came to a great steep hill. There, on the face of it, the White Bear gave a knock, and a door opened, and they came into a castle, where there were many rooms all lit up; rooms gleaming with silver and gold; and there too was a table ready laid, and it was all as grand as grand could be. Then the White Bear gave her a silver bell; and when she wanted anything, she was only to ring it, and she would get it at once.

Well, after she had eaten and drunk, and evening wore on, she got sleepy after her journey, and thought she would like to go to bed, so she rang the bell; and she had scarce taken hold of it before she came into a chamber, where there was a bed made, as fair and white as anyone would wish to sleep in, with silken pillows and curtains, and gold fringe. All that was in the room was gold or silver; but when she had gone to bed, and put out the light, a man came and laid himself alongside her. That was the White Bear, who threw off his beast shape at night; but she never saw him, for he always came after she had put out the light, and before the day dawned he was up and off again. So things went on happily for a while, but at last she began to get silent and sorrowful; for there she went about all day alone, and she longed to go home to see her father and mother, and brothers and sisters. So one day, when the White Bear asked what it was that she lacked, she said it was so dull and lonely there, and how she longed to go home to see her father and mother, and brothers and sisters, and that was why she was so sad and sorrowful, because she couldn't get to them.

'Well, well!' said the Bear, 'perhaps there's a cure for all this; but you must promise me one thing, not to talk alone with your mother, but only when the rest are by to hear; for she'll take you by the hand and try to lead you into a room alone to talk; but you must mind and not do that, else you'll bring bad luck on both of us.'

So one Sunday the White Bear came and said now they could set off to see her father and mother. Well, off they started, she sitting on his back; and they went far and long. At last they came to a grand house, and there her brothers and sisters were running about out of doors at play, and everything was so pretty, 'twas a joy to see.

'This is where your father and mother live now,' said the White Bear; 'but don't forget what I told you, else you'll make us both unlucky.'

'No! bless her, she'd not forget;' and when she had reached the house, the White Bear turned right about and left her.

Then when she went in to see her father and mother, there was such joy, there was no end to it. None of them thought they could thank her enough for all she had done for them. Now, they had everything they wished, as good as good could be, and they all wanted to know how she got on where she lived.

Well, she said, it was very good to live where she did; she had all she wished. What she said beside I don't know; but I don't think any of them had the right end of the stick, or that they got much out of her. But so in the afternoon, after they had done dinner, all happened as the White Bear had said. Her mother wanted to talk with her alone in her bedroom; but she minded what the White Bear had said, and wouldn't go up stairs.

'Oh, what we have to talk about will keep,' she said, and put her mother off. But somehow or other, her mother got round her at last, and she had to tell her the whole story. So she said, how every night, when she had gone to bed, a man came and lay down beside her as soon as she had put out the light, and how she never saw him, because he was always up and away before the morning dawned; and how she went about woeful and sorrowing, for she thought she should so like to see him, and how all day long she walked about there alone, and how dull, and dreary, and lonesome it was.

'My!' said her mother; 'it may well be a Troll you slept with! But now I'll teach you a lesson how to set eyes on him. I'll give you a bit of candle, which you can carry home in your bosom; just light that while he is asleep, but take care not to drop the tallow on him.'

Yes! she took the candle, and hid it in her bosom, and as night drew on, the White Bear came and fetched her away.

But when they had gone a bit of the way, the White Bear asked if all hadn't happened as he had said.

'Well, she couldn't say it hadn't.'

'Now, mind,' said he, 'if you have listened to your mother's advice, you have brought bad luck on us both, and then, all that has passed between us will be as nothing.'

'No,' she said, 'she hadn't listened to her mother's advice.'

So when she reached home, and had gone to bed, it was the old story over again. There came a man and lay down beside her; but at dead of night, when she heard he slept, she got up and struck a light, lit the candle, and let the light shine on him, and so she saw that he was the loveliest Prince one ever set eyes on, and she fell so deep in love with him on the spot, that she thought she couldn't live if she didn't give him a kiss there and then. And so she did, but as she kissed him, she dropped three hot drops of tallow on his shirt, and he woke up.

'What have you done?' he cried; 'now you have made us both unlucky, for had you held out only this one year, I had been freed. For I have a stepmother who has bewitched me, so that I am a White Bear by day, and a Man by night. But now all ties are snapt between us; now I must set off from you to her. She lives in a castle which stands east o' the sun and west o' the moon, and there, too, is a Princess, with a nose three ells long, and she's the wife I must have now.'

She wept and took it ill, but there was no help for it; go he must.

Then she asked if she mightn't go with him.

No, she mightn't.

'Tell me the way, then,' she said, 'and I'll search you out; *that* surely I may get leave to do.'

'Yes, she might do that,' he said; 'but there was no way to that place. It lay east o' the sun and west o' the moon, and thither she'd never find her way.'

So next morning, when she woke up, both Prince and castle were gone, and then she lay on a little green patch, in the midst of the gloomy thick wood, and by her side lay the same bundle of rags she had brought with her from her old home.

So when she had rubbed the sleep out of her eyes, and wept till she was tired, she set out on her way, and walked many, many days, till she came to a lofty crag. Under it sat an old hag, and played with a gold apple which she tossed about. Her the lassie asked if she knew the way to the Prince, who lived with his stepmother in the castle that lay east o' the sun and west o' the moon, and who was to marry the Princess with a nose three ells long.

'How did you come to know about him?' asked the old hag; 'but maybe you are the lassie who ought to have had him?'

Yes, she was.

'So, so; it's you, is it?' said the old hag. 'Well, all I know about him is, that he lives in the castle that lies east o' the sun and west o' the moon, and thither you'll come, late or never; but still you may have the loan of my horse, and on him you can ride to my next neighbour. Maybe she'll be able to tell you; and when you get there, just give the horse a switch under the left ear, and beg him to be off home; and, stay, this gold apple you may take with you.'

So she got upon the horse, and rode a long long time, till she came to another crag, under which sat another old hag, with a gold carding-comb. Her the lassie asked if she knew the way to the castle that lay east o' the sun and west o' the moon, and she answered, like the first old hag, that she knew nothing about it, except it was east o' the sun and west o' the moon.

'And thither you'll come, late or never; but you shall have the loan of my horse to my next neighbour; maybe she'll tell you all about it; and when you get there, just switch the horse under the left ear, and beg him to be off home.'

And this old hag gave her the golden carding-comb; it might be she'd find some use for it, she said. So the lassie got up on the horse, and rode a far far way, and a weary time; and so at last she came to another great crag, under which sat another old hag, spinning with a golden spinning-wheel. Her, too, she asked if she knew the way to the Prince, and where the castle was that lay east o' the sun and west o' the moon. So it was the same thing over again.

'Maybe it's you who ought to have had the Prince?' said the old hag.

Yes, it was.

But she, too, didn't know the way a bit better than the other two. 'East o' the sun and west o' the moon it was,' she knew – that was all.

'And thither you'll come, late or never; but I'll lend you my horse, and then I think you'd best ride to the East Wind and ask him; maybe he knows those parts, and can blow you thither. But when you get to him, you need only give the horse a switch under the left ear, and he'll trot home of himself.'

And so, too, she gave her the gold spinning-wheel.

'Maybe you'll find a use for it,' said the old hag.

Then on she rode many many days, a weary time, before she got to the East Wind's house, but at last she did reach it, and then she asked the East Wind if he could tell her the way to the Prince who dwelt east o' the sun and west o' the moon. Yes, the East Wind had often heard tell of it, the Prince and the castle, but he couldn't tell the way, for he had never blown so far.

'But, if you will, I'll go with you to my brother the West Wind, maybe he knows, for he's much stronger. So, if you will just get on my back, I'll carry you thither.'

Yes, she got on his back, and I should just think they went briskly along.

So when they got there, they went into the West Wind's house, and the East Wind said the lassie he had brought was the one who ought to have had the Prince who lived in the castle east o' the sun and west o' the moon: and so she had set out to seek him, and how he had come with her, and would be glad to know if the West Wind knew how to get to the castle.

'Nay,' said the West Wind, 'so far I've never blown; but if you will, I'll go with you to our brother the South Wind, for he's much stronger than either of us, and he has flapped his wings far and wide. Maybe he'll tell you. You can get on my back, and I'll carry you to him.'

Yes! she got on his back, and so they travelled to the South Wind, and weren't so very long on the way, I should think.

When they got there, the West Wind asked him if he could tell her the way to the castle that lay east o' the sun and west o' the moon, for it was she who ought to have had the Prince who lived there.

'You don't say so! That's she, is it?' said the South Wind.

'Well, I have blustered about in most places in my time, but so far have I never blown; but if you will, I'll take you to my brother the North Wind; he is the oldest and strongest of the whole lot of us, and if he don't know where it is, you'll never find anyone in the world to tell you. You can get on my back, and I'll carry you thither.'

Yes! she got on his back, and away he went from his house at a fine rate. And this time, too, she wasn't long on her way.

So when they got to the North Wind's house, he was so wild and cross, cold puffs came from him a long way off.

'BLAST YOU BOTH, WHAT DO YOU WANT?' he roared out to them ever so far off, so that it struck them with an icy shiver.

'Well,' said the South Wind, 'you needn't be so foul-mouthed, for here I am, your brother, the South Wind, and here is the lassie who ought to have had the Prince who dwells in the castle that lies east o' the sun and west o' the moon, and now she wants to ask you if you ever were there, and can tell her the way, for she would be so glad to find him again.'

'YES, I KNOW WELL ENOUGH WHERE IT IS,' said the North Wind; 'once in my life I blew an aspen-leaf thither, but I was so tired I couldn't blow a puff for ever so many days after. But if you really wish to go thither, and aren't afraid to come along with me, I'll take you on my back and see if I can blow you thither.'

Yes! with all her heart; she must and would get thither if it were possible in any way; and as for fear, however madly he went, she wouldn't be at all afraid.

'Very well, then,' said the North Wind, 'but you must sleep here tonight, for we must have the whole day before us, if we're to get thither at all.'

Early next morning the North Wind woke her, and puffed himself up, and blew himself out, and made himself so stout and big, 'twas gruesome to look at him; and so off they went high up through the air, as if they would never stop till they got to the world's end.

Down here below there was such a storm; it threw down long tracts of wood and many houses, and when it swept over the great sea, ships foundered by hundreds.

So they tore on and on, – no one can believe how far they went, –

and all the while they still went over the sea, and the North Wind got more and more weary, and so out of breath he could scarce bring out a puff, and his wings drooped and drooped, till at last he sunk so low that the crests of the waves dashed over his heels.

'Are you afraid?' said the North Wind.

'No!' she wasn't.

But they weren't very far from land; and the North Wind had still so much strength left in him that he managed to throw her up on the shore under the windows of the castle which lay east o' the sun and west o' the moon; but then he was so weak and worn out, he had to stay there and rest many days before he could get home again.

Next morning the lassie sat down under the castle window, and began to play with the gold apple; and the first person she saw was the Long-nose who was to have the Prince.

'What do you want for your gold apple, you lassie?' said the Long-nose, and threw up the window.

'It's not for sale, for gold or money,' said the lassie.

'If it's not for sale for gold or money, what is it that you will sell it for? You may name your own price,' said the Princess.

'Well! if I may get to the Prince, who lives here, and be with him tonight, you shall have it,' said the lassie whom the North Wind had brought.

Yes! she might; that could be done. So the Princess got the gold apple; but when the lassie came up to the Prince's bedroom at night he was fast asleep; she called him and shook him, and between whiles she wept sore; but all she could do she couldn't wake him up. Next morning as soon as day broke, came the Princess with the long nose, and drove her out again.

So in the daytime she sat down under the castle windows and began to card with her golden carding-comb, and the same thing happened. The Princess asked what she wanted for it; and she said it wasn't for sale for gold or money, but if she might get leave to go up to the Prince and be with him that night, the Princess should have it. But when she went up she found him fast asleep again, and all she called, and all she shook, and wept, and prayed, she couldn't get life into him; and as soon as the first gray peep of day came, then came the Princess with the long nose, and chased her out again.

So in the daytime the lassie sat down outside under the castle

window, and began to spin with her golden spinning-wheel, and that,
too, the Princess with the long nose wanted to have. So she threw up
the window and asked what she wanted for it. The lassie said, as she
had said twice before, it wasn't for sale for gold or money; but if she
might go up to the Prince who was there, and be with him alone that
night, she might have it.

Yes! she might do that and welcome. But now you must know
there were some Christian folk who had been carried off thither, and
as they sat in their room, which was next the Prince, they had heard
how a woman had been in there, and wept and prayed, and called to
him two nights running, and they told that to the Prince.

That evening, when the Princess came with her sleepy drink, the
Prince made as if he drank, but threw it over his shoulder, for he
could guess it was a sleepy drink. So, when the lassie came in, she
found the Prince wide awake; and then she told him the whole story
how she had come thither.

'Ah,' said the Prince, 'you've just come in the very nick of time, for
tomorrow is to be our wedding-day; but now I won't have the Long-
nose, and you are the only woman in the world who can set me free.
I'll say I want to see what my wife is fit for, and beg her to wash the
shirt which has the three spots of tallow on it; she'll say yes, for she
doesn't know 'tis you who put them there; but that's a work only for
Christian folk, and not for such a pack of Trolls, and so I'll say that I
won't have any other for my bride than the woman who can wash
them out, and ask you to do it.'

So there was great joy and love between them all that night. But
next day, when the wedding was to be, the Prince said –

'First of all, I'd like to see what my bride is fit for.'

'Yes!' said the stepmother, with all her heart.

'Well,' said the Prince, 'I've got a fine shirt which I'd like for my
wedding shirt, but somehow or other it has got three spots of tallow
on it, which I must have washed out; and I have sworn never to take
any other bride than the woman who's able to do that. If she can't,
she's not worth having.'

Well, that was no great thing they said, so they agreed, and she
with the long nose began to wash away as hard as she could, but the
more she rubbed and scrubbed, the bigger the spots grew.

'Ah!' said the old hag, her mother, 'you can't wash; let me try.'

But she hadn't long taken the shirt in hand, before it got far worse than ever, and with all her rubbing, and wringing, and scrubbing, the spots grew bigger and blacker, and the darker and uglier was the shirt.

Then all the other Trolls began to wash, but the longer it lasted, the blacker and uglier the shirt grew, till at last it was as black all over as if it had been up the chimney.

'Ah!' said the Prince, 'you're none of you worth a straw: you can't wash. Why there, outside, sits a beggar lassie, I'll be bound she knows how to wash better than the whole lot of you. COME IN, LASSIE! he shouted.

Well, in she came.

'Can you wash this shirt clean, lassie, you?' said he.

'I don't know,' she said, 'but I think I can.'

And almost before she had taken it and dipped it in the water, it was as white as driven snow, and whiter still.

'Yes; you are the lassie, for me,' said the Prince.

At that the old hag flew into such a rage, she burst on the spot, and the Princess with the long nose after her, and the whole pack of Trolls after her, – at least I've never heard a word about them since.

As for the Prince and Princess, they set free all the poor Christian folk who had been carried off and shut up there; and they took with them all the silver and gold, and flitted away as far as they could from the castle that lay east o' the sun and west o' the moon.

The Good Girl and
the Ornery Girl

(NORTH AMERICAN: OZARKS)

ne time there was an old woman lived away out in the
timber, and she had two daughters. One of them was a
good girl and the other one was ornery, but the old woman
liked the ornery one best. So they made the good girl do all
the work, and she had to split wood with a dull axe. The ornery girl
just laid a-flat of her back all day and never done nothing.

The good girl went out to pick up sticks, and pretty soon she seen
a cow. The cow says, 'For God's sake milk me, my bag's about to
bust!' So the good girl milked the cow, but she didn't drink none of the
milk. Pretty soon she seen a apple tree, and the tree says, 'For God's
sake pick these apples, or I'll break plumb down!' So the good girl

picked the apples, but she didn't eat none. Pretty soon she seen some cornbread a-baking, and the bread says, 'For God's sake take me out, I'm a-burning up!' So the good girl pulled the bread out, but she didn't taste a crumb. A little old man come along just then, and he throwed a sack of gold money so it stuck all over her. When the good girl got home she shed gold pieces like feathers off a goose.

Next day the ornery girl went out to get her some gold too. Pretty soon she seen a cow, and the cow says, 'For God's sake milk me, my bag's about to bust!' But the ornery girl just kicked the old cow in the belly, and went right on. Pretty soon she seen a apple tree, and the tree says, 'For God's sake pick these apples, or I'll break plumb down!' But the ornery girl just laughed, and went right on. Pretty soon she seen some cornbread a-baking, and the bread says, 'For God's sake take me out, I'm a-burning up!' But the ornery girl didn't pay no mind, and went right on. A little old man come along just then, and he throwed a kettle of tar so it stuck all over her. When the ornery girl got home she was so black the old woman didn't know who it was.

The folks tried everything they could, and finally they got most of the tar off. But the ornery girl always looked kind of ugly after that, and she never done any good. It served the little bitch right, too.

THE ARMLESS MAIDEN

(RUSSIAN)

I n a certain kingdom, not in our land, there lived a wealthy merchant; he had two children, a son and a daughter. The father and mother died. The brother said to the sister: 'Let us leave this town, little sister; I will rent a shop and trade, and find lodgings for you; we will live together.' They went to another province. When they came there, the brother inscribed himself in the merchants' guild, and rented a shop of woven cloths. The brother decided to marry and took a sorceress to wife. One day he went to trade in his shop and said to his sister: 'Keep order in the house, sister.' The wife felt offended because he said this to his sister. To revenge herself she broke all the furniture and when her husband came back she met him and said: 'See what a sister you have; she has broken all the furniture in the house.' 'Too bad, but we can get some new things,' said the husband.

The next day when leaving for his shop he said farewell to his wife and his sister and said to his sister: 'Please, little sister, see to it that everything in the house is kept as well as possible.' The wife bided her time, went to the stables, and cut off the head of her husband's favorite horse with a saber. She awaited him on the porch. 'See what a sister you have,' she said. 'She has cut off the head of your favorite horse.' 'Ah, let the dogs eat what is theirs,' answered the husband.

On the third day the husband again went to his shop, said farewell, and said to his sister: 'Please look after my wife, so that she does not hurt herself or the baby, if by chance she gives birth to one.' When the wife gave birth to her child, she cut off his head. When her husband came home he found her sitting and lamenting over her baby. 'See what a sister you have! No sooner had I given birth to my baby than she cut off his head with a saber.' The husband did not say anything; he wept bitter tears and turned away.

Night came. At the stroke of midnight he rose and said: 'Little sister, make ready; we are going to mass.' She said: 'My beloved brother, I do not think it is a holiday today.' 'Yes, my sister, it is a holiday; let us go.' 'It is still too early to go, brother,' she said. 'No,' he answered, 'young maidens always take a long time to get ready.' The sister began to dress; she was very slow and reluctant. Her brother said: 'Hurry, sister, get dressed.' 'Please,' she said, 'it is still early, brother.' 'No, little sister, it is not early, it is high time to be gone.'

When the sister was ready they sat in a carriage and set out for mass. They drove for a long time or a short time. Finally they came to a wood. The sister said: 'What wood is this?' He answered: 'This is the hedge around the church.' The carriage caught in a bush. The brother said: 'Get out, little sister, disentangle the carriage.' 'Ah, my beloved brother, I cannot do that, I will dirty my dress.' 'I will buy you a new dress, sister, a better one than this.' She got down from the carriage, began to disentangle it, and her brother cut off her arms to the elbows, struck his horse with the whip, and drove away.

The little sister was left alone; she burst into tears and began to walk in the woods. She walked and walked, a long time or a short time; she was all scratched, but could not find a path leading out of the woods. Finally, after several years, she found a path. She came to a market town and stood beneath the window of the wealthiest merchant to beg for alms. This merchant had a son, an only one, who was the apple of his father's eye. He fell in love with the beggar woman and said: 'Dear Father and Mother, marry me.' 'To whom shall we marry you?' 'To this beggar woman.' 'Ah, my dear child, do not the merchants of our town have lovely daughters?' 'Please marry me to her,' he said. 'If you do not, I will do something to myself.' They were distressed, because he was their only son, their life's treasure. They gathered all the merchants and clerics and asked them to judge the matter: should they marry their son to the beggar woman or not? The priest said: 'Such must be his fate, and God gives your son his sanction to marry the beggar woman.'

So the son lived with her for a year and then another year. At the end of that time he went to another province, where her brother had his shop. When taking his leave he said: 'Dear Father and Mother, do not abandon my wife; as soon as she gives birth to a child, write to me

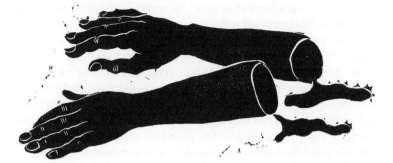

that very hour.' Two or three months after the son left, his wife gave birth to a child; his arms were golden up to the elbows, his sides were studded with stars, there was a bright moon on his forehead and a radiant sun near his heart. The grandparents were overjoyed and at once wrote their beloved son a letter. They dispatched an old man with this note in all haste. Meanwhile the wicked sister-in-law had learned about all this and invited the old messenger into her house: 'Come in, little father,' she said, 'and take a rest.' 'No, I have no time, I am bringing an urgent message.' 'Come in, little father, take a rest, have something to eat.'

She sat him down to dinner, took his bag, found the letter in it, read it, tore it into little pieces, and wrote another letter instead: 'Your wife,' it said, 'has given birth to a half dog and half bear that she conceived with beasts in the woods.' The old messenger came to the merchant's son and handed him the letter; he read it and burst into tears. He wrote in answer, asking that his son be not molested till he returned. 'When I come back,' he said, 'I will see what kind of baby it is.' The sorceress again invited the old messenger into her house. 'Come in, sit down, take a rest,' she said. Again she charmed him with talk, stole the letter he carried, read it, tore it up, and instead ordered that her sister-in-law be driven out the moment the letter was received. The old messenger brought this letter; the father and mother read it and were grieved. 'Why does he cause us so much trouble?' they said. 'We married him to the girl, and now he does not want his wife!' They pitied not so much the wife as the babe. So they gave their blessing to her and the babe, tied the babe to her breast, and sent her away.

She went, shedding bitter tears. She walked, for a long time or a short time, all in the open field, and there was no wood or village anywhere. She came to a dale and was very thirsty. She looked to the right and saw a well. She wanted to drink from it but was afraid to stoop, lest she drop her baby. Then she fancied that the water came closer. She stooped to drink and her baby fell into the well. She began to walk around the well, weeping, and wondering how to get her child out of the well. An old man came up to her and said: 'Why are you weeping, you slave of God?' 'How can I help weeping? I stooped over the well to drink water and my baby fell into it.' 'Bend down and take him out.' 'No, little father, I cannot; I have no hands, only stumps.' 'Do as I tell you. Take your baby.' She went to the well, stretched out her arms, and God helped, for suddenly she had her hands, all whole. She bent down, pulled her baby out, and began to give thanks to God, bowing to all four sides.

She said her prayers, went on farther, and came to the house where her brother and husband were staying, and asked for shelter. Her husband said: 'Brother, let the beggar woman in; beggar women can tell stories and recount real happenings.' The wicked sister-in-law said: 'We have no room for visitors, we are overcrowded.' 'Please, brother, let her come; there is nothing I like better than to hear beggar women tell tales.' They let her in. She sat on the stove with her baby. Her husband said: 'Now, little dove, tell us a tale – any kind of story.'

She said: 'I do not know any tales or stories, but I can tell the truth. Listen, here is a true happening that I can recount to you.' And she began: 'In a certain kingdom, not in our land lived a wealthy merchant; he had two children, a son and a daughter. The father and mother died. The brother said to the sister: "Let us leave this town, little sister." And they came to another province. The brother inscribed himself in the merchants' guild and took a shop of woven cloth. He decided to marry and took a sorceress to wife.' At this point the sister-in-law muttered: 'Why does she bore us with her stories, that hag?' But the husband said: 'Go on, go on, little mother, I love such stories more than anything!'

'And so,' the beggar woman went on, 'the brother went to trade in his shop and said to his sister: "Keep order in the house, sister." The wife felt offended because he had said this to his sister and out of spite broke all the furniture.' And then she went on to tell how her brother took her to mass and cut off her hands, how she gave birth to a baby, how her sister-in-law lured the old messenger – and again the sister-in-law interrupted her, crying: 'What gibberish she is telling!' But the husband said: 'Brother, order your wife to keep quiet; it is a wonderful story, is it not?'

She came to the point when her husband wrote to his parents ordering that the baby be left in peace until his return, and the sister-in-law mumbled: 'What nonsense!' Then she reached the point when she came to their house as a beggar woman, and the sister-in-law mumbled: 'What is this old bitch gibbering about!' And the husband said: 'Brother, order her to keep quiet; why does she interrupt all the time?' Finally she came to the point in the story when she was let in and began to tell the truth instead of a story. And then she pointed at them and said: 'This is my husband, this is my brother, and this is my sister-in-law.'

Then her husband jumped up to her on the stove and said: 'Now, my dear, show me the baby. Let me see whether my father and mother wrote me the truth.' They took the baby, removed its swaddling clothes – and the whole room was illumined! 'So it is true that she did not tell us just a tale; here is my wife, and here is my son – golden up to the elbows – his sides studded with stars, a bright moon on his forehead, and a radiant sun near his heart!'

The brother took the best mare from his stable, tied his wife to its tail, and let it run in the open field. The mare dragged her on the ground until she brought back only her braid; the rest was strewn on the field. Then they harnessed three horses and went home to the young husband's father and mother; they began to live happily and to prosper. I was there and drank mead and wine; it ran down my mustache, but did not go into my mouth.

PART FIVE

WITCHES

THE CHINESE PRINCESS

(KASHMIRI)

n the reign of the Mughal Emperor Shah Jahan the Valley of Kashmir was under the rule of a governor named Ali Mardan Khan. He was very fond of hunting. One day he was in search of game in a forest not far from the beautiful Dal Lake when he saw a stag. Leaving his companions behind, he gave chase to it. After some time the stag eluded him and disappeared into some bushes.

Ali Mardan drew rein, and waited in the hope that it would come out of its hiding place; but there was no sign of it. Tired and disappointed he was returning to his companions when suddenly he heard some one crying. He went in the direction of the sound, and there he found seated under a tree a damsel of surpassing beauty, richly dressed and bejewelled. It was obvious that she did not belong to this country.

Ali Mardan was dazzled by her beauty. He dismounted and inquired of her as to who she was and why she was crying.

'Oh, Sir,' she replied 'I am the daughter of a Chinese King. My father fell in a battle between him and the ruler of a neighbouring province. Many of our noblemen were taken prisoner; but I, somehow, managed to escape. Since then I have been wandering from place to place until I reached here.'

'Fair maiden,' Ali Mardan replied, consoling her, 'Now you need wander no more. No harm will come to you, for I am the ruler of this country.'

The Chinese princess wept on hearing this.

'Oh my lord,' she said, 'I weep for my father, I weep for my mother, I weep for my country and I weep for myself. What will become of me, friendless and homeless, how can I live?'

'Weep no more, lovely one,' the King said compassionately. 'Stay in my palace where you will be safe and comfortable.'

'That gladly will I do,' said the girl, still crying, 'and were you to ask me to become your wife, I should not be able to refuse you.'

On hearing these words Ali Mardan's face brightened. He held the girl's hands.

'Come, my beloved! I will make you my wife,' he said and he took her to his palace and they were married soon after.

Ali Mardan and his wife spent some time happily together when one day she approached him saying:

'Build me a palace by the Lake, where from the balcony I could see my reflection in the water.'

Thereupon Ali Mardan immediately gave orders for the construction of the new palace. Thousands of labourers and masons were engaged to complete the building, and in the shortest possible time a beautiful palace of marble adorned the bank of the Dal Lake. It was enclosed on three sides by gardens full of flowers of the rarest fragrance and beauty, and there beside the lake she lived happily with Ali Mardan whose love for her increased every day.

But their happiness did not last long. One morning Ali Mardan woke up feeling unwell.

'I have a pain in my stomach,' he told his Chinese wife.

He did not worry much about it. But as the pain persisted throughout the day, his wife sent for the royal physician, who examined him and gave him some medicine, but still the pain did not subside. Ali Mardan was confined to his room and the Chinese princess constantly attended to his needs. Many days passed but his malady was no better.

Now it chanced, that a Yogi was passing by way of the Dal Lake carrying a small jar of water. He was surprised to see the new palace.

'I have never seen a palace here before,' he said to himself. 'Who could have built it I wonder.'

As he felt tired and the day was hot, he went into the garden of the palace, and sat down under a tree. So much at peace did he feel among the flowers beds, and so sweetly did the birds sing around him that soon he was lulled to sleep.

Now at this very hour Ali Mardan, feeling slightly better, was having a stroll in the garden. He was walking slowly supported by his courtiers.

Ali Mardan was a man of humble heart and always showed great respect towards holy men irrespective of their belief; so instead of becoming angry with the intruder, he smiled.

'Don't disturb the sleeping Yogi,' he said to his attendants. 'Go bring the best bed you can find, and lay this holy man gently upon it.' Then seeing the jar of water he added:

'Take great care of this too.'

Two hours later when the Yogi awoke he was surprised to find himself on such a comfortable bed.

'Don't worry,' said an attendant who approached, seeing him awake. 'You are the guest of Ali Mardan, the Governor of Kashmir, who desires to see you.'

Then noticing that he was searching for something, the attendant added:

'Your jar of water is in safe custody; rest assured.'

He was then taken to the Governor's room. He found him lying on his bed.

'Have you rested well, holy man.' Ali Mardan asked gently. 'Who are you and from where do you come?'

'Sire,' replied the Yogi, 'I am an humble disciple of my Guru who lives at some distance from here in a forest. My master likes to drink the water of a sacred spring and sends me every now and then to fetch it. The last time I passed this way there was no palace here, so I was surprised to find this one today. But I must now take leave of you as I am already delayed and my master will be anxious if I don't get back before dark.'

The Yogi then thanked him for his kindness, and was just leaving the bedroom when Ali Mardan was seized by a spasm of pain. On inquiring, the Yogi came to know of the Governor's mysterious malady. Then he left the palace.

That evening the Yogi returned to his master, and related to him the events of the day. He particularly mentioned the hospitality shown to him by the Governor. The Guru was very pleased to hear of it. Then the disciple told him of how the Governor was in the grip of a strange illness which no physician had so far been able to cure.

'I am sorry to hear about his illness,' said the Guru. 'Take me to him tomorrow, and we will see if we can do anything to help him.'

Next morning the disciple took his master to the palace and sought an audience with the Governor, who was still confined to his bedroom.

The disciple introduced his master to Ali Mardan and also told him the purpose of their visit.

'I am much honoured by your Holy presence, O! Guru,' said Ali Mardan. 'And if you can cure me of this disease I shall be grateful to you all my life.'

'Show me your body,' said the holy man.

Hardly had he uncovered himself, when the Guru inquired: 'Have you recently married?'

'Yes,' said Ali Mardan, and briefly told the holy man of his encounter with the Chinese princess and of his marriage with her.

'Just as I had suspected,' observed the holy man, then in grave tone he said:

'O Governor! you are really very ill, but I can cure you if you do as I tell you.'

The Governor was alarmed and assured the holy man that he would do as he was bidden.

That evening Ali Mardan, as instructed by the Guru ordered two kinds of *kitcheri* to be cooked, one sweet and the other salty, and

placed on one dish in such a way that the salty *kitcheri* was on one side and the sweet on the other. When, as usual, the Governor and his Chinese wife sat down to eat, he turned the salty side of the dish towards her. She found her portion too salty but seeing that her husband was eating with relish she made no remark and ate in silence.

When the time came for them to retire, Ali Mardan, under the instructions of the Guru, had secretly given orders to the attendants that the drinking water should be removed from their bedroom and that the room should be locked from outside.

As was expected the Chinese princess woke up very thirsty in the middle of the night, and finding no water and no way out she became desperate. She looked at her husband to assure herself that he was fast asleep; then she assumed the shape of a snake, slipped through the window, and went down to the Lake to quench her thirst. After a few minutes she returned by the same way and resuming her human shape, lay down beside her husband again.

Ali Mardan, who in fact had been feigning sleep, was horrified at what he had seen, and was unable to sleep for the rest of the night. Early next morning he sought the holy man and told him what had happened in the night.

'Oh! Governor,' said the holy man, 'as you have seen, your wife is no woman but a Lamia – a snake woman.' Then he explained to Ali Mardan:

'If for one hundred years the glance of no human being falls on a snake a crest forms on its head, and it becomes the king of the snakes, and if for another hundred years it comes not within sight of a man it changes into a dragon, and if for three hundred years it has not been looked upon by a human being it becomes a Lamia. A Lamia possesses enormous powers and can change its appearance at will. It is very fond of assuming the form of a woman. Such is your wife O! Governor,' he concluded.

'Horrors!' exclaimed the Governor. 'But is there no way of escape from this monster?'

'Yes there is,' replied the holy man; 'only we must act cautiously so as not to arouse her suspicions, for if she suspects even remotely that her secret is disclosed she will destroy not only you, but your country as well. Therefore, do precisely what I tell you.'

Then the Guru told the Governor of his plan which was carried out at once. A house of lac was built at some distance from the palace, which had only a bedroom and kitchen. A big oven with a strong lid was built in the kitchen.

The royal physician then advised Ali Mardan to confine himself in this house for forty days. During this period no one but his wife should be allowed to see him.

His wife was only too glad to have Ali Mardan all to herself. A few days passed during which she happily attended to all his needs. One day Ali Mardan told his wife:

'The physician has prescribed a special loaf for me; kindly cook it for me.'

'I dislike ovens,' she said.

'But my life is in danger,' said the Governor. 'If you really love me, do this for me.'

She had no alternative but to cook the loaf. She went to the kitchen and set to work. Just when she stooped over the mouth of the oven to turn the loaf, Ali Mardan, seizing his opportunity, collected all his strength, pushed her in, and clamped down the lid so that she was unable to escape. He then hurried out and as directed by the holy man, set light to the house which, being made of lac, flared up instantaneously.

'You have done well,' said the Guru, who just then came up. 'Now go to your palace and rest there for two days. On the third day come to me and I will show you something.'

The Governor obeyed. In these two days his health was completely restored. He became as cheerful and strong as he had been on the day he met his fake Chinese princess.

On the third day, as appointed, Ali Mardan and the Guru went to the place where the house of lac had stood. All that was left of it was a heap of ashes.

'Look carefully in the ashes,' said the holy man, 'and you will find a pebble among them.'

Ali Mardan searched for a few minutes.

'Here it is,' he said at last.

'Good,' said the Guru, 'now which will you have, the pebble or the ashes?'

'The pebble,' answered the King.

'All right,' said the holy man. 'Then I will take the ashes.'

Whereupon he carefully wrapped the ashes in the hem of his garment and went away with his disciple.

Ali Mardan soon discovered the virtue of the pebble. It was the philosopher's stone the touch of which can change all metals into gold. But what the worth of the ashes was, remained a secret, for Ali Mardan never saw the Guru or his disciple again.

The Cat-Witch

(AFRICAN AMERICAN)

his happened in slavery times, in North Carolina. I've heard my grandmother tell it more than enough.

My grandmother was cook and house-girl for this family of slave-owners – they must have been Bissits, 'cause she was a Bissit. Well, Old Marster had sheep, and he sheared his sheep and put the wool upstairs. And Old Miss accused the cook of stealing her wool. 'Every day my wool gets smaller and smaller; somebody's taking my wool.' She knowed nobody could get up there handy but the house-girl. So they took her out and tore up her back about the wool, and Old Marster give her a terrible whipping.

When Grandma went upstairs to clean up, she'd often see a cat laying in the pile of wool. So she thought the cat laying there packed the wool, and made it look small. And she said to herself, she's going to cut off the cat's head with a butcher knife, if she catches her again. And sure enough she did. She grabbed the cat by her foot, her front foot, and hacked her foot with the knife, and cut if off. And the cat went running down the stairs, and out.

So she kilt the foot she cut off, and it turned natural, it turned to a hand. And the hand had a gold ring on the finger, with an initial in the ring. My grandmother carried the hand down to her Mistress, and showed it to her. Grandma could not read nor write, but old Miss could, and she saw the initial on the ring. So it was an outcry; they begin to talk about it, like people do in a neighborhood, and they look around to see who lost her hand. And they found it was this rich white woman, who owned slaves, and was the wife of a young man hadn't been long married. (Witches don't stay long in one place; they travel.) Next morning she wouldn't get up to cook her husband's breakfast, 'cause she didn't have but one hand. And when he heard the talk, and saw the hand with his wife's gold ring, and found her in bed without a hand, he knew she was the cat-witch. And he said he didn't want her no longer.

So it was a custom of killing old witches. They took and fastened her to an iron stake, they staked her, and poured tar around her, and set her afire, and burnt her up.

She had studied witchcraft, and she wanted that wool, and could get places, like the wind, like a hant. She would slip out after her husband was in bed, go through keyholes, if necessary be a rat – they can change – and steal things, and bring them back.

My grandma told that for the truth.

The Baba Yaga

(RUSSIAN)

nce upon a time there was an old couple. The husband lost his wife and married again. But he had a daughter by the first marriage, a young girl, and she found no favor in the eyes of her evil stepmother, who used to beat her, and consider how she could get her killed outright. One day the father went away somewhere or other, so the stepmother said to the girl, 'Go to your aunt, my sister, and ask her for a needle and thread to make you a shift.'

Now that aunt was a Baba Yaga. Well, this girl was no fool, so she went to a real aunt of hers first, and says she:

'Good morning, Auntie!'

'Good morning, my dear! What have you come for?'

'Mother has sent me to her sister, to ask for a needle and thread to make me a shift.'

Then her aunt instructed her what to do. 'There is a birch tree there, niece, which would hit you in the eye – you must tie a ribbon round it; there are doors which would creak and bang – you must pour oil on their hinges; there are dogs which would tear you in pieces – you must throw them these rolls; there is a cat which would scratch your eyes out – you must give it a piece of bacon.'

So the girl went away, and walked and walked, till she came to the place. There stood a hut, and in it sat weaving the Baba Yaga, the Bony-Shanks.

'Good morning, Auntie,' says the girl.

'Good morning, my dear,' replies the Baba Yaga.

'Mother has sent me to ask you for a needle and thread to make me a shift.'

'Very well; sit down and weave a little in the meantime.'

So the girl sat down behind the loom, and the Baba Yaga went outside, and said to her servant-maid:

'Go and heat the bath, and get my niece washed; and mind you look sharp after her, I want to breakfast off her.'

Well, the girl sat there in such a fright that she was as much dead as alive. Presently she spoke imploringly to the servant-maid, saying:

'Kinswoman dear, do please wet the firewood instead of making it burn; and fetch the water for the bath in a sieve.' And she made her a present of a handkerchief.

The Baba Yaga waited awhile; then she came to the window and asked:

'Are you weaving, niece? Are you weaving, my dear?'

'Oh yes, dear Aunt, I'm weaving.' So the Baba Yaga went away again, and the girl gave the Cat a piece of bacon, and asked:

'Is there no way of escaping from here?'

'Here's a comb for you and a towel,' said the Cat; 'take them, and be off. The Baba Yaga will pursue you, but you must lay your ear on the ground, and when you hear that she is close at hand, first of all throw down the towel. It will become a wide, wide river. And if the Baba Yaga gets across the river, and tries to catch you, then you must lay your ear on the ground again, and when you hear that she is close at hand, throw down the comb. It will become a dense, dense forest; through that she won't be able to force her way anyhow.'

The girl took the towel and the comb and fled. The dogs would have rent her, but she threw them the rolls, and they let her go by; the doors would have begun to bang, but she poured oil on their hinges, and they let her pass through; the birch tree would have poked her eyes out, but she tied the ribbon round it, and it let her pass on. And the Cat sat down to the loom, and worked away; muddled everything about, if it didn't do much weaving. Up came the Baba Yaga to the window, and asked:

'Are you weaving, niece? Are you weaving, my dear?'

'I'm weaving, dear Aunt, I'm weaving,' gruffly replied the Cat.

The Baba Yaga rushed into the hut, saw that the girl was gone, and took to beating the Cat, and abusing it for not having scratched the girl's eyes out. 'Long as I've served you,' said the Cat, 'you've never given me so much as a bone; but she gave me bacon.' Then the Baba Yaga pounced upon the dogs, on the doors, on the birch tree, and on the servant-maid, and set to work to abuse them all, and to knock

them about. Then the dogs said to her, 'Long as we've served you, you've never so much as pitched us a burnt crust; but she gave us rolls to eat.' And the doors said, 'Long as we've served you, you've never poured even a drop of water on our hinges; but she poured oil on us.' The birch tree said, 'Long as I've served you, you've never tied a single thread round me; but she fastened a ribbon around me.' And the servant-maid said, 'Long as I've served you, you've never given me so much as a rag; but she gave me a handkerchief.'

The Baba Yaga, bony of limb, quickly jumped into the mortar, sent it flying along with the pestle, sweeping away the while all traces of its flight with a broom, and set off in pursuit of the girl. Then the girl put her ear to the ground, and when she heard that the Baba Yaga was chasing her, and was now close at hand, she flung down the towel. And it became a wide, such a wide river! Up came the Baba Yaga to the river, and gnashed her teeth with spite; then she went home for her oxen, and drove them to the river. The oxen drank up every drop of the river, and then the Baba Yaga began the pursuit anew. But the girl put her ear to the ground again, and when she heard that the Baba Yaga was near, she flung down the comb, and instantly a forest sprang up, such an awfully thick one! The Baba Yaga began gnawing away at it, but however hard she worked, she couldn't gnaw her way though it, so she had to go back again.

But by this time the girl's father had returned home, and he asked: 'Where's my daughter?'

'She's gone to her aunt's,' replied her stepmother.

Soon afterwards the girl herself came running home.

'Where have you been?' asked her father.

'Ah, Father!' she said, 'Mother sent me to Aunt's to ask for a needle and thread to make me a shift. But Aunt's a Baba Yaga, and she wanted to eat me!'

'And how did you get away, daughter?'

'Why, like this,' said the girl, and explained the whole matter. As soon as her father had heard all about it, he became wroth with his wife, and shot her. But he and his daughter lived on and flourished, and everything went well with them.

MRS NUMBER THREE

(CHINESE)

During the T'ang Period there stood, to the west of the city of K'ai Fêng Fu, an inn called the 'Footbridge Tavern', kept by a woman about thirty years of age. No one knew who she was or whence she came, and she was known locally as 'Mrs Number Three'. She was childless, had no relations, and was supposed to be a widow. It was a comfortable, roomy inn; the hostess was in easy circumstances, and had a herd of very fine asses.

Besides this, she had a generous nature. If a traveller were short of money, she would reduce her prices, or board him for nothing; so her inn was never empty.

Sometime between AD 806 and 820, a man called Chao Chi Ho, on his way to Lo Yang (which was then the capital city of China), stopped at the 'Foot-Bridge Tavern' for the night. There was six or seven guests there already, each of whom had a bed in a large sleeping apartment. Chao, the last arrival, had a bed allotted to him in a corner, against the wall of the hostess's bedroom. Mrs Number Three treated him well, as she did all her guests. At bedtime she offered wine to each, and took a glass with them. Chao alone had none, as he did not generally drink wine. Quite late, when all the guests had gone to bed, the hostess retired to her room, shut the door and blew out the light.

The other guests were soon snoring peacefully, but Chao felt restless.

About midnight he heard the hostess moving things about in her room, and peeped through a crack in the wall. She lit a candle, and took out of a box an ox, a drover and a plough, little wooden models about six or seven inches high. She placed them near the hearth, on the beaten-clay floor of the room, took some water in her mouth, and sprayed it over the figures. Immediately they came to life. The drover goaded the ox, which drew the plough, back and forth, furrowing the floor over a space about equal to that of an ordinary mat. When the ploughing was done, she handed the drover a packet of buckwheat grains. He sowed them, and they at once began to sprout. In a few minutes they flowered, and then bore ripe grain. The drover gathered the grain, threshed it, and handed it to Mrs Number Three, who made him grind it in a little mill. Then she put the drover, his ox and his plough – which had again become little wooden figures – back into their box and used the buckwheat to make cakes.

At cockcrow the guests arose and prepared to leave, but the hostess said, 'You must not go without breakfast,' and set the buckwheat cakes before them.

Chao was very uneasy, so he thanked her and walked out of the inn. Looking over his shoulder, he saw each guest, the moment he tasted the cakes, drop down on all fours and begin to bray. Each had turned into a fine strong donkey; and the hostess forthwith drove them into her stable, and took possession of their belongings.

Chao did not tell a soul about his adventure; but a month later, when his business in Lo Yang was finished, he returned, and stopped

one evening at the 'Foot-Bridge Tavern'. He had with him some fresh buckwheat cakes, of the same size and shape as those made at the time of his former visit by Mrs Number Three.

The inn happened to be empty, and she made him very comfortable. Before he went to bed, she asked him if he wished to order anything.

'Not tonight,' he replied, 'but I should like something to eat first thing in the morning, before I go.'

'You shall have a good meal,' said the hostess.

During the night, the usual magic growth of buckwheat took place, and the next morning she placed before Chao a dish of buckwheat cakes. While she was away for a few minutes, Chao took one of the magic cakes off the dish, replaced it by one of his own, and waited for her to return. When she came back, she said, 'You are not eating anything.'

'I was waiting for you,' he replied. 'I have some cakes. If you will not try one of mine, I shall not eat those you have given me.'

'Give me one,' said Mrs Number Three.

Chao handed her the magic cake he had taken from the dish, and the moment she put her teeth into it she went down on all fours and began to bray. She had become a fine, strong she-ass.

Chao harnessed her, and rode home on her back, taking with him the box of wooden figures; but as he did not know the spell, he was unable to make them move, or to turn other people into asses.

Mrs Number Three was the strongest and most enduring donkey imaginable. She could travel 100 li a day on any road.

Four years later, Chao was riding her past a temple dedicated to Mount Hua, when an old man suddenly began clapping his hands and laughing, crying out, 'Now, Mrs Number Three of the Foot-Bridge, what's happened to you, eh?' Then, seizing the bridle, he said to Chao, 'She has tried to do you a wrong, I grant, but she has performed sufficient penance for her sins. Let me now set her free!' Then he took the halter off her head, and immediately she shed the ass's skin and stood upright in human form. She saluted the old man and vanished. No one has ever heard of her since.

PART SIX

UNHAPPY FAMILIES

THE GIRL WHO
BANISHED SEVEN YOUTHS

(MOROCCAN)

here was a woman who had seven sons. Whenever she felt her labor pains begin, she said, 'This time I shall bear a daughter.' But it always was a boy.

Say that she carried again and her month came round. Her husband's sister came to help as her time drew near. Her seven sons went out to hunt, but before they left they told their aunt: 'If our mother gives birth to a girl, hang the spindle over the door. When we see it, we shall spin around and come home. If she gives birth to another boy, hang up the sickle. When we see it, we shall cut loose and go.' The woman hated her nephews, so although the child was indeed a girl, she hung the sickle over the door. When they saw it, the seven went off into the desert.

The child was given the name Wudei'a Who Sent Away Subei'a, or The Girl Who Banished Seven. She grew and began to play with the other girls. One day she quarreled with her friends, and they said to her, 'If there was any good in you would your seven brothers have left for the desert on the day you were born?'

Wudei'a ran home to her mother. 'Is it true that I have seven brothers?' she asked. 'Seven brothers you have,' her mother said, 'but on the day you were born, they went out hunting and – O sadness and affliction – we have heard nothing of them since.' 'Then I shall go out and find them,' said the girl. 'How can you do so, when we have not seen them these fifteen years?' asked her mother. 'I'll search the world from its beginning to its end until I find them,' said Wudei'a.

So her mother gave her a camel to ride and sent with her a manservant and a maid. A while after they had set out, the manservant said, 'Get off the camel and let the maid ride.' 'Ya Ummi, O my mother,' called Wudei'a. And her mother replied, 'Why do you call?' 'The servant wants me to get off the camel,' said Wudei'a. Her mother told the servant to let Wudei'a ride, and they traveled on a little further. Again the servant tried to make Wudei'a dismount. and again she called 'Ya Ummi!' for her mother to help. The third time, however, her mother did not reply to her call, for they were too far away to be heard. So now the servant forced her off the camel and let the maid ride. Wudei'a walked on the ground with the blood pouring from her bare feet, for she was not used to walking so far.

Three days they traveled in this way, the maidservant riding high on the camel's back while Wudei'a walked below, weeping and tying cloths around her feet. On the third day they met a merchant's caravan. The servant said, 'O lords of this caravan, have you seen seven men hunting in the wilderness?' 'You will reach them before noon; their castle is on the road,' they answered.

Now the manservant heated pitch in the sun, and with it he rubbed the girl Wudei'a until all her skin was dark. Leading the camel to the castle gate, he called out, 'Good news, masters! I have brought your sister to you.' The seven brothers ran to greet their father's servant, but they said, 'We have no sister; our mother gave birth to a son!' The servant made the camel kneel and pointed to the maid. 'Your mother gave birth to a girl, and here she has come.' The brothers had never seen their sister; how could they know? They believed their father's servant when he told them that the maid was their sister and that Wudei'a was their sister's slave girl.

Next day the brothers said, 'Today we shall sit with our sister; we shall not go to hunt.' The oldest brother said to the black slave girl, 'Come and look through my hair for lice.' So Wudei'a laid her brother's head on her knee and wept as she combed his hair. A tear fell on to her arm. Her brother rubbed the spot, and the white flesh beneath the pitch appeared. 'Tell me your story,' said her eldest brother. Sobbing and talking Wudei'a told her tale. Her brother took his sword in his hand, went into the castle and cut off the heads of the servant and the maid. He heated water and brought out soap and Wudei'a washed herself until her skin was white again. Her brothers said, 'Now she looks like our true sister.' And they kissed her and stayed with her that day and the next. But on the third day they said, 'Sister, lock the castle gate, for we are going hunting and will not come back till seven days have passed. Lock the cat in with you and take care of her. Do not eat anything without giving a share to her.'

Seven days Wudei'a waited in the castle with the cat. On the eighth her brothers returned with game. They asked, 'Were you afraid?' 'What should I fear?' said Wudei'a. 'My room has seven doors, six of wood and the seventh made of iron.' After a time the brothers went away to hunt again. 'No one dares to approach our castle,' they told her. 'Be careful only of the cat; whatever you eat, give her half of it. And should anything happen, she knows our hunting grounds – she and the dove on the windowsill.'

Cleaning the rooms while she waited for her brothers to return, Wudei'a found a broad bean on the ground and picked it up. 'What are you eating?' asked the cat. 'Nothing. I found a broad bean among the sweepings,' said Wudei'a. 'Why didn't you give me half?' asked the cat. 'I forgot,' said Wudei'a. 'Watch and see how I'll repay you,' said the cat. 'All for half a bean?' asked Wudei'a. But the cat ran to the kitchen, pissed on the fire, and put it out.

There was no fire now to cook the food. Wudei'a stood on the castle wall, looking till she saw a light far off. She set out in that direction, and when she reached the place she found a Ghoul sitting at his fire. His hair was so long that one whisker was a pallet beneath him and the other a blanket above. 'Greetings, father Ghoul,' said Wudei'a. And the Ghoul replied.

> By Allah, had not your greeting
> Come first before your speaking.
> By now the hills around would hear
> Your young bones crack and your flesh tear!

'I need a fire,' said Wudei'a. The Ghoul answered,

> If you want a large ember, you must give a strip of skin
> From your tallest finger to just below your chin.
> Or if the ember you want is a small one.
> From your ear down to your thumb.

Wudei'a took the large ember and began to walk back, the blood flowing from her wound. A raven followed behind her throwing earth on each bloodstain to bury it. When she reached her gate, the bird flew up to the top of the wall. Wudei'a was startled and she scolded. 'May God give you cause to feel fear as you have frightened me.' 'Is this how kindness is rewarded?' said the raven. Down from the wall he dropped and ran along the ground, baring the blood he had covered all the way from her doorstep to the Ghoul's camp.

In the middle of the night the Ghoul woke up and followed the trail of blood until he came to the brothers' castle. He charged through the gate but he found the girl's room shut with seven doors – six made of wooden panels and the seventh a door of iron. He said,

> Wudei'a Who Sent Away Subei'a,
> What was your old father doing when you came?

She answered,

> Lying on a gold bed frame,
> Of fine silk his counterpane
> And his mattress of the same.

The Ghoul laughed and smashed down one of the wooden doors. Then he went away. But the next night and the next, the same thing happened until he had broken all six doors of wood. Only the seventh door was left, the door of iron.

Now Wudei'a was afraid. She wrote a message on a piece of paper and tied the paper around the neck of her brothers' dove with a thread. 'O dove, whom my brothers love,' she said, 'carry my words to them through the air above.' The tame bird flew off and did not alight until it sat in the lap of the oldest of the brothers. He read from his sister's paper.

> Six doors are broken down; only the seventh remains.
> Come quickly if you want to see your sister again.

The seven youths jumped into their saddles, and before the middle of the afternoon they had returned home. The castle gate was broken, the six wooden doors of their sister's room were splintered. Through the seventh door of iron they shouted, 'Sister, sister, we are your brothers; unlock your door and tell us how it happened.'

When she had repeated her tale, they said, 'May Allah grant you wisdom, did we not tell you never to eat without giving the cat its share? How could you forget?' Then they prepared themselves for the visit of the Ghoul. They dug a deep pit and filled it with firewood. They lit a fire and fed it until the pit was heaped with glowing coals. Then they laid a mat carefully to cover the opening of their trap and waited.

The Ghoul arrived and said,

> *Wudei'a Who Sent Away Subei'a,*
> *What was your old father doing when you came?*

She answered through her door,

> *He was flaying mules and donkeys,*
> *Drinking blood and sucking entrails.*
> *Matted hair so wild and long*
> *It was his bed to lie upon.*
> *O pray he may fall into the fire*
> *To toast and burn till he expire.*

The Ghoul boiled with rage. With a roar he broke down the seventh door and burst in. Wudei'a's brothers met him and said, 'Come neighbor, sit with us a while.' But when the Ghoul folded his legs to squat on the straw mat, he tumbled into the pit of embers. The brothers threw wood on top of him heaping more and more until he was all burned up, even his bones. Nothing remained of him except the nail of his little finger, which had jumped into the middle of the room. It lay on the floor until later, when Wudei'a bent down to wipe the tiles with a cloth. Then it pricked her finger and slipped under the skin of her hand. That same moment the girl fell to the ground without life or movement.

Her brothers found her lying dead. They wept and wailed and made her a bier and tied it on to their father's camel's back and said,

> *Carry her, O camel of our father,*
> *Carry her back to her mother.*
> *Stop not to rest on the way thither*
> *Stop not for man, or woman either.*
> *Kneel only for him who says 'Shoo!'*

The camel lifted itself up to do as they bid. Neither halting nor running, it walked along the road it had traveled before. When half the distance had been crossed, three men spied what looked like a riderless camel lost in the wild. 'Let us catch it for ourselves!' they said, and shouted to make it stop. But the camel continued on.

Suddenly one of the men called to his friends. 'Wait while I tie on my shoe!' As soon as the camel heard the word 'shoe' it began to lower itself on to its knees. Joyfully the men ran to seize its halter. But what did they find? A wooden bier and lying on it a lifeless girl! 'Her people are wealthy,' said one, 'look at the ring on her finger!' And swiftly as the thought entered his head he began to pull off the shining jewel for himself. But in moving the ring the robber dislodged the nail from the Ghoul's little finger which had pierced Wudei'a's skin as she swept. The girl sat up alive and breathing. 'Long life to him who brought me back from death,' she said. Then she turned the camel's head towards her brothers' castle.

Weeping and falling upon Wudei'a's neck, the youths welcomed their lost sister back. 'Let us go and kiss the hands of our father and mother before they die,' said the eldest. 'You have been a father to us,' said the others, 'and your word like a father's.' Mounting their horses, all seven, with their sister on her camel making the eighth, set out for home.

'O sons, what made you leave the world I live in?' said their father when he had kissed and welcomed them. 'What made you leave me and your mother weeping night and day in grief over you?' On the first day and the second and the third, the youths rested and said nothing. But on the fourth when they had eaten, the oldest brother told the story from the time when their aunt had so falsely sent them into the wilderness until they had all found each other again. And from that day, they all lived together and were happy.

So ends the story of Wudei'a Who Sent Away Subei'a.

THE MARKET OF THE DEAD

(WEST AFRICAN: DAHOMEY)

here were two co-wives. The first wife gave birth to twins, but herself died in childbirth. So the second wife took care of them. The elder twin was called Hwese, the other Hwevi. When the stepmother pounded grain, she took away the fine flour on top, and gave them what was not fit to eat.

One day the stepmother gave them each a small gourd, and told them to go for water. They went to the stream, but on the way back Hwese slipped and broke his gourd. The other said, 'If we go home now, she will beat Hwese, and let me go free. So I'll break mine, too.' He threw it down and broke it.

When the stepmother saw what had happened, she got a whip and whipped them.

Hwevi said, 'I am going to buy a bead.' Hwese said, 'Yes, let us each buy a bead for Ku. We will go there and visit the one who watches Death's door. Perhaps he will let us see our mother.'

> *The grave is deep,*
> *Deep, deep,*
> *Stepmother bought some gourds,*
> *But Hwese broke his gourd,*
> *And Hwevi broke his, too.*
> *When we told our stepmother,*
> *She flogged us with a whip,*
> *So Hwese bought a bead*
> *And Hwevi bought one, too.*

Good. So they went to see the guardian of Death's door. He asked them, 'What do you want?'

Hwevsi said, 'Yesterday, when we went to get water, my brother Hwese broke his gourd. So I broke mine, too. Our stepmother beat us, and did not give us anything to eat all day. So we have come to beg you to let us enter here. We want to see our mother.'

When the guardian heard this, he opened the door.

> *The grave is deep,*
> *Deep, deep.*
> *Stepmother bought some gourds,*
> *But Hwese broke his gourd,*
> *And Hwevi broke his, too.*
> *When we told our stepmother,*
> *She flogged us with a whip,*
> *So Hwese bought a bead,*
> *And Hwevi bought one, too.*
> *We gave these to the door's guardian*
> *And the door opened.*

Inside there were two markets, the market of the living, and the market of the dead.

Good. Everybody asked them, 'Where do you come from, where do you come from?' The living asked this, and the dead asked it, too. The children said, 'This is what happened. Yesterday we broke the little gourds our stepmother gave us. She beat us and gave us nothing to eat. We begged the man who watches at the door to let us come in to see our mother, so she might buy two other gourds for us.'

Good. Then their mother came and bought some *acasa* in the market of the living for them. Then she turned her back, and gave money to a living man to buy two gourds in the market of the living for them, and gave these to her children. Then she herself went to the market of the dead, and bought palm nuts to send to her husband's other wife. For she knew that the other liked these nuts very much. Now, once the woman ate the palm nuts, she would surely die.

Good. Then the mother said to the children, 'All right. Go home now, and tell your stepmother good-day. Thank her for looking after you so well.'

> *The grave is deep,*
> *Deep, deep.*

Stepmother bought some gourds,
But Hwese broke his gourd,
And Hwevi broke his, too.
When we told our stepmother,
She flogged us with a whip,
So Hwese bought a bead,
And Hwevi bought one, too.
We gave these to the door's guardian
And the door opened.
Our mother, hearing our story,
Bought us two gourds,
For our stepmother.

The stepmother looked for the two boys. She looked for them everywhere, but she could not find out where they had gone. When they came back, she asked them, 'Where were you?'

They said, 'We went to see our mother.'

But their stepmother scolded them. She said, 'No, you lie. Nobody can visit the dead.'

Good. The children gave her the palm nuts. They said, 'Here, our mother sent these to you.'

The other woman laughed at them. 'So you found a dead one to send me palm nuts?'

But when the stepmother ate these palm nuts, she died.

The grave is deep,
Deep, deep.
Stepmother bought some gourds,
But Hwese broke his gourd,
And Hwevi broke his, too.
When we told our stepmother,
She flogged us with a whip,
So Hwese bought a bead,
And Hwevi bought one, too.
We gave these to the door's guardian
And the door opened.
Our mother, hearing our story,
Bought us two gourds,
For our stepmother.

At home our stepmother wanted to buy life,
But we gave her the fruit
In abundance, abundance.

In Dahomey, when a person dies, the family goes to a diviner and he makes the dead talk so that you hear his voice. So when they called the dead stepmother she said, 'Tell all the other women that my death came from the orphans. Tell them also that Mawu says that when there are several wives, and one dies and leaves children, the others must care for the children of the dead woman.'

This is why, if a man has two wives, and one dies leaving a child, you give that child to the second wife, and the second wife must look after the dead woman's child better than after her own children. And this is why one never mistreats orphans. For once you mistreat them, you die. You die the same day. You are not even sick. I know that myself. I am an orphan. My father never lets me go out alone at night. Whenever I ask him for something, he gives it to me.

The Woman Who
Married Her Son's Wife

(INNUIT)

nce there lived an old woman who desired her son's pretty young wife. This son was a hunter who often would be gone for many days at a time. Once, while he was gone, the old woman sat down and made herself a penis out of seal-bone and skins. She fastened this penis to her waist and showed it to her daughter-in-law, who exclaimed: 'How nice . . .' Then they slept together. Soon the old woman was going out to hunt in a big skin kayak, just like her son. And when she came back, she would take off her clothes and move her breasts up and down, saying: 'Sleep with me, my dear little wife. Sleep with me . . .'

It happened that the son returned from his hunting and saw his mother's seals lying in front of the house. 'Whose seals are these?' he asked of his wife.

'None of your business,' she replied.

Being suspicious of her, he dug a hole behind their house and hid there. He figured that some hunter was claiming his wife in his absence. Soon, however, he saw his mother paddling home in her kayak with a big hooded seal. Mother and son never caught anything but big hooded seals. The old woman reached land and took off her clothes, then moved her breasts up and down, saying: 'My sweet little wife, kindly delouse me . . .'

The son was not pleased by his mother's behaviour. He came out of hiding and struck the old woman so hard that he killed her. 'Now,' he said to his wife, 'you must come away with me because our home place has a curse on it.'

The wife began to quiver and shake all over. 'You've killed my dear husband,' she cried. And would not stop crying.

The Little Red Fish and
the Clog of Gold

(IRAQI)

either here nor there lived a man, a fisherman. His wife had drowned in the great river and left him a pretty little girl not more than two years old. In a house nearby lived a widow and her daughter. The woman began to come to the fisherman's house to care for the girl and comb her hair, and every time she said to the child, 'Am I not like a mother to you?' She tried to please the fisherman, but he always said, 'I shall never marry. Stepmothers hate their husband's children even though their rivals are dead and buried.' When his daughter grew old enough to pity him when she saw him washing his own clothes, she began to say, 'Why don't you marry our neighbor, Father? There is no evil in her, and she loves me as much as her own daughter.'

They say water will wear away stone. In the end the fisherman married the widow, and she came to live in his house. The wedding week was not yet over when sure enough, she began to feel jealous of her husband's daughter. She saw how much her father loved the child and indulged her. And she could not help but see that the child was fair, and quick, while her own daughter was thin and sallow, and so clumsy she did not know how to sew the seam of her gown.

No sooner did the woman feel that she was mistress of the house then she began to leave all the work for the girl to do. She would not give her stepchild soap to wash her hair and feet, and she fed her nothing but crusts and crumbs. All this the girl bore patiently, saying not a word. For she did not wish to grieve her father, and she thought, 'I picked up the scorpion with my own hand; I'll save myself with my own mind.'

Besides her other errands, the fisherman's daughter had to go down to the river each day to bring home her father's catch, the fish they ate and sold. One day from beneath a basket load of three catfish, suddenly one little red fish spoke to her:

> *Child with such patience to endure,*
> *I beg you now, my life secure.*
> *Throw me back into the water,*
> *And now and always be my daughter.*

The girl stopped to listen, half in wonder and half in fear. Then retracing her steps, she flung the fish into the river and said, 'Go! People say, "Do a good deed for, even if it is like throwing gold into the sea, in God's sight it is not lost."' And lifting itself on the face of the water, the little fish replied:

> *Your kindness is not in vain –*
> *A new mother do you gain.*
> *Come to me when you are sad,*
> *And I shall help to make you glad.*

The girl went back to the house and gave the three catfish to her stepmother. When the fisherman returned and asked about the fourth, she told him, 'Father, the red fish dropped from my basket. It may have fallen into the river, for I couldn't find it again.' 'Never mind,' he said, 'it was a very small fish.' But her stepmother began to scold, 'You never told me there were four fishes. You never said that you lost one. Go now and look for it, before I curse you!'

It was past sunset and the girl had to walk back to the river in the dark. Her eyes swollen with tears, she stood on the water's edge and called out,

> *Red fish, my mother and nurse,*
> *Come quickly, and ward off a curse.*

And there at her feet appeared the little red fish to comfort her and say, 'Though patience is bitter, its fruit is very sweet. Now bend down and take this gold piece from my mouth. Give it to your stepmother, and she will say nothing to you.' Which is exactly what happened.

The years came and the years went, and in the fisherman's house life continued as before. Nothing changed except that the two little girls were now young women.

One day a great man, the master of the merchants' guild, announced that his daughter was to be married. It was the custom for the women to gather at the bride's house on the 'day of the bride's henna' to celebrate and sing as they watched the girls' feet, palms, and arms being decorated for the wedding with red henna stain. Then every mother brought her unwed daughters to be seen by the mothers of sons. Many a girl's destiny was decided on such a day.

The fisherman's wife rubbed and scrubbed her daughter and dressed her in her finest gown and hurried her off to the master merchant's house with the rest. The fisherman's daughter was left at home to fill the water jar and sweep the floor while they were gone.

But as soon as the two women were out of sight, the fisherman's daughter gathered up her gown and ran down to the river to tell the little red fish her sorrow. 'You shall go to the bride's henna and sit on the cushions in the center of the hall,' said the little red fish. She gave the girl a small bundle and said, 'Here is everything you need to wear, with a comb of pearl for your hair and clogs of gold for your feet. But one thing you must remember: be sure to leave before your stepmother rises to go.'

When the girl loosened the cloth that was knotted round the clothes, out fell a gown of silk as green as clover. It was stitched with threads and sequins of gold, and from its folds rose a sweet smell like the essence of roses. Quickly she washed herself and decked herself and tucked the comb of pearl behind her braid and slipped the golden clogs on to her feet and went tripping off to the feast.

The women from every house in the town were there. They paused in their talk to admire her face and her grace, and they thought, 'This must be the governor's daughter!' They brought her sherbet and cakes made with almonds and honey and they sat her in the place of honor in the middle of them all. She looked for her stepmother with her daughter and saw them far off, near the door where the peasants were sitting, and the wives of weavers of peddlers.

Her stepmother stared at her and said to herself, 'O Allah Whom we praise, how much this lady resembles my husband's daughter! But then, don't they say, "Every seven men were made from one clod of clay"?' And the stepmother never knew that it was her very own husband's daughter and none other!

Not to spin out our tale, before the rest of the women stood up, the fisherman's daughter went to the mother of the bride to say, 'May it be with God's blessings and bounty, O my aunt!' and hurried out. The sun had set and darkness was falling. On her way the girl had to cross a bridge over the stream that flowed into the king's garden. And by fate and divine decree, it happened that as she ran over the bridge one of her golden clogs fell off her foot and into the river below. It was too far to climb down to the water and search in the dusk; what if her stepmother should return home before her? So the girl took off her other shoe, and pulling her cloak around her head, dashed on her way.

When she reached the house she shucked her fine clothes, rolled the pearly comb and golden clog inside them, and hid them under the woodpile. She rubbed her head and hands and feet with earth to make them dirty, and she was standing with her broom when her step-mother found her. The wife looked into her face and examined her hands and feet and said, 'Still sweeping after sunset? Or are you hoping to sweep our lives away?'

What of the golden clog? Well, the current carried it into the king's garden and rolled it and rolled it until it came to rest in the pool where the king's son led his stallion to drink. Next day the prince was water-ing the horse. He saw that every time it lowered its head to drink, something made it shy and step back. What could there be at the bottom of the pool to frighten his stallion? He called to the groom, and from the mud the man brought him the shining clog of gold.

When the prince held the beautiful little thing in his hand he began to imagine the beautiful little foot that had worn it. He walked back to the palace with his heart busy and his mind full of the girl who owned so precious a shoe. The queen saw him lost in thought and said, 'May Allah send us good news; why so careworn, my son?' 'Yammah, Mother, I want you to find me a wife!' said the prince. 'So much thought over one wife and no more?' said the queen. 'I'll find you a thousand if you wish! I'll bring every girl in the kingdom to be your wife if you want! But tell me, my son, who is the girl who has stolen your reason?' 'I want to marry the girl who owns this clog,' replied the prince, and he told his mother how he had found it. 'You shall have her, my son,' said the queen. 'I shall begin my search tomorrow as soon as it is light, and I shall not stop till I find her.'

The very next day the prince's mother went to work, in at one house and out at the next with the golden clog tucked under her arm.

Wherever she saw a young woman, she measured the shoe against the sole of the maiden's foot. Meanwhile the prince sat in the palace gate waiting for her return 'What news, Mother?' he asked. And she said, 'Nothing yet, my son. Be patient, child, put snow on your breast and cool your passion. I'll find her yet.'

And so the search continued. Entering at one gate and leaving at the next, the queen visited the houses of the nobles and the merchants and the goldsmiths. She saw the daughters of the craftsmen and the tradesmen. She went into the huts of the water carriers and the weavers, and stopped at each house until only the fishermen's hovels in the bank of the river were left. Every evening when the prince asked for news, she said, 'I'll find her, I'll find her.'

When the fisherfolk were told that the queen was coming to visit their houses, that wily fisherman's wife got busy. She bathed her daughter and dressed her in her best, she rinsed her hair with henna and rimmed her eyes with *kohl* and rubbed her cheeks till they glowed red. But still when the girl stood beside the fisherman's daughter, it was like a candle in the sun. Much as the stepchild had been ill-treated and starved, through the will of Allah and with the help of the little red fish, she had grown in beauty from day to day. Now her stepmother dragged her out of the house and into the yard. She pushed her into the bakehouse and covered its mouth with the round clay tray on which she spread her dough. This she held down with the stone of her handmill. 'Don't dare move until I come for you!' said the stepmother. What could the poor girl do but crouch in the ashes and trust in Allah to save her?

When the queen arrived the stepmother pushed her daughter forward, saying, 'Kiss the hands of the prince's mother ignorant child!' As she had done in the other houses, the queen set the girl beside her and held up her foot and measured the golden clog against it. Just at that moment the neighbor's rooster flew into the yard and began to crow,

> *Ki-ki-ki-kow!*
> *Let the king's wife know*
> *They put the ugly one on show*
> *And hid the beauty down below!*
> *Ki-ki-ki-kow!*

He began again with his piercing cry, and the stepmother raced out and flapped her arms to chase him away. But the queen had heard the words, and she sent her servants to search both high and low. When they pushed aside the cover off the mouth of the oven, they found the girl – fair as the moon in the midst of the ashes. They brought her to the queen, and the golden clog fit as if it had been the mold from which her foot was cast.

The queen was satisfied. She said, 'From this hour that daughter of yours is betrothed to my son. Make ready for the wedding. God willing, the procession shall come for her on Friday.' And she gave the stepmother a purse filled with gold.

When the woman realized that her plans had failed, that her husband's daughter was to marry the prince while her own remained in the house, she was filled with anger and rage. 'I'll see that he sends her back before the night is out,' she said.

She took the purse of gold, ran to the perfumer's bazaar and asked for a purge so strong that it would shred the bowels to tatters. At the sight of the gold the perfumer began to mix the powders in his tray. Then she asked for arsenic and lime, which weaken hair and make it fall, and an ointment that smelled like carrion.

Now the stepmother prepared the bride for her wedding. She washed her hair with henna mixed with arsenic and lime and spread the foul ointment over her hair. Then she held the girl by the ear and poured the purge down her throat. Soon the wedding procession arrived, with horses and drums fluttering bright clothes, and the sounds of jollity. They lifted the bride on to the litter and took her away. She came to the palace preceded by music and followed by singing and chanting and clapping of hands. She entered the chamber, the prince lifted the veil off her face and she shone like a fourteen-day moon. A scent of amber and roses made the prince press his face to her hair. He ran his fingers over her locks, and it was like a man playing with cloth of gold. Now the bride began to feel a heaviness in her belly, but from under the hem of her gown there fell gold pieces in thousands till the carpet and the cushions were covered with gold.

Meanwhile the stepmother waited in her doorway, saying 'Now they'll bring her back in disgrace. Now she'll come home all filthy and bald.' But though she stood in the doorway till dawn, from the palace no one came.

The news of the prince's fair wife began to fill the town, and the

master merchant's son said to his mother, 'They say that the prince's bride has a sister, I want her for my bride.' Going to the fisherman's hut, his mother gave the fisherman's wife a purse full of gold and said, 'Prepare the bride, for we shall come for her on Friday if God wills.' And the fisherman's wife said to herself, 'If what I did for my husband's daughter turned her hair to threads of gold and her belly to a fountain of coins, shall I not do the same for my own child?' She hastened to the perfumer and asked for the same powders and drugs, but stronger than before. Then she prepared her child, and the wedding procession came. When the merchant's son lifted her veil, it was like lifting the cover off a grave. The stink was so strong that it choked him, and her hair came away in his hands. So they wrapped the poor bride in her own filth and carried her back to her mother.

As for the prince, he lived with the fisherman's daughter in great happiness and joy, and God blessed them with seven children like seven golden birds.

Mulberry, mulberry,
So ends my story.
If my house were not so far
I'd bring you figs and raisins in a jar.

THE WICKED STEPMOTHER

(WEST AFRICAN: TOGOLAND)

here was once a certain man who had two wives. The first one bore him a boy-child and the other had no children. Now it came to pass that the mother of the boy became sick, and when she knew that death was near she sent for the second wife and placed in her charge her son, saying: 'I am going away now and must leave my boy. Take him and care for him and feed him as if he were your own. The second wife agreed, and shortly after the woman died.

But the surviving wife forgot her promise and ill-treated the motherless boy. She gave him neither food nor clothing, and the wretched child had to seek what he could find for himself.

One day the woman called the child to her and said that he was to accompany her into the bush to get firewood. The boy obeyed and went with the woman. When they were a long way from the village the woman went into the bush for the sticks and the boy sat down in the shade of a big tree. Presently he noticed a lot of fruit had fallen from the tree and he began to eat it. He was very hungry and only when all the fallen fruit had been eaten was his hunger satisfied. He then fell asleep, and after a while when he awoke he found he was again hungry. But there was no fruit on the ground and he was far too small to reach up to the branches to gather some. So he began to sing, and as he sang a song in praise of the tree, lo! the branches of the tree bent down to him and enabled him to climb up. He then took all the food he could eat and collected some to take home in the rag which did service for a cloth. Then, still singing, he climbed down and waited for the woman. She soon came and they both went home.

Some days later the boy was seated outside the house eating the fruit he had gathered when the woman saw him and asked him what

he had there. He told her, and the woman took some and said that it was good. She then told the boy to go with her to the tree so that they could get some more of this new and excellent fruit.

They went, and when they drew near the tree the boy began to sing again, and the tree obediently bent down its branches, and the woman climbed up. Then the boy ceased his song and the branches sprang up, taking with them the woman. The woman called to the boy, but he answered that Nyame had now given him sense and had shown him how to procure food, and that as she had neglected him so he would now neglect her. He then went home to the village.

Now when he arrived all the people asked him where was the woman, and he replied that she had gone to the bush to get firewood. Evening came and still no woman. So the people assembled under the village tree and again asked the boy, but he replied as before.

On the following morning they again collected, and began to beg the boy to show them where he had left his stepmother. When they had begged him for a long time he at last consented and led them into the bush, where the people saw the woman at the top of the tree. They asked her how she had managed to get there and she told them. Then they all begged the boy to sing. For a long time he refused, but at last as they begged him so long he agreed and began to sing his praise of the tree. Immediately the branches bent down and the woman was freed.

Then everyone went back to the village and reported to the chief what they had seen. He at once called all the elders and sent for the woman. He told her that had the boy not consented to sing she would not have been rescued, and he ordered her to give an account of how she had treated the motherless child. She confessed she had done wrong, and then the chief said: 'Now let all men know from this that when a man has many wives the children shall be treated as the children of them all. To each woman her husband's son shall be a son, and each child shall call each of his father's wives mother.'

TUGLIK AND HER GRANDDAUGHTER

(INNUIT)

O nce there was a big narwhal hunt to which everyone went but an old woman named Tuglik and her granddaughter Qujapik. The two of them were getting rather hungry, but they hadn't any idea of how to hunt for their food. Yet old Tuglik knew a few magical words, which she uttered during a trance. All of a sudden she changed into a man. She had a seal-bone for a penis and chunk of *mataq* for testicles. Her vagina became a sledge. She said to her granddaughter:

'Now I can travel to the fjords and get some food for us.'

The girl replied: 'But what about dogs to pull your sledge?'

And so strong was the old woman's magic that she was able to create a team of dogs from her own lice. The dogs were barking and

yelping and ready to go, so Tuglik cracked her whip and off she went with them to the fjords. Day after day she went off like this, and she would always return in the evening with some sort of game, even if it was only a ptarmigan or two. Once, while she was away hunting, a man came to their hut. He looked around and said:

'Whose harpoon is this, little girl?'

'Oh,' said Qujapik, 'it is only my grandmother's.'

'And whose kayak is this?'

'Just my grandmother's.'

'You seem to be pregnant. Who is your husband?'

'My grandmother is my husband.'

'Well, I know someone who would make a better husband for you . . .'

Now the old woman returned home with a walrus thrown over her sledge. 'Qujapik!' she called out, 'Qujapik!' But there was no Qujapik at all. The girl had gathered up all her things and left the village with her new husband.

Tuglik saw no point in being a man any more – man or woman, it's all the same when a person is alone. So she uttered her magic words and once again she was a wrinkled old hag with a vagina instead of a sledge.

THE JUNIPER TREE

(GERMAN)

ll this took place a long time ago, most likely some two thousand years ago. There was a rich man who had a beautiful and pious wife, and they loved each other very much. Though they did not have any children, they longed to have some. Day and night the wife prayed for a child, but still none came, and everything remained the same.

Now, in the front of the house there was yard, and in the yard stood a juniper tree. One day during winter the wife was under the tree peeling an apple, and as she was peeling it, she cut her finger, and her blood dripped on the snow.

'Oh,' said the wife, and she heaved a great sigh. While she looked at the blood before her, she became quite sad, 'If only I had a child as red as blood and as white as snow!' Upon saying that, her mood changed, and she became very cheerful, for she felt something might come of it. Then she went home.

After a month the snow vanished. After two months everything turned green. After three months the flowers sprouted from the ground. After four months all the trees in the woods grew more solid, and the green branches became intertwined. The birds began to sing, and their song resounded throughout the forest as the blossoms fell from the trees. Soon the fifth month passed, and when the wife stood under the juniper tree, it smelled so sweetly that her heart leapt for joy. Indeed, she was so overcome by joy that she fell down on her knees. When the sixth month had passed, the fruit was large and firm and she was quite still. In the seventh month she picked the juniper berries and ate them so avidly that she became sad and sick. After the eighth month passed, she called her husband to her and wept.

'If I die,' she said, 'bury me under the juniper tree.'

After that she was quite content and relieved until the ninth month had passed. Then she had a child as white as snow and as red as blood. When she saw the baby, she was so delighted that she died.

Her husband buried her under the juniper tree, and he began weeping a great deal. After some time he felt much better, but he still wept every now and then. Eventually, he stopped, and after more time passed, he took another wife. With his second wife he had a daughter, while the child from the first wife was a little boy, who was as red as blood and as white as snow. Whenever the woman looked at her daughter she felt great love for her, but whenever she looked at the little boy, her heart was cut to the quick. She could not forget that he would always stand in her way and prevent her daughter from inheriting everything, which was what the woman had in mind. Thus the devil took hold of her and influenced her feelings toward the boy until she became quite cruel toward him: she pushed him from one place to the next, slapped him here and cuffed him there, so that the poor child lived in constant fear. When he came home from school, he found no peace at all.

One time the woman went up to her room, and her little daughter followed her and said, 'Mother, give me an apple.'

'Yes, my child,' said the woman, and she gave her a beautiful apple from the chest that had a large heavy lid with a big sharp iron lock.

'Mother,' said the little daughter,' shouldn't brother get one too?'

The woman was irritated by that remark, but she said, 'Yes, as soon as he comes home from school.' And, when she looked out of the window and saw he was coming, the devil seemed to take possession of her, and she snatched the apple away from her daughter.

'You shan't have one before your brother,' she said and threw the apple into the chest and shut it.

The little boy came through the door, and the devil compelled her to be friendly to him and say, 'Would you like to have an apple, my son?' Yet, she gave him a fierce look.

'Mother,' said the little boy, 'how ferocious you look! Yes, give me an apple.'

Then she felt compelled to coax him.

'Come over here,' she said as she lifted the lid, 'Take out an apple for yourself.'

And as the little boy leaned over the chest, the devil prompted her, and *crash!* she slammed the lid so hard that his head flew off and fell among the apples. Then she was struck by fear and thought, How am I going to get out of this? She went up to her room and straight to her dresser, where she took out a white kerchief from a drawer. She put the boy's head back on to his neck and tied the neckerchief around it so nothing could be seen. Then she set him on a chair in front of the door and put the apple in his hand.

Some time later little Marlene came into the kitchen and went up to her mother, who was standing by the fire in front of a pot of hot water, which she was constantly stirring.

'Mother,' said Marlene, 'brother's sitting by the door and looks very pale. He's got an apple in his hand, and I asked him to give me the apple, but he didn't answer, and I became very scared.'

'Go back to him,' said the mother, 'and if he doesn't answer you, give him a box on the ear.'

Little Marlene returned to him and said, 'Brother, give me the apple.'

But he would not respond. So she gave him a box on the ear, and his head fell off. The little girl was so frightened that she began to cry and howl. Then she ran to her mother and said, 'Oh, Mother, I've knocked my brother's head off!' And she wept and wept and could not be comforted.

'Marlene,' said the mother, 'what have you done! You're not to open your mouth about this. We don't want anyone to know, and besides there's nothing we can do about it now. So we'll make a stew out of him.'

The mother took the little boy and chopped him into pieces. Next she put them into a pot and let them stew. But Marlene stood nearby and wept until all her tears fell into the pot, so it did not need any salt.

When the father came home, he sat down at the table and asked, 'Where's my son?'

The mother served a huge portion of the stewed meat, and Marlene wept and could not stop.

'Where's my son?' the father asked again.

'Oh,' said the mother, 'he's gone off into the country to visit his mother's great uncle. He intends to stay there for a while.'

'What's he going to do there? He didn't even say goodbye to me.'

'Well, he wanted to go very badly and asked me if he could stay there six weeks. They'll take good care of him.'

'Oh, that makes me sad,' said the man. 'It's not right. He should have said goodbye to me.' Then he began to eat and said, 'Marlene, what are you crying for? Your brother will come back soon.' Without pausing he said, 'Oh, wife, the food tastes great! Give me some more!' The more he ate, the more he wanted. 'Give me some more,' he said, 'I'm not going to share this with you. Somehow I feel as if it were all mine.'

As he ate and ate he threw the bones under the table until he was all done. Meanwhile, Marlene went to her dresser and took out her best silk neckerchief from the bottom drawer, gathered all the bones from beneath the table, tied them up in her silk kerchief, and carried them outside the door. There she wept bitter tears and laid the bones beneath the juniper tree. As she put them there, she suddenly felt relieved and stopped crying. Now the juniper tree began to move. The branches separated and came together again as though they were clapping their hands in joy. At the same time smoke came out of the tree, and in the middle of the smoke there was a flame that seemed to be burning. Then a beautiful bird flew out of the fire and began singing magnificently. He soared high in the air, and after he vanished, the juniper tree was as it was before. Yet, the silk kerchief was gone. Marlene was very happy and gay. It was as if her brother were still alive, and she went merrily back into the house, sat down at the table, and ate.

Meanwhile, the bird flew away, landed on a goldsmith's house, and began to sing:

> 'My mother, she killed me.
> My father, he ate me
> My sister, Marlene, she made sure to see
> my bones were all gathered together,
> bound nicely in silk, as neat as can be
> and laid beneath the juniper tree.
> Tweet, tweet! What a lovely bird I am!'

The goldsmith was sitting in his workshop making a golden chain. When he heard the bird singing on his roof, he thought it was very beautiful. Then he stood up, and as he walked across the threshold, he lost a slipper. Still, he kept on going, right into the middle of the street with only one sock and a slipper on. He was also wearing his apron, and in one of his hands he held the golden chain, in the other his tongs. The sun was shining brightly on the street as he walked, and then he stopped to get a look at the bird.

'Bird,' he said, 'how beautifully you sing! Sing me that song again.'

'No,' said the bird, 'I never sing twice for nothing. Give me the golden chain, and I'll sing it for you again.'

'All right,' said the goldsmith. 'Here's the golden chain. Now sing the song again.'

The bird swooped down, took the golden chain in his right claw, went up to the goldsmith, and began singing:

> 'My mother, she killed me.
> My father, he ate me.
> My sister, Marlene, she made sure to see
> my bones were all gathered together,
> bound nicely in silk, as neat as can be,
> and laid beneath the juniper tree.
> Tweet, tweet! What a lovely bird I am!'

Then the bird flew off to a shoemaker, landed on his roof, and sang:

> 'My mother, she killed me.
> My father, he ate me.
> My sister, Marlene, she made sure to see
> my bones were all gathered together,
> bound nicely in silk, as neat as can be,
> and laid beneath the juniper tree.
> Tweet, tweet! What a lovely bird I am!'

When the shoemaker heard the song, he ran to the door in his shirt sleeves and looked up at the roof, keeping his hand over his eyes to protect them from the bright sun.

'Bird,' he said. 'How beautifully you sing!' Then he called into the house, 'Wife, come out here for a second! There's a bird up there. Just look. How beautifully he sings!' Then he called his daughter and her children, and the journeyman, apprentices, and maid. They all came running out into the street and looked at the bird and saw how beautiful he was. He had bright red and green feathers, and his neck appeared to glisten like pure gold, while his eyes sparkled in his head like stars.

'Bird,' said the shoemaker, 'now sing me that song again.'

'No,' said the bird, 'I never sing twice for nothing. You'll have to give me a present.'

'Wife,' said the man, 'go into the shop. There's a pair of red shoes on the top shelf. Get them for me.'

His wife went and fetched the shoes.

'There,' said the man. 'Now sing the song again.'

The bird swooped down, took the shoes in his left claw, flew back up on the roof, and sang:

> *'My mother, she killed me.*
> *My father, he ate me.*
> *My sister, Marlene, she made sure to see*
> *my bones were all gathered together,*
> *bound nicely in silk, as neat as can be,*
> *and laid beneath the juniper tree.*
> Tweet, tweet! *What a lovely bird I am!'*

When the bird finished the song, he flew away. He had the chain in his right claw and the shoes in his left, and he flew far away to a mill. The mill went *clickety-clack, clickety-clack, clicketyclack.* The miller had twenty men sitting in the mill, and they were hewing a stone. Their chisels went *click-clack, click-clack, click-clack.* And the mill kept going *clickety-clack, clickety-clack, clickety-clack.* The bird swooped down and landed on a linden tree outside the mill and sang:

> *'My mother, she killed me.'*

Then one of the men stopped working.

> *'My father, he ate me.'*

Then two more stopped and listened.

> *'My sister, Marlene, she made sure to see . . .'*

Then four more stopped.

'. . . my bones were all gathered together,
bound nicely in silk, as neat as can be.'

Now only eight kept chiseling.

'And laid beneath . . .'

Now only five.

'. . . the juniper tree.'

Now only one.

Tweet, tweet! *What a lovely bird I am!'*

Then the last one also stopped and listened to the final words.

'Bird, how beautifully you sing! Let me hear that too. Sing your song again for me.'

'No,' said the bird. 'I never sing twice for nothing. Give me the millstone, and I'll sing the song again.'

'I would if I could,' he said. 'But the millstone doesn't belong to me alone.'

'If he sings again,' said the others, 'he can have it.'

Then the bird swooped down, and all twenty of the miller's men took beams to lift the stone. 'Heave-ho! Heave-ho! Heave-ho!' Then the bird stuck his neck through the hole, put the stone on like a collar, flew back to the tree, and sang:

'My mother, she killed me.
My father, he ate me.
My sister, Marlene, she made sure to see
my bones were all gathered together,
bound nicely in silk, as neat as can be,
and laid beneath the juniper tree.
Tweet, tweet! *What a lovely bird I am!'*

When the bird finished his song, he spread his wings, and in his right claw he had the chain, in his left the shoes, and around his neck the millstone. Then he flew away to his father's house.

The father, mother, and Marlene were sitting at the table in the parlor, and the father said, 'Oh, how happy I am! I just feel so wonderful!'

'Not me,' said the mother. 'I feel scared as if a storm were about to erupt.'

Meanwhile, Marlene just sat there and kept weeping. Then the bird flew up, and when he landed on the roof, the father said, 'Oh, I'm in such good spirits. The sun's shining so brightly outside, and I feel as though I were going to see an old friend again.'

'Not me,' said his wife, 'I'm so frightened that my teeth are chattering. I feel as if fire were running through my veins.'

She tore open her bodice, while Marlene sat in a corner and kept weeping. She had her handkerchief in front of her eyes and wept until it was completely soaked with her tears. The bird swooped down on the juniper tree, where he perched on a branch and began singing:

> *'My mother, she killed me.'*

The mother stopped her ears, shut her eyes, and tried not to see or hear anything, but there was a roaring in her ears like a turbulent storm, and her eyes burned and flashed like lightning.

> *'My father, he ate me.'*

'Oh, Mother,' said the man, 'listen to that beautiful bird singing so gloriously! The sun's so warm, and it smells like cinnamon.'

> *'My sister, Marlene, she made sure to see . . .'*

Then Marlene laid her head on her knees and wept and wept, but the man said, 'I'm going outside. I must see the bird close up.'

'Oh, don't go!' said the wife. 'I feel as if the whole house were shaking and about to go up in flames!'

Nevertheless, the man went out and looked at the bird.

> *'. . . my bones were all gathered together,*
> *bound nicely in silk, as neat as can be,*
> *and laid beneath the juniper tree.*
> Tweet, tweet! *What a lovely bird I am!'*

After ending his song, the bird dropped the golden chain, and It fell around the man's neck just right, so that it fit him perfectly. Then he went inside and said, 'Just look how lovely that bird is! He gave me this beautiful golden chain, and he's as beautiful as well!'

But the woman was petrified and fell to the floor. Her cap slipped off her head, and the bird sang again:

'My mother, she killed me.'

'Oh, I wish I were a thousand feet beneath the earth so I wouldn't have to hear this!'

'My father, he ate me.'

Then the woman fell down again as if she were dead.

'My sister, Marlene, she made sure to see . . .'

'Oh,' said Marlene, 'I want to go outside too and see if the bird will give me something.' Then she went out.

'. . . my bones were all gathered together,
bound nicely in silk, as neat as can be.'

Then the bird threw her the shoes.

'And laid beneath the juniper tree.
Tweet, tweet! *What a lovely bird I am!'*

Marlene felt gay and happy. She put on the new red shoes and danced and skipped back into the house.

'Oh,' she said, 'I was so sad when I went out, and now I feel so cheerful. That certainly is a splendid bird. He gave me a pair of red shoes as a gift.'

'Not me,' said the wife, who jumped up, and her hair flared up like red-hot flames. 'I feel as if the world were coming to an end. Maybe I'd feel better if I went outside.'

As she went out the door, *crash!* the bird threw the millstone down on her head, and she was crushed to death. The father and Marlene heard the crash and went outside. Smoke, flames, and fire were rising from the spot, and when it was over, the little brother was standing there. He took his father and Marlene by the hand, and all three were very happy. Then they went into the house, sat down at the table, and ate.

NOURIE HADIG

(ARMENIAN)

here was once a rich man who had a very beautiful wife and a beautiful daughter known as Nourie Hadig [tiny piece of pomegranate]. Every month when the moon appeared in the sky, the wife asked: 'New moon, am I the most beautiful or are you?' And every month the moon replied, 'You are the most beautiful.'

But when Nourie Hadig came to be fourteen years of age, she was so much more beautiful than her mother that the moon was forced to change her answer. One day when the mother asked the moon her constant question, the moon answered: 'I am not the most beautiful, nor are you. The father's and mother's only child, Nourie Hadig, is the most beautiful of all.' Nourie Hadig was ideally named because her skin was perfectly white and she had rosy cheeks. And if you have ever seen a pomegranate, you know that it has red pulpy seeds with a red skin which has a pure white lining.

The mother was very jealous – so jealous in fact, that she fell sick and went to bed. When Nourie Hadig returned from school that day, her mother refused to see her or speak to her. 'My mother is very sick today,' Nourie Hadig said to herself. When her father returned home, she told him that her mother was sick and refused to speak to her. The father went to see his wife and asked kindly, 'What is the matter, wife? What ails you?'

'Something has happened which is so important that I must tell you immediately. Who is more necessary to you, your child or myself? You cannot have both of us.'

'How can you speak in this way?' he asked her. 'You are not a step-mother. How can you say such things about your own flesh and blood? How can I get rid of my own child?'

'I don't care what you do,' the woman said. 'You must get rid of her so that I will never see her again. Kill her and bring me her bloody shirt.'

'She is your child as much as she is mine. But if you say I must kill her, then she will be killed,' the father sadly answered. Then he went to his daughter and said, 'Come, Nourie Hadig, we are going for a visit. Take some of your clothes and come with me.'

The two of them went far away until finally it began to get dark. 'You wait here while I go down to the brook to get some water for us to drink with our lunch,' the father told his daughter.

Nourie Hadig waited and waited for her father to return, but he did not return. Not knowing what to do, she cried and walked through the woods trying to find a shelter. At last she saw a light in the distance, and approaching it, she came upon a large house. 'Perhaps these people will take me in tonight,' she said to herself. But as she put her hand on the door, it opened by itself, and as she passed inside, the door closed behind her immediately. She tried opening it again, but it would not open.

She walked through the house and saw many treasures. One room was full of gold; another was full of silver; one was full of fur, one was full of chicken feathers; one was full of pearls; and one was full of rugs. She opened the door to another room and found a handsome youth sleeping. She called out to him, but he did not answer.

Suddenly she heard a voice tell her that she must look after this boy and prepare his food. She must place the food by his bedside and then leave; when she returned, the food would be gone. She was to do this for seven years, for the youth was under a spell for that length of time. So, every day she cooked and took care of the boy. At the first new moon after Nourie Hadig had left home, her mother asked, 'New Moon, am I the most beautiful or are you?'

'I am not the most beautiful and neither are you,' the new moon replied. 'The father's and mother's only child, Nourie Hadig, is the most beautiful of all.'

'Oh, that means that my husband has not killed her after all,' the wicked woman said to herself. She was so angry that she went to bed again and pretended to be sick. 'What did you do to our beautiful child?' she asked her husband. 'Whatever did you do to her?'

'You told me to get rid of her. So I got rid of her. You asked me to bring you her bloody shirt, and I did,' her husband answered.

'When I told you that, I was ill. I didn't know what I was saying,' his wife said. 'Now I am sorry about it and plan to turn you over to the authorities as the murderer of your own child.'

'Wife, what are you saying? You were the one who told me what to do, and now you want to hand me over to the authorities?'

'You must tell me what you did with our child!' the wife cried. Although the husband did not want to tell his wife that he had not killed their daughter, he was compelled to do so to save himself. 'I did not kill her, wife. I killed a bird instead and dipped Nourie Hadig's shirt in its blood.'

'You must bring her back, or you know what will happen to you,' the wife threatened.

'I left her in the forest, but I don't know what happened to her after that.'

'Very well, then, I will find her,' the wife said. She traveled to distant places but could not find Nourie Hadig. Every new moon she asked her question and was assured that Nourie Hadig was the most beautiful of all. So on she went, searching for her daughter.

One day when Nourie Hadig had been at the bewitched house for four years, she looked out the window and saw a group of gypsies camping nearby. 'I am lonely up here. Can you send up a pretty girl of about my own age?' she called to them. When they agreed to do so, she ran to the golden room and took a handful of golden pieces. These she threw down to the gypsies who, in turn, threw up the end of a rope to her. Then a girl started climbing at the other end of the rope and quickly reached her new mistress.

Nourie Hadig and the gypsy soon became good friends and decided to share the burden of taking care of the sleeping boy. One day, one would serve him; and the next day, the other would serve him. They continued in this way for three years. One warm summer day the gypsy was fanning the youth when he suddenly awoke. As he thought that the gypsy had served him for the entire seven years, he said to her: 'I am a prince, and you are to be my princess for having cared for me such a long time.' The gypsy said, 'If you say it, so shall it be.'

Nourie Hadig, who had heard what was said by the two, felt very bitter. She had been in the house alone for four years before the gypsy came and had served three years with her friend, and yet the other girl was to marry the handsome prince. Neither girl told the prince the truth about the arrangement.

Everything was being prepared for the wedding, and the prince was making arrangements to go to town and buy the bridal dress. Before he left, however, he told Nourie Hadig: 'You must have served me a little while at least. Tell me what you would like me to bring back for you.'

'Bring me a Stone of Patience,' Nourie Hadig answered.

'What else do you want?' he asked, surprised at the modest request.

'Your happiness.'

The prince went into town and purchased the bridal gown, then went to a stone cutter and asked for a Stone of Patience.

'Who is this for?' the stonecutter asked.

'For my servant,' the prince replied.

'This is a Stone of Patience,' the stonecutter said. 'If one has great troubles and tells it to the Stone of Patience, certain changes will occur. If one's troubles are great, so great that the Stone of Patience cannot bear the sorrow, it will swell and burst. If, on the other hand, one makes much of only slight grievances, the Stone of Patience will not swell, but the speaker will. And if there is no one there to save this person, he will burst. So listen outside your servant's door. Not everyone knows of the Stone of Patience, and your servant, who is a very unusual person, must have a valuable story to tell. Be ready to run in and save her from bursting if she is in danger of doing so.'

When the prince reached home, he gave his betrothed the dress and gave Nourie Hadig the Stone of Patience. That night the prince listened outside Nourie Hadig's door. The beautiful girl placed the Stone of Patience before her and started telling her story:

'Stone of Patience,' she said, 'I was the only child of a well-to-do family. My mother was very beautiful, but it was my misfortune to be even more beautiful than she. At every new moon my mother asked who was the most beautiful one in the world. And the new moon always answered that my mother was the most beautiful. One day my mother asked again, and the moon told her that Nourie Hadig was the most beautiful one in the whole world. My mother became very jealous and told my father to take me somewhere, to kill me and bring her my bloody shirt. My father could not do this, so he permitted me to go free,' Nourie Hadig said. 'Tell me, Stone of Patience, am I more patient or are you?'

The Stone of Patience began to swell.

The girl continued, 'When my father left me, I walked until I saw this house in the distance. I walked toward it, and when I touched the door, it opened magically by itself. Once I was inside, the door closed behind me and never opened again until seven years later. Inside I found a handsome youth. A voice told me to prepare his food and take care of him. I did this for four years, day after day, night after night, living alone in a strange place, with no one to hear my voice. Stone of Patience tell me, am I more patient or are you?'

The Stone of Patience swelled a little more.

'One day a group of gypsies camped right beneath my window. As I had been lonely all these years, I bought a gypsy girl and pulled her up on a rope to the place where I was confined. Now, she and I took turns in serving the young boy who was under a magic spell. One day she cooked for him and the next day I cooked for him. One day, three years later while the gypsy was fanning him, the youth awoke and saw her. He thought that she had served him through all those years and took her as his betrothed. And the gypsy, whom I had bought and considered my friend, did not say one word to him about me. Stone of Patience, tell me, am I more patient or are you?'

The Stone of Patience swelled and swelled and swelled. The prince, meanwhile, had heard this most unusual story and rushed in to keep the girl from bursting. But just as he stepped into the room, it was the Stone of Patience which burst.

'Nourie Hadig,' the prince said, 'it is not my fault that I chose the gypsy for my wife instead of you. I didn't know the whole story. You are to be my wife, and the gypsy will be our servant.'

'No, since you are betrothed to her and all the preparations for the wedding are made, you must marry the gypsy,' Nourie Hadig said.

'That will not do. You must be my wife and her mistress.' So Nourie Hadig and the prince were married.

Nourie Hadig's mother, in the meanwhile, had never stopped searching for her daughter. One day she again asked the new moon, 'New moon, am I the most beautiful or are you?'

'I am not the most beautiful, nor are you. The princess of Adana is the most beautiful of all,' the new moon said. The mother knew immediately that Nourie Hadig was now married and lived in Adana. So she had a very beautiful ring made, so beautiful and brilliant that no one could resist it. But she put a potion in the ring that would make the wearer sleep. When she had finished her work, she called an old

witch who traveled on a broomstick. 'Witch, if you will take this ring and give it to the princess of Adana as a gift from her devoted mother, I will grant you your heart's desire.'

So the mother gave the ring to the witch, who set out for Adana immediately. The prince was not home when the witch arrived, and she was able to talk to Nourie Hadig and the gypsy alone. Said the witch, 'Princess, this beautiful ring is a gift from your devoted mother. She was ill at the time you left home and said some angry words, but your father should not have paid attention to her since she was suffering from such pain.' So she left the ring with Nourie Hadig and departed.

'My mother does not want me to be happy. Why should she send me such a beautiful ring?' Nourie Hadig asked the gypsy.

'What harm can a ring do?' the gypsy asked.

So Nourie Hadig slipped the ring on her finger. No sooner was it on her finger than she became unconscious. The gypsy put her in bed but could do nothing further.

Soon the prince came home and found his wife in a deep sleep. No matter how much they shook her, she would not awaken; yet she had a pleasant smile on her face, and anyone who looked at her could not believe that she was in a trance. She was breathing, yet she did not open her eyes. No one was successful in awakening her.

'Nourie Hadig, you took care of me all those long years,' the prince said. 'Now I will look after you. I will not let them bury you. You are always to lie here, and the gypsy will guard you by night while I guard you by day,' he said. So the prince stayed with her by day, and the gypsy guarded her by night. Nourie Hadig did not open her eyes once in three years. Healer after healer came and went, but none could help the beautiful girl.

One day the prince brought another healer to see Nourie Hadig, and although he could not help her in the least, he did not want to say so. When he was alone with the enchanted girl, he noticed her beautiful ring. 'She is wearing so many rings and necklaces that no one will notice if I take this ring to my wife,' he said to himself. As he slipped the ring off her finger, she opened her eyes and sat up. The healer immediately returned the ring to her finger. 'Aha! I have discovered the secret!'

The next day he exacted many promises of wealth from the prince for his wife's cure. 'I will give you anything you want if you can cure my wife,' the prince said.

The healer, the prince and the gypsy went to the side of Nourie Hadig. 'What are all those necklaces and ornaments? Is it fitting that a sick woman should wear such finery? Quick,' he said to the gypsy, 'remove them!' The gypsy removed all the jewelry except the ring, 'Take that ring off, too,' the healer ordered.

'But that ring was sent to her by her mother, and it is a dear remembrance,' the gypsy said.

'What do you say? When did her mother send her a ring?' asked the prince. Before the gypsy could answer him, the healer took the ring off Nourie Hadig's finger. The princess immediately sat up and began to talk. They were all very happy: the healer, the prince, the princess and the gypsy, who was now a real friend of Nourie Hadig.

Meanwhile, during all these years, whenever the mother had asked the moon her eternal question, it had replied, 'You are the most beautiful!' But when Nourie Hadig was well again, the moon said, 'I am not the most beautiful, neither are you. The father's and mother's only daughter, Nourie Hadig, the princess of Adana, is the most beautiful of all.' The mother was so surprised and so angry that her daughter was alive that she died of rage there and then.

From the sky fell three apples: one to me, one to the storyteller and one to the person who has entertained you.

BEAUTY AND POCK FACE

(CHINESE)

here were once two sisters; the eldest was very beautiful and everyone called her 'Beauty', but the younger had a face covered with pock marks, and everyone called her 'Pock Face'. She was the daughter of the second wife, and was very spoilt, and had a bad character. Beauty's mother had died when her daughter was very small, and after her death she had turned into a yellow cow, which lived in the garden. Beauty adored the yellow cow, but it had a miserable existence, because the stepmother treated it so badly.

One day, the stepmother took the ugly daughter to the theatre and left the elder one at home. She wanted to accompany them, but her stepmother said: 'I will take you tomorrow, if you tidy the hemp in my room.'

Beauty went off and sat down in front of the stack of hemp but after a long time she had only divided half. Bursting into tears, she took it off to the yellow cow, who swallowed the whole mass and then spat it out again all clearly arranged bit by bit. Beauty dried her tears, and gave the hemp to her mother on her return home: 'Mother, here is the hemp. I can go to the theatre tomorrow, can't I?'

But when the next day came, her stepmother again refused to take her, saying: 'You can go when you have separated the sesame seeds from the beans.' The poor girl had to divide them seed by seed, until the exhausting task made her eyes ache. Again she went to the yellow cow, who said to her: 'You stupid girl, you must separate them with a fan.' Now she understood, and the sesame and beans were soon divided. When she brought the seeds all nicely separated, her stepmother knew that she could no longer prevent her going to the theatre, but she asked her: 'How can a servant girl be so clever? Who helped you?' And Beauty had to admit that the yellow cow had advised her, which made the stepmother very angry. Without, therefore, saying a word, she killed and ate the cow, but Beauty had loved the cow so dearly that she could not eat its flesh. Instead, she put the bones in an earthenware pot and hid them in her bedroom.

Day after day, the stepmother did not take her to the theatre, and one evening, when she had gone there herself with Pock Face, Beauty was so cross that she smashed everything in the house including the earthenware pot. Whereupon there was a crack, and a white horse, a new dress, and a pair of embroidered shoes came out. The sudden appearance of these things gave her a terrible fright, but she soon saw that they were real objects and, quickly pulling on the new dress and the shoes, she jumped on to the horse and rode out of the gate.

While riding along, one of her shoes slipped off into the ditch. She wanted to dismount and fetch it, but could not do so; at the same time she did not want to leave it lying there. She was in a real quandary, when a fishmonger appeared. 'Brother fishmonger! Please pick up my shoe,' she said to him. He answered with a grin: 'With great pleasure, if you will marry me.' 'Who could marry you?' she said crossly. 'Fishmongers always stink.' And seeing that he had no chance, the fishmonger went on his way. Next, an assistant of a rice shop went by, and she said to him: 'Brother rice broker, please give me my shoe.' 'Certainly, if you will marry me,' said the young man. 'Marry a rice broker! Their bodies are all covered with dust.' The rice broker departed, and soon an oil merchant came by, whom she also asked to pick up her shoe. 'I will pick it up if you consent to marry me,' he replied. 'Who could want to marry you?' Beauty said with a sigh. 'Oil merchants are always so greasy.' Shortly after a scholar came by, whom she also asked to pick up her shoe. The scholar turned to look at her, and then said: 'I will do so at once if you promise to marry me.' The scholar was very handsome, so she nodded her head in agreement, and he picked up the shoe and put it on her foot. Then he took her back to his house and made her his wife.

Three days later, Beauty went with her husband to pay the necessary respects to her parents. Her stepmother and sister had quite changed their manner and treated them both in the most friendly and attentive fashion. In the evening, they wanted to keep Beauty at home, and she, thinking they meant it kindly, agreed to stay and to follow her husband in a few days. The next morning her sister took her by the hand and said to her with a laugh: 'Sister, come and look into the well. We will see which of us is the more beautiful.' Suspecting nothing, Beauty went to the well and leant over to look down, but at this moment her sister gave her a shove and pushed her into the well, which she quickly covered up with a basket. Poor Beauty lost consciousness and was drowned.

After ten days, the scholar began to wonder why his wife had still not returned. He sent a messenger to inquire, and the stepmother sent back a message that his wife was suffering from a bad attack of smallpox and was not well enough to return for the moment. The scholar believed this, and every day he sent over salted eggs and other sickbed delicacies, all of which found their way into the stomach of the ugly sister.

After two months, the stepmother was irritated by the continual messages from the scholar and made up her mind to practise a deception, and to send back her own daughter as his wife. The scholar was horrified when he saw her and said: 'Goodness! How changed you are! Surely you are not Beauty. My wife was never such a monster. Good Heavens!' Pock Face replied seriously: 'If I am not Beauty, whom do you think I am then? You know perfectly well I was very ill with smallpox, and now you want to disown me. I shall die! I shall die!' And she began to howl. The tender-hearted scholar could not bear to see her weeping, and although he still had some doubts, he begged her forgiveness and tried to console her, so that gradually she stopped weeping.

Beauty, however, had been transformed into a sparrow, and she used to come and call out when Pock Face was combing her hair: 'Comb once, peep; comb twice, peep; comb thrice, up to the spine of Pock Face.' And the wicked wife answered: 'Comb once, comb twice, comb thrice, to the spine of Beauty.' The scholar was very mystified by this conversation, and he said to the sparrow: 'Why do you sing like that? Are you by any chance my wife? If you are, call three times, and I will put you in a golden cage and keep you as a pet.' The sparrow called out three times, and the scholar bought a golden cage to keep it in. The ugly sister was very angry when she saw that her husband kept the sparrow in a cage, and she secretly killed it and threw it into the garden, where it was once more transformed into a bamboo with many shoots. When Pock Face ate them, an ulcer formed on her tongue, but the scholar found them excellent. The wicked woman became suspicious again and had the bamboo cut down and made into a bed, but when she lay on it, innumerable needles pricked her, while the scholar found it extremely comfortable. Again she became very cross and threw the bed away.

Next door to the scholar lived an old woman who sold money-bags. One day, on her way home, she saw the bed and thought to herself: 'No one has died here, why have they thrown the bed away? I shall take it,' and she took the bed into her house and passed a very comfortable night. The next day, she saw that the food in the kitchen was ready cooked. She ate it up, but naturally she felt a little nervous, not having any idea who could have prepared it. Thus for several days she found she could have dinner the moment she came home, but finally, being no longer able to contain her anxiety, she came back early one afternoon and went into the kitchen, where she saw a dark shadow washing rice. She ran up quickly and clasped the shadow round the waist. 'Who are you?' she asked, 'and why do you cook food for me?' The shadow replied: 'I will tell you everything. I am the wife of your neighbour the scholar and am called "Beauty". My sister threw me into the well and I was drowned, but my soul was not dispersed. Please give me a rice-pot as head, a stick as hand, a dish-cloth as entrails, firehooks as feet, and then I can assume my former shape again.' The old woman gave her what she asked for, and in a moment a beautiful girl appeared, and the old woman was so delighted at seeing such a charming girl, that she questioned her very closely. She told the old woman everything, and then said: 'Old woman, I have got a bag, which you must offer for sale outside the scholar's house. If he comes out, you must sell it to him.' And she gave her an embroidered bag.

The next day the old woman stood outside the scholar's house and shouted that she had a bag for sale. Maddened by the noise, he came out to ask what kind of bags she sold, and she showed him Beauty's embroidered bag. 'Where did you get this bag?' he asked. 'I gave it to my wife.' The old woman then told the whole story to the scholar, who was overjoyed to hear that his wife was still alive. He arranged everything with the old woman, laid down a red cloth on the ground, and brought Beauty back to his house.

When Pock Face saw her sister return, she gave her no peace. She began to grumble and say that the woman was only pretending to be Beauty, and that in point of fact she was a spirit. She wanted to have a trial to see which was the genuine wife. Beauty, also, would not admit herself in the wrong, and said: 'Good. We will have a test.' Pock Face suggested that they should walk on eggs, and whoever broke the shells would be the loser, but although she broke all the eggs, and Beauty none, she refused to admit her loss and insisted on another trial. This time they were to walk up a ladder made of knives. Beauty went up and down first without receiving the tiniest scratch, but before Pock Face had gone two steps her feet were cut to the bone. Although she had lost again, she insisted on another test, that of jumping into a cauldron of hot oil. She hoped that Beauty, who would have to jump in first, would be burnt. Beauty, however, was quite unharmed by the boiling oil, but the wicked sister fell into it and did not appear again.

Beauty put the roasted bones of the wicked sister into a box and sent them over to her stepmother by a stuttering old servant woman, who was told to say: 'Your daughter's flesh.' But the stepmother loved carp and understood 'carp flesh' instead of 'your daughter's flesh'. She thought her daughter had sent her over some carp and opened the box in a state of great excitement; but when she saw the charred bones of her daughter lying inside, she let out a piercing scream and fell down dead.

OLD AGE

(INNUIT)

here was woman who was old, blind and likewise unable to walk. Once she asked her daughter for a drink of water. The daughter was so bored with her old mother that she gave her a bowl of her own piss. The old woman drank it all up, then said: 'You're a nice one, daughter. Tell me – which would you prefer as a lover, a louse or a sea scorpion?'

'Oh, a sea scorpion,' laughed the daughter, 'because he would not be crushed so easily when I slept with him.'

Whereupon the old woman proceeded to pull sea scorpions out of her vagina, one after another, until she fell over dead.

PART SEVEN

MORAL TALES

LITTLE RED RIDING HOOD

(FRENCH)

nce upon a time, there lived a pretty little girl whose mother adored her, and her grandmother adored her even more. This good woman made her a red hood like the ones that fine ladies wear when they go riding. The hood suited the child so much that soon everybody was calling her Little Red Riding Hood.

One day, her mother baked some cakes on the griddle and said to Little Red Riding Hood:

'Your granny is sick; you must go and visit her. Take her one of these cakes and a little pot of butter.'

Little Red Riding Hood went off to the next village to visit her grandmother. As she walked through the wood, she met a wolf, who wanted to eat her but did not dare to because there were woodcutters working nearby. He asked her where she was going. The poor child did not know how dangerous it is to chatter away to wolves and replied innocently:

'I'm going to visit my grandmother to take her this cake and this little pot of butter from my mother.'

'Does your grandmother live far away?' asked the wolf.

'Oh yes,' said Little Red Riding Hood. 'She lives beyond the mill you can see over there, in the first house you come to in the village.'

'Well, I shall go and visit her, too,' said the wolf. 'I will take *this* road and you shall take *that* road and let's see who can get there first.'

The wolf ran off by the shortest path and Red Riding Hood went off the longest way and she made it still longer because she dawdled along, gathering nuts and chasing butterflies and picking bunches of wayside flowers.

The wolf soon arrived at Grandmother's house. He knocked on the door, rat tat tat.

'Who's there?'

'Your granddaughter, Little Red Riding Hood,' said the wolf, disguising his voice. 'I've brought you a cake baked on the griddle and a little pot of butter from my mother.'

Grandmother was lying in bed because she was poorly. She called out:

'Lift up the latch and walk in!'

The wolf lifted the latch and opened the door. He had not eaten for three days. He threw himself on the good woman and gobbled her up. Then he closed the door behind him and lay down in Grandmother's bed to wait for Little Red Riding Hood. At last she came knocking on the door, rat tat tat.

'Who's there?'

Little Red Riding Hood heard the hoarse voice of the wolf and thought that her grandmother must have caught a cold. She answered:

'It's your granddaughter, Little Red Riding Hood. I've brought you a cake baked on the griddle and a little pot of butter from my mother.'

The wolf disguised his voice and said:

'Lift up the latch and walk in.'

Little Red Riding Hood lifted the latch and opened the door.

When the wolf saw her come in, he hid himself under the bedclothes and said to her:

'Put the cake and the butter down on the bread-bin and come and lie down with me.'

Little Red Riding Hood took off her clothes and went to lie down in the bed. She was surprised to see how odd her grandmother looked. She said to her:

'Grandmother, what big arms you have!'

'All the better to hold you with, my dear.'

'Grandmother, what big legs you have!'

'All the better to run with, my dear.'

'Grandmother, what big ears you have!'

'All the better to hear you with, my dear.'

'Grandmother, what big eyes you have!'

'All the better to see you with, my dear!'

'Grandmother, what big teeth you have!'

'All the better to eat you up!'

At that, the wicked wolf threw himself upon Little Red Riding Hood and gobbled her up too.

FEET WATER

(IRISH)

n every house in the country long ago the people of the house would wash their feet, the same as they do now, and when you had your feet washed you should always throw out the water, because dirty water should never be kept inside in the house during the night. The old people always said that a bad thing might come into the house if the feet water was kept inside and not thrown out, and they always said, too, that when you were throwing the water out you should say 'Seachain!' for fear that any poor soul or spirit might be in the way. But that is not here nor there, and I must be getting on with my story.

There was a widow woman living a long time ago in the east of County Limerick in a lonely sort of a place, and one night when she and her daughter were going to bed, didn't they forget to throw out the feet water. They weren't long in bed when the knock came to the door, and the voice outside said: 'Key, let us in!'

Well, the widow woman said nothing, and the daughter held her tongue as well.

'Key, let us in,' came the call again, and, faith! this time the key spoke up: 'I can't let you in, and I here tied to the post of the old woman's bed.'

'Feet water, let us in!' says the voice, and with that, the tub of feet water split and the water flowed around the kitchen, and the door opened and in came three men with bags of wool and three women with spinning-wheels, and they sat down around the fire, and the men were taking tons of wool out of the bags, and the little women were spinning it into thread, and the men putting the thread back into the bags.

And this went on for a couple of hours and the widow woman and the girl were nearly out of their minds with the fright. But the girl kept a splink of sense about her, and she remembered that there was a wise woman living not too far away, and down with her from the room to the kitchen, and she catches up a bucket. 'Ye'll be having a sup of tea, after all the work,' says she, as bold as brass, and out the door with her.

They didn't help or hinder her.

Off with her to the wise woman, and out with her story. ''Tis a bad case, and 'tis lucky you came to me,' says the wise woman, 'for you might travel far before you'd find one that would save you from them. They are not of this world, but I know where they are from. And this is what you must do,' and she told her what to do.

Back with the girl and filled her bucket at the well, and back with her to the house. And just as she was coming over the stile, she flung down the bucket with a bang, and shouted out at the top of her voice: 'There is Sliabh na mBan all on fire!'

And the minute they heard it, out with the strange men and women running east in the direction of the mountain.

And in with the girl, and she made short work of throwing out the broken tub and putting the bolt and the bar on the door. And herself and her mother went back to bed for themselves.

It was not long until they heard the footsteps in the yard once more, and the voice outside calling out: 'Key, let us in!' And the key

answered back: 'I can't let you in. Amn't I after telling you that I'm tied to the post of the old woman's bed?' 'Feet water, let us in!' says the voice.

'How can I?' says the feet water, 'and I here on the ground under your feet!'

They had every shout and every yell out of them with the dint of the rage, and they not able to get in to the house. But it was idle for them. They had no power to get in when the feet water was thrown out.

And I tell you it was a long time again before the widow woman or her daughter forgot to throw out the feet water and tidy the house properly before they went to bed for themselves.

WIVES CURE BOASTFULNESS

(WEST AFRICAN: DAHOMEY)

his happened long ago. When the family head let out his pigeons in the morning, he mixed beans and corn and threw this to them. When the pigeons finished eating, there was a jar of water for them.

No sooner were they satisfied, than the pigeons began to annoy the girls with their boasting. They kept saying, 'If I had someone, I would fight him. If I had someone, I would fight him.' The pigeons always said that.

The women got together and said, 'After they eat, our husbands always say, "If I had someone I would fight him. If I had someone I would fight him." Are they really so strong?'

The women went to see Aklasu, the vulture, and said to him that their husbands were always looking for a fight. They said, 'Tomorrow you come, and when they are finished eating, you fight them. But you must not kill them. You can give them a good scare, though.' They repeated, 'But you must not kill them.'

When vulture came, he settled on a tree nearby. The male pigeons knew nothing about his being there. But the women knew. Now, as usual, the master had them all come out to eat. At sunrise, they had corn and beans thrown to them, and when they finished with that, they drank the water.

Each began again. 'If I had someone, I'd fight him. If I had someone I'd fight him.' When they said this, the vulture threw himself at them, tearing at them, pulling at their feathers.

Now, the women were at the side and watched.

The pigeons cried, 'Let us go. We do not want to fight. We said that only to frighten the women. Let us go.' Vulture plucked all their feathers and then he flew away.

Now, the women came to their husbands. The pigeons were all without feathers. The women repeated mockingly, 'If our husbands saw something, they'd fight. If our husbands had someone, they'd fight him.'

The battered pigeons pushed their wives away and said, 'What are you saying? What are you saying?'

Today Pigeon keeps saying, 'I don't want to fight. I am not here for a fight.'

TONGUE MEAT

(SWAHILI)

A sultan lived with his wife in his palace, but the wife was unhappy. She grew leaner and more listless every day. In the same town there lived a poor man whose wife was healthy and fat and happy. When the sultan heard about this, he summoned the poor man to his court, and asked him what his secret was. The poor man said: 'Very simple. I feed her meat of the tongue.' The sultan at once called the butcher and ordered him to sell all the tongues of all the animals that were slaughtered in town, to him, the sultan, exclusively. The butcher bowed and went. Every day he sent the tongues of all the beasts in his shop to the palace. The sultan had his cook bake and fry, roast and salt these tongues in every known manner, and prepare every tongue dish in the book. This the queen had to eat, three or four times a day – but it did not work. She grew even more thin and poorly. The sultan now ordered the poor man to exchange wives – to which the poor man reluctantly agreed. He took the lean queen home with him and sent his own wife to the palace. Alas, there she grew thinner and thinner, in spite of the good food the sultan offered her. It was clear that she could not thrive in a palace.

The poor man, after coming home at night, would greet his new (royal) wife, tell her about the things he had seen, especially the funny things, and then told her stories which made her shriek with laughter. Next he would take his banjo and sing her songs, of which he knew a great many. Until late at night he would play with her and amuse her. And lo! the queen grew fat in a few weeks, beautiful to look at, and her skin was shining and taut, like a young girl's skin. And she was smiling all day, remembering the many funny things her new husband had told her. When the sultan called her back she refused to come. So the sultan came to fetch her, and found her all changed and happy. He asked her what the poor man had done to her, and she told him. Then he understood the meaning of *meat of the tongue*.

The Woodcutter's Wealthy Sister

(SYRIAN)

There was a man with ten children who lived at the foot of a hill. Every day he climbed to the hilltop and collected firewood to sell in town. At sunset his hungry family would wait, watching for his return, and he would bring them a loaf of bread with perhaps an onion or an olive for flavouring. He was a poor man – but what was worse, he lacked not only gold but brains.

One day when the dead wood on the hilltop was almost gone, he decided to try another hill farther off which was covered with trees. As he was walking home in the evening, his load on his back, he met a finely dressed woman jingling with gold bangles and rustling with rich stuffs. 'Don't you recognize your own sister, O my brother?' she asked. 'I wait and wait in vain for you to visit me, but there, not every heart is tender.' 'I have no sister,' said the man. 'What! Will you deny me altogether now? But tell me, brother, what you are doing here?' 'I am heading home after my day's work,' sighed the woodcutter. 'You should give yourself a rest from drudgery and let me care for you,' said the woman. 'Why not come and share my good fortune? Bring your children and your wife to live with me in my big house. I have plenty of good things: enough to suit your every mood!' 'Is that so?' replied the man, not knowing what to say. 'Would I deceive my own brother?' said the woman. 'Come with me now and see for yourself; then you will know the way tomorrow.' And she pulled him by the hand.

And what a house she had! Sack upon sack of wheat and lentils and dried broad beans! Row upon row of jars filled with olive oil and butterfat! The woman invited the woodcutter to eat and cooked a suckling lamb just for him. 'Now doesn't that remind you of our days of long ago?' she asked him. The poor man pounced on the food like a beggar, because it had been many months since he had tasted meat. 'I have never seen her before, but who can she be except my sister?' he wondered. 'Who else would make me so welcome, who else show me such hospitality? And he hurried back to tell his wife, running so fast that it's a wonder he didn't hurt himself.

But the woodcutter's wife was not convinced. 'Wouldn't I have heard of it if I had a sister-in-law?' she asked. 'And if she is not my sister-in-law, for what good purpose does she want us all to live with her?' She tried to reason with her husband; she tried persuasion; but in the end she had to gather her ten children and, leading their scrawny cow by a rope, follow him to his sister's house.

Feast upon feast awaited them. For a month they did nothing but eat and drink and lie in the shade to rest. The children's faces, which had been thin as knife blades, began to fill out. The woodcutter laughed and said, 'A curse on all toilsome work! May Allah never bring back those weary times, but let us live forever like this – fresh as the cool of the day.'

Then one night while the woodcutter's family slept in the lower room of the house, the sister crept down from her loft and tried the door, muttering,

> *All my fat and my flour eaten and gone,*
> *But now they are plump; I need not wait long.*

For this was a She-Ghoul of the kind that feeds on human flesh. Then the cow who was tethered to the doorpost turned on the monster and said:

> *My eyes can burn you like a flame,*
> *My tail can whip you till you're lame,*
> *My horns can tear and gore and maim.*

And the She-Ghoul had to go back the way she had come.

The next night the monster crept down again, and the cow kept her out as before. But on the third night the cow, moving to fend off the Ghoul, kicked the wooden door with her hoof and woke the woodcutter's wife. So the woman heard her husband's sister when she said,

> *All my fat and my flour eaten and gone,*
> *But now they are plump, I need not wait long.*

And she heard the cow's reply:

> *My eyes can burn you like a flame,*
> *My tail can whip you till you're lame,*
> *My horns can tear and gore and maim.*

She shook her husband to wake him, but he was sunk in sleep from too much eating and would not stir.

In the morning, when the woodcutter's wife told him all she had heard in the night, he said that it must have been a bad dream. Yet at noon his wealthy sister came to him and said, 'O my brother, I have a craving for cow's meat today. Surely you will not begrudge me that bony beast of yours.' How could a man refuse his sister? So he killed his cow and made his wife cook the meat. She set the tastiest portion on a plate, and sent her eldest daughter to take it to her aunt. When the girl looked into the sister's room, she saw not her aunt but a demon. Its hair was wild and its eyes blazed red and from the rafters men and women were hanging dead. Without a sound she tiptoed back, but in her hurry she stumbled on the stair and all the food slipped off the dish and on to the floor. Her mother came to scold her, and the girl reported what she had seen. The mother repeated the tale to their father, but still the woodcutter said, 'That is childish talk. How can you want to kick away such comfort, when you should be thanking God and saying prayers for our blessing?'

That night there was no cow to stop the She-Ghoul from entering. The woodcutter's wife watched as the demon, feeling each of the children in their beds, repeated to herself:

> *All my fat and my flour eaten and gone,*
> *But now they are plump; I need not wait long.*

'Sister-in-law, what do you want?' called the woodcutter's wife, who had not closed an eye. 'I was just covering my nieces and nephews to keep them from the cold,' said the She-Ghoul, and climbed back up the stairs to her own bed.

Next day the woodcutter's wife boiled a ground lentil soup to feed her children and watched them splatter and stain their clothes without a word. Then she went to her sister-in-law and said, 'I want to go to the stream to wash my children's clothes. Lend me your copper pot so

that I can heat water and bathe the children too.' And down she went
to the *wadi* and lit a fire and heaped green wood on it to give off
smoke. She hung a couple of rags where the wind would catch them
and called her children to her. The she prayed, 'Open for us, O spacious gate of Allah's protection!' And holding the hem of her long
gown between her teeth and pulling her children along by the hands,
she ran and ran away from the She-Ghoul's home back to her own
home at the foot of the hill.

From time to time the She-Ghoul stepped out of her house to cast
a glance down into the valley. She saw the thick smoke rising and the

cloth playing in the wind and she said, 'There she is, still busy at her washing!' But when the day waned and the sun began to set and still her guests had not returned, she hastened down to see what could delay them. There she found the place abandoned and mother and children gone. She howled so loud that the hill around her rang. And she cried,

> Why did I fatten and fatten them
> When by now I might have eaten them!

The woodcutter, who was dozing under the grape arbor outside the door, heard her howl. Now he began to be alarmed. He looked around for a place to hide. He could hear the She-Ghoul coming and he knew that her knife was hot and sharpened for him and no one else. In his fright he dived into a rubbish heap and buried himself completely. The She-Ghoul entered the yard like a storm, biting her fingers and snorting when she breathed. Inside and out, from the pigeon houses on the roof to the hen coop under the stairs, she searched for him.

At last the She-Ghoul climbed on to the hill of rubbish to gain a better view. As she shifted her weight to the place where the wood-cutter was hiding, out of his mouth popped a loud belch. 'Was that you sighing, O my headcloth?' shouted the demon. And she pulled it off. She stood on her toes to look as far as she could, and the wood-cutter's stomach rumbled again. 'Was that you complaining, O my robe?' she said. And she threw it off. And now she stood in her own hairy skin, a monstrous She-Ghoul for all to see and run from. She heard the woodcutter beneath her once again, and she said, 'It is the rubbish making a noise! Let me see why.' And she flung one half of the heap to the right and the other to the left and pulled the poor woodcutter out.

'Now,' she said, 'tell me, O my brother, where shall I sink my teeth in first?'

> Start with my two ears
> So deaf to my wife's fears!

he wept. 'And then?' said the demon.

Then go on to both my arms
Which dragged her into such harm.

'And then?'

Then go on to my two legs
Which did not go where she begged.

And so on, until she had eaten him all and nothing of him was left to question or to give an answer. But so it is with lazy men: using their own hands they dig the hole into which they fall.

My story I have told it the best I can.
Now it is for you to tell one in return.

Escaping Slowly

(JAMAICAN)

A goat was walking along with her two kids looking for some nice sweet grass when it began to rain. It was really coming down, so she ran under a big rock ledge to get some shelter, not knowing that it was Lion's house. When Lion saw the three goats coming, he purred to himself in a voice like thunder.

This frightened the mother and her kids and she said, 'Good evening, Minister.' And the lion said, 'Good evening.' She said that she was looking for a minister to baptize these two kids, because she wanted to give them names. Lion said he'd be happy to do that: 'This one's name is Dinner and this one's name is Breakfast Tomorrow and your name is Dinner Tomorrow.'

So now after hearing this roared out by the Lion, the goats were really frightened, and the kids' hearts began to leap, *bup bup bup*. Lion asked the mother goat what was the matter with her two kids and she said, 'Well, they always get feeling this way when the room they are in gets so hot.' So she asked Lion that since they were feeling that way, could they go out and get a little cool air. Lion agreed that they could go out until dinner-time, but then they must come back in. So the mother whispered to the two kids to run as hard as they could until dark came.

So when the lion saw that evening was falling, and he didn't see the kids coming back, he started to roar again. She said that she was wondering why they were staying out so long, so she asked Lion if she shouldn't go out and get them before it got too dark. The lion agreed. And as soon as the mother got out, she really took off running.

Women know more about life than men, especially when it comes to the children.

Nature's Ways

(ARMENIAN)

here was once a king who had only one daughter. He wanted her never to marry so that he could take care of her and have her under his watchful eye. He wanted her to know nothing of the world, nothing of life, and never to love anyone but himself.

After much thought he called in his adviser and discussed this problem. Together they planned a beautiful palace on a lonely island in the middle of a lake. The girl, only seven at this time, was to live there with women servants only and a female teacher.

The king carried out his plan. He had a beautiful palace built for his daughter, and several female servants and a woman teacher were hired. There were no windows in the palace so that the girl could not see out. She had no visitors except her father who saw her for three or four hours on Sunday. All the doors of the building were locked, and only the king had a key to the outside door.

Years went by until this daughter became eighteen years old. She learned a great many things, but it seemed to her that the books she read were dull and said nothing. She began to think for herself. 'What kind of a life is this? All my servants are women; my teacher is a woman. If all the world is peopled only by girls, what is my father?' If she had had more courage, she would have asked her father about this, but as it was she only asked her teacher.

'I am going to ask you a question, but you must tell me the truth. I have no mother, no sister, no friend. You are everything to me. Answer me as a mother. Why am I on this island alone? All the people around me are women, but my father is different. How is this?'

The teacher had been told not even to whisper of such matters to her pupil. So she said, 'I am not to speak or think of such things, and neither are you. Never let your father hear you saying such things or our lives won't be worth even one *para* [Turkish coin].'

But the girl persisted in asking questions and wanted books which would explain life and the world. The teacher finally brought her such a book but asked the girl not to tell anyone about her reading.

The girl began thinking of her future. 'Am I going to spend all my days in this prison?' she asked herself over and over again. Now this girl had learned a good deal about magic. One day she asked her teacher to get her flour, eggs, butter and milk with which she was going to make some dough. After she had kneaded the dough, she modeled the form of a man with it. She drew the features and made the figure of human size.

She used all her magic in making the image and then began praying to God to give this image the soul of a human being. 'I made him with my hands, I drew him with my mind, and with my tears I pray that this image may become a human being,' she said. She repeated this prayer over and over again, always asking God to give this image a soul.

Finally, God heard her voice and granted her wish: the image was given a soul. The teacher managed to bring clothes for the man. The two young people fell in love, and the girl was careful to hide the boy

so that no one saw him except the teacher who, of course, had helped
them.

The girl knew the time of her father's weekly visits and was careful that he should not discover her secret. But one Sunday she
overslept, and so did the man and so did the teacher. The father
entered the palace, and what did he see but a man by his daughter's
side! He was enraged! He had gone through much trouble and expense
to stop this very thing! The king took all of them – daughter, man,
teacher and servants – to prison and ordered that the boy and the girl
be killed immediately.

'Give us an opportunity to defend ourselves,' the girl pleaded with
her father. Finally, because he loved his daughter dearly, the king consented to listen. A court was assembled and the guilty ones brought
before the judge. The princess, as the chief wrong-doer, spoke first,
telling the truth about the matter, from the very beginning to the very
end.

'My father did not want me ever to get married, and so he built a
prison and put me in it. All my servants and my teacher were women.
Yet I could see that my father, who visited me each Sunday, was different. I wanted to live and to know what love was! With my
knowledge of magic, I made the image of a man with flour, butter,
eggs and milk. I made this image with my hands, drew it with my
mind and, with my tears, prayed God to give it a human soul. God,
through His kindness, heard my voice and granted my wish. This man
standing beside me, I have made myself. He has no family, no ties. If
you kill us, you will commit the greatest crime imaginable. I have had
my wish: I have lived, I have loved and been loved. If you kill me, I
have no regrets.'

'Is such a thing possible?' all were saying to one another.

'I will have an investigation made of this,' the king said. However,
the investigation revealed that the princess was telling the truth, that
the man had no family and there was no evidence that he had ever
been born.

'My children, I have committed a great crime. I shall try to undo
the harm and suffering that I have caused you. I am having a beautiful palace built and furnished for you. May you live in peace forever,'
the king told his daughter and her mate.

The king fulfilled his promise. A beautiful palace was built for the
young people, and they lived in happiness forever after.

From the sky fell three apples: one to me, one to the story-teller and one to her who has entertained you.

And so you see: Nature helps man understand God's laws, the way of life. No one can or should change these natural laws.

THE TWO WOMEN
WHO FOUND FREEDOM

(INNUIT)

nce there lived a man who had two wives. His name was Eqqorsuaq. And he was so jealous of these wives that he would keep them locked up in his hut. He would thrash them if they did not behave themselves. Or he would thrash anyone who happened to lay eyes on them. He killed a man named Angaguaq because rumour had it that Angaguaq had slept with one of the wives. Which he hadn't done. Eqqorsuaq was a somewhat mean-spirited person.

Finally the two women got a bit tired of their husband. They left him and fled along the coast until they were all worn out and hungry. When they could go no further, they saw the huge carcass of a whale washed up on a beach. They crawled in through the mouth and hid

inside this carcass. The smell was foul, but better a foul smell than another thrashing.

Now Eqqorsuaq was in a furor. He searched high and low for his wives. He questioned everyone in the village and threatened not a few. But no one seemed to know about the missing women. At last the man paid a visit to the local witch doctor, who told him:

'You must look for the body of a big whale which is on the Skerry of the Heart-Shaped Mountain.'

And so Eqqorsuaq set out for the Skerry of the Heart-Shaped Mountain. He sang old drum-songs all along the way, for he looked forward to the pleasure of thrashing his wives. At last he arrived at his destination and saw the dead whale. But the stench was so awful that he could get nowhere near it. He called out again and again for the women, yet there came no answer. Perhaps they were no longer here. Eqqorsuaq camped on the beach for three days and then went home, determined to thrash the witch doctor.

Meanwhile the two wives lived on inside the whale. They had grown so accustomed to the stench that it did not bother them. They had plenty of food to eat, however rotten, and a warm place to sleep. It is said that they were very happy in their new home.

HOW A HUSBAND WEANED HIS WIFE
FROM FAIRY TALES

(RUSSIAN)

here was once an innkeeper whose wife loved fairy tales above all else and accepted as lodgers only those who could tell stories. Of course the husband suffered loss because of this, and he wondered how he could wean his wife away from fairy tales. One night in winter, at a late hour, an old man shivering with cold asked him for shelter. The husband ran out and said: 'Can you tell stories? My wife does not allow me to let in anyone who cannot tell stories.' The old man saw that he had no

choice; he was almost frozen to death. He said: 'I can tell stories.'
'And will you tell them for a long time?' 'All night.'

So far, so good. They let the old man in. The husband said: 'Wife, this peasant has promised to tell stories all night long but only on condition that you do not argue with him or interrupt him.' The old man said: 'Yes, there must be no interruptions, or I will not tell any stories.' They ate supper and went to bed. Then the old man began: 'An owl flew by a garden, sat on a tree trunk, and drank some water. An owl flew into a garden, sat on a tree trunk, and drank some water.' He kept on saying again and again: 'An owl flew into a garden, sat on a tree trunk, and drank some water.' The wife listened and listened and then said: 'What kind of story is this? He keeps repeating the same thing over and over!' 'Why do you interrupt me? I told you not to argue with me! That was only the beginning; it was going to change later.' The husband, upon hearing this – and it was exactly what he wanted to hear – jumped down from his bed and began to belabor his wife: 'You were told not to argue, and now you have not let him finish his story!' And he thrashed her and thrashed her, so that she began to hate stories and from that time on forswore listening to them.

PART EIGHT

STRONG MINDS AND LOW CUNNING

THE TWELVE WILD DUCKS

(NORWEGIAN)

nce on a time there was a queen who was out driving, when there had been a new fall of snow in the winter; but when she had gone a little way, she began to bleed at the nose, and had to get out of her sledge. And so, as she stood there, leaning against the fence, and saw the red blood on the white snow, she fell a-thinking how she had twelve sons and no daughter, and she said to herself –

'If I only had a daughter as white as snow and as red as blood, I shouldn't care what became of all my sons.'

But the words were scarce out of her mouth before an old witch of the Trolls came up to her.

'A daughter you shall have,' she said, 'and she shall be as white as snow, and as red as blood; and your sons shall be mine, but you may keep them till the babe is christened.'

So when the time came the queen had a daughter, and she was as white as snow, and as red as blood, just as the Troll had promised, and so they called her 'Snow-white and Rosy-red'. Well, there was great joy at the king's court, and the queen was as glad as glad could be; but when what she had promised to the old witch came into her mind, she sent for a silversmith, and bade him make twelve silver spoons, one for each prince, and after that she bade him make one more, and that she gave to Snow-white and Rosy-red. But as soon as ever the princess was christened, the princes were turned into twelve wild ducks, and flew away. They never saw them again – away they went, and away they stayed.

So the princess grew up, and she was both tall and fair, but she was often so strange and sorrowful, and no one could understand what it was that ailed her. But one evening the queen was also sorrowful, for she had many strange thoughts when she thought of her sons. She said to Snow-white and Rosy-red, 'Why are you so sorrowful, my daughter? Is there anything you want? If so, only say the word, and you shall have it.'

'Oh, it seems so dull and lonely here,' said Snow-white and Rosy-red; 'everyone else has brothers and sisters, but I am all alone; I have none; and that's why I'm so sorrowful.'

'But you *had* brothers, my daughter,' said the queen; 'I had twelve sons who were your brothers, but I gave them all away to get you'; and so she told her the whole story.

So when the princess heard that, she had no rest; for, in spite of all the queen could say or do, and all she wept and prayed, the lassie would set off to seek her brothers, for she thought it was all her fault; and at last she got leave to go away from the palace. On and on she walked into the wide world, so far, you would never have thought a young lady could have strength to walk so far.

So, once, when she was walking through a great, great wood, one day she felt tired, and sat down on a mossy tuft and fell asleep. Then she dreamt that she went deeper and deeper into the wood, till she came to a little wooden hut, and there she found her brothers. Just then she woke, and straight before her she saw a worn path in the green moss, and this path went deeper into the wood; so she followed it, and after a long time she came to just such a little wooden house as that she had seen in her dream.

Now, when she went into the room there was no one at home, but there stood twelve beds, and twelve chairs, and twelve spoons – a dozen of everything, in short. So when she saw that she was so glad, she hadn't been so glad for many a long year, for she could guess at once that her brothers lived here, and that they owned the beds, and chairs and spoons. So she began to make up the fire, and sweep the room, and make the beds, and cook the dinner, and to make the house as tidy as she could; and when she had done all the cooking and work, she ate her own dinner, and crept under her youngest brother's bed, and lay down there, but she forgot her spoon upon the table.

So she had scarcely laid herself down before she heard something flapping and whirring in the air, and so all the twelve wild ducks came sweeping in; but as soon as ever they crossed the threshold they became princes.

'Oh, how nice and warm it is in here,' they said. 'Heaven bless him who made up the fire, and cooked such a good dinner for us.'

And so each took up his silver spoon and was going to eat. But when each had taken his own, there was one still left lying on the table, and it was so like the rest that they couldn't tell it from them.

'This is our sister's spoon,' they said; 'and if her spoon be here she can't be very far off herself.'

'If this be our sister's spoon, and she be here,' said the eldest, 'she shall be killed, for she is to blame for all the ill we suffer.'

And this she lay under the bed and listened to.

'No,' said the youngest, ' 'twere a shame to kill her for that. She has nothing to do with our suffering ill; for if anyone's to blame, it's our own mother.'

So they set to work hunting for her both high and low, and at last they looked under all the beds, and so when they came to the youngest prince's bed, they found her, and dragged her out. Then the eldest prince wished again to have her killed, but she begged and prayed so prettily for herself.

'Oh! Gracious goodness! don't kill me, for I've gone about seeking you these three years, and if I could only set you free, I'd willingly lose my life.'

'Well!' said they, 'if you will set us free, you may keep your life; for you can if you choose.'

'Yes; only tell me,' said the princess, 'how it can be done, and I'll do it, whatever it be.'

'You must pick thistledown,' said the princes, 'and you must card it, and spin it and weave it; and after you have done that, you must cut out and make twelve coats, and twelve shirts and twelve neckerchiefs, one for each of us, and while you do that, you must neither talk, nor laugh nor weep. If you can do that, we are free.'

'But where shall I ever get thistledown enough for so many neck-erchiefs, and shirts, and coats?' asked Snow-white and Rosy-red.

'We'll soon show you,' said the princes; and so they took her with them to a great wide moor, where there stood such a crop of thistles, all nodding and nodding in the breeze, and the down all floating and glistening like gossamers through the air in the sunbeams. The princess had never seen such a quantity of thistledown in her life, and she began to pluck and gather it as fast and as well as she could; and when she got home at night she set to work carding and spinning yarn from the down. So she went on a long long time, picking, and carding and spinning, and all the while keeping the princes' house, cooking, and making their beds. At evening home they came, flapping and whirring like wild ducks, and all night they were princes, but in the morning off they flew again, and were wild ducks the whole day.

But now it happened once, when she was out on the moor to pick thistledown – and if I don't mistake, it was the very last time she was to go thither – it happened that the young king who ruled that land was out hunting, and came riding across the moor, and saw her. So he stopped there and wondered who the lovely lady could be that walked along the moor picking thistledown, and he asked her her name, and when he could get no answer he was still more astonished; and at last he liked her so much, that nothing would do but he must take her home to his castle and marry her. So he ordered his servants to take her and put her up on his horse. Snow-white and Rosy-red wrung her hands, and made signs to them, and pointed to the bags in which her work was, and when the king saw she wished to have them with her, he told his men to take up the bags behind them. When they had done that the princess came to herself, little by little, for the king was both a wise man and a handsome man too, and he was as soft and kind to her as a doctor. But when they got home to the palace, and the old queen, who was his stepmother, set eyes on Snow-white and Rosy-red, she got so cross and jealous of her because she was so lovely, that she said to the king, 'Can't you see now, that this thing whom you have picked up, and whom you are going to marry, is a witch? Why, she can't either talk, or laugh or weep!'

But the king didn't care a pin for what she said, but held on with the wedding, and married Snow-white and Rosy-red, and they lived in great joy and glory; but she didn't forget to go on sewing at her shirts.

So when the year was almost out, Snow-white and Rosy-red brought a prince into the world, and then the old queen was more spiteful and jealous than ever. At dead of night she stole in to Snow-white and Rosy-red, while she slept, and took away her babe, and threw it into a pit full of snakes. After that she cut Snow-white and Rosy-red in her finger, and smeared the blood over her mouth, and went straight to the king.

'Now come and see,' she said, 'what sort of a thing you have taken for your queen; here she has eaten up her own babe.'

Then the king was so downcast, he almost burst into tears, and said, 'Yes, it must be true, since I see it with my own eyes; but she'll not do it again, I'm sure, and so this time I'll spare her life.'

So before the next year was out she had another son, and the same thing happened. The king's stepmother got more and more jealous and spiteful. She stole in to the young queen at night while she slept, took away the babe, and threw it into a pit full of snakes, cut the young queen's finger, and smeared the blood over her mouth, and then went and told the king she had eaten up her own child. Then the king was so sorrowful, you can't think how sorry he was, and he said, 'Yes, it must be true, since I see it with my own eyes, but she'll not do it again, I'm sure, and so this time too I'll spare her life.'

Well, before the next year was out, Snow-white and Rosy-red brought a daughter into the world, and her, too, the old queen took and threw into the pit full of snakes, while the young queen slept. Then she cut her finger, smeared the blood over her mouth, and went again to the king and said, 'Now you may come and see if it isn't as I say; she's a wicked, wicked witch, for here she has gone and eaten up her third babe too.'

Then the king was so sad, there was no end to it, for now he couldn't spare her any longer but had to order her to be burnt alive on a pile of wood. But just when the pile was all ablaze, and they were going to put her on it, she made signs to them to take twelve boards and lay them round the pile, and on these she laid the neckerchiefs, and the shirts and the coats for her brothers, but the youngest brother's shirt wanted its left arm, for she hadn't had time to finish it. And as soon as ever she had done that, they heard such a flapping and whirring in the air, and down came twelve wild ducks flying over the forest, and each of them snapped up his clothes in his bill and flew off with them.

'See now!' said the old queen to the king, 'wasn't I right when I told you she was a witch; but make haste and burn her before the pile burns low.'

'Oh!' said the king, 'we've wood enough and to spare, and so I'll wait a bit, for I have a mind to see what the end of all this will be.'

As he spoke, up came the twelve princes riding along as handsome well-grown lads as you'd wish to see; but the youngest prince had a wild duck's wing instead of his left arm.

'What's all this about?' asked the princes.

'My queen is to be burnt,' said the king, 'because she's a witch, and because she has eaten up her own babes.'

'She hasn't eaten them at all,' said the princes. 'Speak now, sister; you have set us free and saved us, now save yourself.'

Then Snow-white and Rosy-red spoke, and told the whole story; how every time she was brought to bed, the old queen, the king's stepmother, had stolen in to her at night, had taken her babes away, and cut her little finger, and smeared the blood over her mouth; and then the princes took the king, and showed him the snake-pit where three babes lay playing with adders and toads, and lovelier children you never saw.

So the king had them taken out at once, and went to his step-mother, and asked her what punishment she thought that woman deserved who could find it in her heart to betray a guiltless queen and three such blessed little babes.

'She deserves to be fast bound between twelve unbroken steeds, so that each may take his share of her,' said the old queen.

'You have spoken your own doom,' said the king, 'and you shall suffer it at once.'

So the wicked old queen was fast bound between twelve unbroken steeds, and each got his share of her. But the king took Snow-white and Rosy-red, and their three children, and the twelve princes, and so they all went home to their father and mother and told all that had befallen them, and there was joy and gladness over the whole king-dom, because the princess was saved and set free, and because she had set free her twelve brothers.

OLD FOSTER

(HILLBILLY: USA)

hey use to be an old man, he lived way over in the forest by hisself, and all he lived on was he caught women and boiled 'em in front of the fire and eat 'em. Now the way my mother told me, he'd go into the villages and tell 'em this and that and get 'em to come out and catch 'em and jest boil they breasts. That's what she told me, and then I've heard hit that he jest eat 'em. Well, they was a beautiful stout woman, he liked 'em the best (he'd a been right atter me un your mother) so every day he'd come over to this woman's house and he'd tell her to please come over to see his house. 'Why, Mr Foster, I can't find the way.' 'Yes, you can. I'll take a spool of red silk thread out of my pocket and I'll start windin' hit on the bushes and it'll carry ye straight to my house.' So she promised him one day she'd come.

So she got her dinner over one day and she started. So she follered the red silk thread and went on over to his house. When she got there, there was a poor little old boy sittin' over the fire a boilin' meat. And he says, 'Laws, Aunt' – she was his aunt – 'what er you doin' here? Foster kills every woman that comes here. You leave here jest as quick as you can.'

She started to jump out the door and she saw Foster a comin' with two young women, one under each arm. So she run back and says, 'Jack, honey, what'll I do, I see him a comin'?' 'Jump in that old closet under the stair and I'll lock you in,' says Jack.

So she jumped in and Jack locked her in. So Foster come in and he was jest talkin' and a laughin' with those two girls and tellin' the most tales, and he was goin' to taken 'em over to a corn shuckin' next day. Foster says, 'Come on in and have supper with me.' So Jack put up some boiled meat and water. That's all they had. As soon as the girls

stepped in and seed the circumstance and seed their time had come
their countenance fell. Foster says, 'You better come in and eat, maybe
the last chance you'll ever have.' Girls both jumped up and started to
run. Foster jumps up and ketched 'em, and gets his tomihawk and
starts upstairs with 'em. Stairs was shackly and rattly, and as they
went up one of the girls retched her hand back and caught hold of a
step and Foster jest tuck his tomihawk and hacked her hand off. It
drapped into whar my mother was. She laid on in there until next day
atter Foster went, then Jack let her out.

She jest bird worked over to where the corn shuckin' was. When
she got there Foster was there. She didn't know how to git Foster
destroyed. The people thought these people got out in the forest and
the wild animals ud ketch 'em. So she says, 'I dreamt an awful dream
last night. I dreamed I lived close to Foster's house and he was always
a-wantin' me to come to his house.'

Foster says, 'Well, that ain't so, and it shan't be so, and God forbid
it ever should be so.'

She went right on, 'And I dreamt he put out a red thread and I

follered hit to his house and there uz Jack broilin' women's breasts in
front of the fire.'

Foster says, 'Well, that ain't so, and it shan't be so, and God forbid
it ever should be so.'

She went right on, 'And he says, "What er you doin' here! Foster
kills every woman uz comes here."'

Foster says, 'Well, that ain't so, and it shan't be so, and God forbid
it ever should be so.'

She went right on, 'And I seed Foster a-comin' with two girls. And
when they git thar the girls their hearts failed 'em and Foster ketched
'em and gets his tomihawk and starts up stairs with 'em.'

Foster says, 'Well, that ain't so, and it shan't be so, and God forbid
it ever should be so.'

She went right on, 'The stairs was shackly and rattly and as they
went up, one of the girls retched her hand back and caught hold of a
step and Foster jest tuk his tomihawk and hacked her hand off.'

Foster says, 'Well, that ain't so, and it shan't be so, and God forbid
it ever should be so.'

She says, 'Hit is so, and it shall be so and here I've got the hand to
show.'

And they knowed the two girls was missin' and they knowed it was
so, so they lynched Foster and then they went and got Jack and bound
him out.

ŠĀHĪN

(PALESTINIAN ARAB)

nce there was a king (and there is no kingship except that which belongs to Allah, may He be praised and exalted!) and he had an only daughter. He had no other children, and he was proud of her. One day, as she was lounging about, the daughter of the vizier came to visit her. They sat together, feeling bored.

'We're sitting around here feeling bored,' said the daughter of the vizier. 'What do you say to going out and having a good time?'

'Yes,' said the other.

Sending for the daughters of the ministers and dignitaries of state, the king's daughter gathered them all together, and they went into her father's orchard to take the air, each going her own way.

As the vizier's daughter was sauntering about, she stepped on an iron ring. Taking hold of it, she pulled, and behold! it opened the door to an underground hallway, and she descended into it. The other girls, meanwhile, were distracted, amusing themselves. Going into the hallway, the vizier's daughter came upon a young man with his sleeves rolled up. And what! there were deer, partridges, and rabbits in front of him, and he was busy plucking and skinning.

Before he was aware of it, she had already saluted him. 'Peace to you!'

'And to you, peace!' he responded, taken aback. 'What do you happen to be, sister, human or jinn?'

'Human,' she answered, 'and the choicest of the race. What are you doing here?'

'By Allah,' he said, 'we are forty young men, all brothers. Every day my brothers go out to hunt in the morning and come home toward evening. I stay home and prepare their food.'

'That's fine,' she chimed in. 'You're forty young men, and we're forty young ladies. I'll be your wife, the king's daughter is for your eldest brother, and all the other girls are for all your other brothers.' She matched the girls with the men.

Oh! How delighted he was to hear this!

'What's your name?'

'Šāhīn,' he answered.

'Welcome, Šāhīn.'

He went and fetched a chair, and set it in front of her. She sat next to him, and they started chatting. He roasted some meat, gave it to her, and she ate. She kept him busy until the food he was cooking was ready.

'Šāhīn,' she said when the food was ready, 'you don't happen to have some seeds and nuts in the house, do you?'

'Yes, by Allah, we do.'

'Why don't you get us some. It'll help pass away the time.'

In their house, the seeds and nuts were stored on a high shelf. He got up, brought a ladder, and climbed up to the shelf. Having filled his handkerchief with seeds and nuts, he was about to come down when she said, 'Here, let me take it from you. Hand it over!' Taking the handkerchief from him, she pulled the ladder away and threw it to the ground, leaving him stranded on the shelf.

She then brought out large bowls, prepared a huge platter, piled all the food on it, and headed straight out of there, taking the food with her and closing the door of the tunnel behind her. Putting the food under a tree, she called to the girls, 'Come eat, girls!'

'Eh! Where did this come from?' they asked, gathering around.

'Just eat and be quiet,' she replied. 'What more do you want? Just eat!'

The food was prepared for forty lads, and here were forty lasses. They set to and ate it all.

'Go on along now!' commanded the vizier's daughter. 'Each one back where she came from. Disperse!'

She dispersed them, and they went their way. Waiting until they were all busy, she took the platter back, placing it where it was before and coming back out again. In time the girls all went home.

Now we go back. To whom? To Šāhīn. When his brothers came home in the evening, they could not find him.

'Oh Šāhīn,' they called. 'Šāhīn!'

And behold! he answered them from the shelf.

'Hey! What are you doing up there?' asked the eldest brother.

'By Allah, brother,' Šāhīn answered, 'I set up the ladder after the food was ready and came to get some seeds and nuts for passing away the time. The ladder slipped, and I was stranded up here.'

'Very well,' they said, and set up the ladder for him. When he came down, the eldest brother said, 'Now, go bring the food so we can have dinner.' Gathering up the game they had hunted that day, they put it all in one place and sat down.

Šāhīn went to fetch the food from the kitchen, but he could not find a single bite.

'Brother,' he said, coming back, 'the cats must have eaten it.'

'All right,' said the eldest. 'Come, prepare us whatever you can.'

Taking the organs of the hunted animals, from this and that he made dinner and they ate. Then they laid their heads down and went to sleep.

The next morning they woke up and set out for the hunt. 'Now brother,' they mocked him, 'be sure to let us go without dinner another evening. Let the cats eat it all!'

'No, brothers,' he said. 'Don't worry.'

No sooner did they leave than he rolled up his sleeves and set to skinning and plucking the gazelles, rabbits and partridges. On time, the vizier's daughter showed up. Having gone to the king's daughter and gathered all the other girls, she waited till they were amusing themselves with something and then dropped in on him.

'Salaam!'

'And to you, peace!' he answered. 'Welcome to the one who took the food and left me stranded on the shelf, making me look ridiculous to my brothers!'

'What you say is true,' she responded. 'And yet I'm likely to do even more than that to the one I love.'

'And as for me,' he murmured, 'your deeds are sweeter than honey.'

Fetching a chair, he set it down for her, and then he brought some seeds and nuts. They sat down to entertain themselves, and she kept him amused until she realised the food was ready.

'Šāhīn,' she said, 'isn't there a bathroom in your house?'

'Yes, there is,' he replied.

'I'm pressed, and must go to the bathroom. Where is it?'

'It's over there,' he answered.

'Well, come and show it to me.'

'This is it, here,' he said, showing it to her.

She went in and, so the story goes, made as if she did not know how to use it.

'Come and show me how to use this thing,' she called.

I don't know what else she said, but he came to show her, you might say, how to sit on the toilet. Taking hold of him, she pushed him inside like this, and he ended up with his head down and his feet up. She closed the door on him and left. Going into the kitchen, she served up the food on to a platter and headed out of there. She put the food under a tree and called to her friends, 'Come eat!'

'And where did you get all this?'

'All you have to do is eat,' she answered.

They ate and scattered, each going her way. And she stole away and returned the platter.

At the end of the day the brothers came home, and there was no sign of their brother. 'Šāhīn, Šāhīn!' they called out. 'O Šāhīn!' But no answer came. They searched the shelf, they searched here, and they searched there. But it was no use.

'You know,' said the eldest, 'I say there's something odd about Šāhīn's behaviour. I suspect he has a girlfriend. Anyway, some of you go into the kitchen, find the food, and bring it so we can eat. I'm sure Šāhīn will show up any moment.'

Going into the kitchen, they found nothing. 'There's no food,' they reported. 'It's all gone! We're now sure that Šāhīn has a girlfriend, and he gives her all the food. Let's go ahead and fix whatever there is at hand so we can eat.'

Having prepared a quick meal, they ate dinner and were content. They prepared for sleep, but one of them (All respect to the listeners!) was pressed and needed to relieve himself. He went to the bathroom, and lo! there was Šāhīn, upside down.

'Hey, brothers!' he shouted. 'Here's Šāhīn, and he's fallen into the toilet!'

They rushed over and lifted him out. What a condition he was in! They gave him a bath.

'Tell me,' said the eldest, 'what's going on?'

'By Allah, brother,' replied Šāhīn, 'after I cooked dinner I went to relieve myself, and I slipped.'

'Very well,' returned the eldest. 'But the food, where is it?'

'By Allah, as far as I know it's in the kitchen, but how should I know if the cats haven't eaten it?'

'Well, all right!' they said, and went back to sleep.

The next morning, as they were setting out, they mocked him again. 'Why don't you leave us without dinner another night?'

'No, brothers!' he said. 'Don't worry.'

Pulling themselves together, they departed. Now, on time, the daughter of the vizier came to see the king's daughter, gathered the others, and they came down to the orchard and spread out. Waiting until they were all caught up with something, she slipped away to him, and listen, brothers! she found him at home.

'Salaam!'

'And to you, peace!' he retorted. 'Welcome! On the shelf the first day, and you made away with the food; and the second day you threw me into the toilet and stole the food, blackening my face in front of my brothers!'

'As for me,' she said, 'I'll do even more than that to the one I love.'

'And to me, it's sweeter than honey,' he responded, bringing her a chair. She sat down, he brought seeds and nuts, and they passed away the time entertaining themselves. She kept chatting with him, until she knew the food was ready.

'Šāhīn,' she said.

'Yes.'

'Don't you have some drinks for us to enjoy ourselves? There's meat here, and seeds and nuts. We could eat and have something to drink.'

'Yes,' he replied, 'we do.'

'Why don't you bring some out, then?' she urged him.

Bringing a bottle, he set it in front of her. She poured drinks and handed them to him. 'This one's to my health,' she egged him on, 'and this one's also for my sake,' until he fell over, as if no one were there. She then went and took some sugar, put it on to boil, and made a preparation for removing body hair. She used it on him to perfection, and, brother, she made him look like the most beautiful of girls. Bringing a woman's dress, she put it on him. Then, bringing a scarf, she wrapped it around his head and laid him down to sleep in bed. She powdered his face, wrapped the scarf well around his head, put the bed covers over him, and left. Then into the kitchen she went, loaded the food, and departed. The girls ate, and the platter was replaced.

When the brothers returned in the evening, they did not find Šāhīn at home.

'O Šāhīn! Šāhīn! Šāhīn!'

No answer. 'Let's search the bathroom,' they said among themselves. But they did not find him there. They searched the shelf, and still no sign of him.

'Didn't I tell you Šāhīn has a girlfriend?' the eldest declared. 'I'd say Šāhīn has a girlfriend and goes out with her. Some of you, go and see if the food's still there.' They did, and found nothing.

Again they resorted to a quick meal of organ meat. When it was time to sleep, each went to his bed. In his bed, the eldest found our well-contented friend stretched out in it. Back to his brothers he ran. 'I told you Šāhīn has a girlfriend, but you didn't believe me. Come and take a look! Here's Šāhīn's bride' Come and see! Come and see!'

He called his brothers, and they all came, clamouring, 'Šāhīn's bride!' Removing his scarf, they looked at him carefully. Eh! A man's features are hard to miss. They recognised him. 'Eh! This is Šāhīn!' they shouted. Bringing water, they splashed his face till he woke up. Looking himself over, what did he find? They fetched a mirror. He looked at himself, and what a sight he was – all rouged, powdered and beautified.

'And now,' they asked him, 'what do you have to say for yourself?'

'By Allah, brother,' answered Šāhīn, 'listen and I'll tell you the truth. Every day, around noon, a girl with such and such features comes to see me. She says, "We're forty young ladies. The king's daughter is for your eldest brother, I am yours, and all the other girls are for all your other brothers." She's the one who's been doing these things to me every day.'

'Is that so?'

'Yes, it is.'

'Fine. All of you go to the hunt tomorrow,' suggested the eldest, and I'll stay behind with Šāhīn. I'll take care of her!'

Pulling out his sword (so the story goes), he sat waiting in readiness. By Allah, brothers, in due time she came. She had gathered the girls as usual, and they had come down to the orchard. Waiting until their attention was caught, she slipped away to him. Before he was even aware of her, she had already saluted him.

'Salaam!'

'And to you, peace!' he answered. 'The first item on the shelf, and I said all right; the second time in the bathroom, and I said all right; but the third time you put make-up on me and turned me into a bride!'

'And yet I'm likely to do even more than that to the one I love.'

No sooner had she said that than up rose the eldest brother and rushed over to her, his sword at the ready.

'Listen,' she reasoned with him. 'You are forty, and we are forty. The king's daughter is to be your wife, and I, Šāhīn's; and so and so among us is for so and so among you, and so on.' She calmed him down.

'Is it true, what you're saying?' he asked.

'Of course it's true,' she replied.

'And who can speak for these girls?'

'I can.'

'You're the one who can speak for them?'

'Yes.'

(Šāhīn, meanwhile, was listening, and since he was already experienced, he mused to himself that his brother had been taken in already.)

'Agreed,' said the eldest brother. 'Come over here and let me pay you the bridewealth for the forty girls. Where are we to meet you?'

'First pay me the bridewealth,' she answered, 'and tomorrow, go and reserve a certain public bath for us at your expense. Stand guard at the gate, and as we go in you yourself can count us one by one – all forty of us. We'll go into the baths and bathe, and after we come out each of you will take his bride home by the hand.'

'Just like that?' he wondered.

'Of course,' she assured him.

He brought out a blanket, she spread it, and – count, count, count – he counted one hundred Ottoman gold coins for each girl. When he had finished counting out the money, she took it and went straight out. Calling her friends over, she said, 'Sit here! Sit under this tree! Each of you open your hand and receive your bridewealth.'

'Eh!' they protested, 'You so and so! Did you ruin your reputation?'

'No one's to say anything,' she responded. 'Each of you will take her bridewealth without making a sound.' Giving each of them her money, she said, 'Come. Let's go home.'

After she had left their place, Šāhīn said to his brother, 'Brother, she tricked me and took only the food. But she tricked you and got away with our money.'

'Who, me?' the brother declared, 'Trick me? Tomorrow you'll see.'

The next day the brothers stayed at home. They went and reserved the baths at their own expense, and the eldest stood watch at the door, waiting for the girls to arrive. Meanwhile, the vizier's daughter had got up the next day, gathered all the girls, the king's daughter among them, and, leading them in front of her, headed for the bath with them. And behold! there was our *effendi* guarding the door. As they were going in, he counted them one by one. Count, count, he counted them all – exactly forty.

Going into the baths, the girls bathed and enjoyed themselves. But after they had finished bathing and put on their clothes, she, the clever one, gave them this advice: 'Each of you is to shit in the tub she has bathed in, and let's line the tubs up all in a row.' Each of them shat in her tub, and they arranged them neatly in a row, all forty of them. Now, the baths had another door, away from the entrance. 'Follow me this way,' urged the vizier's daughter, and they all hurried out.

The eldest brother waited an hour, two, three, then four, but the girls did not emerge. 'Eh!' he said. 'They're taking a long time about it.'

'Brother,' said Šāhīn, 'they're gone.'

'But listen!' he replied, 'where could she have gone? They all went inside the bath-house together.'

'All right,' said Šāhīn, 'let's go in and see.'

Going into the bath-house, brother, they found the owner inside.

'Where did the girls who came into the bath-house go?'

'O uncle!' replied the owner, 'they've been gone a long time.'

'And how could they have left?' asked the eldest brother.

'They left by that door,' he replied.

Now, Šāhīn, who was experienced, looked in the bathing place and saw the tubs all lined up.

'Brother!' he called out.

'Yes. What is it?'

'Come here and take a look,' he answered. 'Here are the forty! Take a good look! See how she had them arranged so neatly?'

Finally the brothers went back home, wondering to themselves, 'And now, what are we going to do?'

'Leave them to me!' volunteered Šāhīn. 'I'll take care of them.'

The next day Šāhīn disguised himself as an old lady. Wearing an old woman's dress, he put a beaded rosary around his neck and headed for the city. The daughter of the vizier, meanwhile, had gathered the girls, and she was sitting with them in a room above the street. As he was coming from afar, she saw and recognised him. She winked to her friends, saying, 'I'll go call him, and you chime in with, "Here's our aunt! Welcome to our aunt!"' As soon as she saw him draw near, she opened the door and came out running. 'Welcome, welcome, welcome to our aunty! Welcome, aunty!' And, taking him by the hand, she pulled him inside to where they were. 'Welcome to our aunty!' they clamoured, locking the door. 'Welcome to our aunty!'

'Now, girls, take off your clothes,' urged the vizier's daughter. 'Take off your clothes. It's been a long time since we've had our clothes washed by our aunty's own hands. Let her wash our clothes!'

'By Allah, I'm tired,' protested Šāhīn. 'By Allah, I can't do it.'

'By Allah, you must do it, aunty,' they insisted. 'It's been such a long time since we've had our clothes washed by our aunty's hands.'

She made all forty girls take off their clothes, each of them leaving on only enough to cover her modesty, and she handed the clothes to him. He washed clothes till noon.

'Come girls,' said the vizier's daughter. 'By Allah, it's been such a long time since our aunty has bathed us with her own hands. Let her bathe us!'

Each of them put on a wrap and sat down, and he went around bathing them in turn. By the time he had finished bathing them all, what a condition he was in! He was exhausted.

When he had finished with one, she would get up and put on her clothes. The vizier's daughter would then wink at her and whisper that she should take the wrap she was wearing, fold it over, twist it, and tie a knot at one end so that it was like a whip.

When all forty girls had finished bathing, the leader spoke out, 'Eh, aunty! Hey girls, she has just bathed us, and we must bathe her in return.'

'No, niece!' he protested. 'I don't need a bath! For the sake of . . .'

'Impossible, aunty!' insisted the vizier's daughter. 'By Allah, this can't be. Eh! You bathe and bathe all of us, and we don't even bathe you in return. Come, girls!'

At a wink from her, they set on him against his will. They were forty. What could he do? They took hold of him and removed his clothes, and lo and behold! he was a man.

'Eh!' they exclaimed. 'This isn't our aunty. It's a man! Have at him, girls!'

And with their whips, each of them having braided her robe and tied knots in it, they put Šāhīn in the middle and descended on his naked body. Hit him from here, turn him around there, and beat him again on the other side! All the while he was jumping among them and shouting at the top of his voice. When she thought he had had enough, she winked at them to clear a path. As soon as he saw his way open, he opened the door and dashed out running, wearing only the skin the Lord had given him.

His brothers were at home, and before they were even aware of it, he showed up, naked. And what a condition he was in! Up they sprang, as if possessed. 'Hey! What happened to you?' they asked. 'Come! Come! What hit you?'

'Wait a minute,' he answered. 'Such and such happened to me.'

'And now,' they asked among themselves, 'what can we do?'

'Now, by Allah,' answered Šāhīn, 'we have no recourse but for each of us to ask for the hand of his bride from her father. As for me, I'm going to ask for her hand. But as soon as she arrives here, I'm going to kill her. No other punishment will do. I'll show her!'

They all agreed, each going to ask for his bride's hand from her father, and the fathers gave their consent.

Now, the daughter of the minister was something of a devil. She asked her father, if anyone should come asking for her hand, not to give his consent before letting her know. When Šāhīn came to propose, the father said, 'Not until I consult with my daughter first.' The father went to consult with his daughter, and she said, 'All right, give your consent, but on condition that there be a waiting period of one month so that the bridegroom can have enough time to buy the wedding clothes and take care of all the other details.'

After the asking for her hand was completed, the minister's daughter waited until her father had left the house. She then went and put on one of his suits, wrapped a scarf around the lower part of her face, and, taking a whip with her, headed for the carpenter's workshop.

'Carpenter!'

'Yes, Your Excellency!'

'In a while I'll be sending you a concubine. You will observe her height and make a box to fit her. I want it ready by tomorrow. Otherwise, I'll have your head cut off. And don't hold her here for two hours!'

'No, sir. I won't.'

She lashed him twice and left, going directly – where? To the halva maker's shop.

'Halva maker!'

'Yes.'

'I'm going to be sending you a concubine momentarily. You will observe her. See her shape and her height. You must make me a halva doll that looks exactly like her. And don't you keep her here for a couple of hours or I'll shorten your life!'

'Your order, O minister,' said the man, 'will be obeyed.'

She lashed him twice with the whip and left. She went and changed, putting on her ordinary clothes, then went to the carpenter's shop and stayed a while. After that she went and stood by the halva maker's shop for a while. Then she went straight home. Changing back into her father's suit, she took the whip with her and went to the carpenter.

'Carpenter!'

'Yes, my lord minister!'

'An ostrich shorten your life!' responded the girl. 'I send you the concubine, and you hold her here for two hours!'

She descended on him with the whip, beating him all over.

'Please, sir!' he pleaded, 'it was only because I wanted to make sure the box was an exact fit.'

Leaving him alone, she headed for the halva maker's. Him too, she whipped several times, and then she returned home.

The next day she sent for her slave and said to him, 'Go bring the wooden box from the carpenter's shop to the halva maker's. Put the halva doll in it, lock it, and bring it to me here.'

'Yes, I'll do it,' he answered.

When the box was brought, she took it in and said to her mother, 'Listen, mother! I'm going to leave this box with you in trust. When the time comes to take me out of the house and to load up and bring along my trousseau, you must have this box brought with the trousseau and placed in the same room where I will be.'

'But, dear daughter!' protested the mother, 'what will people say? The minister's daughter is bringing a wooden box with her trousseau! You will become a laughing-stock.' I don't know what else she said but it was no use.

'This is not your concern,' insisted the daughter. 'That's how I want it.'

When the bridegroom's family came to take the bride out of her father's house, she was made ready, and the wooden box was brought along with her trousseau. They took the wooden box and, as she had told them, placed it in the same room where she was to be. As soon as she came into the room and the box was brought in, she threw out all the women. 'Go away!' she said. 'Each of you must go home now.'

After she had made everyone leave, she locked the door. Then, dear ones, she took the doll out of the box. Taking off her clothes, she put them on the doll, and she placed her gold around its neck. She then set the doll in her own place on the bridal seat, tied a string around its neck, and went and hid under the bed, having first unlocked the door.

Her husband, meanwhile, was taking his time. He stayed away an hour or two before he came in. What kind of mood do you think he was in when he arrived? He was in a foul humour, his sword in hand, ready to kill her, as if he did not want to marry her in the first place. As soon as he passed over the doorstep, he looked in and saw her on the bridal seat.

'Yes, yes!' he reproached her. 'The first time you abandoned me on the shelf and took the food, I said to myself it was all right. The second time you threw me into the toilet and took the food, and I said all right. The third time you removed my body hair and made me look like a bride, taking the food with you, and even then I said to myself it was all right. After all that, you still weren't satisfied. You tricked us all and took the bridewealth for the forty girls, leaving each of us a turd in the washtub.'

Meanwhile, as he finished each accusation, she would pull the string and nod the doll's head.

'As if all that weren't enough for you,' he went on, 'you had to top it all with your aunty act. "Welcome, welcome, aunty! It's been a long time since we've seen our aunty. It's been such a long time since aunty has washed our clothes!" And you kept me washing clothes all day. And after all that, you insisted, "We must bathe aunty." By Allah, I'm going to burn the hearts of all your paternal and maternal aunties!'

Seeing her nod her head in agreement, he yelled, 'You mean you're not afraid? And you're not going to apologise?' Taking hold of his sword, he struck her a blow that made her head roll. A piece of halva (if the teller is not lying!) flew into his mouth. Turning it around in his mouth, he found it sweet.

'Alas, cousin!' he cried out. 'If in death you're so sweet, what would it have been like if you were still alive?'

As soon as she heard this, she jumped up from under the bed and rushed over to him, hugging him from behind.

'O cousin! Here I am!' she exclaimed. 'I'm alive!'

They consummated their marriage, and lived together happily.

This is my tale, I've told it; and in your hands I leave it.

THE DOG'S SNOUT PEOPLE

(LETTISH)

ong ago there lived in a forest country two peoples: people with dogs' snouts and good people. The former were hunters, and the latter tilled the soil. Once the dog's snout people, while hunting, caught a girl belonging to the good people; she did not come from an adjacent settlement, but from a distant village. The people with dogs' snouts took the girl home and fed her on nuts and sweet milk; then after a while, wishing to judge of her condition, they took a long needle and drove it into her forehead. They licked up the blood, as a bear licks honey from a hive. They fed the girl, till at last she seemed to be suitable for their purpose. 'She will be a delicious morsel!' they said, telling their mother to roast the girl while they were away hunting in the forest. The oven had already been heating for two days. The men's mother now sent the girl to a neighbouring farm for a shovel, upon which the victim could be thrown into the oven, but by chance the girl went for the shovel to a farm belonging to the good people. She arrived and said to their mother, 'Little mother, lend our woman with the dog's snout a shovel.' 'Why does she require a shovel?' 'I do not know.' 'You are a stupid girl,' said the mother of the good people. 'Do you not know that the oven is being heated for you? In carrying the shovel you will be assisting your own death, but I will instruct you, little daughter. Take the shovel with you, and when the woman with the dog's snout says, "Lie upon the shovel!" then lie upon it crossways; and when she says, "Lie more conveniently" beg her to show you how to take your position. As soon as she has lain down lengthways on the shovel throw her as quickly as possible into the oven, and shut the door so tight that she cannot open it. When you have done this strew around you some ashes, and taking off your bast shoes, put them on reversed, so that the front shall become the back and the back shall become the front; then run away with all your might; they will not find you by your traces! Take care that you do not fall into the hands of the dog's snout people, or there will be an end of you!'

The girl took the shovel and returned with it, and the dog's snout woman said to her, 'Lie down upon the shovel!' The girl lay crossways. Then the dog's snout woman said, 'Lie down lengthways; it will be better.' 'I do not understand,' said the girl; 'show me.' They disputed a long while, until the dog's snout woman lay down upon the shovel. The girl immediately seized it, thrust the woman rapidly into the oven and shut the door tight. Then she shod herself, as the mother of the good people had instructed her, and ran away. The dog's snout men came home and looked for their mother unsuccessfully. One said to another, 'Perhaps she has gone on a visit to her neighbours; let us see if the roast meat is ready!'

THE OLD WOMAN
AGAINST THE STREAM

(NORWEGIAN)

here was once a man who had an old wife, and she was so cross and contrary that she was hard to get along with. The man, in fact, didn't get along with her at all. Whatever *he* wanted, she always wanted the very opposite.

Now one Sunday in late summer it happened that the man and the wife went out to see how the crop was getting along. When they came to a field on the other side of the river, the man said, 'Well, now it's ripe. Tomorrow we'll have to start reaping.'

'Yes, tomorrow we can start to clip it,' said the old woman.

'What's that? Shall we clip? Aren't we going to be allowed to reap either, now?' said the man.

No, clip it they should, the old woman insisted.

'There's nothing worse than knowing too little,' said the man, 'but this time you certainly must have lost what little wits you had. Have you ever seen anyone *clip* the crop?'

'Little do I know, and little do I care to know,' said the old woman, 'but this I know to be sure: the crop is going to be clipped and not reaped!' There was nothing more to be said. Clip it they should, and that was that.

So they walked back, wrangling and quarrelling, until they came to a bridge over the river, just by a deep pool.

'It's an old saying,' said the man, 'that good tools do good work. But I dare say *that'll* be a queer harvest which they clip with sheepshears!' he said. 'Shan't we be allowed to reap the crop at all, now?'

'Nay, nay! – Clip, clip, clip!' shrieked the old woman, hopping up and down, and snipping at the man's nose with her fingers. But in her fury she didn't look where she was going, and she tripped over the end of a post in the bridge and tumbled into the river.

'Old ways are hard to mend,' thought the man, 'but it'd be nice if I were right for once – me too.'

He waded out in the pool and caught hold of the old woman's top-knot, just when her head was barely above the water. 'Well, are we going to reap the field?' he said.

'Clip, clip, clip!' shrieked the old woman.

'I'll teach you to clip, I will,' thought the man, and ducked her under. But it didn't help. They were going to clip, she said, when he let her up again.

'I can only believe that the old woman is mad!' said the man to himself. 'Many people are mad and don't know it; many have sense and don't show it. But now I'll have to try once more, all the same,' he said. But hardly had he pushed her under before she thrust her hand up out of the water, and started clipping with her fingers as with a pair of scissors.

Then the man flew into a rage, and ducked her both good and

long. But all at once her hand sank down below the surface of the water, and the old woman suddenly became so heavy that he had to let go his hold.

'If you want to drag me down into the pool with you now, you can just lie there, you Troll!' said the man. And so there the old woman stayed.

But after a little while, the man thought it a pity that she should lie there and not have a Christian burial. So he went down along the river, and started looking and searching for her. But for all he looked and for all he searched, he couldn't find her. He took with him folk from the farm, and other folk from the neighbourhood, and they all started digging and dragging down along the whole river. But for all they looked, no old woman did they find.

'No,' said the man. 'That's no use at all. This old woman had a mind of her own,' he said. 'She was so contrary while she was alive that she can't very well be otherwise now. We'll have to start searching upstream, and try above the falls. Maybe she's floated herself upstream.'

Well, they went upstream, and looked and searched above the falls. There lay the old woman!

She was *the old woman against the stream*, she was!

THE LETTER TRICK

(SURINAMESE)

There was a woman who had a husband. Well, then her husband was in the bush, and she had another man. But when her husband went to the city, then the other man said to her, said, 'If you love me, you must let me come sleep in your house.' Then she said to the man, said, 'All right. My husband is in the city, I will let you come. I am going to dress you in one of my skirts and blouses, and I am going to tell my husband that you are my sister from the plantation.' Then when she dressed him in

the dress, then that night he came there. And the woman told her husband this was her sister.

Then at night they went to sleep. But in the morning the woman went to the market because she sold things. Then the man lay down upstairs. But when the woman's husband saw she did not come down, then he went to look, and he saw a man. Then the man was angry. He took a stick and came running to the market towards the woman. But when the woman saw him coming, then the woman took a piece of paper, then she read and cried. Then, when the man came he said, 'What are you doing?' Then she made up a speech. 'Hm! I just received a letter that all my sisters on the plantation have changed into men.' Then the man said, 'They do not lie, because the one who came to sleep with you last night, that one, too, changed into a man.' But the man did not know how to read. That is why the woman deceived him with such a trick.

ROLANDO AND BRUNILDE

(ITALY: TUSCAN)

mother and her daughter lived in a village. The daughter was happy because she was engaged to a boy who lived in the same village, a woodcutter, and they were to be married within a few weeks. So she passed all her time helping her mother a little, working in the fields a little, gathering wood a little; and then in her free time she sat at the window and sang . . . as she spun. She spun and she sang, waiting for her fiancé to return from the forest.

One day, a magician passed through town, and he heard singing; she had a pretty voice. He turned around and saw this girl at the window. Seeing her and falling in love with her was one and the same for the magician And so he sent . . . he sent someone to ask if she would marry him. This prin . . . this girl said, 'No, because I am already engaged to be married. I have a fiancé and I am very fond of him,' she replied, 'and in a few weeks we are getting married,' she said, 'so I don't need a magician or these riches,' because he had told her that he would make her a rich lady because she was poor.

Then the magician, who had become indignant at her refusal, sent an eagle to kidnap the girl, who was called Brunilde, and it carried her to his castle where he showed her all his riches, all his castles, all his gold, all his money, but she didn't care about any of it. She said. 'I will marry Rolando and I want Rolando.' The magician then told her, 'If you don't marry me then you will never leave this castle.' And in fact he locked her up . . . he locked her in a room near his bedroom. Since the magician slept very soundly during the night and snored, for fear that someone would steal her he had an effigy made of himself as big as he was and then he had bells put on it, a thousand tiny bells, so that if anyone bumped into this effigy he would wake up.

Now, her mother and Rolando were worried because the girl didn't come home, and her fiancé wanted to go and kill the magician. But her mother said, 'No, wait, let's wait a little.' She said, 'If not, he could hurt you, too; let's wait a bit.' And they tried one night to get into the garden, but the magician had had a wall built that surrounded the garden and it was so tall that it was impossible to enter. And the girl's mother sat all day and cried.

Finally, one day when she was in the forest she came upon a fairy in the form of an old lady who said to her, 'Tell me, why are you crying so?' And the girl's mother told the old woman about her Brunilde and how she had been carried off. 'Listen,' the fairy said, 'listen, I don't have much power in this case because the magician is much more powerful than I. I can't do anything,' she said. 'However, I can help you,' and she told her that he had closed the girl in a room and that he had had an effigy made of himself. So she said, 'You can't go there because if one of those bells should ring, he'll wake up.' She said: 'Listen to what you should do. This is the season when the cotton falls from the trees. You should go every day and fill a bag with cotton. In the evening when Rolando comes home from the forest, you have him take the cotton to the castle and I'll help you crawl through a hole.' She said: 'I get the bag into the garden and you'll get inside the palace . . . into the castle. In the castle you must stuff a few bells each night with cotton. Until you have stuffed them all, so that they will not ring any more, then we'll see what we can do.' And, in fact, this poor woman said: 'Of course, I'll do it. It will take time but I'll do it gladly.'

So they talked to the young man. During the day the mother gathered the cotton while he went to work, and in the evening they took the bag of cotton to the castle, and the mother stuffed the bells. Until one night the bells had finally all been stuffed. She went back to the old woman in the forest and told her that the last bell had been stuffed that same evening. Then the old woman said, 'Take Rolando with you.' And so the young man was made to enter through the same door that was used to stuff the bells, and the old woman gave him a sword and told him that when they were near enough he should cut off the left ear of the magician. All the power of the magician lies in his left ear, she said . . . In fact they entered the castle and went to get the girl. And the young man went to cut off the magician's ear. After he cut off the ear, the left ear where all his power lay, the entire castle crumbled, everything crumbled. The young couple took all the gold, the silver, and everything that belonged to the magician. They became rich, they got married, and they lived happily ever after.

THE GREENISH BIRD

(MEXICAN)

here were three girls who were orphaned, and Luisa did much sewing. The other two said that they didn't like Luisa's kind of life. They would rather go to bars and such things. Well, that kind of women – gay women. So Luisa stayed home. She kept a jar of water on the window sill, and she sewed and sewed and sewed.

So then he came, the Greenish Bird that was an enchanted prince. And of course he liked Luisa a lot, so he would light there on the window sill and say, 'Luisa, raise your eyes to mine, and your troubles will be over.' But she wouldn't.

On another night he came and said, 'Luisa, give me a drink of water from your little jar.' But she wouldn't look to see if he was a bird or a man or anything. Except she didn't know whether he drank or not, but then she saw he was a man. She gave him some water. So then he came again and proposed to her, and they fell in love. And the bird would come inside; he would lie in her bed. There on the headboard. And he set up a garden for her, with many fruit trees and other things, and a messenger and a maid; so the girl was living in grand style.

What should happen but that her sisters found out. 'Just look at Luisa, how high she has gone overnight. And us,' one of the sisters says, 'just look at us the way we are. Let's spy on her and see who it is that goes in there.' They went and spied on her and saw it was a bird, so they bought plenty of knives. And they put them on the window sill. When the little bird came out, he was wounded all over.

He said, 'Luisa, if you want to follow me, I live in crystal towers on the plains of Merlin. I'm badly wounded,' he said.

So she bought a pair of iron shoes, Luisa did, and she took some clothes with her – what she could carry walking – and a guitar she had.

And she went off after him. She came to the house where the Sun's mother lived. She was a blonde, blonde old woman. Very ugly. So she got there and knocked on the door and it opened. The old woman said, 'What are you doing here? If my son the Sun sees you, he'll devour you,' she said.

'I'm searching for the Greenish Bird,' she said.

'He was here. Look, he's badly wounded. He left a pool of blood there, and he just left a moment ago.'

She said, 'All right, then, I'm going.'

'No,' she said, 'hide and let's see if my son can tell you something. He shines on all the world,' she said.

So he came in, very angry:

> *Whoo! Whoo!*
> *I smell human flesh. Whoo-whoo!*
> *If I can't have it, I'll eat you.*

He said this to his mother.

'What do you want me to do, son? There's nobody here.' She calmed him down and gave him food. Then she told him, little by little.

He said, 'Where's the girl,' he said. 'Let her come out so I can see her.' So Luisa came out and asked him about the Greenish Bird. He said, 'Me, I don't know. I haven't heard of him. I don't know where to find him. I haven't seen anything like that, either. It could be that the Moon's mother, or the Moon herself, would know,' he said.

Well then, 'All right, I'm going now.' Without tasting a bite of food. So then the Sun told her to eat first and then go. And so then they gave her something to eat, and she left.

All right, so she got to the house where the Moon's mother lived. And so, 'What are you doing here? If my daughter the Moon sees you, she will devour you.' And I don't know how many other things the old woman said to her.

'Well then, I'll go. I just wanted to ask her if she hadn't seen the Greenish Bird pass by here.

He was here. Look, there's the blood; he's very badly wounded,' she said.

All right, so she started to go away, but the Moon said, '*Hombre*, don't go. Come eat first, and then you can go.' So they also gave her a bite to eat. As soon as they gave her something, she left. 'Why don't you go where the mother of the Wind lives and wait for the Wind to come home? The Wind goes into every nook and cranny; there isn't a place he doesn't visit.'

The mother of the Wind said, 'All right,' so she hid. She said, 'But you'll have to hide, because if my son the Wind sees you, Heaven help us.'

'All right,' she said.

The Wind came home, all vapoury and very angry, and his mother told him to behave, to take a seat, to sit down and have something to eat. So he quieted down. And then the girl told him that she was looking for the Greenish Bird.

But no. 'I can't tell you anything about that. I've never seen anything,' he said.

Well, so the girl went out again, but they gave her breakfast first and all that. The thing is that by the time she did find out, she had worn out the iron shoes she was wearing. It happened that there was an old hermit way out there, who tended to all the birds. He would call them by blowing on a whistle, and they would all come, and all kinds of animals, too. So she went there, too. And he asked her what she was doing out there, in those lonely wilds, and this and that. So she told the hermit, 'I'm in search of the Greenish Bird. Don't you know where he lives?'

'No,' he said. 'What I do know is that he was here. And he's badly wounded. But let me call my birds, and it may be that they know or have heard where he is, or something.'

Well, no. All the birds were called, but the old eagle was missing. The old eagle was right in the middle of it, eating tripe. The prince was to be married, but he had prayed to God that he would get leprosy, something like sores, and he was ill with sores. He was hoping Luisa would get there. But they were getting ready to marry him. The bride was a princess and very rich, but even so he didn't love her. He wanted to wait for his Luisa. Well then, so the old eagle was missing. The old man, the hermit, began blowing and blowing on his whistle until she came.

'What do you want, *hombre*? There I was, peacefully eating tripe, and you have to carry on like that, with all that blowing.'

'Wait, don't be mean.' he said. 'There's a poor girl here looking for the Greenish Bird. She says she's his sweetheart and is going to marry him.'

'She's looking for the Greenish Bird? The Greenish Bird is about to get married. The only reason he hasn't married yet is that he's very sick of some sores. Hmm, yes. But the wedding feast is going on, and the bride's mother is there and everything. But, anyway, if she wants to go, it's all right. I just came from there. I was there eating tripe and guts and all that stuff they throw away. If she wants to go, all she has to do is butcher me a cow, and we'll go.'

The girl heard, and she was very happy, even if he was getting married and all that. The hermit called her, and she came out, and she saw all kinds of birds. And he said, 'The old eagle says that if you butcher a cow, she will take you all the way to the very palace.'

All right, she said she would. For she had plenty of money with her. The bird had made her well off from the beginning. He would have married her then and there, if it hadn't been for those bratty sisters of hers. So all right, so they did go. She slaughtered the cow, and the eagle took her and the cow on her back. She would fly high, high, high; and then she would start coming down.

'Give me a leg,' she would say. And she would eat the meat. That's why we say a person is 'an old eagle' when they ask for meat. She would give her meat. And, 'What do you see?'

'Nothing,' she would say. 'You can't see anything yet. It's a very pretty palace made of nothing but glass. It will shine in the sun,' the eagle would say. 'I don't see anything yet.' And she would keep on going, straight, straight ahead, who knows how far. And then she would fly up, and up, and up.

'What do you see?'

'Well, something like a peak that shines. But it's very far away.'

'Yes, it's very far.'

So the cow was all eaten up, and still they didn't get there. And she said she wanted more meat. Luisa said, 'Here, take the knife.' She told the eagle that. 'Cut off one of my legs, or I'll cut it off myself,' Luisa told the eagle. But she didn't say it wholeheartedly, of course. Not a chance.

Anyway the eagle said, 'No, no. I only said it to test you. I'm going to leave you just outside because there are many cops around – or something like that – guarding the doors. You ask permission to go in from one of them. Tell them to let the ladies know you are coming in to cook. Don't ask for anything else,' she said. 'Get a job as a cook and then, well, we'll see how things go for you.'

All right, so she left Luisa just outside the yard. It was a great big yard made of pure gold or God knows what. As beautiful as could be. She asked the guard to let her in. 'And what is your reason for going in? What are you going to do?'

She said. 'Well. I'm very poor, and I've come from a long way off. And I'm looking for work. Anything I can do to eat, no matter if it is working in the kitchen.' And her carrying a golden comb, and all that the Greenish Bird had given her. And the guitar.

'Let me go ask the mistress,' he said, to see if they want to hire some kitchen help.' So he went and told her, 'A woman is looking for work.' And who knows what else.

'What kind of woman is she?'

'Well, she is like this, and this way, and that way.'

'All right, tell her to come in, and have her go around that way, so she won't come in through here in the palace,' she said. She didn't want her to go through the house.

So she went over there. And everybody was very kind to her. Meanwhile the Greenish Bird was a person now, but he was all leprous and very sick. There was a little old woman who had raised him. She was the one who took care of him. They had her there as a servant. First she had raised the boy, when she worked for his parents. Then she had moved over here, to the bride's house. She was no bride when the old woman first came there, but the girl had fallen in love with him. But he loved his Luisa.

And well, the wedding feast was in full swing, you might say, and he began to feel much better, for he heard a guitar being played, and he asked the old woman why they hadn't told him there were strangers in the house.

And when he heard the guitar, he told the woman who was taking care of him, who came to see him when he was sick, 'Who is singing and playing the guitar?'

'Oh, I had forgotten to tell you. A lady came wearing a pair of worn-out iron shoes, and she also has a guitar and a comb.'

'Is there anything on the comb?'

'Well, I don't know.' She couldn't read any more than I can.

'I don't know what's on it. They look like little wreaths or letters or I don't know what.'

'Ask her to lend it to you and bring it here.' And once he heard about the guitar, once he heard the guitar playing and all, he began to get well. He got much better. But neither the mother and father of the girl nor anybody else came to see him there.

He was all alone with the woman who took care of him. Because he looked very ugly. But then the woman went and told the princess who was going to be his mother-in-law, 'You should see how much better the prince is, the Greenish Bird. He is quite well now.'

So they all came to see him. And that made him angrier yet, because they came to see him now that he was well. The girl was very rich and a princess and all that, and Luisa was a poor little thing. But he said, 'Go ask her to lend you her comb and bring it to me.'

The old woman went and asked for the comb as if she wanted to comb her hair, and she went back where he was. He didn't say anything; he just looked at it.

'What do you say?'

'No, nothing,' he said. 'Tomorrow, or this afternoon, when they bring me food, have her bring it to me. She's working here, after all,' he said.

So when it was time to take him his dinner, she said, 'Listen, Luisa, go take the prince his dinner. I'm very tired now. I'm getting old.' Luisa didn't want to go; she was putting on. She hung back and she hung back, but at last she went.

Well, they greeted each other and saw each other and everything. And she said, 'Well, so you are already engaged and are going to get married,' Luisa said. 'And one cannot refuse anything to kings and princes.'

'But I have an idea, ever since I heard the guitar,' said the boy.

'What is it?'

'Everybody is going to make chocolate, and the cup I drink, I'll marry the one who made it.'

And she says, 'But I don't even know how to make chocolate!'

The old woman said she would make it for her, the woman who was taking care of him. Because Luisa went and told her about it. 'Just imagine what the prince wants. For all of us to come in, cooks and no cooks and absolutely all the women here, princesses and all. And each one of us must make a cup of chocolate, and the cup he drinks, he'll marry the woman who made it.' And she said. 'I don't know how . . .'

'Now, now,' said the old woman, 'don't worry about that. I'll make it for you. And you can take it to him.'

Well, the first to come in were all the big shots, as is always the case. First the bride, then the mother-in-law, the father-in-law, sisters-in-law, and everybody. And all he said was, 'I don't like it. I don't like it.'

The mother-in-law said, 'Now, I wonder who he wants to marry?' And, 'I wonder who he wants to marry?'

Well . . . nobody. So then the old woman who took care of him came. Neither. Then the other cook went in. And Luisa was the last one. He told them that she was the one he wanted to marry. That she had come searching for him from very far away, and that he would marry her. And he drank all of Luisa's cup of chocolate. Bitter or not, he didn't care. And he married her. And *colorin* so red, the story is finished.

THE CRAFTY WOMAN

(LITHUANIAN)

man and his young wife, who had settled down to life in a village, agreed so well that neither of them pronounced a single unpleasant word, they only caressed and kissed each other. For fully six months the Devil did his best to make the pair quarrel, but, at last, irritated by continued failure, he expressed his rage by making a disagreeable noise in his throat and made ready to depart. However, an old woman who was roaming about met him and said, 'Why are you annoyed?' The Devil explained, and the woman, on the understanding that she would receive some new bast shoes and a pair of boots, endeavoured to make the young couple disagree. She went to the wife while the husband was at work in the fields and, having begged for alms, said, 'Ah, my dear! how pretty and good you are! Your husband ought to love you from the depths of his soul. I know you live more amicably than any other couple in the world, but, my daughter! I will teach you to be yet happier. Upon your husband's head, at the very summit, are a few grey hairs, you must cut them off, taking care that he does not notice what you are about.'

'But how shall I do that?'

'When you have given your husband his dinner, tell him to lie down and rest his head upon your lap, then as soon as he goes to sleep, whip a razor out of your pocket and remove the grey hairs.' The young wife thanked her adviser and gave her a present.

The old woman went immediately to the field and warned the husband that a misfortune threatened him, since his amiable wife not only had betrayed him, but intended that afternoon to kill him and later to marry someone richer than himself. When at midday, the wife arrived and, after his meal, placed her husband's head upon her knees, he pretended to be asleep and she took a razor from her pocket in order to remove the grey hairs. Instantly the exasperated man jumped on to his feet and, seizing his wife by the hair, began to abuse and strike her. The Devil saw all and could not believe his eyes; soon he took a long pole, attached loosely to one end of it the promised bast shoes and boots, and without coming close, passed them to the old woman. 'I will not on any account approach nearer to you,' he said, 'lest you should in some way impose upon me, for you really are more crafty and cunning than I am!' Having delivered the boots and bast shoes, the Devil vanished as quickly as if he had been shot from a gun.

PART NINE

UP TO SOMETHING – BLACK ARTS AND DIRTY TRICKS

PRETTY MAID IBRONKA

(HUNGARIAN)

here was a pretty girl in the village. That is why she was called by the name of Pretty Maid Ibronka. But what of it, if all the other girls – and what a bevy of them used to gather to do their spinning together – had a lover to themselves, and she alone had none? For quite a while she waited patiently, pondering over her chances, but then the thought took hold of her mind: 'I wish God would give me a sweetheart, even if one of the devils he were.'

That evening, when the young were together in the spinning room, in walks a young lad in a sheepskin cape and a hat graced with the feather of a crane. Greeting the others, he takes a seat by the side of Pretty Maid Ibronka.

Well, as is the custom of the young, they start up a conversation, talking about this and that, exchanging news. Then it happened that the spindle slipped from Ibronka's hand. At once she reached down for it and her sweetheart was also bending for it, but as her groping hand touched his foot, she felt it was a cloven hoof. Well, great was her amazement as she picked up her spindle.

Ibronka went to see them out, as on that evening the spinning had been done at her place. Before separating they had a few words together, and then they bid each other goodbye. As is the custom of the young they parted with an embrace. It was then that she felt her hand go into his side, straight through his flesh. That made her recoil with even greater amazement.

There was an old woman in the village. To that woman she went and said, 'Oh mother, put me wise about this. As you may know, for long they have been wagging their tongues in the village, saying that of all the village girls, only Pretty Maid Ibronka is without a sweetheart. And I was waiting and waiting for one, when the wish took hold of my mind that God would give me a sweetheart, even if one of the devils he were. And on that very same evening a young man appeared, in a sheepskin cape and a hat graced with a crane feather. Straight up to me he walked and took a seat by my side. Well, we started up a conversation, as is the custom of the young, talking about this and that. I must have become heedless of my work and let the spindle slip from my hand. At once I reached down to pick it up, and so did he, but as my groping hand chanced to touch his foot, I felt it was a cloven hoof. This was so queer it made me shudder. Now put me wise, mother, what should I be doing now?'

'Well,' she said, 'go and do the spinning at some other place, changing from here to there, so you can see if he will find you.'

She did so and tried every spinning room there was in the village, but wherever she went, he came after her. Again she went to see the old woman. 'Oh mother, didn't he come to every single place I went? I see I shall never get rid of him this way, and I dare not think of what is going to come of all this. I do not know who he is, nor from where he came. And I find it awkward to ask him.'

'Well, here's a piece of advice to you. There are little girls in the village who are just learning to spin, and they find it good practice to wind the thread into balls. Get yourself such a ball, and when they gather again at your place for the spinning, see them out when they leave, and while you are talking to each other before parting, fuss about until you can get the end of the thread tied in a knot round a tuft in his sheepskin cape. When he takes leave and goes his way, let the thread unwind from the ball. When you feel that there is no more to come, make it into a ball again, following the track of the unwound thread.'

Well, they came to her place to do the spinning. The ball of thread she kept in readiness. Her sweetheart was keeping her waiting. The others began teasing her: 'Your sweetheart is going to let you down, Ibronka!'

'To be sure, he won't. He will come; only some business is now keeping him away.'

They hear the door open. They stop in silence and expectation: who is going to open the door? It is Ibronka's sweetheart. He greets them all and takes a seat at her side. And as is the custom of the young, they make conversation, each having something to tell the other. Amid such talk the time passes.

'Let's be going home, it must be close to midnight.'

And they did not tarry long, but quickly rose to their feet and gathered their belongings.

'Good night to you all!'

And they file off and leave the room, one after the other. Outside the house a final goodbye was said, and each went his way and was soon bound homeward.

And the pair drew closer to each other and were talking about this and that. And she was manipulating the thread until she got the end knotted round a tuft of wool in his sheepskin cape. Well, they did not make long with their conversation as they began to feel the chill of the night. 'You better go in now, my dear,' he said to Ibronka, 'or you'll catch cold. When the weather turns mild we may converse at greater leisure.'

And they embraced. 'Good night,' he said.

'Good night,' she said to him.

And he went his way. And she began to unwind the ball as he was walking away. Fast did the thread unwind from the ball. And she began to speculate how much more there would be still to come, but no sooner than this thought came into her head, than it stopped. For a while she kept waiting. But no more thread came off the ball. Then she started to rewind it. And bravely she followed the track of the thread as she went winding it into a ball again. Rapidly the ball was growing in her hand. And she was thinking to herself that she would not have to go very much farther. But where would the thread be leading her? It led her straight to the church.

'Well,' she thought, 'he must have passed this way.'

But the thread led her further on, straight to the churchyard. And she walked over to the door. And through the keyhole the light shone from the inside. And she bent down and peeped through the keyhole. And whom does she behold there? Her own sweetheart. She keeps her eye on him to find out what he was doing. Well, he was busy sawing the head of a dead man in two. She saw him separate the two parts, just the same way we cut a melon in two. And then she saw him feasting on the brains from the halved head. Seeing that, she grew even more horrified. She broke the thread, and in great haste made her way back to the house.

But her sweetheart must have caught sight of her and briskly set out after her. No sooner had she reached home in great weariness and bolted the door safely on the inside, than her sweetheart was calling to her through the window, 'Pretty Maid Ibronka, what did you see looking through the keyhole?'

She answered, 'Nothing did I see.'

'You must tell me what you saw, or your sister shall die.'

'Nothing did I see. If she dies, we'll bury her.'

Then her sweetheart went away.

First thing in the morning she went to the old woman. In great agitation did she appeal to her, as her sister had died. 'Oh mother, I need your advice.'

'What about?'

'Well, I did what you advised me to do.'

'What happened then?'

'Oh, just imagine where I was led in following the thread. Straight to the churchyard.'

'Well, what was his business there?'

'Oh, just imagine, he was sawing a dead man's head in two, just the same way we'd go about cutting up a melon. And there I stayed and kept my eye on him, to see what he'd be doing next. And he set to feasting on the brains from the severed head. I was so horrified that I broke the thread and in great haste made my way back home. But he must have caught sight of me, because as soon as I had the door safely bolted on the inside, he was calling to me through the window, "Pretty Maid Ibronka, what did you see looking through the keyhole?" "Nothing did I see." "You must tell me what you saw, or your sister shall die." I said then, "If she dies, we will bury her, but nothing did I see through the keyhole."'

'Now listen,' the old woman said, 'take my advice and put your dead sister in the outhouse.'

Next evening she did not dare to go spinning with her friends, but her sweetheart was calling again through her window, 'Pretty Maid Ibronka, what did you see through the keyhole?'

'Nothing did I see.'

'You must tell me what you saw,' he said, 'or your mother shall die.'

'If she dies, we will bury her, but nothing did I see looking through the keyhole.'

He turned away from the window and was off. Ibronka was preparing for a night's rest. When she rose in the morning, she found her mother dead. She went to the old woman. 'Oh, mother, what will all this lead to? My mother too – she's dead.'

'Do not worry about it, but put her corpse in the outhouse.'

In the evening her sweetheart came again. He was calling her through the window, 'Pretty Maid Ibronka, tell me, what did you see looking through the keyhole?'

'Nothing did I see.'

'You must tell me what you saw,' he said, 'or your father shall die.'

'If he dies, we will bury him, but nothing did I see looking through the keyhole.'

Her sweetheart turned away from the window and was off, and she retired for the night. But she could not help musing over her lot; what would come of all this? And she went on speculating until she felt sleepy and more at ease. But she could not rest for long. Soon she lay wide awake and was pondering over her fate. 'I wonder what the future keeps in store for me?' And when the day broke she found her father dead. 'Now I am left alone.'

She took the corpse of her father into the outhouse, and then she went as fast as she could to the old woman again. 'Oh, mother, mother! I need your comfort in my distress. What is going to happen to me?'

'You know what's going to happen to you? I may tell you. You are going to die. Now go and ask your friends to be there when you die. And when you die, because die you will for certain, they must not take out the coffin either through the door or the window when they carry it to the churchyard.'

'How then?'

'They must cut a hole through the wall and must push the coffin through that hole. But they should not carry it along the road but cut across through the gardens and the bypaths. And they should not bury it in the burial ground but in the ditch of the churchyard.'

Well, she went home. Then she sent word to her friends, the girls in the village, and they appeared at her call.

In the evening her sweetheart came to the window. 'Pretty Maid Ibronka, what did you see looking through the keyhole?'

'Nothing did I see.'

'You must tell me at once,' he said, 'or you shall die.'

'If I die, they will bury me, but nothing did I see through the keyhole.'

He turned away from the window and took off.

Well, for a while she and her friends kept up their conversation. They were only half inclined to believe that she would die. When they grew tired they went to sleep. But when they awoke, they found Ibronka dead. They were not long in bringing a coffin and cutting a hole through the wall. They dug a grave for her in the ditch of the churchyard. They pushed the coffin through the hole in the wall and went off with it. They did not follow the road, but went cross-country, cutting through the gardens and the bypaths. When they came to the churchyard they buried her. Then they returned to the house and filled in the hole they had cut through the wall. It so happened that before she died, Ibronka enjoined them to take care of the house until further events took place.

Before long, a beautiful rose grew out of Ibronka's grave. The grave was not far from the road, and a prince, driving past in his coach, saw it. So much was he taken by its beauty that he stopped the coachman at once. 'Hey! Rein in the horses and get me that rose from the grave. Be quick about it.'

At once the coachman came to a halt. He jumps from the coach and goes to fetch the rose. But when he wants to break it off, the rose will not yield. He is pulling harder now, but still it does not yield. He is pulling the rose with all his might, but all in vain.

'Oh, what a dummy you are! Haven't you got the brains to pick a rose? Come on here, get back on the coach and let me go and get the flower.'

The coachman got back on to his seat, and the prince gave him the reins, which he had been holding while the other went for the rose. The prince then jumped down from the coach and went to the grave. No sooner had he grasped the rose, than it came off at once and he was holding it in his hand.

'Look here, you idiot, with all your tearing and pulling you could not get me this rose, and hardly did I touch it and off it came into my hand.'

Well, they took off, driving back home at great speed. The prince pinned the rose on his breast. At home, he found a place for it in front of the dining-room mirror so that he should be able to look at it even while he was having his meals.

There the rose stayed. One evening some leftovers remained on the table after supper. The prince left them there. 'I may eat them some other time.'

This happened every now and again. Once the servant asked the prince, 'Did your majesty eat the leftovers?'

'Not I,' said the prince. 'I guessed it was you who finished off what was left.'

'No, I did not,' he says.

'Well, there's something fishy about it.'

Says the servant, 'I am going to find out who's in this – the cat, or whoever.'

Neither the prince nor the servant would have guessed that the rose was eating the remains.

'Well,' said the prince, 'we must leave some more food on the table. And you will lie in wait and see who's going to eat it up.'

They left plenty of food on the table. And the servant was lying in wait, but never for a moment did he suspect the rose. And the rose alighted from her place by the mirror, and shook itself, and at once it turned into such a beautiful maiden that you could not find a second to her, not in all Hungary, not in all the wide world. Well, she sat down on a chair at the table and supped well off the dishes. She even found a glass of water to finish off her supper. Then she shook herself a little and back again she was in her place in front of the mirror, in the shape of a rose.

Well, the servant was impatiently waiting for day to break. Then he went to the prince and reported, 'I've found it out, your royal majesty, it was the rose.'

'This evening you must lay the table properly and leave plenty of food on it. I am going to see for myself whether you are telling me the truth.'

And as they were lying in wait, the prince and the servant, they saw the rose alight from her place. She made a slight movement, then shook herself and at once turned into a fine and beautiful maiden. She takes a chair, sits down at the table, and sups well on the dishes. The prince was watching her as he sat under the mirror. And when she finished her supper and poured herself a glass of water and was about to shake herself into a rose again, the prince clasped his arms round her and took her into his lap.

'My beautiful and beloved sweetheart. You are mine, and I am yours for ever, and nothing but death can us part.'

'Oh, it cannot be so,' said Ibronka.

'To be sure, it can be,' he says. 'And why not?'

'There is more to it than you think.'

Well, I just remember a slip I have made in the story. Here goes then. On the day she was buried, her sweetheart appeared at her window as usual. He called in to her. But no answer came. He goes to the door and kicks it open. 'Tell me, you door, was it through you they took out Ibronka's coffin?'

'No, it was not.'

He goes then to the window. 'Tell me, you window, was it through you they took the coffin out?'

'No, it was not.'

He takes himself off to the road. 'Tell me, you road, was it this way they took the coffin?'

'No, it was not.'

He goes to the churchyard. 'Tell me, you churchyard, was it in your ground they buried Pretty Maid Ibronka?'

'No, it was not.'

Well, that is the missing part.

Fervently the prince is now wooing her and tries to win her consent to their marriage. But she resorts to evasion. And finally she made her condition, 'I will marry you only if you never compel me to go to church.'

Said the prince, 'Well then, we could get along without you going to church. Even if I sometimes go myself. I shall never compel you to come with me.'

Here is another part of the story I missed telling in its proper order. As he did not get any the wiser from the answer of the road, and the churchyard either, her sweetheart said to himself, 'Well, I see I must get myself a pair of iron moccasins and an iron staff and then I shall not stop until I find you, Pretty Maid Ibronka, even if I have to wear them away to naught.'

The time comes when Ibronka is expecting a child. The couple are living happily, only she never goes along with him to church. Day follows day, the years slip by. Again she is with child. They have already two children, and they are no longer babes, but a boy of five and six years of age. And it is their father who takes them to church. True enough, he himself had found it strange enough that only his children went with him while all other folks appeared together with their wives. And he knew that they rebuked him for it and said, 'Why does not your majesty bring along the queen?'

He says, 'Well, that is the custom with us.'

But all the same he felt embarrassed after this rebuke, and next Sunday, when he was getting ready with the boys to go to church, he said to his wife, 'Look here, missus, why won't you come with us too?'

She answered, 'Look here, husband, don't you remember your promise?'

'How then? Must we stick to it for ever and aye? I've been hearing their scorn long enough. And how could I give up going to church when the kids want me to go with them? Whatever we were saying then, let us forget about it.'

'All right, let it be as you wish, but it will give rise to trouble between us two. However, as I see you've set your mind on it, I am willing to go with you. Now let me go and dress for church.'

So they went, and it made the people rejoice to see them together. 'That is the right thing, your majesty,' they said, 'coming to church with your wife.'

The mass is drawing to a close, and when it ends, a man is walking up to the couple wearing a pair of iron moccasins worn to holes, and with an iron staff in his hand. He calls out loudly, 'I pledged myself, Ibronka, that I would put on a pair of iron moccasins and take an iron staff, and go out looking for you, even if I should wear them to naught. But before I had worn them quite away, I found you. Tonight I shall come to you.'

And he disappeared. On their way home the king asked his wife, 'What did that man mean by threatening you?'

'Just wait and see, and you will learn what will come of it.'

So both were anxiously waiting for the evening to come. The day was drawing to a close. Suddenly there was someone calling through the window, 'Pretty Maid Ibronka, what did you see through the key-hole?'

Pretty Maid Ibronka then began her speech: 'I was the prettiest girl in the village, but to a dead and not a living soul am I speaking – and all the other girls had a sweetheart – but to a dead and not to a living soul am I speaking. Once I let it out, I wish God would give me one, even if one of the devils he were. There must have been something in the way I said it, because that evening, when we gathered to do our spinning, there appeared a young lad in a sheepskin cape, and a hat graced with a feather of a crane. He greets us and takes a seat at my side and we are conversing, as is the custom of the young. And then it so happened – but to a dead and not to a living soul am I speaking – that my spindle slipped from my hand. I bent to pick it up and so did my sweetheart, but as my groping hand touched his foot, I felt at once – but to a dead and not to a living soul am I speaking – that it was a cloven hoof. And I recoiled in horror that God had given me a devil for a sweetheart – but to a dead and not to a living soul am I speaking.'

And he is shouting at the top of his voice through the window. 'Pretty Maid Ibronka, what did you see looking through the keyhole?'

'But when at the parting, as is the custom with the young, we embraced, my hand went straight through his flesh. At that I grew even more horrified. There was a woman in the village, and I went to ask for her advice. And she put me wise – but to a dead and not to a living soul am I speaking.'

And he kept shouting through the window, 'Pretty Maid Ibronka, what did you see looking through the keyhole?'

'And then my sweetheart took leave and went away. And I wished he would never come again – but to a dead and not to a living soul am I speaking. The woman said, I was to try to do the spinning at some other place, once here, once there, so that he might not find me. But wherever I went, there he came. And again I went for advice to the woman – but to a dead and not to a living soul am I speaking.'

And he was shouting through the window, 'Pretty Maid Ibronka, what did you see looking through the keyhole?'

'Then the woman advised me to get myself a ball of thread, which I was to fasten on to his sheepskin cape. And when he asked me and I said "Nothing did I see", he said, "Tell me at once, or your sister shall die." "If she dies, we will bury her, but nothing did I see looking through the keyhole." And he came again next evening and asked me what I had seen through the keyhole – but to a dead and not to a living soul am I speaking.'

And all the while he never stops shouting through the window.

'And my sister died. And the next evening he came again and was calling to me through the window – but to a dead and not to a living soul am I speaking. "Tell me what you saw, or your mother shall die." "If she dies, we will bury her." Next evening he is calling to me again, "Pretty Maid Ibronka, what did you see looking through the keyhole?" – but to a dead and not to a living soul am I speaking. "Tell me what you saw, or your father shall die." "If he dies, we will bury him, but nothing did I see looking through the keyhole." On that day I sent word to my friends, and they came and it was arranged that when I died they would not take my coffin either through the door or the window. Nor were they to take me along the road or bury me in the churchyard.'

And he went on shouting through the window, 'Pretty Maid Ibronka, what did you see looking through the keyhole?'

'And my friends cut a hole through the wall and went along the road when they took me to the churchyard where they buried me in the ditch – but to a dead and not to a living soul am I speaking.'

And then he collapsed under the window. He uttered a shout which shook the castle to its bottom, and it was he who died then. Her mother and her father and her sister rose from their long sleep. And that is the end of it.

ENCHANTER AND ENCHANTRESS

(MORDVIN)

man who was a magician took a girl-magician as his wife. The man went to the bazaar, whereupon his wife, who had a lover, called him, and they drank and ate together. In the evening the husband returned late from the bazaar and, looking through the window, saw his wife and her lover drinking and eating. The lover caught a glimpse of the husband and said to the woman, 'Who peered through the window just now?'

'I know,' said the woman; she took a small whip, and going out, struck her husband with the whip and said, 'Be no more a man; become a yellow dog!' The peasant became a yellow dog. It grew day, and the other dogs seeing the yellow dog, began to tear him. The yellow dog galloped along the road; bounded and leapt; he saw some shepherds feeding their flock, and he went to them. Pleased that the yellow dog had joined them, the shepherds fed him and gave him water. The dog looked after the flock so well that there was nothing left for the shepherds to do. As they saw that the dog acted efficiently they began to stay away from the field.

Once, when the dog was guarding the flock, the shepherds were in the tavern. A merchant entered this tavern and said, 'A thief is pestering me; he comes every night.' 'You should have our dog!' said the shepherds, and they related the dog's services. The merchant made an offer for the dog, and though the shepherds did not wish to sell him, they were overcome by the thought of the money. The merchant bought the dog and led him home. Night came, and with it the magician-wife of the yellow dog arrived to commit a theft. The woman entered the merchant's house and began to remove his money chest. The yellow dog threw himself upon his wife, took away the money chest and lay down upon it. In the morning the merchant rose and saw that the chest was gone; pushing the yellow dog, he said, 'I bought a dog to no purpose, for thieves have got hold of my money.' No sooner had the merchant pushed the dog, than he saw his coffer. The yellow dog slept three nights at the merchant's, and each night deprived his wife of the merchant's money. The wife ceased to visit the merchant for the purpose of theft.

The queen bore two sons, but both disappeared in the night; the wife of the yellow dog had stolen them. When the queen was again about to give birth to a child the king, who had heard of the yellow dog, went to the merchant and asked for him. The queen bore a son, but the wife of the yellow dog came by night and tried to steal him. However, no sooner had the wife of the yellow dog entered the royal dwelling and seized the third little prince, than the yellow dog rushed up and snatched the infant from her. In the morning the child was found safe and protected by the dog in the middle of a field. The king took his son and said to the yellow dog, 'If you were a man I would give you half my kingdom.'

The yellow dog lived well now at the king's house; nevertheless, he longed for his wife. He left the king and galloped to his own home, where he looked in at the window and found his wife again drinking with her lover. The lover saw the yellow dog and said, 'Someone looked through the window.' 'I know him,' answered the woman. She went out and struck the yellow dog with a whip, and he became a sparrow. For a long time he flew about as a sparrow.

Then the wife began to long for her husband. She went into the forest and, having made a cage, threw into it some millet seeds and hoped to effect a capture. The husband was roaming about in the form of a sparrow and was very hungry. He flew into the forest, found the cage, and, stepping in to peck at the grains, was caught. The wife came and took the cage, dragged her husband out of it, made him once more a man, and said, 'Return home, take the king's two first children from the cellar, and restore them to him.' The peasant accompanied his wife home, and, having taken the king's children from the cellar, carried them to the king. When the king saw his eldest sons his delight knew no bounds, and he loaded the peasant with gifts.

The peasant took the money and went home and said, 'Well, woman, we have enough money now!' 'Come old man,' his wife replied, 'let us build a stone house and sell the square logs.' But the peasant had not forgotten the tortures inflicted on him by his wife, and he said, 'Woman, become a chestnut mare; I will use you to transport both stones and logs.' The peasant-magician had scarcely spoken when his wife became a chestnut mare, and by harnessing her and setting her to transport stones he was enabled to erect a stone house. When it was completed he harnessed the chestnut, and transported the logs, a great number of them. The yard was now filled with the timber, and the old man said, 'Wife, change again to a woman.' Immediately the mare became a woman. The woman had taught the peasant and the peasant had taught the woman. Now she is always baking pancakes and feeding her husband, and he sells logs and they live very well.

THE TELLTALE LILAC BUSH

(USA: HILLBILLY)

n old man and woman once lived by themselves along the Tygart Valley River. There had been trouble between them for many years. Few people visited them, and it was not immediately noticed that the wife had unaccountably disappeared. People suspected that the old man had killed her, but her body could not be found, and the question was dropped.

The old man lived a gay life after his wife's disappearance, until one night when a group of young men were sitting on his porch, talking of all the parties which the old man was giving. While they were talking, a large lilac bush growing nearby began beating on the window pane and beckoning towards them as though it were trying to tell them something. No one would have thought anything of this if the wind had been blowing. But there was no wind – not even a small breeze.

Paying no attention to the old man's protests, the young men dug up the lilac bush. They were stunned when the roots were found to be growing from the palm of a woman's hand.

The old man screamed and ran down the hill towards the river, never to be seen again.

TATTERHOOD

(NORWEGIAN)

nce on a time there was a king and a queen who had no children, and that gave the queen much grief; she scarce had one happy hour. She was always bewailing and bemoaning herself, and saying how dull and lonesome it was in the palace.

'If we had children there'd be life enough,' she said.

Wherever she went in all her realm she found God's blessing in children, even in the vilest hut; and wherever she came she heard the Goodies scolding the bairns, and saying how they had done that and that wrong. All this the queen heard, and thought it would be so nice to do as other women did. At last the king and queen took into their palace a stranger lassie to rear up, that they might have her always with them, to love her if she did well, and scold her if she did wrong, like their own child.

So one day the little lassie whom they had taken as their own, ran down into the palace-yard, and was playing with a gold apple. Just then an old beggar wife came by, who had a little girl with her, and it wasn't long before the little lassie and the beggar's bairn were great friends, and began to play together, and to toss the gold apple about between them. When the queen saw this, as she sat at a window in the palace, she tapped on the pane for her foster-daughter to come up. She went at once, but the beggar girl went up too; and as they went into the queen's bower, each held the other by the hand. Then the queen began to scold the little lady, and to say, 'You ought to be above running about and playing with a tattered beggar's brat.' And so she wanted to drive the lassie downstairs.

'If the queen only knew my mother's power, she'd not drive me out, said the little lassie; and when the queen asked what she meant more plainly, she told her how her mother could get her children if she chose. The queen wouldn't believe it, but the lassie held her own, and said every word of it was true, and bade the queen only to try and make her mother do it. So the queen sent the lassie down to fetch up her mother.

'Do you know what your daughter says?' asked the queen of the old woman, as soon as ever she came into the room.

No; the beggar wife knew nothing about it.

'Well, she says you can get me children if you will,' answered the queen.

'Queens shouldn't listen to beggar lassies' silly stories,' said the old wife, and strode out of the room.

Then the queen got angry, and wanted again to drive out the little lassie; but she declared it was true every word that she had said.

'Let the queen only give my mother a drop to drink,' said the lassie. 'When she gets merry she'll soon find out a way to help you.

The queen was ready to try this; so the beggar wife was fetched up again once more, and treated both with wine and mead as much as she chose; and so it was not long before her tongue began to wag. Then the queen came out again with the same question she had asked before.

'One way to help you perhaps I know,' said the beggar wife. 'Your Majesty must make them bring in two pails of water some evening before you go to bed. In each of them you must wash yourself, and afterwards throw away the water under the bed. When you look under the bed next morning, two flowers will have sprung up, one fair and one ugly. The fair one you must eat, the ugly one you must let stand; but mind you don't forget the last.'

That was what the beggar wife said.

Yes; the queen did what the beggar wife advised her to do. She had the water brought up in two pails, washed herself in them, and emptied them under the bed; and lo! when she looked under the bed next morning, there stood two flowers. One was ugly and foul, and had black leaves; but the other was so bright and fair, and lovely, she had never seen its like; so she ate it up at once. But the pretty flower tasted so sweet, that she couldn't help herself. She ate the other up too, for, she thought, 'It can't hurt or help one much either way, I'll be bound.'

Well, sure enough, after a while the queen was brought to bed. First of all, she had a girl who had a wooden spoon in her hand, and rode upon a goat; loathly and ugly she was, and the very moment she came into the world she bawled out 'Mamma.'

'If I'm your mamma,' said the queen, 'God give me grace to mend my ways.'

'Oh, don't be sorry,' said the girl, who rode on the goat, for one will soon come after me who is better looking.'

So, after a while, the queen had another girl, who was so fair and sweet, no one had ever set eyes on such a lovely child, and with her you may fancy the queen was very well pleased. The elder twin they called 'Tatterhood', because she was always so ugly and ragged, and because she had a hood which hung about her ears in tatters. The queen could scarce bear to look at her, and the nurses tried to shut her up in a room by herself, but it was all no good; where the younger twin was, there she must also be, and no one could ever keep them apart.

Well, one Christmas eve when they were half grown up, there rose such a frightful noise and clatter in the gallery outside the queen's bower. So Tatterhood asked what it was that dashed and crashed so out in the passage.

'Oh!' said the queen, 'it isn't worth asking about.'

But Tatterhood wouldn't give over till she found out all about it; and so the queen told her it was a pack of Trolls and witches who had come there to keep Christmas. So Tatterhood said she'd just go out and drive them away, and in spite of all they could say, and however much they begged and prayed her to let the Trolls alone, she must and would go out to drive the witches off; but she begged the queen to mind and keep all the doors close shut, so that not one of them came so much as the least bit ajar. Having said this, off she went with her wooden spoon, and began to hunt and sweep away the hags; and all this while there was such a pother out in the gallery, the like of it was never heard. The whole palace creaked and groaned as if every joint and beam were going to be torn out of its place.

Now, how it was, I'm sure I can't tell; but somehow or other one door did get the least bit ajar. Then her twin sister just peeped out to see how things were going with Tatterhood, and put her head a tiny bit through the opening. But, POP! up came an old witch, and whipped off her head, and stuck a calf's head on her shoulders instead; and so the princess ran back into the room on all fours, and began to 'moo' like a calf. When Tatterhood came back and saw her sister, she scolded them all round, and was very angry because they hadn't kept better watch, and asked them what they thought of their heedlessness now, when her sister was turned into a calf.

'But still I'll see if I can't set her free,' she said.

Then she asked the king for a ship in full trim, and well fitted with stores; but captain and sailors she wouldn't have. No, she would sail away with her sister all alone; and as there was no holding her back, at last they let her have her own way.

Then Tatterhood sailed off, and steered her ship right under the land where the witches dwelt, and when she came to the landing place, she told her sister to stay quite still on board the ship; but she herself rode on her goat up to the witches' castle. When she got there, one of the windows in the gallery was open, and there she saw her sister's head hung up on the window frame; so she leapt her goat through the window into the gallery, snapped up the head, and set off with it. After her came the witches to try to get the head again, and they flocked about her as thick as a swarm of bees or a nest of ants; but the goat snorted and puffed, and butted with his horns, and Tatterhood beat and banged them about with her wooden spoon; and so the pack of witches had to give it up. So Tatterhood got back to her ship, took the calf's head off her sister, and put her own on again, and then she became a girl as she had been before. After that she sailed a long, long way, to a strange king's realm.

Now the king of that land was a widower, and had an only son. So when he saw the strange sail, he sent messengers down to the strand to find out whence it came, and who owned it; but when the king's men came down there, they saw never a living soul on board but Tatterhood, and there she was, riding round and round the deck on her goat at full speed, till her elf locks streamed again in the wind. The folk from the palace were all amazed at this sight, and asked were there not more on board. Yes, there were; she had a sister with her, said Tatterhood. Her, too, they wanted to see, but Tatterhood said 'No.'

'No one shall see her, unless the king comes himself,' she said, and so she began to gallop about on her goat till the deck thundered again.

So when the servants got back to the palace, and told what they had seen and heard down at the ship, the king was for setting out at once, that he might see the lassie that rode on the goat. When he got down, Tatterhood led out her sister, and she was so fair and gentle, the king fell over head and ears in love with her as he stood. He brought them both back with him to the palace, and wanted to have the sister for his queen; but Tatterhood said 'No': the king couldn't have her in any way, unless the king's son chose to have Tatterhood. That you may fancy the prince was very loath to do, such an ugly hussy as Tatterhood was; but at last the king and all the others in the palace talked him over, and he yielded, giving his word to take her for his queen; but it went sore against the grain, and he was a doleful man.

Now they set about the wedding, both with brewing and baking, and when all was ready they were to go to church; but the prince thought it the weariest churching he had ever had in all his life. First, the king drove off with his bride, and she was so lovely and so grand, all the people stopped to look after her all along the road, and they stared at her till she was out of sight. After them came the prince on horseback by the side of Tatterhood, who trotted along on her goat with her wooden spoon in her fist, and to look at him, it was more like going to a burial than a wedding, and that his own; so sorrowful he seemed, and with never a word to say.

'Why don't you talk?' asked Tatterhood, when they had ridden a bit.

'Why, what should I talk about?' answered the prince.

'Well, you might at least ask me why I ride upon this ugly goat,' said Tatterhood.

'Why do you ride on that ugly goat?' asked the prince.

'Is it an ugly goat? why, it's the grandest horse a bride ever rode on,' answered Tatterhood; and in a trice the goat became a horse, and that the finest the prince had ever set eyes on.

Then they rode on again a bit, but the prince was just as woeful as before, and couldn't get a word out. So Tatterhood asked him again why he didn't talk, and when the prince answered, he didn't know what to talk about, she said, 'You can at least ask me why I ride with this ugly spoon in my fist.'

'Why do you ride with that ugly spoon?' asked the prince.

'Is it an ugly spoon? why, it's the loveliest silver wand a bride ever bore,' said Tatterhood; and in a trice it became a silver wand, so dazzling bright, the sunbeams glistened from it.

So they rode on another bit, but the prince was just as sorrowful, and said never a word. In a little while Tatterhood asked him again why he didn't talk, and bade him ask why she wore that ugly grey hood on her head.

'Why do you wear that ugly grey hood on your head?' asked the prince.

'Is it an ugly hood? why, it's the brightest golden crown a bride ever wore,' answered Tatterhood, and it became a crown on the spot.

Now they rode on a long while again, and the prince was so woeful that he sat without sound or speech, just as before. So his bride asked him again why he didn't talk and bade him ask now why her face was so ugly and ashen-grey?

'Ah!' asked the prince, 'why is your face so ugly and ashen-grey?'

'I ugly?' said the bride. 'You think my sister pretty, but I am ten times prettier'; and lo! when the prince looked at her, she was so lovely he thought there never was so lovely a woman in all the world. After that, I shouldn't wonder if the prince found his tongue, and no longer rode along hanging down his head.

So they drank the bridal cup both deep and long, and, after that, both prince and king set out with their brides to the princess's father's palace, and there they had another bridal feast, and drank anew, both deep and long. There was no end to the fun; and, if you make haste and run to the king's palace, I dare say you'll find there's still a drop of the bridal ale left for you.

The Witchball

(USA: HILLBILLY)

nce there was a poor boy who wanted to marry a girl, but her folks didn't want him. His grandma was a witch, an' she said she'd fix it up. She made a horsehair witchball, an' put it under the girl's doorstep. The girl come outside, passin' over the witchball, an' went back in the house. She started to say somethin' to her mother, an' ripped out, an' every time she spoke a word, she'd rip out. Her mother told her to stop that or she'd lick her. Then the mother went out for somethin', an' when she came back in,

she broke wind, too, every time she spoke. The father come in an' he did the same thing.

He thought somethin' was the matter, so he called the doctor, an' when the doctor come in over the doorstep, he started to poop with every word he said, and they were all atalkin' an' apoopin' when the ole witch come in, an' told 'em God had probably sent that on them as a curse because they wouldn' allow their daughter to marry the poor boy. They told her to run an' git the boy, 'cause he could marry their girl right away, if God would only take that curse offa them. The ole witch went an' got the boy, an' on her way out, she slipped the witch-ball out from under the doorstep. The boy an' girl got married an' lived happy ever after.

THE WEREFOX

(CHINESE)

any years ago, a Buddhist monk, named Chi Hsüan, led a very holy and mortified life. He never wore silk, tramped from town to town on foot, and slept in the open. One moonlight night, he was preparing to sleep in a copse adjoining a grave, ten miles from a city in Shan Si. By the light of the moon he saw a wild fox place on its head a skull and some withered bones, go through several mysterious movements, and then deck itself out with grass and leaves. Presently the fox assumed the form of a beautiful woman, very quietly and plainly dressed, and in this guise it wandered out of the copse on to the adjoining high road. As the trampling of a horseman's mount became audible, coming from the north-west, the woman began to weep and wail, her attitude and gestures showing extreme grief. A man on horseback approached, pulled his horse up, and alighted.

'Lady, he cried, 'what brings you here, alone, in the night. Can I help you?'

The woman stopped crying and told her tale. 'I am the widow of So-and-so. My husband died suddenly last year, leaving me penniless; my parents live a long way off. I do not know the way, and there is no one I can turn to, to help me to get back to my home.'

When he heard where her parents lived, the horseman said, 'I come from that place, and I am now on my way home again. If you do not mind rough travelling, you may ride my horse, and I will walk beside it.'

The woman accepted gratefully, and vowed she would never forget the horseman's kindness. She was just on the point of mounting, when the monk, Chi Hsüan, came out of the copse, crying to the horseman, 'Beware! She is not human; she is a werefox. If you do not

believe me, wait a few moments and I will make her resume her
true shape.'

So he made a sign, or mudra, with his fingers, uttered a *dhârani* (or
spell) and cried in a loud voice, 'Why do you not return at once to
your original form?'

The woman immediately fell down, turned into an old fox, and
expired. Her flesh and blood flowed away like a stream, and nothing
remained but the dead fox, a skull, a few dry bones and some leaves
and blades of grass.

The cavalier, quite convinced, prostrated himself several times
before the priest, and went away full of astonishment.

THE WITCHES' PIPER

(HUNGARIAN)

y elder brother was piping for some people at a certain place, while another fellow, a man from Etes, was playing for the children at the same house. It must have been on a day before Ash Wednesday. At eleven o'clock or so, the children were taken home. The man who had been playing for them, Uncle Matyi, was paid for his piping. He took leave of my brother and left for home.

On his way home, three women stepped up to him and said, 'Come along, Uncle Matyi! We want you to play for us. Let's go to that house over there, at the end of the street. And have no fear, we're going to pay for your piping.'

When he went in, they took him by the arms (by the way, the man is still living in the village) and made him stand on the bench near the wall. And there he was piping for them. Money came in showers at his feet. 'Gee, I'm not doing badly at all!' he said to himself.

At about midnight, there came a terrible crash, and in a wink he found himself standing right in the top of the white poplar, at the end of the village.

'Damn it! How the dickens can I get down from this tree?'

Suddenly a cart came up the road. When it reached the tree, he called down, 'Oh, brother, do help me!' But the man drove on, taking no heed of Uncle Matyi. Before long another cart drove up towards the tree. On the cart was Péter Barta, a fellow from Karancsság. 'I say, brother, stop your horses and help me get down.' The man brought his horses to a halt and said, 'Is that you, Uncle Matyi?'

'Damn it, to be sure it's me.'

'What on earth are you doing up there?'

'Well, brother, three women stopped me on my way home. They

asked me to follow them to a house at the end of the street. When I went in, they made me stand on a bench and there I was to pipe for them. And they've given me a lot of money for it.'

When the man got him down from the tree, Uncle Matyi began looking for the money he had tucked into the hem of his cloak. But there was no money. There was only a lot of broken crockery and little chips of glass.

Such strange things sometimes still happen.

Vasilissa the Fair

(RUSSIAN)

merchant and his wife living in a certain country had an only daughter, the beautiful Vasilissa. When the child was eight years old the mother was seized with a fatal illness, but before she died she called Vasilissa to her side and, giving her a little doll, said, 'Listen, dear daughter! remember my last words. I am dying, and bequeath to you now, together with a parent's blessing, this doll. Keep it always beside you, but show it to nobody; if at any time you are in trouble, give the doll some food and ask its advice.' Then the mother kissed her daughter, sighed deeply and died.

After his wife's death the merchant grieved for a long time, and next began to think whether he should not wed again. He was handsome and would have no difficulty in finding a bride; moreover, he was especially pleased with a certain little widow, no longer young, who possessed two daughters of about the same age as Vasilissa.

The widow was famous as both a good housekeeper and a good mother to her daughters, but when the merchant married her he quickly found she was unkind to his daughter. Vasilissa, being the chief beauty in the village, was on that account envied by her stepmother and stepsisters. They found fault with her on every occasion, and tormented her with impossible tasks; thus, the poor girl suffered from the severity of her work and grew dark from exposure to wind and sun. Vasilissa endured all and became every day more beautiful; but the stepmother and her daughters who sat idle with folded hands, grew thin and almost lost their minds from spite. What supported Vasilissa? This. She received assistance from her doll; otherwise she could not have surmounted her daily difficulties.

Vasilissa, as a rule, kept a dainty morsel for her doll, and in the evening when everyone had gone to bed she would steal to her closet and regale her doll and say, 'Now, dear, eat and listen to my grief! Though I am living in my father's house, my life is joyless; a wicked stepmother makes me wretched; please direct my life and tell me what to do.'

The doll tasted the food, and gave advice to the sorrowing child, and in the morning performed her work, so that Vasilissa could rest in the shade or pluck flowers; already the beds had been weeded, and the cabbages watered, and the water carried, and the stove heated. It was nice for Vasilissa to live with her doll.

Several years passed. Vasilissa grew up, and the young men in the town sought her hand in marriage; but they never looked at the step-sisters. Growing more angry than ever, the stepmother answered Vasilissa's suitors thus: 'I will not let you have my youngest daughter before her sisters.' She dismissed the suitors and vented her spite on Vasilissa with harsh words and blows.

But it happened that the merchant was obliged to visit a neigh-bouring country, where he had business; and in the meanwhile the stepmother went to live in a house situated close to a thick forest. In the forest was a glade, in which stood a cottage, and in the cottage lived Baba-Yaga, who admitted nobody to her cottage, and devoured people as if they were chickens. Having moved to the new house, the merchant's wife continually, on some pretext or other, sent the hated Vasilissa into the forest, but the girl always returned home safe and unharmed, because the doll directed her and took care she did not enter Baba-Yaga's cottage.

Spring arrived, and the stepmother assigned to each of the three girls an evening task; thus, she set one to make lace, a second to knit stockings, and Vasilissa to spin. One evening, having extinguished all the lights in the house except one candle in the room where the girls sat at work, the stepmother went to bed. In a little while the candle needed attention, and one of the stepmother's daughters took the snuffers and, beginning to cut the wick, as if by accident, put out the light.

'What are we to do now?' said the girls. 'There is no light in the whole house, and our tasks are unfinished; someone must run for a light to Baba-Yaga.'

'I can see my pins,' said the daughter who was making lace. 'I shall not go.'

'Neither shall I,' said the daughter who was knitting stockings; 'my needles are bright.'

'You must run for a light. Go to Baba-Yaga's,' they both cried, pushing Vasilissa from the room.

Vasilissa went to her closet, placed some supper ready for the doll, and said, 'Now, little doll, have something to eat and hear my trouble. They have sent me to Baba-Yaga's for a light, and she will eat me.'

'Do not be afraid!' answered the doll. 'Go on your errand, but take me with you. No harm will befall you while I am present.' Vasilissa placed the doll in her pocket, crossed herself and entered the thick forest, but she trembled.

Suddenly a horseman galloped past; he was white and dressed in white, his steed was white and had a white saddle and bridle. The morning light was appearing.

The girl went further and another horseman rode past; he was red and dressed in red and his steed was red. The sun rose.

Vasilissa walked all night and all day, but on the following evening she came out in a glade, where stood Baba-Yaga's cottage. The fence around the cottage was made of human bones, and on the fence there were fixed human skulls with eyes. Instead of doorposts at the gates there were human legs; instead of bolts there were hands, instead of a lock there was a mouth with sharp teeth. Vasilissa grew pale from terror and stood as if transfixed. Suddenly another horseman rode up; he was black and dressed in black and upon a black horse; he sprang through Baba-Yaga's gates and vanished, as if he had been hurled into the earth. Night came on. But the darkness did not last long; the eyes in all the skulls on the fence lighted up, and at once it became as light throughout the glade as if it were midday. Vasilissa trembled from fear, and not knowing whither to run, she remained motionless.

Suddenly she heard a terrible noise. The trees cracked, the dry leaves rustled, and out of the forest Baba-Yaga appeared, riding in a mortar which she drove with a pestle, while she swept away traces of her progress with a broom. She came up to the gates and stopped; then sniffing about her, cried, 'Phoo, phoo, I smell a Russian! Who is here?'

Vasilissa approached the old woman timidly and gave her a low bow; then she said, 'It is I, granny! My stepsisters have sent me to you for a light.'

'Very well,' said Baba-Yaga, 'I know them. If you first of all live with me and do some work, then I will give you a light. If you refuse,

I will eat you.' Then she turned to the gates and exclaimed, 'Strong bolts, unlock; wide gates, open!' The gates opened, and Baba-Yaga went out whistling. Vasilissa followed, and all again closed.

Having entered the room, the witch stretched herself and said to Vasilissa, 'Hand me everything in the oven; I am hungry.' Vasilissa lit a torch from the skulls upon the fence and, drawing the food from the oven, handed it to the witch. The meal would have been sufficient for ten men. Moreover, Vasilissa brought up from the cellar kvass, and honey, and beer and wine. The old woman ate and drank almost everything. She left nothing for Vasilissa but some fragments, end-crusts of bread and tiny morsels of sucking-pig. Baba-Yaga lay down to sleep and said, 'When I go away tomorrow, take care that you clean the yard, sweep out the cottage, cook the dinner and get ready the linen. Then go to the cornbin, take a quarter of the wheat and cleanse it from impurities. See that all is done! otherwise I shall eat you.'

After giving these injunctions Baba-Yaga began to snore. But Vasilissa placed the remains of the old woman's meal before her doll and, bursting into tears, said, 'Now, little doll, take some food and hear my grief. Baba-Yaga has set me a terrible task, and has threatened to eat me if I fail in any way; help me!'

The doll answered, 'Have no fear, beautiful Vasilissa! Eat your supper, say your prayers and lie down to sleep; morning is wiser than evening.'

It was early when Vasilissa woke, but Baba-Yaga, who had already risen, was looking out of the window. Suddenly the light from the eyes in the skulls was extinguished; then a pale horseman flashed by, and it was altogether daylight. Baba-Yaga went out and whistled; a mortar appeared before her with a pestle and a hearth broom. A red horseman flashed by, and the sun rose. Then Baba-Yaga took her place in the mortar and went forth, driving herself with the pestle and sweeping away traces of her progress with the broom.

Vasilissa remained alone and, eyeing Baba-Yaga's house, wondered at her wealth. The girl did not know which task to begin with. But when she looked she found that the work was already done: the doll had separated from the wheat the last grains of impurity.

'Oh, my dear liberator,' said Vasilissa to the doll, 'you have rescued me from misfortune!'

'You have only to cook the dinner,' said the doll, climbing into Vasilissa's pocket. 'God help you to prepare it; then rest in peace!'

Towards evening Vasilissa laid the table and awaited Baba-Yaga's return. It became dusk, and a black horseman flashed by the gates; it had grown altogether dark. But the eyes in the skulls shone and the trees cracked and the leaves rustled. Baba-Yaga came. Vasilissa met her. 'Is all done?' asked the witch. 'Look for yourself, granny!'

Baba-Yaga examined everything and, vexed that she had no cause for anger, said, 'My true servants, my bosom friends, grind my wheat!' Three pairs of hands appeared, seized the wheat and bore it from sight.

Baba-Yaga ate to repletion, prepared for sleep, and again gave an order to Vasilissa. 'Tomorrow repeat your task of today; in addition remove the poppies from the cornbin and cleanse them from earth, seed by seed; you see, someone has maliciously mixed earth with them!' Having spoken, the old woman turned to the wall and snored.

Vasilissa began to feed her doll, who said, as on the previous day, 'Pray to God and go to sleep; morning is wiser than evening; all will be done, dear Vasilissa!'

In the morning Baba-Yaga departed again in her mortar, and immediately Vasilissa and the doll set to work at their tasks. The old woman returned, observed everything and cried out, 'My faithful servants, my close friends, squeeze the oil from the poppies!' Three pairs of hands seized the poppies and bore them from sight. Baba-Yaga sat down to dine, and Vasilissa stood silent.

'Why do you say nothing?' remarked the witch. 'You stand as if you were dumb.'

Timidly Vasilissa replied, 'If you would permit me, I should like to ask you a question.'

'Ask, but remember, not every question leads to good. You will learn much; you will soon grow old.'

'I only wish to ask you,' said the girl, 'about what I have seen. When I came to you a pale horseman dressed in white on a white horse overtook me. Who was he?'

'He is my clear day,' answered Baba-Yaga.

'Then another horseman, who was red and dressed in red, and who rode a red horse, overtook me. Who was he?'

'He was my little red sun!' was the answer.

'But who was the black horseman who passed me at the gate granny?'

'He was my dark night; all three are my faithful servants.'

Vasilissa recalled the three pairs of hands, but was silent. 'Have you nothing more to ask?' said Baba-Yaga.

'I have, but you said, granny, that I shall learn much as I grow older.'

'It is well,' answered the witch, 'that you have enquired only about things outside and not about anything here! I do not like my rubbish to be carried away, and I eat over-inquisitive people! Now I will ask you something. How did you succeed in performing the tasks which I set you?'

'My mother's blessing assisted me,' answered Vasilissa.

'Depart, favoured daughter! I do not require people who have been blessed.' Baba-Yaga dragged Vasilissa out of the room and pushed her beyond the gate, took down from the fence a skull with burning eyes and, putting it on a stick, gave it to the girl and said, 'Take this light to your stepsisters; they sent you here for it.'

Vasilissa ran off, the skull giving her light, which only went out in the morning; and at last, on the evening of the second day, she reached home. As she approached the gates, she was on the point of throwing away the skull, for she thought that there would no longer be any need for a light at home. Then suddenly a hollow voice from the skull was heard to say, 'Do not cast me aside, but carry me to your stepmother.' Glancing at the house, and not seeing a light in any of the windows, she decided to enter with the skull.

At first her stepmother and stepsisters met her with caresses, telling her that they had been without a light from the moment of her departure; they could not strike a light in any way, and if anybody brought one from the neighbours, it went out directly it was carried into the room. 'Perhaps your light will last,' said the stepmother. When they carried the skull into the room its eyes shone brightly and looked continually at the stepmother and her daughters. All their efforts to hide themselves were vain; wherever they rushed they were ceaselessly pursued by the eyes, and before dawn had been burnt to ashes, though Vasilissa was unharmed.

In the morning the girl buried the skull in the ground, locked up the house and visited the town, where she asked admission into the home of a certain old woman who was without kindred. Here she lived quietly and awaited her father. But one day she said to the old woman, 'It tires me to sit idle, granny! Go off and buy me some of the best flax; I will busy myself with spinning.'

The old woman purchased the flax and Vasilissa sat down to spin. The work proceeded rapidly, and the thread when spun was as smooth and fine as a small hair. The thread lay in heaps, and it was time to begin weaving, but a weaver's comb could not be found to suit Vasilissa's thread, and nobody would undertake to make one. Then the girl had recourse to her doll, who said, 'Bring me an old comb that has belonged to a weaver, and an old shuttle, and a horse's mane, and I will do everything for you.' Vasilissa obtained everything necessary, and lay down to sleep. The doll, in a single night, made a first-rate loom. Towards the end of winter linen had been woven of so fine a texture that it could be drawn through the needle where the thread should pass.

In spring the linen was bleached, and Vasilissa said to the old woman, 'Sell this linen, granny, and keep the money for yourself.'

The old woman glanced at the work and said with a sigh, 'Ah! my child, nobody but a tsar would wear such linen. I will take it to the palace.'

She went to the royal dwelling, and walked up and down in front of the windows. When the tsar saw her he said, 'What do you desire, old woman?'

'Your Majesty,' she answered, 'I have brought some wonderful material, and will show it to nobody but yourself.'

The tsar ordered that she should be admitted, and marvelled when he saw the linen. 'How much do you ask for it?' he enquired.

'It is not for sale, Tsar and Father! I have brought it as a gift.' The tsar thanked her, and sent her away with some presents.

Some shirts for the tsar were cut out from this linen, but a seamstress could nowhere be found to complete them. At last the tsar summoned the old woman and said to her, 'You were able to spin and weave this linen, so you will be able to sew together some shirts from it.'

'Tsar, it was not I who spun and wove the linen; it is the work of a beautiful maiden.'

'Well, let her sew them!'

The old woman returned home and related everything to Vasilissa. The girl said in reply, 'I knew that this work would not pass out of my hands.' She shut herself in her room and began the undertaking; soon without resting her hands, she had completed a dozen shirts.

The old woman bore them to the tsar, while Vasilissa washed herself and combed her hair, dressed and then took a seat at the window, and there awaited events. She saw a royal servant come to the old woman's house. He entered the room and said, 'The Tsar-Emperor desires to see the skilful worker who made his shirts, and to reward her out of his royal hands.'

Vasilissa presented herself before the tsar. So much did she please him that he said, 'I cannot bear to separate from you; become my wife!' The tsar took her by her white hands, placed her beside himself, and the wedding was celebrated.

Vasilissa's father quickly returned to rejoice at his daughter's good fortune and to live with her. Vasilissa took the old woman into the palace, and never separated from the little doll, which she kept in her pocket.

THE MIDWIFE AND THE FROG

(HUNGARIAN)

y grandmother's mother was a midwife – the queen's midwife, as we used to say, because she drew her pay from the parish, which in our eyes meant the whole country.

One night she was called away to assist at a childbirth. It was about midnight. It was pitch dark on the road and it was raining. When the woman was delivered of her babe – God let her have a good one – my great-grandmother started off homeward. On the road she came across a big frog. It was hopping along right in front of her. My great-grandmother had always had a holy fear of frogs, and she cried out in terror, 'Get out of my way, you hideous creature! Why on earth are you hopping around me? Is it a midwife you may be wanting?'

And thus she was conversing with the frog as she proceeded on her way, and the frog jumped closer and closer to her. Once it got right under her feet, and she stepped on it. It gave such a shriek that my great-grandmother almost jumped out of her shoes. Well, she went home leaving the frog on the road, and the frog hopped off to some place, wherever it had its abode.

Back at home, my great-grandmother went to bed. Suddenly she heard a cart driving into the yard. She thought there was another childbirth where her assistance would be needed. Soon she saw the door open. Two men came in; both were very dark-skinned. They were both spindleshanks; their legs looked like a pair of pipestems, and their heads were as big as a bushel. They greeted her with, 'Good evening,' and then said, 'We want to take you along, mother; you must come and help with a birth.'

She said, 'Who is it?' as it is the custom of a midwife to enquire where her assistance is wanted.

One of the men said, 'On the road you promised my wife to help her with the child when her time came.'

And this gave my great-grandmother something to think of, because she had not met a single soul on her way back, except the frog. 'It's true' she thought to herself, 'I asked her by way of a joke "Is it a midwife you're looking for? I might come and help you too."'

The two men said to her, 'Do not tarry, mother.'

But she said to them, 'I'm not going with you because I've met no human creature and I've promised nothing.'

But they were so insistent that she should keep her promise that finally she said, 'Well, as you are so keen on taking me along, I'll go with you.'

She thought to herself that in any case she'd take her rosary with her, and that if she would pray, God would not forsake her, wherever she'd be taken by the two men. And then the men left her alone, and she began to dress. She dressed herself quite neatly, and when she was ready she asked the men, 'Is it a long journey? Shall I put on more warm clothes?'

'We aren't going far. It will take us an hour and a half or so to get back. But hurry up, mother, because my wife was in a bad state when I left her.'

Then she finished dressing and went out with the two men. They put her in their black coach and soon were driving up a big mountain. It was Magyarós Mountain, not far from the banks of the Szucsáva. As they were driving along, suddenly the mountain opened up before them, and they drove straight through the split, right into the centre of the mountain. They pulled up before a house and one of the men opened the door for her.

'Well, you go in to her,' he said. 'You'll find my wife there. She's lying on the floor.'

And as she stepped through the door, she beheld a small woman lying on the floor. She, too, had a head as big as a bushel. She looked ill and was groaning terribly.

My great-grandmother said to her, 'You're in a bad state, daughter, aren't you? But have no fear. God will deliver you of your burden, and then you'll feel well again.'

The woman then said to my great-grandmother, 'Don't say that God will help me. My husband must not hear you saying it.'

The midwife asked, 'What else could I say?'

'Say the *gyivák* [a type of devil] will help you.'

Then my great-grandmother – we had it from her own mouth – felt as if the words had frozen on her lips, so alarmed did she grow at the thought of what place she had been brought to. No sooner had she thought about it than the child was born, a spindleshanks, with legs as thin as pipestems and a head as big as a stewpot. My great-grandmother thought to herself, 'Well, I was brought here, but how am I to get back?' So she turned to the woman. 'Well, your men have brought me to your place, but how can I get back? It's pitch dark outside. I couldn't find my way back home alone.'

The sick woman then said, 'Do not worry about that. My husband will take you back to the same place he brought you from.' And then she asked my great-grandmother, 'Well, mother, do you know who I am?'

'I couldn't say I do. I've asked your husband a few questions about you, but he didn't tell me a thing. He said I should go with them and I'd learn in time who you were.'

'Well, you know who I am? I am the frog you kicked about on the road and trod under your feet. Now, this should serve as a lesson that if you happen to come across some creature like me at about midnight or an hour past it, do not speak to it, nor take heed of what you see. Just pass along on your way. You see, you stopped to talk to me and made a promise to me. So you had to be brought here, because I was that frog you met on the road.'

Then my great-grandmother said, 'I've done my job here; now get me back to my home.'

Then the man came in and asked her, 'Well, what would you want me to pay for your troubles?'

Then the old midwife said, 'I don't want you to pay me anything. Get me right back to the place you brought me from.'

The man said, 'Do not worry. We still have half an hour or so to get you back. But now let me take you to our larder so that you may see for yourself that we are doing well. You needn't fear that we haven't the wherewithal to pay for your services.'

And my great-grandmother followed him to the larder. In the larder she beheld all sorts of food heaped on the shelves: flour and bacon and firkins of lard here, and loaves of bread and cream there and a lot of other things, all arranged in neat order, to say nothing of veritable mounds of gold and silver.

'Now you can see for yourself what plenty there is. Whatever the rich men and the wealthy farmers deny to the poor in their greed becomes ours and goes into our storeroom.' And he turned to my great-grandmother and said, 'Well, mother, let's get along. There isn't much time left for us to get you back to your home. Take of this gold an apronful, as I see you have on your Sunday apron.'

And he insisted on her taking an apronful of gold. He wouldn't let her leave the larder until she had filled her apron with it.

When she had put the gold in her apron, she was taken to the top of Magyarós Mountain by the same coach in which she had first come. But dawn was already coming on, and soon the cock uttered its first crow. Then the men pushed her from the black coach – though they were still near the top – and said to her, 'Trot along, mother, you can find your way home from here.'

And when she took a look at her apron to make sure that she had the gold, there was nothing whatever in her apron; that heap of gold had vanished into thin air.

And that is all there is to the story; you can take it from me.

PART TEN

BEAUTIFUL PEOPLE

FAIR, BROWN AND TREMBLING

(IRISH)

ing Aedh Cúrucha lived in Tir Conal, and he had three daughters, whose names were Fair, Brown, and Trembling.

Fair and Brown had new dresses, and went to church every Sunday. Trembling was kept at home to do the cooking and work. They would not let her go out of the house at all; for she was more beautiful than the other two, and they were in dread she might marry before themselves.

They carried on in this way for seven years. At the end of seven years the son of the king of Omanya fell in love with the eldest sister.

One Sunday morning, after the other two had gone to church, the old henwife came into the kitchen to Trembling, and said, 'It's at church you ought to be this day, instead of working here at home.'

'How could I go?' said Trembling. 'I have no clothes good enough to wear at church. And if my sisters were to see me there, they'd kill me for going out of the house.'

'I'll give you,' said the henwife, 'a finer dress than either of them has ever seen. And now tell me what dress will you have?'

'I'll have,' said Trembling, 'a dress as white as snow, and green shoes for my feet.'

Then the henwife put on the cloak of darkness, clipped a piece from the old clothes the young woman had on, and asked for the whitest robes in the world and the most beautiful that could be found, and a pair of green shoes.

That moment she had the robe and the shoes, and she brought them to Trembling, who put them on. When Trembling was dressed and ready, the henwife said, 'I have a honey-bird here to sit on your right shoulder, and a honey-finger to put on your left. At the door stands a milk-white mare, with a golden saddle for you to sit on, and a golden bridle to hold in your hand.'

Trembling sat on the golden saddle. And when she was ready to start, the henwife said, 'You must not go inside the door of the church, and the minute the people rise up at the end of mass, do you make off, and ride home as fast as the mare will carry you.'

When Trembling came to the door of the church there was no one inside who could get a glimpse of her but was striving to know who she was; and when they saw her hurrying away at the end of mass, they ran out to overtake her. But no use in their running; she was away before any man could come near her. From the minute she left the church till she got home, she overtook the wind before her, and out-stripped the wind behind.

She came down at the door, went in, and found the henwife had dinner ready. She put off the white robes, and had on her old dress in a twinkling.

When the two sisters came home the henwife asked, 'Have you any news today from the church?'

'We have great news,' said they. 'We saw a wonderful, grand lady at the church door. The like of the robes she had we have never seen on woman before. It's little that was thought of our dresses beside what she had on. And there wasn't a man at the church, from the king to the beggar, but was trying to look at her and know who she was.'

The sisters would give no peace till they had two dresses like the robes of the strange lady; but honey-birds and honey-fingers were not to be found.

Next Sunday the two sisters went to church again, and left the youngest at home to cook the dinner.

After they had gone, the henwife came in and asked, 'Will you go to church today?'

'I would go,' said Trembling, 'if I could get the going.'

'What robe will you wear?' asked the henwife.

'The finest black satin that can be found, and red shoes for my feet.'

'What colour do you want the mare to be?'

'I want her to be so black and so glossy that I can see myself in her body.'

The henwife put on the cloak of darkness, and asked for the robes and the mare. That moment she had them. When Trembling was dressed, the henwife put the honey-bird on her right shoulder and the honey-finger on her left. The saddle on the mare was silver, and so was the bridle.

When Trembling sat in the saddle and was going away, the henwife ordered her strictly not to go inside the door of the church. but to rush away as soon as the people rose at the end of mass, and hurry home on the mare before any man could stop her.

That Sunday the people were more astonished than ever, and gazed at her more than the first time, and all they were thinking of was to know who she was. But they had no chance. for the moment the people rose at the end of mass she slipped from the church, was in the silver saddle, and home before a man could stop her or talk to her.

The henwife had the dinner ready. Trembling took off her satin robe, and had on her old clothes before her sisters got home.

'What news have you today?' asked the henwife of the sisters when they came from the church.

'Oh, we saw the grand strange lady again! And it's little that any man could think of our dresses after looking at the robes of satin that she had on! And all at church, from high to low, had their mouths open, gazing at her, and no man was looking at us.'

The two sisters gave neither rest nor peace till they got dresses as nearly like the strange lady's robes as they could find. Of course they were not so good, for the like of those robes could not be found in Erin.

When the third Sunday came, Fair and Brown went to church dressed in black satin. They left Trembling at home to work in the kitchen, and told her to be sure and have dinner ready when they came back.

After they had gone and were out of sight, the henwife came to the kitchen and said, 'Well, my dear, are you for church today?'

'I would go if I had a new dress to wear.'

'I'll get you any dress you ask for. What dress would you like?' asked the henwife.

A dress red as a rose from the waist down, and white as snow from the waist up; a cape of green on my shoulders; and a hat on my head with a red, a white, and a green feather in it; and shoes for my feet with the toes red, the middle white, and the backs and heels green.'

The henwife put on the cloak of darkness, wished for all these things, and had them. When Trembling was dressed, the henwife put the honey-bird on her right shoulder and the honey-finger on her left, and placing the hat on her head, clipped a few hairs from one lock and a few from another with her scissors, and that moment the most beautiful golden hair was flowing down over the girl's shoulders. Then the henwife asked what kind of a mare she would ride. She said white, with blue and gold-coloured diamond-shaped spots all over her body, on her back a saddle of gold, and on her head a golden bridle.

The mare stood there before the door, and a bird sitting between her ears, which began to sing as soon as Trembling was in the saddle, and never stopped till she came home from the church.

The fame of the beautiful strange lady had gone out through the world, and all the princes and great men that were in it came to church that Sunday, each one hoping that it was himself would have her home with him after mass.

The son of the king of Omanya forgot all about the eldest sister, and remained outside the church, so as to catch the strange lady before she could hurry away.

The church was more crowded than ever before, and there were three times as many outside. There was such a throng before the church that Trembling could only come inside the gate.

As soon as the people were rising at the end of mass, the lady slipped out through the gate, was in the golden saddle in an instant, and sweeping away ahead of the wind. But if she was, the prince of Omanya was at her side, and seizing her by the foot, he ran with the mare for thirty perches, and never let go of the beautiful lady till the shoe was pulled from her foot, and he was left behind with it in his hand. She came home as fast as the mare could carry her, and was thinking all the time that the henwife would kill her for losing the shoe.

Seeing her so vexed and so changed in the face, the old woman asked, 'What's the trouble that's on you now?'

'Oh! I've lost one of the shoes off my feet,' said Trembling.

'Don't mind that; don't be vexed,' said the henwife. 'Maybe it's the best thing that ever happened to you.'

Then Trembling gave up all the things she had to the henwife, put on her old clothes, and went to work in the kitchen. When the sisters came home, the henwife asked, 'Have you any news from the church?'

'We have indeed,' said they; 'for we saw the grandest sight today. The strange lady came again, in grander array than before. On herself and the horse she rode were the finest colours of the world, and between the ears of the horse was a bird which never stopped singing from the time she came till she went away. The lady herself is the most beautiful woman ever seen by man in Erin.'

After Trembling had disappeared from the church, the son of the king of Omanya said to the other kings' sons, 'I will have that lady for my own.'

They all said, 'You didn't win her just by taking the shoe off her foot, you'll have to win her by the point of the sword. You'll have to fight for her with us before you can call her your own.'

'Well,' said the son of the king of Omanya, 'when I find the lady that shoe will fit, I'll fight for her, never fear, before I leave her to any of you.'

Then all the kings' sons were uneasy, and anxious to know who was she that lost the shoe; and they began to travel all over Erin to know could they find her. The prince of Omanya and all the others went in a great company together, and made the round of Erin. They went everywhere – north, south, east and west. They visited every place where a woman was to be found, and left not a house in the kingdom they did not search, to know could they find the woman the shoe would fit, not caring whether she was rich or poor, of high or low degree.

The prince of Omanya always kept the shoe. And when the young women saw it they had great hopes, for it was of proper size, neither large nor small, and it would beat any man to know of what material it was made. One thought it would fit her if she cut a little from her great toe; and another, with too short a foot, put something in the tip of her stocking. But no use, they only spoiled their feet, and were curing them for months afterwards.

The two sisters, Fair and Brown, heard that the princes of the world were looking all over Erin for the woman that could wear the shoe, and every day they were talking of trying it on. And one day Trembling spoke up and said, 'Maybe it's my foot that the shoe will fit.'

'Oh, the breaking of the dog's foot on you! Why say so when you were at home every Sunday?'

They were that way waiting, and scolding the younger sister, till the princes were near the place. The day they were to come, the sisters put Trembling in a closet, and locked the door on her. When the company came to the house, the prince of Omanya gave the shoe to the sisters. But though they tried and tried, it would fit neither of them.

'Is there any other young woman in the house?' asked the prince.

'There is,' said Trembling, speaking up in the closet. 'I'm here.'

'Oh! we have her for nothing but to put out the ashes,' said the sisters.

But the prince and the others wouldn't leave the house till they had seen her. So the two sisters had to open the door. When Trembling came out, the shoe was given to her, and it fitted exactly.

The prince of Omanya looked at her and said, 'You are the woman the shoe fits, and you are the woman I took the shoe from.'

Then Trembling spoke up, and said, 'Do you stay here till I return.'

Then she went to the henwife's house. The old woman put on the cloak of darkness, got everything for her she had the first Sunday at church, and put her on the white mare in the same fashion. Then Trembling rode along the highway to the front of the house. All who saw her the first time said, 'This is the lady we saw at church.'

Then she went away a second time, and a second time came back on the black mare in the second dress which the henwife gave her. All who saw her the second Sunday said, 'That is the lady we saw at church.'

A third time she asked for a short absence, and soon came back on the third mare and in the third dress. All who saw her the third time said, 'That is the lady we saw at church.' Every man was satisfied, and knew that she was the woman.

Then all the princes and great men spoke up, and said to the son of the king of Omanya, 'You'll have to fight now for her before we let her go with you.'

'I'm here before you, ready for combat,' answered the prince.

Then the son of the king of Lochlin stepped forth. The struggle began, and a terrible struggle it was. They fought for nine hours. And then the son of the king of Lochlin stopped, gave up his claim, and left the field. Next day the son of the king of Spain fought six hours, and yielded his claim. On the third day the son of the king of Nyerfói fought eight hours, and stopped. The fourth day the son of the king of Greece fought six hours, and stopped. On the fifth day no more strange princes wanted to fight. And all the sons of kings in Erin said they would not fight with a man of their own land, that the strangers had had their chance, and as no others came to claim the woman, she belonged of right to the son of the king of Omanya.

The marriage day was fixed, and the invitations were sent out. The wedding lasted for a year and a day. When the wedding was over, the king's son brought home the bride, and when the time came a son was born. The young woman sent for her eldest sister, Fair, to be with her and care for her. One day, when Trembling was well, and when her husband was away hunting, the two sisters went out to walk. And when they came to the seaside, the eldest pushed the youngest sister in. A great whale came and swallowed her.

The eldest sister came home alone, and the husband asked, 'Where is your sister?'

'She has gone home to her father in Ballyshannon. Now that I am well, I don't need her.'

'Well,' said the husband, looking at her, 'I'm in dread it's my wife that has gone.'

'Oh! no,' said she. 'It's my sister Fair that's gone.'

Since the sisters were very much alike, the prince was in doubt. That night he put his sword between them, and said, 'If you are my wife, this sword will get warm; if not, it will stay cold.'

In the morning when he rose up, the sword was as cold as when he put it there.

It happened when the two sisters were walking by the seashore that a little cowboy was down by the water minding cattle, and saw Fair push Trembling into the sea; and next day, when the tide came in, he saw the whale swim up and throw her out on the sand. When she was on the sand she said to the cowboy, 'When you go home in the evening with the cows, tell the master that my sister Fair pushed me into the sea yesterday; that a whale swallowed me, and then threw me out, but will come again and swallow me with the coming of the next tide; then he'll go out with the tide, and come again with tomorrow's tide, and throw me again on the strand. The whale will cast me out three times. I'm under the enchantment of this whale, and cannot leave the beach or escape myself. Unless my husband saves me before I'm swallowed a fourth time, I shall be lost. He must come and shoot the whale with a silver bullet when he turns on the broad of his back. Under the breast-fin of the whale is a reddish-brown spot. My husband must hit him in that spot, for it is the only place in which he can be killed.'

When the cowboy got home, the eldest sister gave him a draught of oblivion, and he did not tell.

Next day he went again to the sea. The whale came and cast Trembling on shore again. She asked the boy, 'Did you tell the master what I told you to tell him?'

'I did not,' said he. 'I forgot.'

'How did you forget?' asked she.

'The woman of the house gave me a drink that made me forget.'

'Well, don't forget telling him this night. And if she gives you a drink, don't take it from her.'

As soon as the cowboy came home, the eldest sister offered him a drink. He refused to take it till he had delivered his message and told all to the master. The third day the prince went down with his gun and a silver bullet in it. He was not long down when the whale came and threw Trembling upon the beach as the two days before. She had no power to speak to her husband till he had killed the whale. Then the whale went out, turned over once on the broad of his back, and showed the spot for a moment only. That moment the prince fired. He had but the one chance, and a short one at that. But he took it, and hit the spot, and the whale, mad with pain, made the sea all around red with blood, and died.

That minute Trembling was able to speak, and went home with her husband, who sent word to her father what the eldest sister had done. The father came, and told him any death he chose to give her to give it. The prince told the father he would leave her life and death with

himself. The father had her put out then on the sea in a barrel, with provisions in it for seven years.

In time Trembling had a second child, a daughter. The prince and she sent the cowboy to school, and trained him up as one of their own children, and said, 'If the little girl that is born to us now lives, no other man in the world will get her but him.'

The cowboy and the prince's daughter lived on till they were married. The mother said to her husband, 'You could not have saved me from the whale but for the little cowboy. On that account I don't grudge him my daughter.'

The son of the king of Omanya and Trembling had fourteen children, and they lived happily till the two died of old age.

DIIRAWIC AND HER
INCESTUOUS BROTHER

(SUDAN: DINKA)

girl called Diirawic was extremely beautiful. All the girls
of the tribe listened to her words. Old women all listened
to her words. Small children all listened to her words. Even
old men all listened to her words. A man called Teeng
wanted to marry her, but her brother, who was also called Teeng,
refused. Many people each offered a hundred cows for her
bridewealth, but her brother refused. One day Teeng spoke to his
mother and said, 'I would like to marry my sister Diirawic.'

His mother said, 'I have never heard of such a thing. You should go
and ask your father.'

He went to his father and said, 'Father, I would like to marry my
sister.'

His father said, 'My son, I have never heard of such a thing. A man
marrying his sister is something I cannot even speak about. You had
better go and ask your mother's brother.'

He went to his mother's brother and said, 'Uncle, I would like to
marry my sister.'

His maternal uncle exclaimed, 'My goodness! Has anybody ever
married his sister? Is that why you have always opposed her marriage? Was it because you had it in your heart to marry her yourself?
I have never heard of such a thing! But what did your mother say
about this?'

'My mother told me to ask my father. I agreed and went to my
father. My father said he had never heard such a thing and told me to
come to you.'

'If you want my opinion,' said his uncle, 'I think you should ask
your father's sister.'

He went around to all his relatives that way. Each one expressed surprise and suggested that he should ask another. Then he came to his mother's sister and said, 'Aunt, I would like to marry my sister.'

She said, 'My child, if you prevented your sister from being married because you wanted her, what can I say! Marry her if that is your wish. She is your sister.'

Diirawic did not know about this. One day she called all the girls and said, 'Girls, let us go fishing.' Her words were always listened to by everyone, and when she asked for anything, everyone obeyed. So all the girls went, including little children. They went and fished.

In the mean time, her brother Teeng took out his favourite ox, Mijok, and slaughtered it for a feast. He was very happy that he was allowed to marry his sister. All the people came to the feast.

Although Diirawic did not know her brother's plans, her little sister had overheard the conversation and knew what was happening. But she kept silent; she did not say anything.

A kite flew down and grabbed up the tail of Teeng's ox, Mijok. Then it flew to the river where Diirawic was fishing and dropped it in her lap. She looked at the tail and recognised it. 'This looks like the tail of my brother's ox, Mijok,' she said. 'What has killed him? I left him tethered and alive!'

The girls tried to console her, saying, 'Diirawic, tails are all the same. But if it is the tail of Mijok, then perhaps some important guests have arrived. It may be that they are people wanting to marry you. Teeng may have decided to honour them with his favourite ox. Nothing bad has happened.'

Diirawic was still troubled. She stopped the fishing and suggested that they return to find out what had happened to her brother's ox.

They went back. As they arrived, the little sister of Diirawic came running to her and embraced her, saying, 'My dear sister Diirawic, do you know what has happened?'

'I don't know,' said Diirawic.

'Then I will tell you a secret,' continued her sister, 'but please don't mention it to anyone, not even to our mother.'

'Come on, sister, tell me,' said Diirawic.

'Teeng has been preventing you from being married because *he* wants to marry you,' her sister said. 'He has slaughtered his ox, Mijok, to celebrate his engagement to you. Mijok is dead.'

Diirawic cried and said, 'So that is why God made the kite fly with

Mijok's tail and drop it in my lap. So be it. There is nothing I can do.'

'Sister,' said her little sister, 'let me continue with what I have to tell you. When your brother bedevils you and forgets that you are his sister, what do you do? I found a knife for you. He will want you to sleep with him in the hut. Hide the knife near the bed. And at night when he is fast asleep, cut off his testicles. He will die. And he will not be able to do anything to you.'

'Sister,' said Diirawic, 'you have given me good advice.'

Diirawic kept the secret and did not tell the girls what had occurred. But she cried whenever she was alone.

She went and milked the cows. People drank the milk. But when Teeng was given milk, he refused. And when he was given food, he refused. His heart was on his sister. That is where his heart was.

At bedtime, he said, 'I would like to sleep in that hut, Diirawic, sister, let us share the hut.'

Diirawic said, 'Nothing is bad, my brother. We can share the hut.'

They did. Their little sister also insisted on sleeping with them in the hut. So she slept on the other side of the hut. In the middle of the night, Teeng got up and moved the way men do! At that moment, a lizard spoke and said, 'Come, Teeng, have you really become an imbecile? How can you behave like that towards your sister?'

He felt ashamed and lay down. He waited for a while and then got up again. And when he tried to do what men do, the grass on the thatching spoke and said. 'What an imbecile! How can you forget that she is your sister?'

He felt ashamed and cooled down. This time, he waited much longer. Then his desire rose and he got up. The rafters spoke and said, 'O, the man has really become an idiot! How can your heart be on your mother's daughter's body? Have you become a hopeless imbecile?'

He cooled down. This time he remained quiet for a very long time, but then his mind returned to it again.

This went on until very close to dawn. Then he reached that point when a man's heart fails him. The walls spoke and said, 'You monkey of a human being, what are you doing?' The utensils rebuked him. The rats in the hut laughed at him. Everything started shouting at him, 'Teeng, imbecile, what are you doing to your sister?'

At that moment, he fell back ashamed and exhausted and fell into a deep sleep.

The little girl got up and woke her older sister, saying, 'You fool, don't you see he is now sleeping? This is the time to cut off his testicles.'

Diirawic got up and cut them off. Teeng died.

Then the two girls got up and beat the drums in a way that told everybody that there was an exclusive dance for girls. No men could attend that dance. Nor could married women and children. So all the girls came out running from their huts and went to the dance.

Diirawic then spoke to them and said, 'Sisters, I called you to say that I am going into the wilderness.' She then went on to explain to them the whole story and ended, 'I did not want to leave you in secret. So I wanted a chance to bid you farewell before leaving.'

All the girls decided they would not remain behind.

'If your brother did it to you,' they argued, 'what is the guarantee that our brothers will not do it to us? We must all leave together!'

So all the girls of the tribe decided to go. Only very small girls remained. As they left, the little sister of Diirawic said, 'I want to go with you.'

But they would not let her. 'You are too young,' they said. 'You must stay.'

'In that case,' she said, 'I will cry out loud and tell everyone your plan!' And she started to cry out.

'Hush, hush,' said the girls. Then turning to Diirawic they said, 'Let her come with us. She is a girl with a heart. She has already taken our side. If we die, we die together with her!'

Diirawic accepted and they went. They walked; they walked and walked and walked, until they came to the borders between the human territory and the lion world. They carried their axes and their spears: they had everything they might need.

They divided the work among themselves. Some cut the timber for rafters and poles. Others cut the grass for thatching. And they built for themselves an enormous house – a house far larger even than a cattle-byre. The number of girls was tremendous. They built many beds for themselves inside the hut and made a very strong door to make sure of their safety.

Their only problem was that they had no food. But they found a large anthill, full of dried meat, grain, and all the other foodstuffs that they needed. They wondered where all this could have come from. But Diirawic explained to them, 'Sisters, we are women and it is the woman who bears the human race. Perhaps God has seen our plight, and not wanting us to perish, has provided us with all this. Let us take it in good grace!'

They did. Some went for firewood. Others fetched water. They cooked and ate. Every day they would dance the women's dance in great happiness and then sleep.

One evening a lion came in search of insects and found them dancing. But seeing such a large number of girls, he became frightened and left. Their number was such as would frighten anyone.

It then occurred to the lion to turn into a dog and go into their compound. He did. He went there looking for droppings of food. Some girls hit him and chased him away. Others said, 'Don't kill him. He is a dog and dogs are friends!'

But the sceptical ones said, 'What kind of dog would be in this isolated world? Where do you think he came from?'

Other girls said, 'Perhaps he came all the way from the cattle camp, following us! Perhaps he thought the whole camp was moving and so he ran after us!'

Diirawic's sister was afraid of the dog. She had not seen a dog following them. And the distance was so great that the dog could not have travelled all the way alone. She worried but said nothing. Yet she could not sleep; she stayed awake while all the others slept.

One night the lion came and knocked at the door. He had overheard the names of the older girls, one of them, Diirawic. After knocking at the door he said, 'Diirawic, please open the door for me.' The little girl who was awake answered, chanting:

> 'Achol is asleep,
> Adau is asleep,
> Nyankiir is asleep,
> Diirawic is asleep,
> The girls are asleep!'

The lion heard her and said, 'Little girl, what is the matter with you, staying up so late?'

She answered him, saying, 'My dear man, it is thirst. I am suffering from a dreadful thirst.'

'Why?' asked the lion. 'Don't the girls fetch water from the river?'

'Yes,' answered the little girl, 'they do. But since I was born, I do not drink water from a pot or a gourd. I drink only from a container made of reeds.'

'And don't they bring you water in such a container?' asked the lion.

'No,' she said. 'They only bring water in pots and gourds, even though there is a container of reeds in the house.'

'Where is that container?' asked the lion.

'It is outside there on the platform!' she answered.

So he took it and left to fetch water for her.

The container of reeds would not hold water. The lion spent much time trying to fix it with clay. But when he filled it, the water washed the clay away. The lion kept on trying until dawn. Then he returned with the container of reeds and put it back where it was. He then rushed back to the bush before the girls got up.

This went on for many nights. The little girl slept only during the daytime. The girls rebuked her for this, saying, 'Why do you sleep in the daytime? Can't you sleep at night? Where do you go at night?'

She did not tell them anything. But she worried. She lost so much weight that she became very bony.

One day Diirawic spoke to her sister and said, 'Nyanaguek, my mother's daughter, what is making you so lean? I told you to remain at home. This is too much for a child your age! Is it your mother you are missing? I will not allow you to make the other girls miserable. If necessary, daughter of my mother, I will kill you.'

But Diirawic's sister would not reveal the truth. The girls went on rebuking her but she would not tell them what she knew.

One day, she broke down and cried, and then said, 'My dear sister, Diirawic, I eat, as you see. In fact, I get plenty of food, so much that I do not finish what I receive. But even if I did not receive enough food, I have an enduring heart. Perhaps I am able to endure more than any of you here. What I am suffering from is something none of you has seen. Every night a lion gives me great trouble. It is just that I am a person who does not speak. That animal you thought to be a dog is a lion. I remain awake at night to protect us all and then sleep in the daytime. He comes and knocks at the door. Then he asks for you by name to open the door. I sing back to him and tell him that you are all asleep. When he wonders why I am awake, I tell him it is because I am thirsty. I explain that I only drink out of a container made of reeds and that the girls bring water only in pots and gourds. Then he goes to fetch water for me. And seeing that he cannot stop the water from flowing out of the container, he returns towards dawn and disappears, only to be back the following night. So that is what is destroying me, my dear sister. You blame me in vain.'

'I have one thing to tell you,' said Diirawic. 'Just be calm and when he comes, do not answer. I will remain awake with you.'

They agreed. Diirawic took a large spear that they had inherited from their ancestors and remained awake, close to the door. The lion came at his usual hour. He came to the door, but somehow he became afraid and jumped away without knocking. He had a feeling that something was going on.

So he left and stayed away for some time. Then he returned to the door towards dawn. He said, 'Diirawic, open the door for me!' There was only silence. He repeated his request. Still there was only silence. He said, 'Well! The little girl who always answered me is at last dead!'

He started to break through the door, and when he succeeded in pushing his head in, Diirawic attacked him with the large spear, forcing him back into the courtyard.

'Please, Diirawic,' he pleaded, 'do not kill me.'

'Why not?' asked Diirawic. 'What brought you here?'

'I only came in search of a sleeping place!'

'Well, I am killing you for that,' said Diirawic.

'Please allow me to be your brother,' the lion continued to plead. 'I will never attempt to hurt anyone again. I will go away if you don't want me here. Please!'

So Diirawic let him go. He went. But before he had gone a long way, he returned and said to the girls then gathered outside, 'I am going, but I will be back in two days with all my horned cattle.'

Then he disappeared. After two days, he came back with all his horned cattle, as he had promised. Then he addressed the girls, saying, 'Here I have come. It is true that I am a lion. I want you to kill that big bull in the herd. Use its meat for taming me. If I live with you untamed, I might become wild at night and attack you. And that would be bad. So kill the bull and tame me by teasing me with the meat.'

They agreed. So they fell on him and beat him so much that his fur made a storm on his back as it fell off.

They killed the bull and roasted the meat. They would bring a fat piece of meat close to his mouth, then pull it away. A puppy dog would jump out of the saliva which dripped from the lion's mouth. They would give the puppy a fatal blow on the head. Then they would beat the lion again. Another piece of fat meat would be held close to his mouth, then pulled away, and another puppy would jump out of the falling saliva. They would give it a blow on the head and beat the lion some more. Four puppies emerged, and all four were killed.

Yet the lion's mouth streamed with a wild saliva. So they took a large quantity of steaming hot broth and poured it down his throat, clearing it of all the remaining saliva. His mouth remained wide open and sore. He could no longer eat anything. He was fed only milk, poured down his throat. He was then released. For four months, he was nursed as a sick person. His throat continued to hurt for all this time. Then he recovered.

The girls remained for another year. It was now five years since they had left home.

The lion asked the girls why they had left their home. The girls asked him to address his questions to Diirawic, as she was their leader. So he turned to Diirawic and asked the same question.

'My brother wanted to make me his wife,' explained Diirawic. 'I killed him for that. I did not want to remain in a place where I had killed my own brother. So I left. I did not care about my life. I expected such dangers as finding you. If you had eaten me, it would have been no more than I expected.'

'Well, I have now become a brother to you all,' said the lion. 'As an older brother, I think I should take you all back home. My cattle have since multiplied. They are yours. If you find that your land has lost its herds, these will replace them. Otherwise they will increase the cattle already there, because I have become a member of your family. Since your only brother is dead, let me be in the place of Teeng, your brother. Cool your heart and return home.'

He pleaded with Diirawic for about three months. Finally she agreed, but cried a great deal. When the girls saw her cry, they all cried. They cried and cried because their leader, Diirawic, had cried.

The lion slaughtered a bull to dry their tears. They ate the meat. Then he said to them, 'Let us wait for three more days, and then leave!'

They slaughtered many bulls in sacrifice to bless the territory they crossed as they returned, throwing meat away everywhere they passed. As they did so, they prayed, 'This is for the animals and the birds that have helped keep us healthy for all this time without death or illness in our midst. May God direct you to share in this meat.'

They had put one bull into their big house and locked the house praying, 'Our dear house, we give you this bull. And you bull, if you should break the rope and get out of the house, that will be a sign of grace from the hut. If you should remain inside, then we bequeath you this hut as we leave.' And they left.

All this time the people at home were in mourning. Diirawic's father never shaved his head. He left the ungroomed hair of mourning on his head and did not care about his appearance. Her mother, too, was in the same condition. She covered herself with ashes so that she looked grey. The rest of the parents mourned, but everyone mourned especially for Diirawic. They did not care as much for their own daughters as they did for Diirawic.

The many men who had wanted to marry Diirawic also neglected themselves in mourning. Young men and girls wore only two beads. But older people and children wore no beads at all.

All the girls came and tethered their herds a distance from the village. They all looked beautiful. Those who had been immature had grown into maturity. The older ones had now reached the peak of youth and beauty. They had blossomed and had also become wiser and adept with words.

The little boy who was Diirawic's youngest brother had now grown up. Diirawic resembled her mother, who had been an extremely beautiful girl. Even in her old age, she still retained her beauty and her resemblance to her daughter still showed.

The little boy had never really known his sister, as he was too young when the girls left. But when he saw Diirawic in the newly arrived cattle camp, he saw a clear resemblance to his mother. He knew that his two sisters and the other girls of the camp had disappeared. So he came and said, 'Mother, I saw a girl in the cattle camp who looks like she could be my sister, even though I do not remember my sisters.'

'Child, don't you feel shame? How can you recognise people who left soon after you were born? How can you recall people long dead? This is evil magic! This is the work of an evil spirit!' She started to cry, and all the women joined her in crying.

Age-sets came running from different camps to show her sympathy. They all cried, even as they tried to console her with words.

Then came Diirawic with the girls and said, 'My dear woman, permit us to shave off your mourning hair. And all of you, let us shave off your mourning hair!'

Surprised by her words, they said, 'What has happened that we should shave off our mourning hair?'

Then Diirawic asked them why they were in mourning. The old woman started to cry as Diirawic spoke, and said, 'My dear girl, I lost a girl like you. She died five years ago, and five years is a long time. If she had died only two or even three years ago, I might have dared to say you are my daughter. As it is, I can't. But seeing you, my dear daughter, has cooled my heart.'

Diirawic spoke again, saying, 'Dear Mother, every child is a daughter. As I stand in front of you, I feel as though I were your daughter. So please listen to what I say as though I were your own daughter. We have all heard of you and your famed name. We have come from a very far-off place because of you. Please allow us to shave your head. I offer five cows as a token of my request.'

'Daughter,' said the woman, 'I shall honour your request, but not because of the cows – I have no use for cattle. Night and day, I think of nothing but my lost Diirawic. Even this child you see means nothing to me compared to my lost child, Diirawic. What grieves me is that God has refused to answer my prayers. I have called upon our clan spirits and I have called upon my ancestors, and they do not listen. This I resent. I will listen to your words, my daughter. The fact that God has brought you along and put these words into your mouth is enough to convince me.'

So she was shaved. Diirawic gave the woman beautiful leather skirts made from skins of animals they killed on the way. They were not from the hides of cattle, sheep or goats. She decorated the edges of the skirts with beautiful beads and made bead designs of cattle figures on the skirts. On the bottom of the skirts she left the beautiful natural furs of the animals.

The woman cried and Diirawic pleaded with her to wear them. She and the girls went and brought milk from their own cattle and made a feast. Diirawic's father welcomed the end of mourning. But her mother continued to cry as she saw all the festivities.

So Diirawic came to her and said, 'Mother, cool your heart. I am Diirawic.'

Then she shrieked with cries of joy. Everyone began to cry – old women, small girls, everyone. Even blind women dragged themselves out of their huts, feeling their way with sticks, and cried. Some people died as they cried. Drums were taken out and for seven days, people danced with joy. Men came from distant villages, each with seven bulls to sacrifice for Diirawic. The other girls were almost abandoned. All were concerned with Diirawic.

People danced and danced. They said, 'Diirawic, if God has brought you, then nothing is bad. That is what we wanted.'

Then Diirawic said, 'I have come back. But I have come with this man to take the place of my brother Teeng.'

'Very well,' agreed the people. 'Now there is nothing to worry about.'

There were two other Teengs. Both were sons of chiefs. Each one came forward, asking to marry Diirawic. It was decided that they should compete. Two large kraals were to be made. Each man was to fill his kraal with cattle. The kraals were built. The men began to fill them with cattle. One Teeng failed to fill his kraal. The other Teeng succeeded so well that some cattle even remained outside.

Diirawic said, 'I will not marry anyone until my new brother is given four girls to be his wives. Only then shall I accept the man my people want.'

People listened to her words. Then they asked her how the man became her brother. So she told the whole story from its beginning to its end.

The people agreed with her and picked four of the finest girls for her new brother. Diirawic then accepted the man who had won the competition. She was given to her husband and she continued to treat the lion-man as her full brother. She gave birth first to a son and then to a daughter. She bore twelve children. But when the thirteenth child was born, he had the characteristics of a lion. Her lion-brother had brought his family to her village and was living there when the child was born. The fields of Diirawic and her brother were next to each other. Their children played together. As they played, the small lion-child, then still a baby, would put on leather skirts and sing. When Diirawic returned, the children told her, but she dismissed what they said. 'You are liars. How can such a small child do these things?'

They would explain to her that he pinched them and dug his nails into their skins and would suck blood from the wounds. Their mother simply dismissed their complaints as lies.

But the lion-brother began to wonder about the child. He said, 'Does a newly born human being behave the way this child behaves?' Diirawic tried to dispel his doubts.

But one day her brother hid and saw the child dancing and singing in a way that convinced him that the child was a lion and not a human being. So he went to his sister and said, 'What you bore was a lion! What shall we do?'

The woman said, 'What do you mean? He is my child and should be treated as such.'

'I think we should kill him,' said the lion-brother.

'That is impossible,' she said. 'How can I allow my child to be killed? He will get used to human ways and will cease to be aggressive.'

'No,' continued the lion. 'Let us kill him by poison if you want to be gentle with him.'

'What are you talking about?' retorted his sister. 'Have you forgotten that you yourself were a lion and were then tamed into a human being? Is it true that old people lose their memory?'

The boy grew up with the children. But when he reached the age of herding, he would go and bleed the children by turn and suck blood from their bodies. He would tell them not to speak, and that if they said anything to their elders, he would kill them and eat them. The children would come home with wounds, and when asked, would say their wounds were from thorny trees.

But the lion did not believe them. He would tell them to stop lying and tell the truth, but they would not.

One day he went ahead of them and hid on top of the tree under which they usually spent the day. He saw the lion-child bleed the children and suck their blood. Right there, he speared him. The child died.

He then turned to the children and asked why they had hidden the truth for so long. The children explained how they had been threatened by the lion-child. Then he went and explained to his sister, Diirawic, what he had done.

THE MIRROR

(JAPANESE)

here is a pretty Japanese tale of a small farmer who bought his young wife a mirror. She was surprised and delighted to know that it reflected her face, and cherished her mirror above all her possessions. She gave birth to one daughter, and died young; and the farmer put the mirror away in a press, where it lay for long years.

The daughter grew up the very image of her mother; and one day, when she was almost a woman, her father took her aside, and told her of her mother, and of the mirror which had reflected her beauty. The

girl was devoured with curiosity, unearthed the mirror from the old press, and looked into it.

'Father!' she cried. 'See! Here is mother's face!'

It was her own face she saw; but her father said nothing.

The tears were streaming down his cheeks, and the words would not come.

THE FROG MAIDEN

(BURMESE)

n old couple was childless, and the husband and the wife longed for a child. So when the wife found that she was with child, they were overjoyed; but to their great disappointment, the wife gave birth not to a human child, but to a little she-frog. However, as the little frog spoke and behaved as a human child, not only the parents but also the neighbours came to love her and called her affectionately 'Little Miss Frog'.

Some years later the woman died, and the man decided to marry again. The woman he chose was a widow with two ugly daughters and they were very jealous of Little Miss Frog's popularity with the neighbours. All three took a delight in ill-treating Little Miss Frog.

One day the youngest of the king's four sons announced that he would perform the hair-washing ceremony on a certain date and he invited all young ladies to join in the ceremony, as he would choose at the end of the ceremony one of them to be his princess.

On the morning of the appointed day the two ugly sisters dressed themselves in fine raiment, and with great hopes of being chosen by the prince they started for the palace. Little Miss Frog ran after them, and pleaded, 'Sisters, please let me come with you.'

The sisters laughed and said mockingly, 'What, the little frog wants to come? The invitation is to young ladies and not to young frogs.' Little Miss Frog walked along with them towards the palace, pleading for permission to come. But the sisters were adamant, and so at the palace gates she was left behind. However, she spoke so sweetly to the guards that they allowed her to go in. Little Miss Frog found hundreds of young ladies gathered round the pool full of lilies in the palace grounds; and she took her place among them and waited for the prince.

The prince now appeared, and washed his hair in the pool. The ladies also let down their hair and joined in the ceremony. At the end of the ceremony, the prince declared that as the ladies were all beautiful, he did not know whom to choose and so he would throw a posy of jasmines into the air; and the lady on whose head the posy fell would be his princess. The prince then threw the posy into the air, and all the ladies present looked up expectantly. The posy, however, fell on Little Miss Frog's head, to the great annoyance of the ladies, especially the two stepsisters. The prince also was disappointed, but he felt that he should keep his word. So Little Miss Frog was married to the prince, and she became Little Princess Frog.

Some time later, the old king called his four sons to him and said, 'My sons, I am now too old to rule the country, and I want to retire to the forest and become a hermit. So I must appoint one of you as my successor. As I love you all alike, I will give you a task to perform, and he who performs it successfully shall be king in my place. The task is, bring me a golden deer at sunrise on the seventh day from now.'

The youngest prince went home to Little Princess Frog and told her about the task. 'What, only a golden deer!' exclaimed Princess Frog. 'Eat as usual, my prince, and on the appointed day I will give you a golden deer.'

So the youngest prince stayed at home, while the three elder princes went into the forest in search of the deer.

On the seventh day before sunrise, Little Princess Frog woke up her husband and said, 'Go to the palace, prince, and here is your golden deer.'

The young prince looked, then rubbed his eyes, and looked again. There was no mistake about it; the deer which Little Princess Frog was holding by a lead was really of pure gold. So he went to the palace, and to the great annoyance of the elder princes who brought ordinary deers, he was declared to be the heir by the king. The elder princes, however, pleaded for a second chance, and the king reluctantly agreed.

'Then perform this second task,' said the king. 'On the seventh day from now at sunrise, you must bring me the rice that never becomes stale, and the meat that is ever fresh.'

The youngest prince went home and told Princess Frog about the new task. 'Don't you worry, sweet prince,' said Princess Frog. 'Eat as usual, sleep as usual, and on the appointed day I will give you the rice and meat.'

So the youngest prince stayed at home, while the three elder princes went in search of the rice and meat.

On the seventh day at sunrise, Little Princess Frog woke up her husband and said, 'My Lord, go to the palace now, and here is your rice and meat.'

The youngest prince took the rice and meat, and went to the palace, and to the great annoyance of the elder princes who brought only well-cooked rice and meat, he was again declared to be the heir. But the two elder princes again pleaded for one more chance, and the king said, 'This is positively the last task. On the seventh day from now at sunrise, bring me the most beautiful woman on this earth.'

'Ho, ho!' said the three elder princes to themselves in great joy. 'Our wives are very beautiful, and we will bring them. One of us is sure to be declared heir, and our good-for-nothing brother will be nowhere this time.'

The youngest prince overheard their remark, and felt sad, for his wife was a frog and ugly. When he reached home, he said to his wife, 'Dear Princess, I must go and look for the most beautiful woman on this earth. My brothers will bring their wives, for they are really beautiful, but I will find someone who is more beautiful.'

'Don't you fret, my prince,' replied Princess Frog. 'Eat as usual, sleep as usual, and you can take me to the palace on the appointed day; surely I shall be declared to be the most beautiful woman'.

The youngest prince looked at the princess in surprise; but he did not want to hurt her feelings, and he said gently, 'All right, Princess, I will take you with me on the appointed day.'

On the seventh day at dawn, Little Princess Frog woke up the prince and said, 'My Lord, I must make myself beautiful. So please wait outside and call me when it is nearly time to go.' The prince left the room as requested. After some moments, the prince shouted from outside, 'Princess, it is time for us to go.'

'Please wait, my Lord,' replied the princess, 'I am just powdering my face.'

After some moments the prince shouted, 'Princess, we must go now.'

'All right, my Lord,' replied the princess, 'please open the door for me.

The prince thought to himself, 'Perhaps, just as she was able to obtain the golden deer and the wonderful rice and meat, she is able to make herself beautiful,' and he expectantly opened the door, but he was disappointed to see Little Princess Frog still a frog and as ugly as ever. However, so as not to hurt her feelings, the prince said nothing and took her along to the palace. When the prince entered the audience chamber with his Frog Princess the three elder princes with their wives were already there. The king looked at the prince in surprise and said, 'Where is your beautiful maiden?'

'I will answer for the prince, my king,' said the Frog Princess. 'I am his beautiful maiden.' She then took off her frog skin and stood a beautiful maiden dressed in silk and satin. The king declared her to be the most beautiful maiden in the world, and selected the prince as his successor on the throne.

The prince asked his princess never to put on the ugly frog skin again, and the Frog Princess, to accede to his request, threw the skin into the fire.

THE SLEEPING PRINCE

(SURINAMESE)

father had a daughter, but the child loved nothing so much as the field of grass which her father had planted. Only that she loved. Every morning her nurse took her to look at the grass. One morning when they went, the horses were feeding on the grass. Then they fought and fought, and blood fell on the grass. The girl said, 'My nurse, look how the horses are eating my grass till they fight. But look how nice the red is on the earth.'

At once a voice answered her, it said, 'Look how nice the red is on top of the earth. Well, if you were to see the Sleeping Prince! But the one who said the thing must come before eight days are up, and she will see the Sleeping Prince. And she will see a fan, and she should fan the prince until the prince shall awaken. Then she should kiss the prince. And she will see a bottle of water, and she shall sprinkle all the sticks which she sees.'

But, when she went she took her clothes, and she had a black doll and a broken razor. Then she took them and carried them there, too. Then she saw the prince, and she took the fan and began to fan the prince. She fanned so till . . . an old woman sat by at the side. She was a witch. Then she asked her, she said, if she was not tired of fanning? But she said, 'No, no.'

Not long after, the old woman came back, and she asked her, she said, 'Don't you want to go and urinate?' And so at once she got up to go and urinate.

The old woman took up the fan and began to fan. And so, before the girl came back, the prince awakened, and the old woman kissed the prince. And so the old woman had to marry the prince, because the law was that the one who kissed the prince should be the one to marry him.

But when they were already married, then the woman made her look after the fowls. She was very sad, because in her father's country she was a princess, and here she had to look after the fowls. They built a nice little house for her to live in. Then at night when she returned from her work, she put on her fine clothes, and she played a singing box. But when she finished playing, then she took up the black doll and the razor, and she asked it, she said, 'My black doll, my black doll, tell me if that is justice, or I will cut off your neck.' Then she put them back and she went to sleep.

But a soldier passed one night. Then he heard how sweetly the singing box played. He hid at the side of the house, and he heard everything the girl asked the black doll. And so he went and told the king that the girl who looked after the chickens did thus.

The selfsame night the king went to listen. Just as the woman asked the black doll if that was justice, the king knocked on the door that she open the door at once. As the door opened the king saw the woman and at once he fainted, because he did not know that this woman was a princess. She was wearing her fine clothes. And when the king came to himself, he called the woman and said he would call a big audience, and she must explain what made her ask that of the black doll.

When they came to the audience, she said before all the important people, 'Yes, in my father's country I was a princess, and here I must look after the fowls.' And she related everything that had happened between her and the old woman, and she had acted towards her, to cause her (the witch) to marry the prince. And so they found her in the right, and they killed the old woman.

From her bones they made a stepladder to climb to the top of her bed. And from the skin of the old woman she made a carpet to spread on the ground. And from the head she made a wash-basin in which to wash her face.

And so she came to marry the prince later. It was her destiny.

The Orphan

(AFRICAN: MALAWI)

 long time ago a certain man married. His wife gave birth to a baby girl whom they named Diminga. When Diminga's mother died, her father married again, and his new wife bore him several more children.

Although her husband asked her to care for Diminga, the stepmother cursed the child and would not treat her as her own. She would not bathe her, she fed her only husks, and made her sleep in a kraal. So Diminga looked a dirty miserable little girl, a skeleton dressed in rags. All she longed for was to die so that she might join her real mother.

One night Diminga dreamed that her mother was calling her: Diminga! Diminga my child! You need not starve,' said the voice. 'Tomorrow at noon, when you are grazing the cattle, take your big cow Chincheya and tell her to do what I have asked.'

The next day Diminga took her cattle into the fields as usual. When midday came and her hunger was at its worst, she remembered her dream. She went to Chincheya, patted her back, and said, 'Chincheya. Do what my mother told you.'

No sooner had she said this than many plates of food appeared before her. There was rice, beef, chicken, tea and much more. Diminga ate until she was full – and still there was food left over. She made the surplus disappear, and returned home that day so satisfied that she surprised her stepmother by refusing to eat the husks which were offered for her supper. 'Have them yourself,' she said.

Now this happened many times as each day Chincheya produced food for Diminga when they were alone in the fields. As Diminga grew fatter, her stepmother grew more suspicious, asking, 'Why are you growing fat even though you refuse to eat at home? What do you eat?'

But Diminga would not tell her secret and at last the stepmother insisted that her own daughter must accompany Diminga when she grazed her cattle the next day. Diminga was reluctant to take the girl, but she had no choice. When the time came for the midday meal, she told her stepsister to say nothing of what she was about to see.

The girl watched as Diminga took Chincheya aside and spoke to her. She was amazed when suddenly there was food everywhere. Her mouth watered; she tasted all the dishes, then she hid a bit of each under her fingernails before Diminga made the remains vanish.

That night after Diminga had gone to sleep, the girl told her mother to fetch plates, and when these were brought she heaped upon them all the food that she had hidden, saying, 'This food comes from that cow, Chincheya. Abundant and delicious food appears when Diminga speaks to her.'

The old woman was thunderstruck. She gobbled up the food and set about making plans to get all the rest that was still inside the cow. A few days later, she told her husband that she was feeling unwell. Now, for this reason a traditional dance was held and during this dance the stepmother seemed to fall into a trance. She cried out, 'The spirits demand the sacrifice of the cow Chincheya.'

Diminga was furious. She refused to allow the killing. Her stepmother pleaded with her husband, 'Should I die because of your daughter's infatuation with a cow?'

And her husband pleaded with his daughter, but Diminga was determined that Chincheya should not be killed. Then as she slept, one night she heard her mother's voice again. It said, 'My daughter Diminga, let them slaughter Chincheya. But do not eat the meat yourself. Take the stomach. Bury it on an island. You will see what will happen.'

So Diminga allowed the sacrifice to take place. The stepmother was sadly disappointed to find not even a single grain of rice inside the cow, indeed the meat itself was tasteless. Diminga wept at Chincheya's death; but she followed her mother's instructions and planted the cow's stomach on an island.

Where the stomach was planted a golden tree grew. Its leaves were pound notes and its fruits were coins: pennies, shillings, sixpences and florins. The tree glittered and dazzled the eyes of anyone who dared to look at it.

One day a ship passed the island. When the owner saw the golden tree he ordered his men to go ashore and collect the money. They shook the tree and tried to pick off the money, but they could not move it. The owner asked the local chief to shake the tree, then each of his villagers in turn to do the same. Still no one was successful in harvesting the money.

Then the ship's owner, who was a European, asked the chief, 'Is there anyone who has not tried to shake the tree? Go and search your village in case you have left anyone behind.'

The search took place, and the one remaining person who had not tried to shake the tree was found – a ragged dirty girl with sad eyes. It was Diminga. Everyone laughed when she was taken to the tree. 'Can this miserable girl succeed when we have failed!'

'Let her try,' said the European.

The tree swayed as Diminga approached. As she touched it, the tree began to shake, and when she held it, coins and notes showered to the ground in great piles, enough to fill several bags.

Instant marriage was arranged between Diminga and the European, and they went to live at his house. When she had bathed, dressed in new clothes and perfumed herself, Diminga was unrecognisably beautiful. And she was happy with her new life.

After some time Diminga visited her home, taking with her servants, carrying cases of clothes, food and money for her family. They welcomed her warmly, especially when they saw her gifts. And her father was glad that his daughter's troubles were now finished.

But her stepmother was full of envy and began planning once more to get the better of Diminga. Thus it happened that, when Diminga was sitting with her family, her one-eyed stepsister came to her with a needle in her hands, saying, 'Let me find lice in your hair, sister.'

'I have no lice,' said Diminga.

But her stepmother insisted and the girl began her search. Then suddenly, she drove the needle into Diminga's head. Diminga jerked, and was transformed into a bird, which flew away.

The old woman dressed her daughter in Diminga's clothes and veiled her face. She told Diminga's servants that their mistress was sick. They took 'Diminga' home, and told their master of his wife's illness. Whenever he tried to remove the veil, his 'wife' said, 'You must leave it for I am not well.'

One day his servant Guao went to the river to wash clothes and saw a small, bright beautiful bird perched on a tree. It began to sing:

Guao, Guao, Guao
Is Manuel at home
With one eyed-wife
This terrible one-eyed wife?

Guao listened, enchanted by the music and his curiosity was aroused.
Each day he saw the little bird and heard the song, then finally he took
his master to witness the strange event. The master trapped the bird
and took it home, where he made a pet of it. Whenever he touched the
bird's head, he noticed, it trembled. He looked closely and saw a
needle. When he pulled out the needle the bird was transformed into
a beautiful girl – Diminga, his wife.

When Diminga told him of her sufferings her husband ran and
unveiled the 'sick wife' – and shot her. He ordered his servants to cut

the body into pieces, which were dried then mixed with rice and put into bags. The bags of food were sent to Diminga's stepmother with the message, 'Diminga has arrived safely and sends you this gift.'

The old woman was satisfied to hear the news and shared the food amongst her family. It was only when she looked into the last bag of meat that she realised that she had been truly punished. Inside the bag was a human head, with its one eye fixed upon her in a terrible gaze.

PART ELEVEN

MOTHERS AND DAUGHTERS

ACHOL AND HER WILD MOTHER

(SUDAN: DINKA)

chol, Lanchichor (The Blind Beast) and Adhalchingeeny (The Exceedingly Brave One) were living with their mother. Their mother would go to fetch firewood. She gathered many pieces of wood and then put her hands behind her back and said, 'O dear, who will help me lift this heavy load?'

A lion came passing by and said, 'If I help you lift the load, what will you give me?'

'I will give you one hand,' she said.

She gave him a hand; he helped her lift the load and she went home. Her daughter, Achol, said, 'Mother, why is your hand like that?'

'My daughter, it is nothing,' she answered.

Then she left again to fetch firewood. She gathered many pieces of wood and then put her hand behind her back and said, 'O dear, who will now help me lift this heavy load?'

The lion came and said, 'If I help you lift the load, what will you give me?'

'I will give you my other hand!' And she gave him the other hand. He lifted the load on to her head and she went home without a hand.

Her daughter saw her and said, 'Mother, what has happened to your hands? You should not go to fetch firewood again! You must stop!'

But she insisted that there was nothing wrong and went to fetch firewood. Again she collected many pieces of firewood, put her arms behind her back and said, 'Who will now help me lift this heavy load?'

Again the lion came and said, 'If I help you lift the load, what will you give me?'

She said, 'I will give you one foot!'

She gave him her foot; he helped her, and she went home.

Her daughter said, 'Mother, this time, I insist that you do not go for the firewood! Why is all this happening? Why are your hands and your foot like this?'

'My daughter, it is nothing to worry about,' she said. 'It is my nature.'

She went back to the forest another time and collected many pieces of firewood. Then she put her arms behind her back and said, 'Who will now help me lift this load?'

The lion came and said, 'What will you now give me?'

She said, 'I will give you my other foot!'

So she gave him the other foot; he helped her, and she went home.

This time she became wild and turned into a lioness. She would not eat cooked meat; she would only have raw meat.

Achol's brothers went to the cattle camp with their mother's relatives. So only Achol remained at home with her mother. When her mother turned wild, she went into the forest, leaving Achol alone. She would only return for a short time in the evening to look for food. Achol would prepare something for her and put it on the platform in the courtyard. Her mother would come at night and sing in a dialogue with Achol.

> 'Achol, Achol, where is your father?'
> 'My father is still in the cattle camp!'
> 'And where is Lanchichor?'
> 'Lanchichor is still in the cattle camp!'
> 'And where is Adhalchingeeny?'
> 'Adhalchingeeny is still in the cattle camp!'
> 'And where is the food?'
> 'Mother, scrape the insides of our ancient gourds.'

She would eat and leave. The following night, she would return and sing. Achol would reply; her mother would eat and return to the forest. This went on for a long time.

Meanwhile, Lanchichor came from the cattle camp to visit his mother and sister. When he arrived home, he found his mother absent. He also found a large pot over the cooking fire. He wondered about these things and asked Achol, 'Where is Mother gone, and why are you cooking in such a big pot?'

She replied, 'I am cooking in this big pot because our mother has turned wild and is in the forest, but she comes at night for food.'

'Take that pot off the fire,' he said.

'I cannot,' she replied. 'I must cook for her.'

He let her. She cooked and put the food on the platform before they went to bed. Their mother came at night and sang. Achol replied as usual. Her mother ate and left. Achol's brother got very frightened. He emptied his bowels and left the next morning.

When he was asked in the cattle camp about the people at home, he was too embarrassed to tell the truth; so he said they were well.

Then Achol's father decided to come home to visit his wife and his daughter. He found the big pot on the fire and his wife away. When he asked Achol, she explained everything to him. He also told her to take the pot off the fire, but she would not. She put the food on the platform, and they went to bed. Achol's father told her to let him take care of the situation. Achol agreed. Her mother came and sang as usual. Achol replied. Then her mother ate. But her father was so frightened that he returned to the camp.

Then came Adhalchingeeny (The Exceedingly Brave One) and brought with him a very strong rope. He came and found Achol cooking with the large pot, and when Achol explained to him their mother's condition, he told her to take the pot off the fire, but she would not give in. He let her proceed with her usual plan. He placed the rope near the food in a way that would trap his mother when she took the food. He tied the other end to his foot.

Their mother came and sang as usual. Achol replied. As their mother went towards the food, Adhalchingeeny pulled the rope, gagged her and tied her to a pole. He then went and beat her with part

of the heavy rope. He beat her and beat her and beat her. Then he gave her a piece of raw meat, and when she ate it, he beat her again. He beat her and beat her and beat her. Then he gave her two pieces of meat, one raw and one roasted. She refused the raw one and took the roasted one, saying, 'My son, I have now become human, so please stop beating me.'

They then reunited and lived happily.

TUNJUR, TUNJUR

(PALESTINIAN ARAB)

TELLER: Testify that God is One!
AUDIENCE: There is no god but God.

here was once a woman who could not get pregnant and have children. Once upon a day she had an urge; she wanted babies. 'O Lord!' she cried out, 'why of all women am I like this? Would that I could get pregnant and have a baby, and may Allah grant me a girl even if she is only a cooking pot!'

One day she became pregnant. A day came and a day went, and behold! she was ready to deliver. She went into labour and delivered, giving birth to a cooking pot. What was the poor woman to do? She washed it, cleaning it well, put the lid on it, and placed it on the shelf.

One day the pot started to talk. 'Mother,' she said, take me down from this shelf!'

'Alas, daughter!' replied the mother, 'where am I going to put you?'

'What do you care?' said the daughter. 'Just bring me down, and I will make you rich for generations to come.'

The mother brought her down. 'Now put my lid on,' said the pot, 'and leave me outside the door.' Putting the lid on, the mother took her outside the door.

The pot started to roll, singing as she went, 'Tunjur, tunjur, clink, clink, O my mama!' She rolled until she came to a place where people usually gather. In a while people were passing by. A man came and found the pot all settled in its place. Eh!' he exclaimed, 'who has put this pot in the middle of the path? I'll be damned! What a beautiful pot! It's probably made of silver. He looked it over well. 'Hey, people!' he called, 'whose pot is this. Who put it here?' No one claimed it. 'By Allah,' he said, 'I'm going to take it home with me.'

On his way home, he went by the honey vendor. He had the pot filled with honey and brought it home to his wife. 'Look, wife,' he said, 'how beautiful is this pot!' The whole family was greatly pleased with it.

In two or three days they had guests, and they wanted to offer them some honey. The woman of the house brought the pot down from the shelf. Push and pull on the lid, but the pot would not open! She called her husband over. Pull and push, but open it he could not. His guests pitched in. Lifting the pot and dropping it, the man tried to break it open with hammer and chisel. He tried everything, but it was no use.

They sent for the blacksmith, and he tried and tried, to no avail. What was the man to do?

'Damn your owners!' he cursed the pot. 'Did you think you were going to make us wealthy?' And, taking it up, he threw it out the window.

When they turned their back and could no longer see it, she started to roll, saying as she went.

> 'Tunjur, tunjur, O my mama.
> In my mouth I brought the honey.
> Clink, clink, O my mama.
> In my mouth I brought the honey.'

'Bring me up the stairs!' she said to her mother when she reached home.

'Yee!' exclaimed the mother. 'I thought you had disappeared, that someone had taken you.'

'Pick me up!' said the daughter.

Picking her up, my little darlings, the mother took the lid off and found the pot full of honey. Oh! How pleased she was!

'Empty me!' said the pot.

The mother emptied the honey into a jar, and put the pot back on the shelf.

'Mother,' said the daughter the next day, 'take me down!'

The mother brought her down from the shelf.

'Mother, put me outside the door!'

The mother placed her outside the door, and she start rolling – tunjur, tunjur, clink, clink – until she reached a place where people were gathered, and then she stopped. A man passing by found her.

'Eh!' he thought. 'what kind of a pot is this?' He looked it over. How beautiful he found it! 'To whom does this belong?' he asked.

'Hey, people! Who are the owners of this pot?' He waited, but no one said, 'It's mine.' Then he said, 'By Allah, I'm going to take it.'

He took it, and on his way home stopped by the butcher and had it filled with meat. Bringing it home to his wife, he said, 'Look, wife, how beautiful is this pot I've found! By Allah, I found it so pleasing I bought meat and filled it and brought it home.'

'Yee!' they all cheered, 'how lucky we are! What a beautiful pot!' They put it away.

Towards evening they wanted to cook the meat. Push and pull on the pot, it would not open! What was the woman to do? She called her husband over and her children. Lift, drop, strike – no use. They took it to the blacksmith, but with no result.

The husband became angry. 'God damn your owners!' he cursed it. 'What in the world are you?' And he threw it as far as his arm would reach.

As soon as he turned his back, she started rolling, and singing:

> *'Tunjur, tunjur, O my mama,*
> *In my mouth I brought the meat.*
> *Tunjur, tunjur, O my mama,*
> *In my mouth I brought the meat.'*

She kept repeating that till she reached home.

'Lift me up!' she said to her mother. The mother lifted her up, took the meat, washed the pot, and put it away on the shelf.

'Bring me out of the house!' said the daughter the next day. The mother brought her out, and she said, 'Tunjur, tunjur, clink, clink' as she was rolling until she reached a spot close by the king's house, where she came to a stop. In the morning, it is said, the son of the king was on his way out, and behold! there was the pot settled in its place.

'Eh! What's this? Whose pot is it?' No one answered. 'By Allah,' he said, 'I'm going to take it.' He took it inside and called his wife over.

'Wife,' he said, 'take this pot! I brought it home for you. It's the most beautiful pot!'

The wife took the pot. 'Yee! How beautiful it is! By Allah, I'm going to put my jewellery in it.' Taking the pot with her, she gathered all her jewellery, even that which she was wearing, and put it in the pot. She also brought all their gold and money and stuffed them in the pot till it was full to the brim, then she covered it and put it away in the wardrobe.

Two or three days went by, and it was time for the wedding of her brother. She put on her velvet dress and brought the pot out so that she could wear her jewellery. Push and pull, but the pot would not open. She called to her husband, and he could not open it either. All the people who were there tried to open it, lifting and dropping. They took it to the blacksmith, and he tried but could not open it.

The husband felt defeated, 'God damn your owners!' he cursed it, what use are you to us?' Taking it up, he threw it out the window. Of course he was not all that anxious to let it go, so he went to catch it from the side of the house. No sooner did he turn around than she started to run:

> *Tunjur, tunjur, O my mama,*
> *In my mouth I brought the treasure.*
> *Tunjur, tunjur, O my mama.*
> *In my mouth I brought this treasure.'*

'Lift me up!' she said to her mother when she reached home. Lifting her up, the mother removed the lid.

'Yee! May your reputation be blackened!' she cried out. 'Wherever did you get this? What in the world is it?' The mother was now rich. She became very, very happy.

'It's enough now,' she said to her daughter, taking away the treasure. 'You shouldn't go out any more. People will recognise you.'

'No, no!' begged the daughter. 'Let me go out just one last time.'

The next day, my darlings, she went out, saying 'Tunjur, tunjur, O my mama.' The man who found her the first time saw her again.

'Eh! What in the world is this thing?' he exclaimed. 'It must have some magic in it, since it's always tricking people. God damn its owners! By Allah the Great, I'm going to sit and shit in it.' He went ahead, my darlings, and shat right in it. Closing the lid on him, she rolled along:

> *Tunjur, tunjur, O my mama,*
> *In my mouth I brought the caca.*
> *Tunjur, tunjur, O my mama,*
> *In my mouth I brought the caca.'*

'Lift me up!' she said to her mother when she reached home. The mother lifted her up.

'You naughty thing, you!' said the mother. 'I told you not to go out again, that people would recognise you. Don't you think it's enough now?'

The mother then washed the pot with soap, put perfume on it, and placed it on the shelf.

This is my story, I've told it, and in your hands I leave it.

THE LITTLE OLD WOMAN
WITH FIVE COWS

(YAKUT)

ne morning a little old woman got up and went to the field containing her five cows. She took from the earth a herb with five sprouts and, without breaking either root or branch, carried it home and wrapped it in a blanket and placed it on her pillow.

Then she went out again and sat down to milk her cows. Suddenly she heard tambourine bells jingle and scissors fall, on account of which noise she upset the milk. Having run home and looked, she found that the plant was uninjured. Again she issued forth to milk the cows, and again thought she heard the tambourine bells jingle and scissors fall, and once more she spilt her milk. Returning to the house, she looked into the bedchamber. There sat a maiden with eyes of chalcedony and lips of dark stone, with a face of light-coloured stone and with eyebrows like two dark sables stretching their forefeet towards each other; her body was visible through her dress; her bones were visible through her body; her nerves spreading this way and that, like mercury, were visible through her bones. The plant had become this maiden of indescribable beauty.

Soon afterwards Kharjit-Bergen, son of the meritorious Khan Kara, went into the dark forest. He saw a grey squirrel sitting on a curved twig, near the house of the little old woman with five cows, and he began to shoot, but as the light was bad, for the sun was already setting, he did not at once succeed in his purpose. At this time one of his arrows fell into the chimney.

'Old woman! take the arrow and bring it me!' he cried, but received no answer. His cheeks and forehead grew flushed and he became angry; a wave of arrogance sprang from the back of his neck, and he rushed into the house.

When he entered and saw the maiden he lost consciousness. But he revived and fell in love. Then he went out and, jumping on his horse, raced home at full gallop. 'Parents!' said he, 'there is such a beautiful maiden at the house of a little old woman with five cows! Get hold of this maiden and give her to me!'

The father sent nine servants on horseback, and they galloped at full speed to the house of the little old woman with five cows. All the servants became unconscious when they beheld the maiden's beauty. However, they recovered, and all went away except the best one of them.

'Little old woman!' said he, 'give this girl to the son of the meritorious Khan Khara!'

'I will give her,' was the answer.

They spoke to the maiden. 'I will go,' she announced.

'Now, as the bridegroom's wedding gift,' said the old woman, 'drive up cattle, and fill my open fields with horses and horned stock!'

Immediately the request was uttered and before the agreement was concluded the man gave an order to collect and drive up the animals as the bridegroom's gift.

'Take the maiden and depart!' said the little old woman, when the stock of horses and cattle had been given as arranged.

The maiden was quickly adorned, and a finely speckled horse that spoke like a human being was led up to her skilfully. They put on it a silver halter, saddled it with a silver saddle, which was placed over an upper silver saddle-cloth and a lower silver saddle-cloth, and they attached a little silver whip. Then the son-in-law led the bride from the mother's side by the whip, mounted his horse and took the bride home.

They went along the road, and the young man said, 'In the depth of the forest there is a trap for foxes; I will go there. Proceed along this road! It divides into two paths. On the road leading to the east is hanging a sable skin. But on the road leading to the west there should be the skin of a male bear with the paws and head and with white fur at the neck. Go on the path where the sable skin is hanging.' He pointed out the road and went away.

The girl made her way to the fork in the road, but on coming to it forgot the directions. Going along the path where the bear skin was hanging, she reached a small iron hut. Suddenly out of the hut came a devil's daughter, dressed in an iron garment above the knee. She had only one leg, and that was twisted; a single bent hand projected from below her breast, and her single furious eye was situated in the middle of her forehead. Having shot forth a fifty-foot iron tongue on to her breast, she pulled the girl from the horse, dropped her to the ground and tore all the skin from her face and threw it on her own face. She dragged off all the girl's finery and put it on herself. Then mounting, the devil's daughter rode away.

The husband met the devil's daughter when she arrived at the house of the meritorious Khan Khara. Nine youths came to take her horse by the halter; eight maidens did likewise. It is said that the bride wrongly fastened her horse to the willow tree where the old widow from Semyaksin used to tether her spotted ox. The greater part of those who thus received the bride became sorely depressed and the remainder were disenchanted; sorrow fell on them.

All who met the bride abominated her. Even the red weasels ran away from her, thus showing she was repugnant to them. Grass had been strewn on the pathway up to her hut, and on this grass she was led by the hand. Having entered, she replenished the fire with the tops of three young larch trees. Then they concealed her behind a curtain, while they themselves also drank and played and laughed and made merry.

But the marriage feast came to an end, and there was a return to ordinary life The little old woman with five cows, on going into open country to seek her cows, found that the plant with five sprouts was growing better than usual. She dug it up with its roots and, carrying it home, wrapped it up and placed it on her pillow. Then she went back and began to milk the cows, but the tambourine with the bells began to tinkle, and the scissors fell with a noise. Going back to the house, the old woman found the lovely maiden seated and looking more lovely than ever.

'Mother,' she said, 'my husband took me away from here. My dear husband said, "I must go away on some business," but before he went he said, "Walk along the path where the sable's skin is hanging, and do not go where the bear's skin is hanging." I forgot and went along the second path to a little iron house. A devil's daughter tore the skin from my face and put it on her own face; she dragged off all my fine things and put them on; and next this devil's daughter mounted my horse and set out. She threw away skin and bones and a grey dog seized my lungs and heart with his teeth and carried them to open country. I grew here as a plant, for it was decreed that I should not die altogether. Perhaps it has been settled that later I shall bear children. The devil's daughter has affected my fate, for she has married my husband and contaminated his flesh and blood; she has absorbed his flesh and blood. When shall I see him?'

The meritorious Khan Khara came to the field belonging to the little old woman with five cows. The speckled white horse, who was endowed with human speech, knew that his mistress had revived, and he began to speak.

He complained to Khan Khara thus: 'The devil's daughter has killed my mistress, torn all the skin from her face and covered her own face with it; she has dragged away my mistress's finery and clothed herself in it. The devil's daughter has gone to live with Khan Khara's son and become his bride. But my mistress has revived and now lives. If your son does not take this fair girl as his bride, then I will complain to the white Lord God on his seat of white stone, by the lake that has silver waves and golden floating ice, and blocks of silver and black ice; and I will shatter your house and your fire, and will leave you no means of living. A divine man must not take a devil's daughter. Fasten this devil's-daughter bride to the legs of a wild horse. Let a stream of rushing water fall on your son and cleanse him during thirty days; and let the worms and reptiles suck away his contaminated blood. Afterwards draw him from the water and expose him to the wind on the top of a tree for thirty nights, so that breezes from the north and from the south may penetrate his heart and liver, and purify his contaminated flesh and blood. When he is cleansed let him persuade and retake his wife!'

The khan heard and understood the horse's words. It is said he threw aside tears from both eyes; then he galloped home. On seeing him the bride changed countenance.

'Son!' said Khan Khara, 'whence and from whom did you take your wife?'

'She is the daughter of the little old woman with five cows.'

'What was the appearance of the horse on which you brought her? What kind of woman did you bring? Do you know her origin?'

To these questions the son answered, 'Beyond the third heaven, in the upper region which has the white stone seat is the white God; his younger brother collected migratory birds and united them into one society. Seven maidens, his daughters in the form of seven cranes, came to earth and feasted and entered a round field and danced; and an instructress descended to them. She took the best of the seven cranes and said, "Your mission is to go out to people; to be a Yakut on this middle land; you must not dislike this impure middle land! You are appointed worthy of the son of the meritorious Khan Khara and are to wear a skin made of eight sables. On account of him you will become human and bear children, and bring them up." After speaking she cut off the end of the crane's wings. The maiden wept. "Turn into a mare's tail-grass, and grow!" said the instructress; "A little old woman with five cows will find the herb and turn it into a maiden and give her in marriage to Khan Khara's son." I took her according to this direction and as she was described to me; but I accepted a strange being; in reality, as appears to me, I took nothing!'

After his son's reply the khan said, 'Having seen and heard, I have come. The speckled horse with the human voice has complained to me. When you bore away your wife you spoke to her of a forked road. You said, "On the eastern path there is hanging a sable's skin and on the western path a bear's skin." You said, "Do not go on the path with the bear's skin, but go along the path showing a sable skin!" But she forgot, and passed along the path which had a bear's skin. She reached the iron house and then a devil's daughter jumped out to meet her, dragged her from her horse and threw her down, tore the whole of the skin from her face and placed it on her own face. The devil's daughter dressed herself in the girl's finery and silver ornaments and rode hither as a bride. She fastened the horse to the old willow; it is already a mark. "Attach the devil's daughter to the feet of a wild stallion!" said the horse to me, "and wash your son in a swift stream for a whole month of thirty nights; let worms and reptiles suck away his contaminated body and blood. Carry him away and expose him to the breeze on the top of a tree during a month of thirty nights. Let the breezes search him from the north and from the south; let it blow through his heart and liver!" said the horse to me. "Let him go and persuade his wife and take her! But away with this woman! Do not show her! She will devour people and cattle. If you do not get rid of her," said the horse, "I will complain to the white God."

On hearing this the son became much ashamed, and a workman called Boloruk seized the bride, who was sitting behind a curtain, and, dragging her by the foot, fastened her on the legs of a wild horse. The horse kicked the devil's daughter to pieces and to death. Her body and blood were attacked on the ground by worms and reptiles, and became worms and reptiles moving about till the present time. After being placed in a stream of rushing water the khan's son was placed on a tree, so that the spring breezes coming from the north and from the south blew through him. Thus his contaminated body and blood were purified and, when he was brought home, dried up and scarcely breathing, only his skin and bones remained.

He rode to the region of the wedding gift as before and, having picketed his horse, dismounted at his mother-in-law's house. The little old woman who owned the five cows fluttered out joyfully; she rejoiced as if the dead had come to life and the lost had been found. From the picketing spot to the tent she strewed green grass and spread on the front bed a white horse-skin with hoofs. She killed a milch cow and a large-breasted mare and made a wedding feast.

The girl approached her husband with tears. 'Why have you come to me?' she asked. 'You spilt my dark blood, you cut my skin deeply. You gave me up as food for dogs and ducks. You gave me to the daughter of an eight-legged devil. After that, how can you seek a wife here? Girls are more numerous than perch, and women than grayling; my heart is wounded and my mind is agitated! I will not come!'

'I did not send you to the daughter of an eight-legged devil and when I went away on an important matter I pointed out your path. I did not knowingly direct you to a perilous place and I did not know what would happen when I said to you "Go and meet your fate!" The lady-instructress and protectress, the creatress, chose you and appointed you for me; therefore you revived and are alive,' he said; 'and whatever may happen, good or ill, I shall unfailingly take you!'

The little old woman with five cows wiped aways tears from both eyes and sat down between these two children. 'How is it that, having met, you do not rejoice when you have returned to life after death, and been found after having been lost? Neither of you must oppose my will!'

The maiden gave her word, but said 'Agreed!' unwillingly. Then the young man sprang up and danced and jumped and embraced and kissed and drew in his breath. The couple played the best games and burst into loud laughter and talked unceasingly. Outside they fastened the speckled horse that spoke like a human being, laid on him the silver saddle-cloth, saddled him with the silver saddle, bridled him with the silver bridle, hung on him the silver saddle bags and attached to him the little silver whip.

When the maiden had been dressed and all was complete on her she was sent off. She and her husband knew as they went along that it was winter by the fine snow that was falling; they knew it was summer by the rain; they knew it was autumn by the fog.

The servants from the nine houses of Khan Khara, the house servants from eight houses and the room attendants from seven houses, and nine lords' sons who came out like nine cranes thought, 'How will the bride arrive? Will she march out or will she saunter? And will sables arise from her footsteps?'

Thinking thus, they prepared arrows so vigorously that the skin came off their fingers; they attended so closely to their work that their sight became dull. Seven grown-up daughters like seven cranes, born at one time, twisted threads so that the skin came from their knees, and said, 'If, when the bride comes, she blows her nose loudly, dear little kings will be plentiful.'

The son arrived with his bride, and two maidens took their horses by the bridle at the picket rope. The son and his bride dismounted and she blew her nose; therefore dear little kings would come! Instantly the women began to weave garments. Sables ran along the place from which the bride stepped forward, and some of the young men hastened into the dark forest to shoot them.

From the foot of the picketing post to the tent the way had been spread with green grass. On arriving, the bride kindled the fire with three branches of larch. Then they hid her behind a curtain. They stretched a strap in nine portions and tied to it ninety white speckled foals. On the right side of the house they thrust into the ground nine posts and fastened to them nine white foals and put on the foals nine friendly sorcerers who drank kumyss. On the left side of the house they set up eight posts.

Wedding festivities were begun in honour of the bride's entry into the home. Warriors collected and experts came together. It is said that nine ancestral spirits came from a higher place and twelve ancestral spirits rose from the ground. It is said that nine tribes came from under the ground and, using whips of dry wood, trotted badly. Those having iron stirrups crowded together and those having copper stirrups went unsteadily.

All had collected from the foreign tribes and from the tents of the nomad villages; there were singers, there were dancers, there were storytellers; there were those who jumped one on foot and there were leapers; there were crowds possessing five-kopeck pieces, there were saunterers. Then the dwellers-on-high flew upwards; those dwelling in the lower regions sank into the earth; and inhabitants of the middle region, the earth, separated and walked away. The litter remained till the third day; but before the morrow most of the fragments had been collected, all animals had been enclosed and children were sporting in the place. Their descendants are said to be alive today.

Achol and Her
Adoptive Lioness-Mother

(SUDAN: DINKA)

chieng gave birth to two children, Maper and Achol. They had three paternal half-brothers. Achol was betrothed to a man called Kwol. The family moved to the lion territory. As Achol was still small, her brother carried her.

Their half-brothers were jealous of Achol's good fortune in being betrothed so young. They agreed on a plan to abandon Achol and her brother Maper in the wilderness. One evening, they secretly put some medicine in their milk. Achol and Maper fell into a heavy sleep. That night, a gourd full of milk was placed near them, and the cattle camp moved on, leaving them behind.

Achol was the first to wake up the next morning. When she saw that they had been left behind, she cried and woke her brother up. 'Maper, son of my mother, the camp has gone and we have been left behind!'

Maper woke up, looked around and said, 'So our own brothers have left us! Never mind, drink your milk.'

They drank some milk and then moved into a ditch made by an elephant. This provided them with shelter and protection. There they slept.

Along came a lioness looking for remains in the camp. When she saw the ditch, she looked into it and saw the children. They cried, 'O, Father, we are dead – we are eaten!'

The lioness spoke and said, 'My children, do not cry. I will not eat you. Are you children of human beings?'

'Yes,' they said.

'Why are you here?' she asked.

'We were abandoned by our half-brothers,' said Maper.

'Come along with me,' said the lioness. 'I will look after you as my own children; I have no children of my own.'

They agreed and went with her. On the way, Maper escaped and returned home. Achol remained with the lioness. They went to the lioness's house, and she looked after Achol and raised her until she became a big girl.

In the mean time, Achol's relatives were mourning her loss. The half-brothers denied having played a foul trick. But Maper explained that he and his sister were left behind and found by a lioness, from whom he had escaped.

Some years later, the camp again moved to the lion territory. By this time Maper had become a grown man. One day as he and his age-mates were herding, they came to the home of the lioness. Maper did not recognise the village. The lioness had gone to hunt. Achol was there. But Maper did not recognise her.

One of the age-mates spoke to Achol, saying 'Girl, will you please give us water to drink?'

Achol said, 'This is not a house where people ask for water. I see you are human beings; this place is dangerous for you!'

'We are very thirsty,' they explained. 'Please, let us drink.'

She brought them water, and they drank. Then they left. Achol's mother, the lioness, returned, carrying an animal she had killed. She threw the animal down and sang:

> 'Achol, Achol,
> Come out of the hut,
> My daughter whom I raised in plenty
> When people were gathering wild grain.
> My daughter was never vexed;
> Daughter, come out, I am here.
> My little one who was left behind,
> My little one whom I found unhurt,
> My little one whom I raised,
> Achol, my beloved one
> Come, meet me my daughter.'

They met and embraced, and then cooked for themselves and ate. Achol's mother told her, 'Daughter, if human beings come, do not run away from them; be nice to them. That is how you will get married.'

Maper was attracted to Achol, and that same evening he returned with a friend to court her. Achol's mother gave her a separate hut in which to entertain her age-mates. So when Maper came with his friend and asked to be accommodated, she let them into that hut. She made their beds on one side of the hut, while she herself slept on the other side.

At night, Maper's desire for Achol increased and he wanted to move over to her side of the hut. But whenever he tried to move, a lizard on the wall spoke, saying, 'The man is about to violate his own sister!' So he stopped. Then he tried to move again, and a rafter on the ceiling spoke and said, 'The man is about to violate his sister!' When he tried again, the grass said the same.

Maper's friend woke up and said, 'Who is speaking? What are they saying?' Maper said, 'I do not know and I do not understand what they mean by "sister".'

So they asked the girl to tell them more about who she was. Achol then told them the story of how she and her brother had been abandoned and how the lioness had found them.

'Really?' said Maper with excitement.

'Yes,' said Achol.

'Then, let us leave for home. You are my sister.'

Achol embraced him and cried and cried. When she became calm she told Maper and his friend that she could not leave the lioness, for the lioness had taken very good care of her. But they persuaded her to leave with them. Their camp moved on the next morning to avoid meeting the lioness.

That morning, the lioness left very early to hunt. When she returned in the evening, she sang to Achol as usual, but Achol did not reply. She repeated the song several times, and Achol did not answer. She went inside the hut and found that Achol was gone. She cried and cried and cried: 'Where has my daughter gone? Has a lion eaten her or have the human beings taken her away from me?'

Then she ran, following the cattle camp. She ran and ran and ran.

The cattle camp arrived at the village, and Achol was hidden.

The lioness continued to run and run and run until she reached the village. She stopped outside the village and began to sing her usual song.

As soon as Achol heard her voice, she jumped out of her hiding place. They ran towards one another and embraced.

Achol's father took out a bull and slaughtered it in hospitality for the lioness. The lioness said she would not go back to the forest but would rather stay among the human beings with her daughter, Achol.

Achol was married and was given to her husband. Her mother, the lioness, moved with her to her marital home. And they all lived happily together.

PART TWELVE

MARRIED WOMEN

Story of a Bird Woman

(SIBERIAN TRIBAL: CHUKCHI)

 lad went to a lake in the open country. There he saw many birds, of which some were geese and some were gulls, but both geese and gulls left their garments on the shore. The youth seized their clothing, whereupon all the geese and gulls said, 'Restore it.'

He gave back the stolen things of all the goose-girls, but kept the clothes of one gull-maiden and took her for himself. She bore him two children, real human children. When the women went to collect leaves the gull-wife went with them into the fields, but as she gathered grasses badly, her mother-in-law scolded her. All the birds were flying away, and the wife, who pined to return to her own land, went with her children behind the tent as the geese passed by.

'How would it be,' she said, 'for me to carry away my children?' The geese plucked their wings and stuck feathers on the children's sleeves, and the wife and her children flew away together.

When the husband came he could not find his wife, for she was gone. He could learn nothing about her, so he said to his mother, 'Make me ten pairs of very good boots.' Then he departed to the birds' country and saw an eagle who said to him, 'Go to the seashore; there you will find an old man cutting down wood; he is making firewood. He is of a monstrous aspect behind, so do not draw near to him from that direction; he would swallow you. Approach him face to face.'

The old man said, 'Whence have you come, and whither are you going?'

The lad answered, 'I married a gull-maiden, who bore me two children, but she has now disappeared with them. I am looking for her.'

'How will you travel?'

'I have ten pairs of boots,' was the reply.

The old man said, 'I will make you a canoe.' He made a beautiful canoe, with a cover like a snuff-box. The young man took his place in it, and the old one said, 'If you desire to go to the right, say to the canoe, "Wok, wok", and move your right foot. A little later, if you wish to go to the left, you will say, "Wok, wok!" and move your left foot.'

The canoe was swift as a bird. The old man continued, 'When you reach the shore and wish to land, say "Kay!" and push the cover with your hand!'

The young man approached the shore, pressed the cover, and the canoe grounded. He saw many bird-children at play on the ground. It was bird-land. He found his children and they recognised their father. 'Father has come!'

He said, 'Tell your mother I have arrived.'

They soon returned, and with them came the wife's brother, who approached the young man and said, 'Your wife has been taken as the wife of our chief, a great sea-bird.'

The man entered his wife's house. The chief bird kissed her on the cheek, and said to the young man, 'Why have you come? I will not restore your wife to you.'

The brother-in-law sat down in the tent. The husband and the great bird grappled with one another, and the young man, seizing his opponent by the neck, thrust him out. The chief bird departed to his country and was loud in complaint, whereupon many birds flew hither, and many gulls of various kinds.

While the young man was sleeping with his wife she called out, 'Countless warriors have come, wake up quickly!'

But he remained asleep and, as there were cries and noise around the house, she grew alarmed. Soon the birds drew feathers and poised them like arrows, but the young man went out and, seizing a stick, waved it in various directions; he struck one bird's wing, another's neck and another's back. Then all the birds fled, but on the morrow there came twice as many; they seemed as numerous as a swarm of gnats. But the young man filled a flat vessel with water and sprinkled the birds with it. Afterwards they could not fly, being frozen to the spot, and no more came.

The young man now bore his wife and children home to his own people. Taking his seat in the canoe, he covered it over as before, and coming to the shore, found the little old man.

'Well?' said the latter.

'I have brought them!' was the reply.

'Then depart! Here are your boots, take them and set off.'

When, in time, they forsook the canoe, they found the eagle in the old place. They were exhausted. The eagle said, 'Put on my clothing.' The young man attired himself in the eagle's clothing and flew home. The eagle had said to him, 'You will assume my attire, but do not take it into the house; leave it a little way off in a field!'

So the young man left the garment on the ground, and it flew back to the eagle. They arrived home. The youth now pushed some fallen wood with his foot, and it became a great herd. He drove the herd before him, then anointed his wife with blood and married her. Ceasing to be a bird, she became human and dressed herself as a woman.

FATHER AND MOTHER BOTH 'FAST'

(USA: HILLBILLY)

h, yes. Well a fella stayed with a girl, and by and by he went to his father and he said, 'Father, I'm going to marry that girl.' He says, 'John, let me tell you – I'se fast when I was young, and that girl's your sister.'

Well, he felt bad and he left her. By and by, he picked up another one, and he stayed with her for a while, and he went to his father and he said, 'Father, I'm going to marry that girl.' He said, 'Johnny, I was fast when I was young – that girl's your sister.'

Felt awful bad, and so one day he's setting up by the stove with his head hung down, and his mother said, 'What's the trouble, John?' 'No

nothing.' She says, 'There's something, and I want to know what it is. Why did you leave that girl, the first one you stayed with, and you left your second one?' 'Well,' he said, 'Father told me he was fast when he was young, and they's both my sisters.' Says, 'Johnny, I want to tell you something, I was fast when I'se young, and your father ain't your father at all.'

REASON TO BEAT YOUR WIFE

(EGYPTIAN)

wo friends met. The first said to the second, 'How are you, So-and-so? We have not met for a long time. Those were the days. How are things going for you now?'

The second answered, 'Well, by God, I got married, and my wife is the "daughter of good people". Just as one wishes a wife to be.'

The first asked, 'Have you beaten her yet or not?'

'No, by God, there is no reason to beat her. She does everything as I wish.'

'She has to get at least one beating, just so that she may know who the master of the house is!'

'By God, yes! You are right.'

A week passed, and they met again. The first asked the second, 'Hey, what did you do? Did you beat her?'

'No! I just can't find a reason!'

'I will give you a reason. Buy fish, plenty of it, and take it to her and say, "Cook it, because we will have a guest for dinner", and leave the house. When you go home later, whatever she has cooked, say that you wanted it some other way!'

The man said, 'Fine.' He bought some catfish and went home. At the door, he shoved the fish at his wife and said, 'Cook it, for we will have guests', and he flew outside.

The woman said to herself, 'My girl, what are you going to do with all this fish? He didn't tell you how to fix it.' She thought and thought and finally said, 'I will fry some, bake some, and make some in a casserole with onions and tomatoes.'

She cleaned the house and prepared everything As dinner time approached, her infant son made a mess on the floor right next to the table where they sit cross-legged on the floor to eat. As she went to get something to clean it, she heard her husband and his friend knocking at the door. She ran to the door, and in order not to leave the mess like that, she covered it with a dish which happened to be in her hand.

They walked in and sat down on the floor at the table and said to her, 'Bring the food, mother of So-and-so.'

First she took out the fried fish. He said, 'Fried! I want it baked!' Immediately she took out the baked fish. He shouted, 'Not baked; I mean in a casserole!' Immediately she took out the casserole. He became frustrated and confused. He said, 'I want – I want—'

She asked, 'What?'

He replied in bafflement, 'I want shit!'

She immediately said, lifting the dish off the floor, 'Here it is!'

THE THREE LOVERS

(USA: NEW MEXICO)

nce there was a woman who lived in a city and was married to a man named José Pomuceno. This man owned sheep. He was obliged to look after his business in the country. And whenever he would go out of the city, his wife never missed a chance to betray him. So it was that things got so bad that she had three lovers.

It so happened that one night when the husband wasn't at home the three were going to come the same night. That's the way this woman had things arranged when the first one came. Then the second one arrived. He knocked at the door. The wife said to the first one who was there, 'My husband.'

'Where shall I hide?'

'Hide in that wardrobe.'

The man hid in the wardrobe. The other man entered. A little while later the third one arrived and knocked at the door. The woman says to the second one, 'My husband.'

'No,' he says. 'If it is your husband, let him kill me. I'll do as I please. I am sure that it isn't your husband. You are giving several of us the run-around.'

When the woman saw that he didn't believe that it could be her husband, she tried to drive the other one off, telling him to go away, that everything was off, that he should return some other time.

Then this fellow said to her from outside, 'Since you can't do anything else, why don't you at least give me a kiss?'

'Yes,' the one who is with her tells her. 'It's all right. Tell him to come to the window.'

The one outside comes to the window and the other one holds up his rump for him there, and the fellow outside kisses it.

When the latter saw that he had kissed the other's posterior, he felt rather bad and tried to get even some way; so he again called to him that he liked it, and for him to come back again. The second time that he appeared at the window he didn't try to kiss as he had done the first time, but struck a match and set fire to him.

When the one inside felt the flame, he came away from there yelling and leaping through the room, 'Fire! Fire! Fire!'

Then the one who was shut up in the wardrobe answered, 'Throw your furniture outside, lady.'

So ends the story of the wife of José Pomuceno.

THE SEVEN LEAVENINGS

(PALESTINIAN ARAB)

There was once in times past an old woman who lived in a hut all by herself. She had no one at all. One day when the weather was beautiful she said, 'Ah, yes! By Allah, today it's sunny and beautiful, and I'm going to take the air by the seashore. But let me first knead this dough.'

When she had finished kneading the dough, having added the yeast, she put on her best clothes, saying, 'By Allah, I just have to go and take the air by the seashore.' Arriving at the seashore, she sat down to rest, and lo! there was a boat, and it was already filling with people.

'Hey, uncle!' she said to the man, the owner of the boat. 'Where in Allah's safekeeping might you be going?'

'By Allah, we're heading for Beirut.'

'All right, brother. Take me with you.'

'Leave me alone, old woman,' he said. 'The boat's already full, and there's no place for you.'

'Fine,' she said. 'Go. But if you don't take me with you, may your boat get stuck and sink!'

No one paid her any attention, and they set off. But their boat had not gone twenty metres when it started to sink. 'Eh!' they exclaimed. 'It looks as if that old woman's curse has been heard.' Turning back, they called the old woman over and took her with them.

In Beirut, she did not know anybody or anything. It was just before sunset. The passengers went ashore, and she too came down and sat a while, leaning against a wall. What else could she have done? People were passing by, coming and going, and it was getting very late. In a while a man passed by. Everyone was already at home, and here was this woman sitting against the wall.

'What are you doing here, sister?' he asked.

'By Allah, brother,' she answered, 'I'm not doing anything. I'm a stranger in town, with no one to turn to. I kneaded my dough and leavened it, and came out for pleasure until it rises, when I'll have to go back.'

'Fine,' he said. 'Come home with me then.'

He took her home with him. There was no one there except him and his wife. They brought food, laughed and played – you should have seen them enjoying themselves. After they had finished, lo! the man brought a bundle of sticks this big and set to it – Where's the side that hurts most? – until he had broken them on his wife's sides.

'Why are you doing this, grandson?' the old woman asked, approaching in order to block his way.

'Get back!' he said. 'You don't know what her sin is. Better stay out of the way!' He kept beating his wife until he had broken the whole bundle.

'You poor woman!' exclaimed the old lady when the man had stopped. 'What's your sin, you sad one?'

'By Allah,' replied the wife, 'I've done nothing, and it hadn't even occurred to me. He says it's because I can't get pregnant and have children.'

'Is that all?' asked the old woman. 'This one's easy. Listen, and let me tell you. Tomorrow, when he comes to beat you, tell him you're pregnant.'

'The next day, as usual, the husband came home, bringing with him the needed household goods and a bundle of sticks. After dinner, he came to beat his wife, but he had not hit her with the first stick when she cried out, 'Hold your hand! I'm pregnant!'

'Is it true?'

'Yes, by Allah!'

From that day on, he stopped beating her. She was pampered, her husband not letting her get up to do any of the housework. Whatever she desired was brought to her side.

Every day after that the wife came to the old woman and said, 'What am I going to do, grandmother? What if he should find out?'

'No matter,' the old woman would answer. 'Sleep easy. The burning coals of evening turn to ashes in the morning.' Daily the old woman stuffed the wife's belly with rags to make it look bigger and said, 'Just keep on telling him you're pregnant, and leave it to me. The evening's embers are the morning's ashes.'

Now, this man happened to be the sultan, and people heard what was said: 'The sultan's wife is pregnant! The sultan's wife is pregnant!' When her time to deliver had come, the wife went to the baker and said, 'I want you to bake me a doll in the shape of a baby boy.'

'All right,' he agreed, and baked her a doll which she wrapped and brought home without her husband seeing her. Then people said, 'The sultan's wife is in labour, she's ready to deliver.'

The old woman came forth. 'Back in my country, I'm a midwife,' she said. 'She got pregnant as a result of my efforts, and I should be the one to deliver her. I don't want anyone but me to be around.'

'Fine,' people agreed. In a while, word went out: 'She gave birth! She gave birth!'

'And what did she give birth to?'

'She gave birth to a boy.'

Wrapping the doll up, the wife placed it in the crib. People were saying, 'She gave birth to a boy!' They went up to the sultan and said she had given birth to a boy. The crier made his rounds, announcing to the townspeople that it was forbidden to eat or drink except at the sultan's house for the next week.

Now, the old woman made it known that no one was permitted to see the baby until seven days had passed. On the seventh day it was announced that the sultan's wife and the baby were going to the public baths. Meanwhile, every day the wife asked the old woman, 'What am I going to do, grandmother? What if my husband should find out?' And the old woman would reply, 'Rest easy, my dear! The evening's coals are the morning's ashes.'

On the seventh day the baths were reserved for the sultan's wife. Taking fresh clothes with them, the women went, accompanied by a servant. The sultan's wife went into the bath, and the women set the servant in front of the doll, saying to her, 'Take care of the boy! Watch out that some dog doesn't stray in and snatch him away!'

In a while the servant's attention wandered, and a dog came, grabbed the doll, and ran away with it. After him ran the servant, shouting, 'Shame on you! Leave the son of my master alone!' But the dog just kept running, munching on the doll.

It is said that there was a man in that city who was suffering from extreme depression. He had been that way for seven years and no one could cure him. Now, the moment he saw a dog running with a servant fast behind him shouting, 'Leave the son of my master alone!' he started to laugh. And he laughed and laughed till his heartsickness melted away and he was well again. Rushing out, he asked her, 'What's your story? I see you running behind a dog who has snatched away a doll, and you're shouting at him to leave the son of your master alone. What's going on?'

'Such and such is the story,' she answered.

This man had a sister who had just given birth to twin boys seven days before. Sending for her, he said, 'Sister, won't you put one of your boys at my disposal?'

'Yes,' she said, giving him one of her babies.

The sultan's wife took him and went home. People came to congratulate her. How happy she was!

After some time the old woman said, 'You know, grandchildren, I think my dough must have risen, and I want to go home and bake the bread.'

'Why don't you stay?' they begged her. 'You brought blessings with you.' I don't know what else they said, but she answered, 'No. The land is longing for its people. I want to go home.'

They put her on a boat, filling it with gifts, and said, 'Go in Allah's safekeeping!'

When she came home, she put her gifts away and rested for a day or two. Then she checked her dough. 'Yee, by Allah!' she exclaimed. My dough hasn't risen yet. I'm going to the seashore for a good time.' At the shore she sat for a while, and lo! there was a boat.

'Where are you going, uncle?'

'By Allah, we're going to Aleppo,' they answered.

'Take me with you.'

'Leave me alone, old woman. The boat's full and there's no room.'

'If you don't take me with you, may your boat get stuck and sink in the sea!'

They set out, but in a while the boat was about to sink. They returned and called the old lady over, taking her with them. Being a stranger, where was she to go? She sat down by a wall, with people coming and going until late in the evening. After everybody had gone home for the night, a man passed by.

'What are you doing here?'

'By Allah, I'm a stranger in town. I don't know anyone, and here I am, sitting by this wall.'

'Is it right you should be sitting here in the street? Come, get up and go home with me.'

Getting up, she went with him. Again, there was only he and his wife. They had no children or anybody else. They ate and enjoyed themselves, and everything was fine, but when time came for sleep he fetched a bundle of sticks and beat his wife until he had broken the sticks on her sides. The second day the same thing happened. On the third day the old woman said, 'By Allah, I want to find out why this man beats his wife like this.'

She asked her, and the wife replied, 'By Allah, there's nothing the matter with me, except that once my husband brought home a bunch of black grapes. I put them on a bone-white platter and brought them in. "Yee!" I said, "How beautiful is the black on the white!" Then he sprang up and said, "So! May so-and-so of yours be damned! You've been keeping a black slave for a lover behind my back!" I protested that I had only meant the grapes, but he wouldn't believe me. Every day he brings a bundle of sticks and beats me.'

'I'll save you,' said the old woman. 'Go and buy some black grapes and put them on a bone-white platter.'

In the evening, after he had had his dinner, the wife brought the grapes and served them. The old woman then jumped in and said, 'Yee! You see, son. By Allah, there's nothing more beautiful than the black on the white!'

'So!' he exclaimed, shaking his head. 'It's not only my wife who says this! You're an old lady and say the same thing. It turns out my wife hasn't done anything, and I've been treating her like this!'

'Don't tell me you've been beating her just for that!' exclaimed the old woman. 'What! Have you lost your mind? Look here! Don't you see how beautiful are these black grapes on this white plate?'

It is said they became good friends, and the husband stopped beating his wife. Having stayed with them a few more months, the old woman said, 'The land has been longing for its people. Maybe my dough has risen by now. I want to go home.'

'Stay, old lady!' they said. 'You brought us blessings.'

'No,' she answered. 'I want to go home.'

They prepared a boat for her and filled it with food and other provisions. She gathered herself together and went home. There, in her own house, after she had sat down, rested, and put her things away, she checked the dough. 'By Allah,' she said, 'it has just begun to rise, and I might as well take it to the baker.' She took it to the baker, who baked her bread.

This is my tale, I've told it, and in your hands I leave it.

The Untrue Wife's Song

(USA: NORTH CAROLINA)

nce a man an' his wife were ridin' on a ship. One day the man was talkin' to the captain, an' they got to talkin' about women. The captain said he'd never seen a virtuous woman. The man said his wife was virtuous, and the captain bet the ship's cargo against the man's fiddle that he could seduce the man's wife within three hours. The man sent his wife up to the captain's cabin. After waiting for two hours the man became a little uneasy, so he walked by the captain's cabin, an' played on his fiddle an' sang:

For two long hours
You've resisted the captain's powers.
The cargo will soon be ours.

His wife heard him, an' from within she sang back:

> *Too late, too late, my dear,*
> *He has me around the middle;*
> *Too late, too late, my dear,*
> *You've lost your damned old fiddle.*

THE WOMAN WHO MARRIED HER SON

(PALESTINIAN ARAB)

nce upon a time there was a woman. She went out to gather wood, and gave birth to a daughter. She wrapped the baby in a rag, tossed her under a tree, and went on her way. The birds came, built a nest around the baby, and fed her.

The girl grew up. One day she was sitting in a tree next to a pool. How beautiful she was! (Praise the creator of beauty, and the Creator is more beautiful than all!) Her face was like the moon. The son of the sultan came to the pool to water his mare, but the mare drew back, startled. He dismounted to find out what the matter was, and he saw the girl in the tree, lighting up the whole place with her beauty. He took her with him, drew up a marriage contract, and married her.

When the time for pilgrimage came, the son of the sultan decided to go on the hajj. 'Take care of my wife until I return from the hajj,' he said to his mother.

Now the mother was very jealous of her daughter-in-law, and as soon as her son departed she threw his wife out of the house. Going over to the neighbour's house, the wife lived with them, working as a servant. The mother dug a grave in the palace garden and buried a sheep in it. She then dyed her hair black and put on make-up to make herself look young and pretty. She lived in the palace, acting as if she were her son's wife.

When he came back from the hajj, the son was taken in by his mother's disguise and thought her his wife. He asked her about his mother, and she said, 'Your mother died, and she is buried in the palace garden.'

After she slept with her son, the mother became pregnant and started to crave things. 'My good man,' she said to her son, 'bring me a bunch of sour grapes from our neighbour's vine!' The son sent one of the women servants to ask for the grapes. When the servant knocked on the neighbour's door, the wife of the sultan's son opened it.

'O mistress of our mistress,' said the servant, 'you whose palace is next to ours, give me a bunch of sour grapes to satisfy the craving on our side!'

'My mother gave birth to me in the wilderness,' answered the wife, 'and over me birds have built their nests. The sultan's son has taken his mother to wife, and now wants to satisfy her craving at my expense! Come down, O scissors, and cut out her tongue, lest she betray my secret!' The scissors came down and cut out the servant's tongue. She went home mumbling so badly no one could understand what she was saying.

The son of the sultan then sent one of his men servants to fetch the bunch of sour grapes. The servant went, knocked on the door, and said, 'O mistress of our mistress, you whose palace is next to ours, give me a bunch of sour grapes to satisfy the craving on our side!'

'My mother gave birth to me in the wilderness,' answered the wife of the sultan's son, 'and over me birds have built their nests. The

sultan's son has taken his mother to wife, and now wants to satisfy her craving at my expense! Come down, O scissors, and cut out his tongue, lest he betray my secret!' The scissors came down and cut out his tongue.

Finally the son of the sultan himself went and knocked on the door. 'O mistress of our mistress,' he said, 'you whose palace is next to ours, give me a bunch of sour grapes to satisfy the craving on our side!'

'My mother gave birth to me in the wilderness, and over me birds have built their nests. The king's son has taken his mother to wife, and now wants to satisfy her craving at my expense! Come down, O scissors, and cut out his tongue. But I can't find it in myself to let it happen!' The scissors came down and hovered around him, but did not cut out his tongue.

The sultan's son understood. He went and dug up the grave in the garden, and behold! there was a sheep in it. When he was certain that his wife was actually his mother, he sent for the crier. 'Let him who loves the Prophet,' the call went out, 'bring a bundle of wood and a burning coal!'

The son of the sultan then lit the fire.

Hail, hail! Finished is our tale.

DUANG AND HIS WILD LIFE

(SUDAN: DINKA)

mou was so beautiful. She was betrothed to a man from the tribe. But she was not yet given to her betrothed. She still lived with her family.

There was a man called Duang in a neighbouring village. Duang's father said to him, 'My son, Duang, it is high time you married.'

'Father,' replied Duang, 'I cannot marry; I have not yet found the girl of my heart.'

'But my son,' argued his father, 'I want you to marry while I am alive. I may not live long enough to attend your marriage.'

'I will look, Father,' said Duang, 'but I will marry only when I find the girl of my heart.'

'Very well, my son,' said his father with understanding.

They lived together until the father died. Duang did not marry. Then his mother died. He did not marry.

These deaths made him abandon himself in mourning; so he no longer took care of his appearance. His mourning hair grew long and wild. He never shaved or groomed his hair. He was a very rich man. His cattle-byres were full of cattle, sheep and goats.

One day he left for a trip to a nearby tribe. On the way he heard the drums beating loud. He followed the sounds of the drums and found people dancing. So he stood and watched the dance.

In the dance was the girl called Amou. When she saw him standing, she left the dance and went near him. She greeted him. They stood talking. When the relatives of the man who was betrothed to Amou saw her, they became disturbed. 'Why should Amou leave the dance to greet a man who was merely watching? And then she dared to stand and talk with him! Who is the man, anyway?'

They called her and asked her. She answered, 'I don't see anything wrong! I saw the man looking as though he were a stranger who needed help. So I went to greet him in case he wanted something. There is nothing more to it.'

They dismissed the matter, although they were not convinced. Amou did not go back to the dance. She went and talked to the man again. She invited him to her family's home. So they left the dance and went. She seated him and gave him water. She cooked for him and served him.

The man spent two days in her house and then left and returned home. He went and called his relatives and told them that he had found the girl of his heart. They took cattle and returned to Amou's village.

The man who had betrothed Amou had paid thirty cows. Amou's relatives sent them back and accepted Duang's cattle. The marriage was completed, and Amou was given to her husband.

She went with him and gave birth to a daughter, called Kiliingdit. Then she had a son. She and her husband lived alone with their children. Then she conceived her third child. While she was pregnant, her husband was in the cattle camp. But when she gave birth, he came home to visit her and stay with them for the first few days after her delivery.

After she delivered, she felt a very strong craving for meat. She was still newly delivered. She said to her husband, 'I am dying of craving for meat. I cannot even eat.'

Her husband said to her, 'If it is my cattle you have your eyes on, I will not slaughter an animal merely because of your craving! What sort of a craving is this which requires the killing of livestock? I will not slaughter anything.'

That ended the discussion. But she still suffered and could not eat or work. She would just sit there.

Her husband became impatient and embittered by her craving. He slaughtered a lamb openly so that she and the others could see it. Then he went and killed a puppy dog secretly. He roasted both the lamb and the puppy in smouldering smudge.

When they were ready he took the dog meat to his wife in her women's quarters. He grabbed his children by the hands and took them away with him to the male quarters. His wife protested, 'Why are you taking the children away? Aren't they eating with me?'

He said, 'I thought you said you were dying of craving. I think it would be better for you and the children if you ate separately. They will share with me.'

He seated them next to him, and they ate together. She never doubted what he said, even though she felt insulted. That he would poison her was out of the question. So she ate her meat.

As soon as she ate her fill, her mouth started to drip with saliva. In a short while, she became rabid. Then she ran away, leaving her little baby behind.

Her husband took the boy to the cattle camp and left only the girl at home. She suffered very much taking care of her baby brother. Fearing that her mother might return rabid, she took the remainder of her mother's dog meat, dried it, and stored it. She would cook a portion of it and place it on a platform outside the hut together with some other food she had prepared.

For a while, her mother did not come. Then one night, she came. She stood outside the fence of the house and sang:

> 'Kiliingdit, Kiliingdit,
> Where has your father gone?'

Kiliingdit answered:

> 'My father has gone to Juachnyiel,
> Mother, your meat is on the platform,
> Your food is on the platform,
> The things with which you were poisoned.
> Mother, shall we join you in the forest?
> What sort of home is this without you?'

Her mother would take the food and share it with the lions. This went on for some time.

In the mean time, the woman's brothers had not heard of her giving birth. One of them, called Bol because he was born after twins, said to the others, 'Brothers, I think we should visit our sister. Maybe she has given birth and is now in some difficulties taking care of herself and the house.'

The little girl continued to labour hard looking after the baby and preparing food for the mother and themselves. She also had to protect herself and the baby so their mother would not find them and, having become a lioness, eat them.

She came again another night and sang. Kiliingdit replied as usual. Her mother ate and left.

In the mean time, Bol took his gourds full of milk and left for his sister's home. He arrived in the daytime. When he saw the village so quiet, he feared that something might have gone wrong. 'Is our sister really at home?' he said to himself. 'Perhaps what I was afraid of in my heart has occurred. Perhaps our sister died in childbirth and her husband with the children have gone away and abandoned the house!'

Another part of him said, 'Don't be foolish! What has killed her? She is a newly delivered mother and is confined inside the hut.'

'I see the little girl,' he said to himself, 'but I do not see her mother.' As soon as the little girl saw him, she raced towards him, crying.

'Where is your mother, Kiliingdit?' he asked her in haste.

She told him the story of how her mother turned wild, beginning with her mother's craving for meat and her father's poisoning her with dog meat.

'When she comes in the evening,' she explained, 'her companions are the wives of lions.'

'Will she come tonight?' asked her uncle.

'She comes every night,' answered Kiliingdit. 'But, Uncle, when she comes, please do not reveal yourself to her. She is no longer your sister. She is a lioness. If you reveal yourself to her, she will kill you and the loss will be ours. We shall then remain without anyone to take care of us.'

'Very well,' he said.

That night, she came again. She sang her usual song. Kiliingdit sang her response.

As she approached the platform to pick up her food, she said, 'Kiliingdit, my daughter, why does the house smell like this? Has a human being come? Has your father returned?'

'Mother, my father has not returned. What would bring him back? Only my little brother and I are here. And were we not human beings when you left us? If you want to eat us, then do so. You will save me from all the troubles I am going through. I have suffered beyond endurance.'

'My darling Kiliingdit,' she said, 'how can I possibly eat you? I know I have become a beast of a mother, but I have not lost my heart for you, my daughter. Is not the fact that you cook for me evidence of our continuing bond? I cannot eat you!'

When Bol heard his sister's voice, he insisted on going out to meet her, but his niece pleaded with him, saying, 'Don't be deceived by her voice. She is a beast and not your sister. She will eat you!'

So he stayed; she ate and left to join the wives of the lions.

The next morning, Bol returned to the cattle camp to tell his brothers that their sister had become a lioness. Bewildered by the news, they took their spears and came to their sister's home. They took a bull with them. They walked and walked and then arrived.

They went and sat down. The little girl went ahead and prepared the food for her mother in the usual way. Then they all went to sleep. The little girl went into the hut with her baby brother, as usual, but the men slept outside, hiding in wait for their sister.

She came at night and sang as usual. Kiliingdit responded. She picked up her food and ate with the wives of the lions. Then she brought the dishes back. As she put them back, she said, 'Kiliingdit!'

'Yes, Mother,' answered Kiliingdit.

'My dear daughter,' she continued, 'why does the house feel so heavy? Has your father returned?'

'Mother,' said Kiliingdit, 'my father has not returned. When he abandoned me with this little baby, was it his intention to return to us?'

'Kiliingdit,' argued the mother, 'if your father has returned, why do you hide it from me, dear daughter? Are you such a small child that you cannot understand my suffering?'

'Mother,' Kiliingdit said again, 'I mean what I say, my father has not come. It is I alone with the little baby. If you want to eat us, then eat us.'

As the mother turned to go, her brothers jumped on her and caught her. She struggled in their hands for quite a long time, but could not break away. They tied her to a tree. The next morning, they slaughtered the bull they had brought. Then they beat her and beat her. They would tease her with raw meat by bringing it close to her mouth and pulling it away from her. Then they would continue to beat her. As she was teased with meat, saliva fell from her mouth and formed little puppies. They continued to tease her and beat her until three puppies had emerged from her saliva. Then she refused raw meat. She was given roast meat from the bull and she ate it. The brothers beat her some more until she shed all the hairs that had grown on her body.

Then she opened her eyes, looked at them closely, sat down and said, 'Please hand me my little baby.'

The baby was brought. He could no longer suck his mother's breasts.

When the mother had fully recovered, her brothers said, 'We shall take you to our cattle camp. You will not go to the cattle camp of such a man again!'

But she insisted on going to her husband's cattle camp, saying, 'I must go back to him. I cannot abandon him.'

Her brothers could not understand her. They wanted to attack her husband and kill him, but she argued against that. When she saw that they did not understand her, she told them that she wanted to take care of him in her own way. She was not going back to him out of love but to take revenge. So they left her and she went to her husband.

When she got to the cattle camp, he was very pleased to have her back. She did not show any grievance at all. She stayed with him, and he was very happy with her.

One day she filled a gourd with sour milk. She pounded grain and made porridge. Then she served him, saying, 'This is my first feast since I left you. I hope you give me the pleasure of finding it your heartiest meal.'

First he drank the milk. Then came the porridge with ghee and sour milk mixed into it. He ate. Then she offered him some more milk to drink on top of the porridge. When he tried to refuse, she pleaded with him. The man ate and ate and ate, until he burst and died.

A Stroke of Luck

(HUNGARIAN)

He went ploughing. He was a poor man. The plough cut a furrow and turned up a lot of money. When he set eyes on it, he began to speculate about what to say to his wife. He feared that she might blurt it out to the neighbours, and they would be served a summons to appear before the magistrate.

He went and bought a hare and a fish.

When she brought him his midday meal, he said to her after he had dined, 'Let's fry a fish.'

She said, 'What do you think! How could we catch a fish here in the field?'

'Come on, woman, I've just seen a couple of them, when I was ploughing around the blackthorn shrub.' He led her to the blackthorn shrub.

Says the woman, 'Look, old man, there's a fish.'

'Haven't I told you so?' And he flung the ox goad at the shrub so that the fish turned out at once.

Then he said, 'Let's catch a hare.'

'Don't be kidding me. You haven't got a gun.'

'Never mind. I'll knock it off with the ox goad.'

They were going along when she cried out, 'Look! There's a hare on the tree yonder there.'

The man flung his goad at the tree and the hare fell down.

They were working till the day drew to a close, and in the evening they made their way home. When they went past the church, they heard an ass braying.

The man said to the woman, 'You know what the ass is braying? He is saying, "The priest says in his sermon that soon a comet will appear and that will be the end of the world!"'

They went on. When they passed the city hall, the ass uttered another loud bray. The man said, 'The ass says that "The magistrate and the town clerk have just been caught embezzling public funds."'

As time wore on they were making good use of their money.

The neighbours kept asking them, 'Where did that lot of money come from?'

Then she said to one of the neighbour women, 'I wouldn't mind telling you, but you mustn't pass it on to anyone.' And she told her that they had found the money. Their neighbour reported it to the magistrate, and they were summoned to appear before him. And when he was questioned about the money, the man denied it. By no means did they find any money. Not a penny had been found by them.

The magistrate then said, 'Your wife will tell me.'

'What's the use asking her. She's just a silly woman,' he said.

The woman flew into a temper and began to shout at him. 'Don't you dare say that again. Didn't we find the money when we caught the fish under the blackthorn bush?'

'Now Your Honour may hear for yourself. Catching a fish in a bush. What next!'

'Can't you remember how you shot down a hare from the tree with the ox goad?'

'Well, haven't I told Your Honour? It's no use asking that fool of a woman.'

'A fool you are yourself. Have you forgotten that on our way home we heard an ass braying when we passed the church, and you said that the priest was preaching that a comet would appear and that would be the end of the world.'

'Now wasn't I right, Your Honour? It would be better to leave her alone, or she might give offence with her silly talk.'

The woman flew into a rage and said, 'Don't you remember that when we were passing the city hall and the ass uttered a loud bray you were telling me, "that the magistrate and the town clerk have been just caught out . . ."' The magistrate jumped to his feet and said to the man, 'Take her home, my good man, she seems to have lost her wits.'

The Beans in the Quart Jar

(USA: HILLBILLY)

The old man had taken sick and thought he's gonna die anyway, so he called his wife in and confessed, he said, 'I been stepping out, and I want to be honest with you, and I want to ask your forgiveness before I go.' And she said, 'All right', and 'I'll forgive you.' She forgive him.

By and by, she was taken sick and she called him in and she said, 'No, look, I stepped out quite a lot, and I want to ask forgiveness.' He said, 'Yes, I'll forgive you.' She said, 'Every time I stepped out I put a bean in a quart jar. And you'll find they're all there on that mantelpiece, except that quart I cooked the other Saturday.'

PART THIRTEEN

USEFUL STORIES

A Fable of a Bird and Her Chicks

(YIDDISH)

Once upon a time a mother bird who had three chicks wanted to cross a river. She put the first one under her wing and started flying across. As she flew she said, 'Tell me, child, when I'm old, will you carry me under your wing the way I'm carrying you now?'

'Of course,' replied the chick. 'What a question!'

'Ah,' said the mother bird, 'you're lying.' With that she let the chick slip, and it fell into the river and drowned.

The mother went back for the second chick, which she took under her wing. Once more as she was flying across the river, she said, 'Tell me, child, when I'm old, will you carry me under your wing the way I'm carrying you now?'

'Of course,' replied the chick. 'What a question!'

'Ah,' said the mother bird, 'you're lying.' With that she let the second chick slip, and it also drowned.

Then the mother went back for the third chick, which she took under her wing. Once more she asked in mid-flight, 'Tell me, child, when I am old, will you carry me under your wing the way I'm carrying you now?'

'No, mother,' replied the third chick. 'How could I? By then I'll have chicks of my own to carry.'

'Ah, my dearest child,' said the mother bird, 'you're the one who tells the truth.' With that she carried the third chick to the other bank of the river.

THE THREE AUNTS

(NORWEGIAN)

nce upon a time there was a poor man who lived in a hut far away in the wood, and got his living by shooting. He had an only daughter, who was very pretty, and as she had lost her mother when she was a child, and was now half grown up, she said she would go out into the world and earn her bread.

'Well, lassie!' said the father, 'true enough you have learnt nothing here but how to pluck birds and roast them, but still you may as well try to earn your bread.'

So the girl went off to seek a place, and when she had gone a little while, she came to a palace. There she stayed and got a place, and the queen liked her so well that all the other maids got envious of her. So they made up their minds to tell the queen how the lassie said she was good to spin a pound of flax in four-and-twenty hours, for you must know the queen was a great housewife, and thought much of good work.

'Have you said this? Then you shall do it,' said the queen; 'but you may have a little longer time if you choose.'

Now, the poor lassie dared not say she had never spun in all her life, but she only begged for a room to herself. That she got, and the wheel and the flax were brought up to her. There she sat sad and weeping, and knew not how to help herself. She pulled the wheel this way and that, and twisted and turned it about, but she made a poor hand of it, for she had never even seen a spinning-wheel in her life.

But all at once, as she sat there, in came an old woman to her. 'What ails you, child?' she said.

'Ah!' said the lassie, with a deep sigh, 'it's no good to tell you, for you'll never be able to help me.'

'Who knows?' said the old wife. 'Maybe I know how to help you after all.'

Well, thought the lassie to herself, I may as well tell her, and so she told her how her fellow-servants had given out that she was good to spin a pound of flax in four-and-twenty hours.

'And here am I, wretch that I am, shut up to spin all that heap in a day and a night, when I have never even seen a spinning-wheel in all my born days.'

'Well, never mind, child,' said the old woman. 'If you'll call me Aunt on the happiest day of your life, I'll spin this flax for you, and so you may just go away and lie down to sleep.'

Yes, the lassie was willing enough, and off she went and lay down to sleep.

Next morning when she awoke, there lay all the flax spun on the table, and that so clean and fine, no one had ever seen such even and pretty yarn. The queen was very glad to get such nice yarn, and she set greater store by the lassie than ever. But the rest were still more envious, and agreed to tell the queen how the lassie had said she was good to weave the yarn she had spun in four-and-twenty hours. So the queen said again, as she had said it she must do it; but if she couldn't quite finish it in four-and-twenty hours, she wouldn't be too hard upon her, she might have a little more time. This time, too, the lassie dared not say no, but begged for a room to herself, and then she would try. There she sat again, sobbing and crying, and not knowing which way to turn, when another old woman came in and asked, 'What ails you, child?'

At first the lassie wouldn't say, but at last she told her the whole story of her grief.

'Well, well!' said the old wife, 'never mind. If you'll call me Aunt on the happiest day of your life, I'll weave this yarn for you, and so you may just be off, and lie down to sleep.'

Yes, the lassie was willing enough; so she went away and lay down to sleep. When she awoke, there lay the piece of linen on the table, woven so neat and close, no woof could do better. So the lassie took the piece and ran down to the queen, who was very glad to get such beautiful linen, and set greater store than ever by the lassie. But as for the others, they grew still more bitter against her, and thought of nothing but how to find out something to tell about her.

At last they told the queen the lassie had said she was good to make up the piece of linen into shirts in four-and-twenty hours. Well, all happened as before; the lassie dared not say she couldn't sew; so she was shut up again in a room by herself, and there she sat in tears and grief. But then another old wife came, who said she would sew the shirts for her if she would call her Aunt on the happiest day of her life. The lassie was only too glad to do this, and then she did as the old wife told her, and went and lay down to sleep.

Next morning when she awoke she found the piece of linen made up into shirts, which lay on the table – and such beautiful work no one had ever set eyes on; and more than that, the shirts were all marked and ready for wear. So, when the queen saw the work, she was so glad at the way in which it was sewn, that she clapped her hands, and said, 'Such sewing I never had, nor even saw, in all my born days'; and after that she was as fond of the lassie as of her own children; and she said to her, 'Now, if you like to have the prince for your husband, you shall have him; for you will never need to hire work-women. You can sew, and spin, and weave all yourself.'

So as the lassie was pretty, and the prince was glad to have her, the wedding soon came on. But just as the prince was going to sit down with the bride to the bridal feast, in came an ugly old hag with a long nose – I'm sure it was three ells long.

So up got the bride and made a curtsy, and said, 'Good-day, Auntie.'

'*That* auntie to my bride?' said the prince.

'Yes, she was!'

'Well, then, she'd better sit down with us to the feast,' said the prince; but to tell you the truth, both he and the rest thought she was a loathsome woman to have next you.

But just then in came another ugly old hag. She had a back so humped and broad, she had hard work to get through the door. Up jumped the bride in a trice, and greeted her with 'Good-day, Auntie!'

And the prince asked again if that were his bride's aunt. They both said, yes; so the prince said, if that were so, she too had better sit down with them to the feast.

But they had scarce taken their seats before another ugly old hag came in, with eyes as large as saucers, and so red and bleared, 'twas gruesome to look at her. But up jumped the bride again, with her 'Good-day, Auntie', and her, too, the prince asked to sit down; but I can't say he was very glad, for he thought to himself, 'Heaven shield me from such aunties as my bride has!'

So when he had sat a while, he could not keep his thoughts to himself any longer, but asked 'But how, in all the world can my bride, who is such a lovely lassie, have such loathsome misshapen aunts?'

'I'll soon tell you how it is,' said the first. 'I was just as good-looking when I was her age; but the reason why I've got this long nose is, because I was always kept sitting, and poking, and nodding over my spinning, and so my nose got stretched and stretched, until it got as long as you now see it.'

'And I,' said the second, 'ever since I was young, I have sat and scuttled backwards and forwards over my loom, and that's how my back has got so broad and humped as you now see it.'

'And I,' said the third, 'ever since I was little, I have sat, and stared and sewn, and sewn and stared, night and day; and that's why my eyes have got so ugly and red, and now there's no help for them.'

'So, so!' said the prince, ' 'twas lucky I came to know this; for if folk can get so ugly and loathsome by all this, then my bride shall neither spin, nor weave, nor sew all her life long.'

TALE OF AN OLD WOMAN

(AFRICA: BONDES)

here was once an old woman who had no husband and no relations, no money and no food. One day she took her axe and went to the forest to cut a little firewood to sell, so that she could buy something to eat. She went very far, right into the heart of the bush, and she came to a large tree covered with flowers, and the tree was called *Musiwa*. The woman took her axe and began to fell the tree.

The tree said to her, 'Why are you cutting me? What have I done to you?'

The woman said to the tree, 'I am cutting you down to make some firewood to sell, so that I can get some money, so that I can buy food to keep from starving, for I am very poor and have no husband or relations.'

The tree said to her, 'Let me give you some children to be your own children to help you in your work, but you must not beat them, nor are you to scold them. If you scold them you will see the consequences.'

The woman said, 'All right, I won't scold them.' Then the flowers of that tree turned into many boys and girls. The woman took them and brought them home.

Each child had its own work – some tilled, others hunted elephants, and still others fished. There were girls who had the work of cutting firewood, and girls who had the work of collecting vegetables, and girls who pounded flour and cooked it. The old woman didn't have to work any more, for now she was blessed.

Among the girls, there was one smaller than all the rest. The others said to the woman, 'This little girl must not work. When she is hungry and cries for food, give it to her and don't be angry at her for all of this.'

The woman said to them, 'All right, my children, whatever you tell me I will do.'

In this way, they lived together for some time. The woman didn't have to work except to feed the littlest child when it wanted to eat. One day the child said to the woman, 'I am very hungry. Give me some food to eat.'

The woman scolded the child, saying, 'How you pester me, you children of the bush! Get it out of the pot yourself.'

The child cried and cried because it had been scolded by the woman. Some of her brothers and sisters came, and asked her what was the matter. She told them, 'When I said I was hungry and asked for food, our mother said to me, "How I am worried by these bush children."'

Then the boys and girls waited until those who had gone hunting returned, and they told them how the matter stood. So they said to the woman, 'So you said we are children of the bush. We'll just go back to our mother, *Musiwa*, and you can dwell alone.' The woman pleaded with them every way, but they wouldn't stay. They all returned to the tree and became flowers again, as it was before, and all the people laughed at her. She dwelt in poverty till she died, because she did not heed the instruction given to her by the tree.

THE HEIGHT OF PURPLE PASSION

(USA)

here was this sailor walking down the street and he met a Lady Wearing Lipstick. And she said to him, 'Do you know what the Height of Purple Passion is?' And he said, 'No.' And she said, 'Do you want to find out?' And he said, 'Yes.' So she told him to come to her house at five o'clock *exactly*. So he did, and when he rang the doorbell, birds flew out all around the house. And they went around the house three times and the door opened and they all flew in again. And there was the Lady Wearing

Lipstick. And she said, 'Do you still want to know what the Height of Purple Passion is?' And he said he wanted to find out. So she told him to go and take a bath and be very clean. So he did, and he came running back and slipped on the soap and broke his neck. That's the end. He never found out what it was. My girl friend Alice told me this story. It happened to somebody she knows.

SALT, SAUCE AND SPICE, ONION
LEAVES, PEPPER AND DRIPPINGS

(AFRICA: HAUSA)

his story is about Salt, and Sauce and Spice, and Onion Leaves, and Pepper and Drippings. A story, a story! Let it go, let it come. Salt and Sauce and Spice and Onion Leaves and Pepper and Drippings heard a report of a certain youth who was very handsome, but the son of the evil spirit. They all rose up, turned into beautiful maidens, and then they set off.

As they were going along, Drippings lagged behind the others, who drove her still further off, telling her she stank. But she crouched down and hid until they had gone on, and then she kept following them. When they had reached a certain stream, where they came across an old woman who was bathing, Drippings thought they would rub down her back for her if she asked, but one said, 'May Allah save me that I should lift my hand to touch an old woman's back.' The old woman did not say anything more, and the five passed on.

Soon Drippings came along, encountered the old woman washing, and greeted her. She answered, and said, 'Maiden, where are you going?' Drippings replied, 'I am going to find a certain youth.' And the old woman asked her, too, to rub her back, but unlike the others, Drippings agreed. After she had rubbed her back well for her, the old woman said, 'May Allah bless you.' And she said, too, 'This young man to whom you are all going, do you know his name?' Drippings said, 'No, we do not know his name.' Then the old woman told her, 'He is my son, his name is Daskandarini, but you must not tell the others,' then she fell silent.

Drippings continued to follow far behind the others till they got to the place where the young man dwelled. They were about to go in when he called out to them, 'Go back, and enter one at a time,' which they did.

Salt came forward first and was about to enter, when the voice asked, 'Who is there?' 'It is I,' she replied, 'I, Salt, who make the soup tasty.' He said, 'What is my name?' She said, 'I do not know your name, little boy, I do not know your name.' Then he told her, 'Go back, young lady, go back,' and she did.

Next Sauce came forward. When she was about to enter, she, too, was asked, 'Who are you?' She answered, 'My name is Sauce and I make the soup sweet.' And he said, 'What is my name?' But she did not know, either, and so he said, 'Turn back, little girl, turn back.'

Then Spice rose up and came forward, and she was about to enter when she was asked, 'Who is this, young lady, who is this?' She said, 'It is I who greet you, young man, it is I who greet you.' 'What is your name, young girl, what is your name?' 'My name is Spice, who makes the soup savoury.' 'I have heard your name, young woman, I have heard your name. Speak mine.' She said, 'I do not know your name little boy, I do not know your name.' 'Turn back, young lady, turn back.' So she turned back, and sat down.

Then Onion Leaves came and stuck her head into the room. 'Who is this, young girl, who is this?' asked the voice. 'It is I who salute you young man, it is I who salute you.' 'What is your name, little girl, what is your name?' 'My name is Onion Leaves, who makes the soup smell nicely.' He said, 'I heard your name, little girl. What is my name?' But she didn't know it and so she also had to turn back.

Now Pepper came along. She said, 'Your pardon, young man, your pardon.' She was asked who was there. She said, 'It is I, Pepper, young man, it is I, Pepper, who make the soup hot.' 'I have heard your name, young lady. Tell me my name.' 'I do not know your name, young man, I do not know your name.' He said, 'Turn back, young maid, turn back.'

Now only Drippings was left. When the others asked her if she was going in she said, 'Can I enter the house where such good people as you have gone and been driven away? Would not they sooner drive out one who stinks?' They said, 'Rise up and go in,' for they wanted Drippings, too, to fail.

So she got up and went in there. When the voice asked her who she was, she said, 'My name is Drippings, little boy, my name is *Batso* which makes the soup smell.' He said, 'I have heard your name. There remains my name to be told.' She said, 'Daskandarini, young man, Daskandarini.' And he said, 'Enter.' A rug was spread for her, clothes were given to her, and slippers of gold. And then of Salt, Sauce, Spice, Onion Leaves and Pepper, who before had despised her, one said, 'I will always sweep for you', another, 'I will pound for you', another, 'I will draw water for you', another, 'I will pound the ingredients of the soup for you', and another, 'I will stir the food for you.' They all became her handmaidens. And the moral of all this is that it is from such common things that our most blessed foods are made. So just as such common stuff may be transformed under the right circumstance, if you see a man is poor, do not despise him. You do not know but that some day he may be better than you. That is all.

TWO SISTERS AND THE BOA

(CHINESE)

nce there was an old, Kucong *binbai*, or old woman, who had buried her husband in her youth. Her sole possession was two daughters, the elder, nineteen years old, and the younger, seventeen. One afternoon, she returned home from working in the mountains, feeling thirsty and tired. So she sat down under a mango tree to rest. This mango tree was laden with ripe, golden-yellow fruit hanging down from the branches. A breeze blew from the mountains, carrying the exquisite fragrance of ripe mangoes to her nose, making her mouth water.

Suddenly, the *binbai* heard a swishing sound, 'sha-sha', up in the mango tree, and then thin pieces of bark fell on her. The old woman thought that somebody must be up there, so without even taking a look, she called out, jokingly, 'Who's the young man up in the tree whittling arrows out of mango branches? Whoever you are, if you would honour me by presenting me with a few mangoes, you can have your choice of my two daughters.'

Hardly had the *binbai*'s words escaped her lips, when there came the rustling of leaves, 'hua-hua', and a fully ripe mango fell plop, right on the ground. Feeling delighted and thankful at once, the old woman picked up the mango and began eating it, all the while looking up in the tree. Better for her she had not looked, for she was all agog with what she saw. Coiled all around the mango tree was a boa as thick as a bull's thigh, knocking mangoes free, its tail swishing back and forth. The *binbai* could not care less about picking up any more mangoes, and she scurried down the mountain in leaps and bounds, her bamboo basket on her back.

Wheezing and gasping for breath, the old woman entered her door. As she saw her two darling daughters coming up to meet her she called to mind what had happened under the mango tree. She couldn't help feeling nervous and confused, as if she were stuck in a briar patch. She walked outside and was met by a strange sight. Though it was already dark, all her chickens were still circling around outside the chicken coop. She tried repeatedly to drive them inside, but they would not go. She went up to the coop and peeped in. Gosh! The very same boa which had been coiled around the mango was right there, lying in the chicken coop! As she was about to run away, the huge, long boa began to speak.

'*Binbai*, just now, you made a promise under the mango tree: whoever picked a mango and gave it to you to eat, could have his choice of one of your two daughters. Now please, keep your promise. Give me one of your girls! If you should go back on your word, don't blame me for getting impolite!'

Seeing that boa in the chicken coop, with its brightly patterned, scaly skin, gleaming eyes, and that long, forked tongue sticking out, the *binbai* shivered from head to foot. She couldn't say yes, but she couldn't say no, either. So all she said was, 'Now don't get mad, boa! be patient, please, Let me talk this over with my girls, so I can tell you what they think.'

The *binbai* went back into the house and recounted all that had happened to her two daughters. 'Oh, my little darlings!' she exclaimed. 'It's not that Mama doesn't love you or dote on you, but I have no choice other than to push you in the burning fire. Now you two sisters have to think it over – who is willing to marry the boa?'

No sooner had the old woman finished speaking than the older daughter started screaming, 'No, no! I won't go! Who could marry such an ugly, dreadful thing?'

The younger sister thought for a while. She saw that her mother's life was threatened, while her older sister was adamant.

'Mama,' she said, 'to prevent the boa from doing you and sister any harm, and so you two can live in peace, I'm willing to marry the boa.' And with that, she cried many a sad, sad tear.

The *binbai* led her second child to the gate of the chicken coop and told the boa he could have her. That very night, the old woman took the snake into her home, and the boa and Second Daughter were married.

The next morning, when the boa was about to take her second daughter away, mother and child wept in one another's arms. How hard it was to part! Off went the boa, leading the *binbai*'s dear child to the virgin forest, deep in the mountains, where he brought her to a cave. She groped about in the dark, dark cave, following after the boa. On and on they went, never coming to the end. So worried and afraid was Second Daughter, that her teardrops fell like strings of pearls. Rounding a bend in the cave there was a gleam of light, and suddenly, a resplendent, magnificent palace came in view. There were endless, vermilion walls and yellow tiles without number, long verandas and tiny pavilions, tall buildings and spacious courtyards. Everywhere one could see carved beams, painted rafters, piles of gold, carved jade and wall hangings of red and green silk. Second Daughter was simply dazzled. As she turned around, that terrifying, dreadful boa which had been close by had disappeared. Walking beside her now was a gorgeously dressed young man, looking ever so vigorous and handsome.

'Oh!' she exclaimed, completely outdone. 'How could this be?'

The young man beside her replied, 'Dear Miss! I am the king of the snakes of this region. Not long ago, when I went out to make an inspection tour of the snake tribes, I saw you two sisters. How I admired your wisdom and beauty! I made up my mind right then to have one of you as my wife, and that's how I thought of a way to win your mother's approval. Now, my hopes have come true, Oh, dear Miss! In my palace you'll have gold and silver without end, more cloth than you can ever use, and more rice than you can ever eat. Let us love each other dearly, enjoying a glorious life, to the end of our days!'

As she listened to the snake king's words, Second Sister's heart flooded with warmth. She took hold of his hand, and smiling sweetly, walked towards the resplendent, magnificent palace.

Second Sister and the snake king lived happily as newly-weds for a time. Then, one day, she took leave of her husband to go back home and visit her mother and sister. She told them all about her rich, full married life with the king of the snakes.

How could the elder daughter not be full of regret? 'Ay!' she thought. 'I'm to blame for being so foolish. If I had promised to marry the boa in the first place, would not I have been the one now enjoying glory, honour and riches in that palace, instead of my younger sister?' So she made up her mind, then and there. 'Right! That's what I'll do. I'll find a way to wed a boa too!'

After the younger sister left to return to the snake king, the elder sister walked deep into the mountains, carrying a basket on her back. To find a boa, she would only go where the grass was tall or the jungles were dense. From dawn to dusk and dusk to dawn, she kept on searching until, at last, after great difficulty, she found a boa under a bush. Its eyes were shut, for the boa was enjoying a good snooze.

First Sister gingerly raked the snake into her basket and left for home in high spirits, the boa on her back. She had only gone halfway when the boa woke up. It stuck out its tongue and licked the back of her neck. Instead of being frightened by what the snake was doing, First Sister secretly felt quite delighted. 'Hey!' she whispered softly. 'Don't be so affectionate just yet! Wait till we get home!'

After getting back home, she laid the boa in her bed, then rushed to make the fire and do the cooking. After supper, First Sister told her mother, 'Mama, I found a boa today too, and I shall marry him tonight. From now on, I can live a rich, comfortable life, just like my baby sister!' And off she went to sleep with her boa.

Not long after the mother went to bed, she heard her daughter's voice, 'Mama, it's up to my thighs!'

The *binbai* did not say a word, thinking all she was hearing was a pair of newly-weds having fun playing around.

After a while, First Sister called out, her voice trembling, 'Mama, it's up to my waist!'

The old woman did not understand what such words could mean, so she did not budge an inch.

Yet more time passed, until this time she heard a mournful voice from the inner room, 'Mama, it's up to my neck now . . .' And then, all was silence.

The *binbai* felt something was not quite right, so she quickly rolled out of bed, lit a pine torch and went to take a look. That dreadful boa had swallowed down her elder daughter, leaving but a lock of her hair!

The old woman felt sad and nervous. She paced back and forth in the room, not knowing what to do to rescue her daughter. In the end, all she could think of doing was to pull down her dear, thatched hut, set it afire, and burn up the boa. In the raging flames a loud 'bang' was heard. As the boa was being burned to death, it burst into many pieces. In a later age, these came to be countless snakes, big and little.

The next morning, the *binbai* picked out of the ashes a few of her daughter's bones that had not been consumed by the fire. She dug a hole in the ground and buried them, holding back her tears.

Afterwards, she declared, 'My elder daughter! This is all because of your greed!' With these words, she went off into the dense jungle, and deep into the mountains, to look for her second daughter and her son-in-law, the king of the snakes.

SPREADING THE FINGERS

(SURINAMESE)

n the early times Ba Yau was a plantation overseer. He had two wives in the city. But as he found provisions on the plantation, he brought them to his wives. But when he brought things, then he said to them, 'When you eat, you must spread your fingers.' But when he said this, the first one did not understand very well what that meant to say. He told the second wife the same thing, and that one understood. What he meant was that when he brought them things, they were not to eat them alone, they were to give others half.

Now the one who did not understand what that said, in the afternoon when she cooked, she ate. Then she went outside, and spread her fingers, and said, 'Ba Yau said when I eat I must spread my fingers.' Ba Yau brought her much bacon and salt fish. She alone ate it. But when Ba Yau brought the things for the other one she shared half with other people, because she had understood what the proverb had said.

Not long afterwards Ba Yau died. But when Ba Yau was dead, nobody brought anything to the wife who had spread her fingers for the air. She sat alone. But to the other one who had shared things with other people, many people brought things. One brought her a cow, one brought her sugar, one brought her coffee. So she received many things from others.

Now one day, the one wife went to the other, and she said, 'Yes, sister, ever since Ba Yau died, I have suffered hunger. No one brought me anything. But look, how is it that so many people have brought things to you?'

Then the other one asked her, 'Well, when Ba Yau had brought you things, what did you do with them?'

She said, 'I alone ate them.'

Then the other one said again, 'When Ba Yau said to you, "You must spread your fingers", what did you do?'

She said, 'When I ate, I spread my fingers in the air.'

The other one said, 'So ... Well then, the air must bring you things, because you spread your fingers for the air. As for myself, the same people to whom I gave things, bring me things in return.'

The proverb, when you eat you must spread fingers, means, when you eat, you must eat with people, you must not keep all for yourself. Otherwise, when you have nothing, nobody else is going to give you, because you had not given people what was yours.

AFTERWORD

Italo Calvino, the Italian writer and fabulist and collector of fairy tales, believed strongly in the connection between fantasy and reality: 'I am accustomed to consider literature a search for knowledge,' he wrote. 'Faced with [the] precarious existence of tribal life, the shaman responded by ridding his body of weight and flying to another world, another level of perception, where he could find the strength to change the face of reality.'[1] Angela Carter would not have made the same wish with quite such a straight face, but her combination of fantasy and revolutionary longings corresponds to the flight of Calvino's shaman. She possessed the enchanter's lightness of mind and wit – it's interesting that she explored, in her last two novels, images of winged women. Fevvers, her *aërialiste* heroine of *Nights at the Circus*, may have hatched like a bird, and in *Wise Children*, the twin Chance sisters play various fairies or feathered creatures, from their first foot on the stage as child stars to their dalliance in Hollywood for a spectacular extravaganza of *A Midsummer Night's Dream*.

Fairy tales also offered her a means of flying – of finding and telling an alternative story, of shifting something in the mind, just as so many fairy tale characters shift something in their shape. She wrote her own – the dazzling, erotic variations on Perrault's *Mother Goose Tales* and other familiar stories. In *The Bloody Chamber* she lifted Beauty and Red Riding Hood and Bluebeard's last wife out of the pastel nursery into the labyrinth of female desire.

She had always read very widely in folklore from all over the world and found the stories collected here in sources ranging from Siberia to Suriname. There are few fairies, in the sense of sprites, but the stories move in fairyland – not the prettified, kitschified, Victorians' elfland – but the darker, dream realm of spirits and tricks, magical, talking animals, riddles and spells. In 'The Twelve Wild Ducks', the heroine vows not to speak or to laugh or to cry until she has rescued her brothers from their enchanted animal forms. The issue of women's speech, of women's noise, of their/our clamour and laughter and weeping and shouting and hooting runs through all Angela Carter's writings, and informed her love of the folk tale. In *The Magic Toyshop* the lovely Aunt Margaret cannot speak because she is strangled by the silver torque which the malign puppet-master her husband has made her as a bridal gift. Folklore, by contrast, speaks, and speaks volumes about women's experience; women are often the storytellers, as in one of the dashingly comic and highly Carteresque tales in this collection ('Reason to Beat Your Wife').

Angela Carter's partisan feeling for women, which burns in all her work, never led her to any conventional form of feminism; but she continues here one of her original and effective strategies, snatching out of the jaws of misogyny itself 'useful stories' for women. Her essay *The Sadeian Woman* (1979) found in Sade a liberating teacher of the male–female status quo and made him illuminate the far reaches of women's polymorphous desires; here she turns topsy-turvy some cautionary folk tales and shakes out the fear and dislike of women they once expressed to create a new set of values, about strong, outspoken, zestful, sexual women who can't be kept down (see 'The Old Woman Against the Stream'; 'The Letter Trick'). In *Wise Children* she created a heroine, Dora Chance, who's a showgirl, a soubrette, a vaudeville dancer, one of the low, the despised, the invisible poor, an old woman who was illegitimate and never married (born the wrong side of the blanket, the wrong side of the tracks), and each of these stigmas is taken up with exuberant relish and scattered in the air like so much wedding confetti.

The last story here, 'Spreading the Fingers', a tough morality tale from Suriname about sharing what one has been given with others, also discloses the high value Angela Carter placed on generosity. She gave herself – her ideas, her wit, her incisive, no-bullshit mind – with open but never sentimental prodigality. One of her favourite fairy tales here was a Russian riddle story 'The Wise Little Girl', in which the tsar asks her heroine for the impossible, and she delivers it without batting an eyelid. Angela liked it because it was as satisfying as 'The Emperor's New Clothes', but 'no one was humiliated and everybody gets the prizes'. The story comes in the section called 'Clever

Women, Resourceful Girls and Desperate Stratagems', and its heroine is an essential Carter figure, never abashed, nothing daunted, sharp-eared as a vixen and possessed of dry good sense. It is entirely characteristic of Angela's spirit that she should delight in the tsar's confounding, and yet not want him to be humiliated.

She did not have the strength, before she died, to write the Introduction she had planned to *The Second Virago Book of Fairytales*, which makes up the latter part of this volume. She did, however, leave four cryptic notes among her papers:

> 'every real story contains something useful', says Walter Benjamin
> the *unperplexedness* of the story
> "No one dies so poor that he does not leave something behind," said Pascal.
> fairy tales – cunning and high spirits'.

Fragmentary as they are, these phrases convey the Carter philosophy. She was scathing about the contempt the 'educated' can show, when two-thirds of the literature of the world – perhaps more – has been created by the illiterate. She liked the solid common sense of folk tales, the straightforward aims of their protagonists, the simple moral distinctions, and the wily stratagems they suggest. They are tales of the underdog, about cunning and high spirits winning through in the end, they are practical, and they are not high-flown. For a fantasist with wings, Angela kept her eyes on the ground, with reality firmly in her sights. She once remarked, 'A fairy tale is a story where one king goes to another king to borrow a cup of sugar.'

Feminist critics of the genre – especially in the 1970s – jibbed at the socially conventional 'happy endings' of so many stories (for example, 'When she grew up he married her and she became the tsarina'). But Angela knew about satisfaction and pleasure; and at the same time she believed that the goal of fairy tales was not 'a conservative one, but a utopian one, indeed a form of heroic optimism – as if to say: One day, we might be happy, even if it won't last.' Her own heroic optimism never failed her – like the spirited heroine of one of her tales, she was resourceful and brave and even funny during the illness which brought about her death. Few writers possess the best qualities of their work; she did, in spades.

Her imagination was dazzling, and through her daring, vertiginous plots, her precise yet wild imagery, her gallery of wonderful bad-good girls, beasts, rogues and other creatures, she causes readers to hold their breath as a mood of heroic optimism forms against the odds. She had the true writer's gift of remaking the world for her readers.

She was a wise child herself, with a mobile face, a mouth which sometimes pursed with irony, and, behind the glasses, a wryness, at times a twinkle, at times a certain dreaminess; with her long, silvery hair and ethereal delivery, she had something of the Faerie Queene about her, except that she was never wispy or fey. And though the narcissism of youth was one of the great themes in her early fiction, she was herself exceptionally unnarcissistic. Her voice was soft, with a storyteller's confidingness, and lively with humour; she spoke with a certain syncopation, as she stopped to think – her thoughts made her the most exhilarating companion, a wonderful talker, who wore her learning and wide reading with lightness, who could express a mischievous insight or a tough judgment with scalpel precision and produce new ideas by the dozen without effort, weaving allusion, quotation, parody and original invention, in a way that echoed her prose style. 'I've got a theory that . . .' she would say, self-deprecatorily, and then would follow something that no one else had thought of, some sally, some rich paradox that would encapsulate a trend, a moment. She could be Wildean in her quickness and the glancing drollery of her wit. And then she would pass on, sometimes leaving her listeners astonished and stumbling.

Angela Carter was born in May 1940, the daughter of Hugh Stalker, a journalist for the Press Association, who was a Highlander by birth, had served the whole term of the First World War, and had come south to Balham to work. He used to take her to the cinema, to the Tooting Granada, where the glamour of the building (Alhambra-style) and of the movie stars (Jean Simmons in *The Blue Lagoon*) made an impression which lasted – Angela has written some of the most gaudy, stylish, sexy passages about seduction and female beauty on record, and 'snappy' and 'glamorous' are key words of pleasure and praise in her vocabulary. Her mother was from South Yorkshire, on her own mother's side; this grandmother was tremendously important to her: 'every word and gesture of hers displayed a natural dominance, a native savagery, and I am very grateful for all that, now, though the core of steel was a bit inconvenient when I was looking for boyfriends in the South'. Angela's mother was a scholarship girl, and 'liked things to be nice'; she worked as a cashier in Selfridges in the 1920s, and had passed exams and wanted the same for her daughter. Angela went to Streatham Grammar School, and for a time entertained a fancy of becoming an Egyptologist, but left school to take up an apprenticeship on the *Croydon Advertiser* arranged by her father.

As a reporter on the news desk, she had trouble with her imagination (she used to like the Russian storyteller's formula, 'The story is over, I can't lie any more') and switched to writing a record column as well as features. She got married for the first time when she was twenty-one, to a chemistry teacher at Bristol technical college, and began studying English at Bristol University in the same year, choosing to concentrate on medieval literature, which was then definitely uncanonical. Its forms – from allegory to tales – as well as its heterogeneity of tone – from bawdy to romance – can be found everywhere in her own œuvre; Chaucer and Boccaccio remained among her favourite writers. She also remembered those days, in a recent interview with her great friend Susannah Clapp, for the talking in cafés 'to situationists and anarchists . . . It was the Sixties . . . I was very very unhappy but I was perfectly happy at the same time.'

During this period, she first began developing her interest in folklore, discovering with her husband the folk and jazz music scenes of the 1960s. (At a more recent, staid, meeting of the Folklore Society, she fondly recalled those countercultural days when a member would attend with a pet raven on one shoulder.) She began writing fiction: in her twenties she published four novels (*Shadow Dance*, 1966; *The Magic Toyshop*, 1967; *Several Perceptions*, 1968; *Heroes and Villains*, 1969; as well as a story for children, *Miss Z, the Dark Young Lady*, 1970). She was heaped with praise and prizes; one of them – the Somerset Maugham – stipulated travel, and she obeyed, using the money to run away from her husband ('I think Maugham would have approved'). She chose Japan, because she revered the films of Kurosawa.

Japan marks an important transition; she stayed for two years, from 1971. Her fiction till then, including the ferocious, taut elegy *Love* (1971; revised 1987), showed her baroque powers of invention, and her fearless confrontation of erotic violence, arising from female as well as male sexuality: she marked out her territory early, and men and women clash on it, often bloodily, and the humour is mostly of the gallows variety. From the beginning, her prose was magnificently rich, intoxicated with words – a vivid and sensual lexicon of bodily attributes, minerals, flora and fauna – and she dealt in strangeness. But Japan gave her a way of looking at her own culture which intensified her capacity to conjure strangeness out of the familiar. She also deepened her contact with the Surrealist movement at this time, through French exiles from *les évènements* of 1968 who had fetched up in Japan.

Two novels arose from her time in Japan, though they do not deal with Japan directly: *The Infernal Desire Machines of Doctor Hoffman* (1972) and *The Passion of New Eve* (1977), in which contemporary conflicts are transmuted into bizarre, multiple, picaresque allegories. Though she never won the bestseller fortunes of some of her contemporaries (she would reflect ruefully that it was still a Boys' Club out there, and did not *really* mind much), and was never selected for one of the major prizes, she enjoyed greater international esteem: her name tells from Denmark to Australia, and she was repeatedly invited to teach – accepting invitations from Sheffield (1976–8), Brown University, Providence (1980–1), the University of Adelaide (1984), and the University of East Anglia (1984–7). She helped change the course of postwar writing in English – her influence reaches from Salman Rushdie to Jeanette Winterson to American fabulists like Robert Coover.

Distance from England helped her lay bare women's collusion with their own subjection. In a collection of her criticism, *Expletives Deleted*, she remembers, 'I spent a good many years being told what I ought to think, and how I ought to behave . . . because I was a woman . . . but then I stopped listening to them [men] and . . . I started answering back.'[2] On her return from Japan, she examined in her wonderfully pungent articles (collected as *Nothing Sacred* in 1982) various sacred cows as well as the style of the times (from scarlet lipstick to stockings in D.H. Lawrence). Angela was never someone to offer an easy answer, and in her frankness she was important to the feminist movement: she liked to quote, semi-ironically, 'Dirty Work – but someone has to do it' when talking about facing hard truths, and she would say of someone, in a spirit of approval, 'S/He doesn't temper the wind to the new-shorn lamb.' Her publisher and friend Carmen Callil published her at Virago and her presence there since the start of the house helped establish a woman's voice in literature as special, as *parti pris*, as a crucial instrument in the forging of an identity for post-imperial, hypocritical, fossilized Britain. For in spite of her keen-eyed, even cynical grasp of reality, Angela Carter always believed in change: she would refer to her 'naive leftie-ism', but she never let go of it.

The American critic Susan Suleiman has celebrated Angela Carter's fiction as truly breaking new ground for women by occupying the male voice of narrative authority and at the same time impersonating it to the point of parody, so that the rules are changed and the dreams become unruly, transformed, open to 'the multiplication of narrative possibilities', themselves a promise of a possibly different future; the novels also 'expand our notions of what it is possible to dream in the domain of sexuality, criticizing all dreams that are too narrow'.[3] Angela's favourite icon of the feminine was Lulu, in Wedekind's play, and her favourite star was Louise Brooks who played her in *Pandora's Box*; Louise/Lulu was hardly someone who rejected traditional femaleness, but rather took it to such extremes that its nature was transformed. 'Lulu's character is very attractive to me,' she would say drily, and she borrowed from it to create her wanton, rumbustious and feisty heroines of the boards in *Wise Children*. Lulu never ingratiated herself, never sought fame, or fortune, and suffered neither guilt nor remorse. According to Angela, 'her particular quality is, she makes being polymorphously perverse look like the only way to be'. If she had had a daughter, she once said, she would have called her Lulu.

She liked to refer to her opinions as 'classic GLC' but in spite of these demurrals she was an original and committed political thinker too. *Wise Children* (1989) was born out of her democratic and socialist utopianism, her affirmation of 'low' culture, of the rude health of popular language and humour as a long-lasting, effective means of survival: her Shakespeare (the novel contains almost all his characters and their plots in one form or another) does not compose for the elite, but roots his imagination springing out of folklore, with energy and know-how.

She found happiness with Mark Pearce, who was training to become a primary schoolteacher when she became ill. She often spoke of the radiance of children, their unutterable beauty and their love; their son Alexander was born in 1983.

Sometimes, in the case of a great writer, it is easy to lose sight of the pleasure they give, as critics search for meaning and value, influence and importance; Angela Carter loved cinema and vaudeville and songs and the circus, and she herself could entertain like no other. She included a story from Kenya in this collection about a sultana who is withering away while a poor man's wife is kept happy because her husband feeds her 'meat of the tongue' – stories, jokes, ballads. These are what make women thrive, the story says; they are also what Angela Carter gave so generously to make others thrive. *Wise Children* ends with the words, 'What a joy it is to dance and sing!' That she should not have thrived herself is sad beyond words.

Since her death, tributes have filled the papers and the airwaves. She would have been astonished by the attention, and pleased. It did not come to her in her lifetime, not with such wholeheartedness. It's partly a tribute to her potency that while she was alive people felt discomfited by her, that her wit and witchiness and subversiveness made her hard to handle, like some wonderful beast of the kind she enjoyed in fairy tales. Her friends were lucky knowing her, and her readers too. We have been left a feast and she laid it out with 'spread fingers' for us to share.

Marina Warner
1992

1. Italo Calvino, *Six Memos for the Next Millennium*, trans. William Weaver (London, 1992), p. 26.
2. Angela Carter, *Expletives Deleted* (London, 1992), p. 5.
3. Susan Rubin Suleiman, *Subversive Intent: Gender, Politics and the Avant-Garde* (Harvard, 1990), pp. 136–40.

This introduction contains material from Marina Warner's obituary of Angela Carter which appeared in the *Independent*, 18 February 1992.

NOTES ON PARTS 1–7

These notes are not so much scholarly as idiosyncratic. I have included my sources and what I could find out about the various sources; sometimes it wasn't much, sometimes a lot. Sometimes the stories were self-explanatory and didn't need any notes. Sometimes they opened up into other stories, sometimes they seemed complete in themselves.

1. Sermerssuaq

'Told as a joke at a birthday party, Innuit Point, Northwest Territories.' Arctic Canada. *A Kayak Full of Ghosts,* Innuit tales 'Gathered and Retold' by Lawrence Millman (California, 1987), p. 140.

PART ONE: BRAVE, BOLD AND WILFUL

2. The Search for Luck

This text comes from Pontos, in eastern Greece, reprinted from *Modern Greek Folktales*, chosen and translated by R.M. Dawkins (Oxford, 1953), p. 459. The story is widely told throughout Greece and Bulgaria, says Dawkins, although usually it is a man who goes off to find his luck, or fate – or, rather, who goes off in search of the *reason* for his bad luck or miserable fate.

3. Mr Fox

> *'The wind blew high, my heart did ache*
> *To see the hole the fox did make,'*

says the girl in the version of 'Mr Fox' told to Vance Randolph in the Ozark mountains in Arkansas in the early 1940s.

'After that, poor Elsie wouldn't go with nobody, because she figured men were all son-of-a-bitches. And so she never did get married at all, but just stayed around with the kinfolks. They was glad to have her, of course.'

The Arkansas storytelling manner is relaxed, easy, confidential; this storyteller is attempting to massage you into the suspension of disbelief. The fairy tale is changing, almost imperceptibly, into the tall tale, the outrageous lie imparted with an utterly straight face for the pure pleasure of it.

But this story was already ancient when the first English settlers took their invisible cargo of stories and songs across the Atlantic in the sixteenth and seventeenth centuries; Benedick, in *Much Ado About Nothing*, refers to Mr Fox's hypocritical denial: 'Like the old tale my Lord, "it is not so, nor 'twas not so, but, indeed, God forbid it should be so" (Act. 1, sc. i). This Mr Fox was originally contributed to Malone's variorum edition of Shakespeare in 1821 to elucidate that very speech, which probably accounts for the text's 'literary' flavour.

Cunning, greed and cowardice make the fox's name a universal byword in popular lore, although in China and Japan they believe that foxes can take the form of beautiful women (cf. current US slang use of 'fox' and 'vixen' to denote an attractive woman). The fox's incarnation as psychopathic murderer in this story and its relations gives an added *frisson* to veterans of British childhoods who recall the 'foxy gentleman' who wanted to eat Jemima Puddleduck. (Joseph Jacobs, *English Fairy Tales* [London, 1895].)

4. Kakuarshuk

Collected from Severin Lunge, Rittenback, West Greenland (Millman, p. 47).

5. The Promise

Reprinted from a manuscript collection of ancient stories illustrating the finer points of legal practice in old Burma: Maung Htin Aung, *Burmese Law Tales* (Oxford, 1962), p. 9.

6. Kate Crackernuts

Joseph Jacobs printed this in *English Fairy Tales*, taking it from an edition of *Folk-Lore*, September 1890, contributed by Andrew Lang, of *Red, Blue, Green, Violet*, etc., *Fairy Book* fame. 'It is very corrupt,' complained Jacobs, 'both girls being called Kate, and I have had largely to rewrite.'

This is an authentic fairy tale. Those interested in the origin of the fairies may look up the appropriate reference in Katharine Briggs's A *Dictionary of Fairies* [1976]. Are they spirits of the dead or fallen angels – or, as J.F. Campbell *(Popular Tales of the West Highlands*, edited and translated by J.F. Campbell [London, 1890]) thought, race memories of the Picts, the swarthy and diminutive Stone Age inhabitants of North Britain? Be that as it may, the fairy life cycle closely mimics the human one, with births (that fairy baby!), marriages and deaths. The poet William Blake claimed to have seen a fairy funeral. These fairies do not have spangled wings; traditionally, they ride through the air on ragwort stems, or twigs, astride like witches on broomsticks, levitating themselves by means of magic passwords. John Aubrey *(Miscellanies)* heard one, once: 'Horse and hattock.' These beings, of a brusque and unromantic nature, are, literally, earthy – they prefer to live *inside* hills, or earthen mounds, and are rarely benign.

7. The Fisher-Girl and the Crab

A story from Chitrakot, Bastar State, from the Kuruk, one of the tribal peoples of middle India: Verrier Elwin, *Folk-Tales of Mahakoshal* (Oxford, 1944), p. 134.

'The crab is generally regarded as monogamous and a model of domestic fidelity,' assures Elwin. 'The affection and care shown by the male crab when the female is moulting has been noted in the case of swimming crabs, as also the fact that among burrowing crabs a burrow is occupied by only one male and one female.'

PART TWO: CLEVER WOMEN, RESOURCEFUL GIRLS AND DESPERATE STRATAGEMS

1. Maol a Chliobain

This is a collation, from Western Scotland – mainly from the Gaelic of Ann McGilbray, Islay – translated by J.F. Campbell, with additional passages interpolated from versions by Flora MacIntyre, of Islay, and by an unnamed young girl, 'nurse-maid to Mr Robertson, Chamberlain of Argyll', at Inverary. This girl's version ended with the drowning of the giant. '"And what became of Maol a Chliobain?" asked Campbell. "Did she marry the farmer's youngest son?" "Oh, no; she did not marry at all."'

This is a variant of 'Hop O' My Thumb', with a full-sized heroine instead of a pint-sized hero (Campbell, vol. 1, p. 259).

2. The Wise Little Girl

From the collection made by Aleksandr Nikolayevich Afanas'ev (1826–71), the Russian counterpart of the Grimms, who published his collection from 1866 onwards. Federal Russia was an extraordinarily rich source of oral literature at this time, owing to widespread illiteracy among the rural poor. As late as the close of the eighteenth century, Russian newspapers still carried advertisements from blind men applying for work in the homes of the gentry as tellers of tales, recalling how, two hundred years before, three blind ancients had followed one another in rotation at the bedside of Ivan the Terrible, telling the insomniac monarch fairy tales until at last he managed to sleep.

This story is a battle of wits in three rounds. There is something purely satisfactory about the spectacle of the child taking on the judge, and winning; the story is as satisfying as Hans Andersen's 'The Emperor's New Clothes', but better, because nobody is humiliated and everybody gets prizes. This is my favourite of all the stories in this book.

But there is more to it than meets the eye. The anthropologist Claude Lévi-Strauss says that a close relationship exists between riddles and incest because a riddle unites two irreconcilable terms and incest unites two irreconcilable people.

Robert Graves, in his half-crazed but well-annotated study of pagan anthropology *The White Goddess*, quotes the following story from Saxo Grammaticus's late-twelfth-century *History of Denmark*:

> Aslog, the last of the Volsungs, Brynhild's daughter by Sigurd, was living on a farm at Spangerejd in Norway, disguised as a sooty-faced kitchenmaid . . . Even so, her beauty made such an impression on the followers of the hero Ragnar Lodbrog that he thought of marrying her, and as a test of her worthiness told her to come to him neither on foot nor riding, neither dressed nor naked, neither fasting nor feasting, neither

attended nor alone. She arrived on goatback, one foot trailing on the
ground, clothed only in her hair and a fishing-net, holding an onion to her
lips, a hound by her side.

(*The White Goddess*, p. 401)

Graves also describes a miserere seat in Coventry Cathedral (presumably the building destroyed in the Second World War), which the guidebook he refers to calls 'a
figure emblematic of lechery'; it is 'a long-haired woman wrapped in a net, riding
sideways on a goat and preceded by a hare'.

Which reminds me that Louise Brooks, the great silent-movie actress, proposed to
title her tell-all autobiography 'Naked on My Goat', a quotation from Goethe's
Faust, the *Walpurgisnacht* scene, where the young witch says: 'Naked on my goat, I
display my fine young body.' ('You'll rot,' the old witch tells her.)

The main function of riddles is to show us how a logical structure can be made up
entirely of words.

3. Blubber Boy

Collected throughout the Arctic and Greenland. Compare with the Armenian story
'Nature's Ways' (p. 232) (Millman, p. 100).

4. The Girl Who Stayed in the Fork of a Tree

This story comes from the Bena Mukini people, who inhabit what is now Zambia.
(*African Folktales and Sculpture*, ed. Paul Radin [New York, 1952], p. 181.)

5. The Princess in the Suit of Leather

This Egyptian story comes from *Arab Folktales*, translated and edited from a variety
of – mostly – written sources by Inea Bushnaq (New York, 1986), p. 193. Here is the
'She Stoops to Conquer' theme; princesses disguise themselves in all manner of
ways – in donkey skins, in wooden barrels, even as boxes – and bedaub themselves
with cinders, pitch, etc.

6. The Hare

Jan Knappert writes:

> The Swahili lived at the crossroads of two worlds. An unknown number of
> African peoples have settled along the east coast of Africa . . . An equally
> unknown number of Oriental peoples, sailors and traders, with or without
> their families, have settled on the same coast, blown towards it from
> Arabia, Persia, India or Madagascar.

The result is a people combining African (Bantu) language with an Islamic culture, spread out along a thousand miles of coast between Mogadishu and
Mozambique. Swahili storytellers believe that women are incorrigibly wicked,
diabolically cunning and sexually insatiable; I hope this is true, for the sake of
the women. (Jan Knappert, *Myths and Legend of the Swahili*, [London, 1970],
p. 142.)

7. Mossycoat

The gypsy Cinderella. Collected from the gypsy – Taimie Boswell – at Oswaldwhistle, Northumberland, England, in 1915. Reprinted from *Folktales of England*, ed. Katharine M. Briggs and Ruth L. Tongue (London, 1965), p. 16.

'It is the technique of gypsies and tinkers to go to the front door, and try to see the mistress of the house,' say the editors of *Folktales of England*. 'They have a rooted distrust of servants and underlings. In many versions of the tale, it is the young master who ill-treats the heroine and not the servants.

8. Vasilisa the Priest's Daughter

Afanas'ev, p. 131.

9. The Pupil

Knappert, p. 142.

10. The Rich Farmer's Wife

In the nineteenth century Norway, like many other European countries hitherto dominated by greater powers, began to seek a form of expression uniquely its own. Peter Christen Asbjørnsen and Jørgen Moe modelled their procedures on those of the Brothers Grimm and were moved by the same nationalistic impulse; their collection of tales was published in 1841. This translation was made by Helen and John Gade for the American-Scandinavian Foundation in 1924 (*Norwegian Fairy Tales*, p. 185).

11. Keep Your Secrets

From what is now Ghana, told by A.W. Cardinall, once district commissioner of the Gold Coast, in *Tales Told in Togoland* (Oxford, 1931), p. 213.

The witch duel, or duel of transformations, commemorated in the European children's game 'Scissors, paper, stone', is a recurring phenomenon among supernatural beings. Compare the contest between the afreet and the princess in the tale of the Second Calendar in the *Arabian Nights;* the pursuit of the pygmy, Gwion, by the goddess, Kerridgwen, in the Welsh mythological cycle the *Mabinogion*; the Scots ballad 'The Twa Magicians': 'Then she became a gay grey mare,/And stood in younder slack,/And he became a gilt saddle/And sat upon her back,' etc. (*English and Scottish Popular Ballads*, ed. F.J. Child [Boston, 1882], vol. 1, no. 44.)

At her trial in 1662, Isobel Gowdie of Auldearne, Scotland, gave the witch formula for turning oneself into a hare: 'I shall go into a hare/With sorrow and sighing and mickle care/And I shall go in the Devil's name/Aye, till I come home again.'

This is the best of all 'Mother knows best' stories.

12. The Three Measures of Salt

Dawkins, p. 292; from the island of Naxos. 'This story is a novel on a small scale,' says Dawkins, and indeed it is the pure stuff of soap opera, with its misunderstandings, its lost children, its deserted wives, and its casual wealth – 'in those days everyone was a king'.

13. The Resourceful Wife

Elwin, p. 314.

14. Aunt Kate's Goomer-Dust

Collected in the Ozark mountains in Arkansas, USA, by Vance Randolph; included in *The Devil's Pretty Daughter and Other Ozark Folk Tales*, collected by Vance Randolph with notes by Herbert Halpert (New York, 1955).

15. The Battle of the Birds

J.F. Campbell did not edit this story, so neither did I, although the interestingly self-mutilated heroine does not enter the picture until the second part of this discursive tale. It was told by John Mackenzie, in April 1859; Mackenzie lived near Inverary, on the estate of the Duke of Argyll. He had known the story from his youth, and 'has been in the habit of repeating it to his friends on winter nights, as a pastime'. He was about sixty at that time and could read English, play the bagpipes, and had 'a memory like Oliver and Boyd's Almanac'. (Campbell, vol. 1, p. 25.)

16. Parsley-girl

Collected by Daniela Almansi, aged six, from her babysitter, in Cortona, near Arezzo, Tuscany, Italy, and contributed to the editor by Daniela's mother, Claude Beguin. Claude Beguin adds the information that parsley is a popular abortifacient in Italy. *A Dictionary of Superstitions*, ed. Iona Opie and Moira Tatem (Oxford, 1989), contains two English recipes for this purpose, but also examples of the widespread belief that babies were found in the parsley bed.

17. Clever Gretel

Jacob Ludwig Grimm (1785–1863) and Wilhelm Carl Grimm (1786–1859) were instrumental in the creation of our idea of what a fairy tale is, transforming it from rustic entertainment to reading matter directed primarily, though not exclusively, at children, for both didactic and romantic reasons – to instruct them in the German genius, in morality and justice, certainly, but also in wonder, terror and magic. The Grimms were scholars, grammarians, lexicographers, philologists, antiquarians, but also poets. Indeed, the poet Brentano had first suggested they collect fairy tales from oral sources.

The Grimms' *Kinder und Hausmärchen* [Children and Household Tales], first published in 1812 and continually revised and, indeed, rewritten in an increasingly 'literary' manner until the final edition in 1857, is one of the key volumes to the sensibility of nineteenth-century Romanticism in Europe, and the stories remain indelibly marked on the imaginations of children who read them, helping to shape our consciousness of the world. But as well as the blood-spattered, mysterious, ferociously romantic, enigmatic stories that appealed to the poets in the souls of the Grimms, they could not forbear to publish such genial tales as this one, about sassy Gretel with her red-heeled shoes and her gourmandise, a direct reflection of middle-class fears of what the servants get up to down there in the kitchen.

From *The Complete Fairy Tales of the Brothers Grimm*, translated and with an introduction by Jack Zipes (New York, 1987), p. 75.

18. The Furburger

Those familiar with Chaucer or Boccaccio will recognize this story as a 'merry tale', or exercise in broad humour applied to human relations. The 'merry tale' is an area relatively unexplored by folklorists, although ancient in origin, ubiquitous in distribution, endless in variety, easy to remember, and flourishing today as bravely as ever, wherever two or three people of any gender are gathered in informal circumstances. The sexual joke is easily the most widespread form of folk tale in advanced, industrialized societies, and even when told among women it is often marked by a profound misogyny; it is the reservoir for a vast amount of sexual anxiety and surmise.

The vindictiveness and anger in this story make its heroine's the most desperate stratagem of all. Note the intended rape of the husband.

From *Jokelore: Humorous Folktales from Indiana*, ed. Ronald L. Baker (Indiana, 1986), p. 73.

PART THREE: SILLIES

1. A Pottle o' Brains

Joseph Jacobs, *More English Fairy Tales* (London, 1894), p. 125. 'The noodle family is strongly represented in English folk-tales,' observes Jacobs. Not among the female members, though.

2. Young Man in the Morning

The story was told, with a reprehensible lack of sisterly feeling, by Mrs Mary Richardson – 'a wisp of a woman', says Richard Dorson, 'her nose squashed in by hoodoo evil'. Mrs Richardson, aged seventy when she talked to Dorson in the early 1950s, was born in North Carolina and later moved to Chicago, then to Calvin, in Southwestern Michigan, a black farming settlement founded by freedmen before the American Civil War. During the Depression in the 1930s, Southern-born Black men and women who fled poverty only to find it again on Chicago's South Side settled in Calvin and communities around it, bringing with them a fund of stories with roots in a complex fusion of Black African and European traditions. The musical legacy, Gospel and rhythm and blues, bore fruit later in the decade in the musicians who created the Detroit sound.

This story is also found in Russia, Estonia and Finland. Dorson's other informants told other versions; Georgia Slim Germany said that the old woman sang out: 'I'm shivering cold tonight, but I'm going to marry a young man in the morning, and I'm going to play rat-trap tomorrow night.' (*Negro Folktales in Michigan*, collected and edited by Richard M. Dorson [Cambridge, MA, 1956], p. 193.)

3. Now I Should Laugh, If I Were Not Dead

Please note that if a wedding is the ultimate destination of so many fairy tales, marriage itself and its conditions are universally depicted as a joke.

From *Icelandic Legends*, collected by Jon Arnason, translated by George Powell and Eirikr Magnusson (London, 1866), vol. 2, pp. 627–30.

4. The Three Sillies

Jacobs, *English Fairy Tales*, p. 9.

5. The Boy Who Had Never Seen Women

Told by a Mrs E.L. Smith. Dorson, p. 193.

6. The Old Woman Who Lived in a Vinegar Bottle

Heard around a camp fire in 1924 and published in Katharine M. Briggs, *A Sampler of British Folktales* (London, 1977), p. 40.

7. Tom Tit Tot

The people of Suffolk, whence this story, have long held a reputation for foolishness. When my maternal grandfather, from Lavenham, took the queen's shilling in the 1890s, he joined a regiment with the soubriquet the 'Silly Suffolks'. (Jacobs, *English Fairy Tales*, p. 1.)

8. The Husband Who Was to Mind the House

From Asjbørnsen and Moe again, this time in a handsome Victorian translation by Sir George Webb Darsent (*Popular Tales From the Norse* [Edinburgh, 1903], p. 269.)

PART FOUR: GOOD GIRLS AND WHERE IT GETS THEM

1. East o' the Sun and West o' the Moon

Asjbørnsen and Moe once more, again in the Darsent translation (Darsent, p. 22). This is one of the most lyrically beautiful and mysterious of all Northern European fairy tales, and one that has proved irresistible to 'literary' writers for two thousand years, with its relation to the classical Cupid and Psyche story as retold in *The Golden Ass by* Apuleius, as well as to the lovely literary fairy tale 'Beauty and the Beast', written by Madame Leprince de Beaumont in the eighteenth century.

But Madame Leprince de Beaumont's Beauty is a well-brought-up young lady, designed to conform in a bourgeois, virtuous fashion. Madame Leprince de Beaumont worked as a governess for twenty years; she wrote extensively on good behaviour. But *this* young woman does not hesitate to go to bed with a strange bear and is betrayed by her own desire when she first sees the young man under the bearskin: '. . . she thought she couldn't live if she didn't give him a kiss there and then'. Then he disappears. But she gets him in the end.

2. The Good Girl and the Ornery Girl

'Told by Miss Callista O'Neill, Day, Mo, September 1941,' to Vance Randolph. The story is called 'Mother Holle' in Grimm. (Randolph, *The Devil's Pretty Daughter*.)

3. The Armless Maiden

This horrid story depicts the misfortunes of virtue with the glee of a Marquis de Sade – cf. the Grimms' 'Armless Maiden'. (Afanas'ev, p. 294.)

PART FIVE: WITCHES

1. The Chinese Princess

The French medieval fairy Mélusine changed into a snake from the waist down once a week. The English Romantic poet John Keats has a poem, 'Lamia', about a snake that turns into a beautiful woman. In Freudian terms, this is the return of the repressed with a vengeance.

From *Folk Tales of Pakistan*, compiled by Zainab Ghulam Abbas (Karachi, 1957).

2. The Cat-Witch

Mary Richardson again (Dorson, p. 146).

3. The Baba Yaga

Baba Yaga, the Russian witch, lives in the forest in a hut with chicken's legs that run around when she wants them to. Some say she is the devil's grandmother. She is bad, but stupid, and was characterized thus during the Stalinist period by the Soviet folklorist E.A. Tudorovskaya: 'Baba Yaga, the mistress of the forest and animals, is represented as a real exploiter, oppressing her animal servants.' (W.R. Ralston, *Russian Folk Tales* [London, 1873], pp. 139–42.)

4. Mrs Number Three

This comes from G. Willoughby-Meade, *Chinese Ghouls and Goblins* [London, 1928], a collection of popular lore (p. 191). Names and locations are given with unusual precision. Compare the fate of Mrs Number Three's guests with that of the hero of Apuleius's 'The Golden Ass', and compare Mrs Number Three herself with Circe, the enchantress in Homer's *Odyssey*, who transformed her clients into swine.

PART SIX: UNHAPPY FAMILIES

1. The Girl Who Banished Seven Youths

Bushnaq, p. 119.

2. The Market of the Dead

Melville J. and Frances S. Herskovits, *Dahomean Narrative* (Northwestern University African Studies, Evanston, 1958), p. 290.

3. The Woman Who Married Her Son's Wife

Millman, p. 127. Told by Gustav Broberg, Kulusuk, East Greenland.

4. The Little Red Fish and the Clog of Gold

Bushnaq, p. 181.

5. The Wicked Stepmother

Cardinall, p. 87.

6. Tuglik and Her Granddaughter

Heard from Anarfik, Sermiligaq, East Greenland. (Millman, p. 191.)

7. The Juniper Tree

The definitive version of a tale of child abuse and sibling solidarity known all over the world, in very similar forms. Verrier Elwin prints one from Tribal India. In no other story does the happy ending have more of an ache of wish-fulfilment; it is obvious that this solution can only be imagined, not experienced in reality. (Grimm, p. 171.)

8. Nourie Hadig

This Armenian 'Snow White' was collected by Susie Hoogasian-Villa from Mrs Akabi Mooradian, in the Armenian community in the city of Detroit, Michigan, to which they both belonged. Mrs Mooradian settled in Detroit in 1929, after various wanderings imposed on her by the turbulent history of her homeland since her birth in 1904. (*100 Armenian Tales*, collected and edited by Susie Hoogasian-Villa [Detroit, 1966, p. 84].)

9. Beauty and Pock Face

Chinese Fairy Tales and Folk Tales, collected and translated by Wolfram Eberhard (London, 1937), p. 17.

10. Old Age

Millman, p. 192.

PART SEVEN: MORAL TALES

1. Little Red Riding Hood

From Charles Perrault's *Histoires ou contes du temps passé* (Paris, 1697). I put it into English; my maternal grandmother used to say, 'Lift up the latch and walk in,' when she told it me when I was a child; and at the conclusion, when the wolf jumps on Little Red Riding Hood and gobbles her up, my grandmother used to pretend to eat me, which made me squeak and gibber with excited pleasure.

For an in-depth sociological, historical and psychological discussion of this story, plus thirty-one different literary versions including a feminist revision by the Merseyside Fairy Story Collective, see Jack Zipes, *The Trials and Tribulations of Little Red Riding Hood* (London, 1983). Jack Zipes thinks that 'The Story of Grandmother', recorded in Nièvre, France, around 1885, is part of a 'Red Riding Hood' tradition of a thoroughly emancipated kind; this little girl, colour of clothing unknown, is not an awful warning but an example of quick thinking:

> There was a woman who had some bread. She said to her daughter: 'Go carry this hot loaf and a bottle of milk to your granny.'
> So the little girl departed. At the crossway she met *bzou*, the werewolf, who said to her:

'Where are you going?'

'I'm taking this hot loaf and a bottle of milk to my granny.'

'What path are you taking,' said the werewolf, 'the path of needles or the path of pins?'

'The path of needles,' the little girl said.

'All right, then I'll take the path of pins.'

The little girl entertained herself by gathering needles. Meanwhile the werewolf arrived at the grandmother's house, killed her, put some of her meat in the cupboard and a bottle of her blood on the shelf. The little girl arrived and knocked at the door.

'Push the door,' said the werewolf, 'it's barred by a piece of wet straw.'

'Good day, Granny. I've brought you a hot loaf of bread and a bottle of milk.'

'Put it in the cupboard, my child. Take some of the meat which is inside and the bottle of wine on the shelf.'

After she had eaten, there was a little cat which said: 'Phooey! . . . A slut is she who eats the flesh and drinks the blood of her granny.'

'Undress yourself, my child,' the werewolf said, 'and come lie down beside me.'

'Where should I put my apron?'

'Throw it into the fire, my child, you won't be needing it any more.'

And each time she asked where she should put all her other clothes, the bodice, the dress, the petticoat, and the long stockings, the wolf responded:

'Throw them into the fire, my child, you won't be needing them any more.'

When she laid herself down in the bed, the little girl said:

'Oh, Granny, how hairy you are!'

'The better to keep myself warm, my child!'

'Oh, Granny, what big nails you have!'

'The better to scratch me with, my child!'

'Oh, Granny, what big shoulders you have!'

'The better to carry the firewood, my child!'

'Oh, Granny, what big ears you have!'

'The better to hear you with, my child!'

'Oh, Granny, what big nostrils you have!'

'The better to snuff my tobacco with, my child!'

'Oh, Granny, what a big mouth you have!'

'The better to eat you with, my child!'

'Oh, Granny, I've got to go badly. Let me go outside.'

'Do it in the bed, my child!'

'Oh, no, Granny, I want to go outside.'

'All right, but make it quick.'

The werewolf attached a woollen rope to her foot and let her go outside.

When the little girl was outside, she tied the end of the rope to a plum tree in the courtyard. The werewolf became impatient and said: 'Are you making a load out there? Are you making a load?'

When he realized that nobody was answering him, he jumped out of bed and saw that the little girl had escaped. He followed her but arrived at her house just at the moment she entered.

2. Feet Water

Kevin Danaher, *Folktales of the Irish Countryside* (Cork, 1967), pp. 127–9.

3. Wives Cure Boastfulness

Herskovits and Herskovits, p. 400.

4. Tongue Meat

Knappert, p. 132.

5. The Woodcutter's Wealthy Sister

Bushnaq, p. 137.

6. Escaping Slowly

Afro-American Folktales, stories from Black traditions in the New World edited and selected by Roger D. Abrahams (New York, 1985), p. 240.

7. Nature's Ways

Hoogasian-Villa, p. 338.

8. The Two Women Who Found Freedom

Millman, p. 112; from Akpaleeapik, Pond Inlet, Baffin Island.

9. How a Husband Weaned His Wife from Fairy Tales

Afanas'ev, p. 308.

NOTES ON PARTS 8–13

PART EIGHT: STRONG MINDS AND LOW CUNNING

1. The Twelve Wild Ducks

From the collection of Norwegian folk tales made by Peter Christian Asbjørnsen and Jørgen Moe, in George Webb Darsent's handsome Victorian translation, *Popular Tales from the Norse* (Edinburgh, 1903).

The film-maker Alfred Hitchcock thought nothing was more ominous than the look of blood on daisies. Blood on snow catches even more directly at the viscera. The raven, the blood, the snow – these are the elements of the unappeasable northern formulae of desire. In 'The Story of Conall Gulban' in J.F. Campbell's *Popular Tales of the West Highlands* Conall 'would not take a wife forever whose head should be black as the raven, and her face as fair as the snow, and her cheeks as red as blood'.

Campbell crisply suggests the raven must have been eating something, because of all the blood, and offers a variant from Inverness:

> When he got up in the morning there was young snow, and the raven was upon a spray near him, and a bit of flesh in his beak. The piece of flesh fell and Conall went to lift it, and the raven said to him, that Fair Beauteous Smooth was as white as the snow upon the spray, her cheek as red as the flesh that was in his hand, and her hair as black as the feather that was in his wing. (*Popular Tales of the West Highlands*, orally collected with a translation by J.F. Campbell, vol. III, Paisley, 1892.)

This carnivorous imagery expresses the depths of a woman's desire for a child in traditional stories. 'Snow-White' in the familiar version collected by the Brothers Grimm starts off the same way. Please note that, according to the editors of Palestinian Arab stories, childless mothers in fairy tales wish for daughters far more frequently than they do for sons.

'The Twelve Wild Ducks', with its savage beginning and theme of sibling devotion, forms the basis of the Danish Hans Christian Andersen's lovely literary story, 'The Wild Swans'. Andersen upgraded the ducks to romantic swans although I feel that if wild ducks were good enough for Ibsen, they should have been good enough for him.

2. Old Foster

Collected from Jane Gentry in 1923 in Hot Springs, North Carolina, by Isobel Gordon Carter. Text from *Journal of American Folklore*, 38 (1925), 360–1.

This ancient story of sex murder and serial killing travelled across the Atlantic with the first English settlers of the US in the sixteenth and seventeenth centuries. 'Old Foster' is first cousin to the sinister Mr Fox (see this volume, p. 9), and to 'The Robber Bridegroom' of the Brothers Grimm.

3. Šāhīn

From *Speak, Bird, Speak Again: Palestinian Arab Folktales*, collected and edited by Ibrahim Muhawi and Sharif Kanaana, and published by the University of California Press, 1988.

These stories were collected on tape between 1978 and 1980 in Galilee, since 1948 part of the state of Israel, the West Bank and Gaza. In the Palestinian tradition, women are the custodians of narrative; if men tell stories, they must adopt the narrative style of women. Since storytelling style matures with age, old women have the edge on everybody else. Tales are told on winter nights, when there is little work in the fields, and extended families gather together for mutual entertainment. The oldest woman usually starts. The gatherings are dominated by women; there is a pronounced pro-woman bias to all these Palestinian stories, although the Palestinian family is, as Muhawi and Kanaana explain, 'patrilineal, patrilateral, polygynous, endogamous and patrilocal'.

In their introduction, they note that the pattern of free mate choice by women 'is so consistently at odds with the facts of social life that we must finally conclude that a deeply felt emotional need is being articulated'.

Nevertheless, 'Šāhīn', with its exuberantly self-assertive heroine, was told by a sixty-five-year-old man from Galilee, a ploughman and shepherd all his life. In another variant, the exhausted hero, newly married, says to Šāhīn, 'Believe me you are the man and I am the bride.' And it is nothing but the truth.

4. The Dog's Snout People

A story from the Baltic country of Latvia collected in the 1880s and published in a majestic collection called *Siberian and Other Folktales: Primitive Literature of the Empire of the Tsars*, collected and translated with an introduction and notes by C. Fillingham-Coxwell (London, C.W. Daniel, 1925).

Christian culture was slow to influence the people of heavily forested Latvia, who are said to have retained pagan altars as late as 1835. According to tradition, marriage was obtained by abduction, a risky business. Geographically between, and politically at the mercy of, Germany and Russia for centuries, the Letts, according to Fillingham-Coxwell, regarded the Germans and Russians 'with hatred and despair'. Fillingham-Coxwell also thought the enigmatic 'dog's snout people' themselves might contain memories of aboriginal Lettish inhabitants.

5. The Old Woman Against the Stream

Norwegian, again; from the same Asbjørnsen and Moe collection as 'The Twelve Wild Ducks', in a modern translation by Pat Shaw and Carl Noman (New York, Pantheon Books). Originally published in Oslo by Dreyers Verlag in 1960.

6. The Letter Trick

The people who were taken from West Africa as slaves to the place formerly called Dutch Guiana, now Suriname, took with them an invisible treasure of memory and culture. In the late 1920s, the anthropologists Melville J. Herskovits and Frances S. Herskovits collected a vast number of tales and songs, in the coastal city of Paramaribo. The language of the city was a thick, rich Creole; the Herskovits translated their material into English.

The city of Paramaribo possessed a mixed-race culture – Dutch, Indian, Carib, Arawak, Chinese and Javanese people mingled with those of African descent, but, among the latter, a strong African influence remained, expressing itself not only in voodoo beliefs and practices but in such matters as the tying of a headscarf. Descent was traced through the maternal line; the men were often absent as migrant workers.

Storytelling had an important place in this community. Tales were told to entertain the dead as they lay in state. And there was a taboo against telling stories in the daytime, because, if you did so, death would come and sit beside you, and you would die, too.

(*Suriname Folklore*, collected by Melville J. Herskovits and Frances S. Herskovits [New York, Columbia University Press, 1936], p. 351.

7. Rolando and Brunilde

This type of industrious spinner or seamstress is often rewarded with an illustrious lover simply for sitting at her window sewing or singing. (See 'The Greenish Bird', this volume p. 275.) Here though, she attracts an evil magician who abducts and thereafter deactivates her. Quite unusually, it is her mother who embarks on the Path of Trials as a sort of trickster-heroine. A fairy-hag is her helper and Rolando her assistant. The tale includes some interesting images of the two old women humping heavy bags over a garden wall and breaking into the castle – activities generally reserved for the young.

8. The Greenish Bird

A Mexican variant of the story most familiar in the beautiful Norwegian form, 'East o' the Sun, West o' the Moon', in Peter Christan Asbjørnsen and Jørgen Moe's collection (see this volume, p. 129).

Like the last tale, this Mexican one begins with an industrious spinner at a window. Luisa is swiftly won over by her bird-wooer and begins an indeterminate sexual relationship. Like the Greek love god, hero of Apuleius's third-century Latin novella 'Cupid and Psyche' contained in the Golden Ass, the greenish bird is magical, generous and wonderful in bed. Luisa knows nothing about him, which does not particularly bother her. Like Psyche's sisters Luisa's too are jealous, and mar the relationship, causing the severely wounded prince to abandon her with an injunction to come in search of him. The iron shoe clad heroine who visits the sun and the moon in search of her offended lover occurs in Eastern Europe too, most notably attempting to redeem a Pig-prince. The Cap O' Rushes ending to this tale is similar to the Egyptian Cinderella story 'The Princess in the Suit of Leather', (this volume, p. 43), when the Prince, having realized his sweetheart is a servant in his palace, demands that she bring his meals to him. (*Folktales of Mexico*, by Americo Paredes [Chicago, 1970], p. 95.)

9. The Crafty Woman

From the Baltic state of Lithuania, again from C. Fillingham-Coxwell's collection. He quotes a Russian variation, from around Moscow, in which the part of the old woman is played by a young Jew.

PART NINE: UP TO SOMETHING – BLACK ARTS AND DIRTY TRICKS

1. Pretty Maid Ibronka

This popular Hungarian story has been narrated in almost every village in the country in fairly similar form. It is also known in Lithuania and Yugoslavia. Hungarian popular belief has a particular dread of a revived corpse but the terrible lover, with his hat 'graced with a crane's feather' and his cloven hoof is reminiscent of the demon lover who returns to claim his faithless mistress in the great Scots ballad, 'The House Carpenter' (in Francis Child's collection *The English and Scottish Popular Ballads*, 3 vols., New York, 1957). The demon takes the Scotswoman away on shipboard and destroys her: but Ibronka gets away with it.

This story was narrated by Mihály Fédics, an illiterate day-labourer, in 1938, when he was eighty-six years old. He had gone to the United States at the time of the First World War and worked as a labourer there but soon returned to Hungary. He learned his stories during the long winter evenings, in the village houses where people went to spin together. Later, working as a lumberjack, his stories were the principal source of entertainment in the forest camp. 'It was his custom to interrupt his own story, by calling out "Bones" to his listeners, to see whether they had gone to sleep: if the encouraging answer "tiles" came, he went on with the story, but if there was no answer, he knew that his companions had dropped off, and the tale was to be continued the following day' (p. 130 *Folktales of Hungary*).

This information, together with the story, comes from *Folktales of Hungary*, edited by Linda Degh and translated by Judith Halasz (London, Routledge & Kegan Paul, 1965).

Copyright University of Chicago, 1965. In the series 'Folktales of the World', edited by Richard M. Dorson.

2. Enchanter and Enchantress

A witch duel, or transformation contest, tale from tribal Russia. For more about transformation contests see notes to 'Keep Your Secrets' in this volume, p. 459. This story comes from a Finno-Turkish people called the Mordvins, who lived between the rivers Volga and Oka in the heart of Russia when this story was collected in the nineteenth century. The Mordvinian idea of the cosmos was that of the beehive.

Fillingham-Coxwell, p. 568.

3. The Telltale Lilac Bush

As told to Keith Ketchum in 1963 by Mrs Sarah Dadisman of Union, Monroe Country, West Virginia. (From *The Telltale Lilac Bush and Other West Virginian*

Ghost Tales, collected by Ruth Ann Musick [University of Kentucky Press, 1965], p. 12.)

4. Tatterhood

A Norwegian story from Asbjørnsen and Moe, in George Webb Darsent's translation.

5. The Witchball

An old-fashioned farting story from rural America, as told by seventy-six-year-old V. Ledford, of Clay County, Kentucky. This text is reprinted from *Buying the Wind: Regional Folklore in the United States*, edited and collected by Richard M. Dorson (University of Chicago Press, 1964).

Vance Randolph found another wise woman with access to farting powder in the Ozark mountains in Arkansas; this story may be found in this volume p. 73.

6. The Werefox

From *Chinese Ghouls and Goblins*, edited by G. Willoughby-Meade (London, 1928), p. 123.

7. The Witches' Piper

Narrated by Mihály Bertok, aged sixty-seven, a herdsman of Kishartyan, Nograd County, Hungary, and collected by Linda Degh in 1951.

Once upon a time, the bagpiper provided the music for the Shrove Tuesday dance. Witches would force the piper to play for them and then pay him back with a dirty trick.

8. Vasilissa the Fair

The heroine Vasilissa is as familiar in Russian folklore as the European Ella i.e. Cinderella. (See this volume, 'Vasilissa the Priest's Daughter', p. 61 and 'The Baba Yaga', p. 158.) The tale contains powerful indicators that the Baba Yaga's origins are probably in the Mother goddess of various mythologies. She refers to the morning, day and night as her 'own' and her mortar and pestle are reminiscent of corn and wheat grinding. In addition, she possesses fire, a basic element. (A more obscure tale tells how she stole fire.) She is stern and harsh in her judgement but just and not devoid of ethics, conforming to the deathly aspect of the Mother goddess. The skulls surrounding her home represent the dead in general, though 'The Witch and her Servants' (*The Yellow Story Book*, ed. Andrew Lang) contains a more specific explanation. When the ubiquitous Iwanich of Russian tales goes to work for a witch, she delivers the following warning:

> If you look after them both for a year I will give you anything you like to ask; but if, on the other hand, you let any of the animals escape you, your last hour is come, and your head shall be stuck on the last spike of my fence. The other spikes, as you see, are already adorned, and the skulls are all those of different servants I have had who have failed to do what I demanded (p. 161).

The remaining riddle is that of the invisible pairs of hands. It is clear that the hag is alluding to the secrecy of women's mysteries when she expresses approval that Vasilissa has stopped short of asking the question that would force her to reveal what is inside her house. Her aversion to blessings may well represent the fear of a pagan goddess being driven out by Christianity. Fillingham-Coxwell's note referring to Russian society at the time of collection, says: 'The priest has a difficult, ill-paid and not very exalted position. So superstition and a belief in witchcraft abound, though the efforts of the orthodox church to suppress pagan practices and traditions have not been without a large measure of success' (p. 671 *Siberian and Other Folktales*). A poem entitled 'Russian Folk-Tales' includes the lines:

> Cannibal witches will scarcely attack or make ready to eat us
> Easily, quickly we conquer if enemies dare approach us.

For details of the Baba Yaga herself, see Angela Carter's note to 'The Baba Yaga' (this volume, p. 463). C. Fillingham-Coxwell, p. 680.)

9. The Midwife and the Frog

This story, set in the Magyar Mountains not far from the banks of the Szuscava, was collected by Gyula Orlutory from thirty-three-year-old Mrs Gergely Tamas in 1943. The *gyivak* of this story is glossed in the book as 'a minor devil'.

This tale-type counts as a legend the world over since it continues to be believed. A Middle Eastern variant, in which a midwife delivers a djinn's wife, is always told as if it occurred to an acquaintance of the teller. There the terrified woman accepts a handful of stones which turn to gold when she returns home. A Norse version appears in *Folktales of Norway* edited by Reidar Christiansen (translated by Pat Shaw Iversen, The University of Chicago Press, 1964, p. 105). Numerous variants exist in the British Isles. According to Katharine Briggs, 'the earliest version is from *Gervase of Tilbury* in the 13th C', *Folktales of England*, The University of Chicago Press, 1965. See 'The Fairy Midwife', p. 38 and 'The Midwife', in *The Best-Loved Folktales of the World*, edited by Joanna Cole, Anchor, Doubleday, New York, 1983, p. 280.

(Degh, p. 296.)

PART TEN: BEAUTIFUL PEOPLE

1. Fair, Brown and Trembling

This Irish Cinderella was collected by Jeremiah Curtin in 1887 in Galway. The unkind sisters here are Trembling's own. The henwife is the Celtic equivalent of the fairy godmother. Storytellers sometimes preferred to avoid the use of the word 'witch' in Ireland and Scotland. It was too much like 'tempting fate' so they tended to call her a bird-woman or a henwife. Though henwives are usually good (see Duncan Williams's collections, where the henwife is Jack's greatest helper in the Jack tales) they do occasionally let slip a remark that triggers a sequence of malign events (see Frank McKenna, *The Steed of the Bells* [cassette], selected from the archives of the Ulster Folk and Transport Museum). The henwife asks Trembling to stay outside the church rather than going in, perhaps suggesting practices outside the approval of the Church. Magic good, bad or indifferent had the status of the Devil's work in Christianity so magical practices such as the use of the cloak of darkness would have been frowned on. Trembling's husband is the son of the King of the ancient city of Emania in Ulster, called Omania here. He changed his loyalties from Fair to Trembling after seeing her magical regalia. Another story in Curtin's repertoire has the King of Greece marrying an Irish king's eldest daughter then falling in love with the younger, Gil an Og. He curses them both turning Gil an Og into a 'cat within her castle' and her sister into a serpent in the bay. Gil an Og consults a druid and initiates a series of fights in order to free them both (*Myths and Folktales of Ireland*, Jeremiah Curtin, [reprinted from the 1890 Little, Brown and Co. edition by Dover Publications Inc.,] Toronto, London, 1975, p. 212).

The golden hair cut adrift occurs as far afield as India (cf. Prince Lionheart, in 'There Was Once a King' [in *Folk Tales of Pakistan*, retold by Sayyid Fayyaz Mahmud, Lok Virsa (Pakistan, undated), p. 117]. Strands of Princess Yasmin's golden hair are seen floating downstream by a king, who determines to marry the owner of the hair.

The willingness of the King and Trembling to allow their daughter to marry the cow-herd may have something to do with this statement in Curtin's telling of Kil Arthur: 'In that time there was a law in the world that if a young man came to woo a young woman and her people wouldn't give her to him, the young woman should get her death by law' (Curtin, p. 113).

(*Irish Folk-Tales*, edited by Henry Glassie, Penguin Folklore Library [Harmondsworth, UK, 1985], p. 257.)

2. Diirawac and Her Incestuous Brother

This story was told by a twenty-year-old man (who was not a member of editor, Francis Mading Deng's family).

Angela Carter notes that the Dinka are cattle herders and subsistence farmers of the Sudan. Their land – about 10 per cent of the Sudan – is crossed by the Nile and its tributaries, making communications difficult. 'The main goal of a Dinka is to marry and have children' (p. 166).

Adults and children sleep together in huts. One person is asked to tell a story, then people tell stories in succession, notes Angela Carter, then quotes from Francis Mading Deng: 'As the storytelling progresses, people begin to fall asleep one by one. Sometimes they fall asleep, wake up in the middle of a story, and then fall asleep again . . . People who wake up in the middle of a story are usually brought up to date briefly. As time passes and some people begin to sleep and perhaps snore, the storyteller starts to ask from time to time: Are you asleep? . . . As long as there are people still awake, storytelling continues. The last storyteller is quite likely to be the last person awake and so the final story will be left incomplete' (p. 29).

The lions in most Dinka stories are clearly not real lions but represent a wild, untamed side of human nature. Neither are the puppies, who according to a footnote, symbolise wildness and therefore merit such brutal treatment in folk tales. The victim is subdued by severe beating and 'teasing'. The animal's partiality to raw meat indicates his wildness and its selection of cooked meat signifies it has been tamed (see 'Duang and His Wild Wife', p. 411 of the present book).

It is mostly women and young people who tell the stories. Stories tend to be associated with bedtime and are geared towards the children, the primary educators of childhood (p. 198).

It is likely that the sibling incest taboo is powerfully reinforced not only from the community but the most insignificant sources, because of the children's communal sleeping environment. It is for the heroine Diirawac who killed her brother that the village mourns, the elderly allowing their hair to grow matted and the young abandoning their beads to signify disaster. Violation of the incest taboo is considered more unnatural than murder. No single entity in the tale disputes the validity of the taboo.

(*Dinka Folktales: African Stories from the Sudan*, edited by Francis Mading Deng [New York and London, 1974], p. 78.)

3. The Mirror

Though this variant is poignant, even tragic, the motif of the mistaken mirror image is generally found in humorous tales. In one version a man quarrels with his wife after buying a mirror he mistakes for an image of his dead father. A nun mediates. This version of the tale is also found in India, China and Korea.

The Sun goddess of Japanese myth once took exile from the chaotic world in the Heavenly Rock Dwelling and was enticed back when the celestial smith fashioned a mirror of iron and told her that her reflection was a rival goddess. Beguiled by its beauty and brightness, she returned to light up the world.

(Willoughby-Meade p. 184.)

4. The Frog Maiden

The start of the tale, with its wicked stepmother and two stepsisters, is complemented by further echoes of the Cinderella story when the Frog Maiden arrives to see the prince in a carrot coach with mice for horses. Variations of this story are found all over the world. 'The Three Feathers' (Brothers Grimm), 'The White Cat' (France) and 'The Monkey Princess' (Pakistan) are all standard tales featuring the *Dummling* (simpleton) hero. In her *Introduction to the Interpretation of Fairytales* (Spring Publications Inc., Dallas, USA, 1970), Marie Louise von Franz says that 'the bride is either a toad, a frog, a white cat, an ape, a lizard, puppet, rat, a stocking or a hopping nightcap – not even living objects – and sometimes a turtle'. A few lines down she explains that

> The main action is concerned with the finding of the right female, upon which depends the inheritance of the female and further, that the hero does not perform any masculine deeds. He is not a hero in the proper sense of the word. He is helped all the time by the feminine element, which solves the whole problem for him . . . The story ends with a marriage – a balanced union of the male and female elements. So the general structure seems to point to a problem in which there is a dominating male attitude, a situation which lacks the feminine element, and the story tells us how the missing feminine is brought up and restored (p. 36).

(*Burmese Folktales*, edited and collected by Maung Htin Aung [Calcutta, 1948], p. 137.)

5. The Sleeping Prince

The motive for the princess's journey is provided by the sight of horses' blood on the grass and her comment about its beauty. This seems a strange sentiment except that the blood and the beauty of it on the grass is probably connected with menstrual initiation and fertility. This is borne out by the invisible voice guiding the princess to go in search of a mate. The voice also mentions sticks and the sprinkling of water – elements that never actually materialise in the story – suggesting a sexual initiation which comes to pass only much later. The gory use to which the princess puts the witch's remnants could again be related to puberty – the pain and trauma of sexual deprivation and isolation represented by the witch are now objects of access to womanhood and sexual fruition, particularly the ladder which leads to her bed.

This tale is found in India too, beginning like the famous British tale 'Cap O'Rushes' with the expulsion of the youngest princess who gives an unacceptable response to her king-father's question. The princess asks the prince for some puppets and he overhears her enacting the incidents of her life. The impostor, her maid, is buried to the waist and trampled by horses.

(Herskovits and Herskovits p. 381.)

6. The Orphan

The motif of the mother feeding her daughter from beyond the grave occurs the world over. An almost exact parallel with this aspect of the tale is the Grimm Brothers' 'One Eye, Two Eye and Three Eye'. Treasure associated with the tree is also a feature of both, focusing primarily on the heroine's imminent rise in social status. She is not a conjurer though her stepmother proves to have access to spells and enchantment. The heroine's own inner magic emanates from her innocence. The second common motif here is the type found in 'The Goose Girl', where an envious woman deceitfully takes the place of the true bride. See 'The Woman Who Married Her Son' and 'The Sleeping Prince' in this volume (pp. 408 and 357). A third standard element in fairy tales is the metamorphosis of women into birds, either at will or by enchantment – for example, 'The White Duck' (European), 'The Crane Wife' (Japanese). See also 'Story of a Bird Woman', included in this collection (p. 391). A more exciting parallel is found in 'Devil Woman', in Tales of the Cochiti Indians, collected by Ruth Benedict (Smithsonian Institution, 1930). Here a demon transforms a new mother into a bird – a dove in this instance – by sticking a pin in her head. The removal of the pin ends the enchantment.

(Tales of Old Malawi, retold and edited by E. Singano and A.A. Roscoe [Limbe, Malawi, 1986], p. 69.)

PART ELEVEN: MOTHERS AND DAUGHTERS

1. Achol and Her Wild Mother

Another Dinka story featuring a human lion. This one is told by the daughter of Chief Deng Majok, Nyankoc Deng, who was then aged eighteen to twenty. Perhaps Achol's mother's grisly compulsion to gather wood and forfeit her hands and feet to the lion actually represent some other kind of misdemeanour, such as adultery. Angela Carter's notes copied from Dinka Folktales would seem to support this: 'lions are what the Dinka fear most' (p. 25) and 'A person who violates fundamental precepts of the Dinka moral code is often identified in the folk tales as an outsider and an animal' (p. 161). She comments: 'this differentiates the animal from the human, the lions of the stories are not really lions. Hence the emphasis on human interaction with lions. As in the other stories, the lioness is fed nightly by her daughter until her son arrives and beats the wildness out of her' (see 'Duang and His Wild Wife', p. 411 in this collection).

(Deng, p. 95.)

2. Tunjur, Tunjur

A fifty-five-year-old woman called Fatime, from the village of Arrabe in Galilee, told the story of Tunjur, a cooking pot. Angela Carter's notes quote the description of another teller from *Speak Bird, Speak Again* (p. 31): 'When she came to the part about the man defecating in the cooking pot and the pot closing on him, Im Nabil laughed; then, still laughing she said the pot chopped off the man's equipment.' Angela Carter comments that 'men don't like the stories, partly because some of the mores of which they are guardians, e.g. the "woman's honour" thing, are consistently challenged in the tales – in which *heroines predominate*'. She goes on to quote again from *Speak Bird, Speak Again* (p. 14): 'the ideological basis of the system lies in the father-son bond. The female is identified as the "other".'

In this story, the daughter – a cooking pot – is quite clearly the 'other', but sparklingly in step with the cunning and playful heroine of 'Šāhīn' (see p. 252 note p. 468) in her ability to match every man in wits and strength. She is a recognizable female trickster of the famous British Molly Whuppie type (a female Jack-the-Giant-Killer), even to the extent of going that little bit further than she has to, for the sake of a bit of fun. The story is well in keeping with the woman's need in society to articulate her capabilities without being in the custody of the male infrastructure, so men are entirely peripheral to this story except as fools.

(Muhawi and Kanaana, p. 55.)

3. The Little Old Woman with Five Cows

A Yakut creation myth tells of a Supreme Being who created a small and level world, which was scratched up by evil demons and spirits making the hills and valleys. The evil spirits were regularly appeased and thanked by Yakut shamans. Today they inhabit the Lena basin and intermarry with Russians.

The magical maiden in this Yakut tale has her origins in what would appear to be a foundation myth of sorts. The 'middle land' inhabited by the human race, here represented by the Yakuts, is clearly in need of honour or redemption and the maiden is sent down as the saviour, duly suffering trials, death and resurrection. Unlike 'The Finn King's Daughter' (Christiansen, p. 147) and other tales, in which the reader is informed in a phrase or sentence about the metamorphosis, this tale contains the horrific and explicit process of transformation. The demoness herself is, like the *muzayyara*, an Egyptian water-nymph with iron breasts. (*Folktales of Egypt*, edited and translated by Hasan M. El-Shamy, University of Chicago, 1938, p. 180.) Angela Carter comments: 'The ancient Indian stories contain many horrible descriptions of Rakshasas' (ogres).

The goddess Kali herself is depicted at her most ferocious, with her tongue hanging from her mouth like the demoness of this story who shoots out an iron tongue.

Like the troll-woman in 'The Finn King's Daughter', this demoness is not quite familiar with the social customs of the society she is attempting to infiltrate. There is a cryptic reference to the fact that 'she wrongly fastened her horse to the willow tree where the old widow from Semyaksin used to tether her spotted ox', and this merits the hostility of her husband's clan. The editor of *Siberian and Other Folktales* notes that 'each species of tree has a master of its own except the larch' and it is with a larch branch that the plant maiden kindles the fire when she arrives, suggesting that she is in tune with humans and comes in fulfilment of a greater plan. She also knows of an interesting cleansing ritual vital to get rid of the internal and external pollution of her husband caused by coupling with the demoness. The hanging of the Khan's son from the tree for purification is reminiscent of Christ on the crucifix and other suspended gods such as Attis (Anatolia), Sluy (Wales) and Wotan (Germanic), all of whom returned after a few days.

(Fillingham-Coxwell, p. 262.)

4. Achol and Her Adoptive Lioness-Mother

In this tale told by a twenty-year-old woman, the incest taboo is once again threatened but maintained through the intervention of non-human creatures. (Cf. 'Diirawac and Her Incestuous Brother', p. 338.) Angela Carter comments: 'Incest taboos are particularly complex and important in polygamous societies. Here for example, Achol and her brother cannot recognize each other, having been separated in early childhood through the deceit of their half brothers.'

PART TWELVE: MARRIED WOMEN

1. Story of a Bird Woman

Angela Carter jotted down some salient quotes from *Siberian and Other Folktales* in her notes. 'Stories of bird-women occur among the Yakuts, the Lapps and the Samoyedes'; 'It is not unknown for a Siberian folktale hero to order a large supply of boots when he undertakes a great feat'; and 'Generally speaking, the Chukchis believe that all nature is animated and that every material object can act, speak and walk by itself.'

The transformations of animal goddesses into human wives is the primary component of this story. Japanese and Chinese folklore abound in these. The journey and magical battle of redemption found here are unusual, though. Generally the husband has to content himself with his children or – possibly – rare encounters with the departed wife. The Welsh classic, 'The Song of Taliesin', includes a series of incidents in which the goddess Ceredwen takes the form of birds, ranging from a mighty eagle to a macabre raven and a lowly hen.

(Fillingham-Coxwell, p. 82.)

2. Father and Mother Both 'Fast'

The true purpose of this joke, which challenges the incest taboo, is to rebound on the main protagonist. It contains bawdy references to adultery and illegitimacy, as do most cuckolded husband jokes. It was collected from Jim Alley by Richard Dorson.

(Dorson, p. 79.)

3. Reason to Beat Your Wife

This piece of scatological humour comes from a thirty-year-old peasant woman from a village in the Nile delta, who remembered hearing it from her mother when she was ten. Her husband put up some resistance to her offer of telling the story to the (male) editor Hasan El-Shamy and acceded to his appeal only on condition that her voice would not be recorded. He enjoyed the story though, and joked that his wife had put it to good use.

The editor adds:

> The climactic event in this humorous anecdote belongs under the general motif 'absurd wish'. The overall motif may be contrasted to 'The Taming of the Shrew', which carries the local title of 'Kill Your Cat on Your Wedding Night'.

In fact it is the notion of a husband establishing his superiority over an already dutiful wife that gets its comeuppance here, so it is appropriate that the tale comes from a woman who got it from an older woman. The tale seems to advocate indulgence of the weaknesses of men and the fact that being dutiful pays off – but it hints at concealed guile with the robust, earthy humour familiar in Arab tales. For the audacious use of shit, see 'Šāhīn' (p. 252) and 'Tunjur, Tunjur' (p. 371 and note p. 476).

(Hasan El-Shamy, p. 217.)

4. The Three Lovers

The paramour at the window in this tale from south-west Mexico receives a similar fate to Chaucer's character in 'The Miller's Tale', after having his rump kissed.

(*Cuentos Españoles de Colorado y de Nuevo Mejico Vol. I*, original text by Juan B. Rael [Stanford University Press, 1957], p. 105. This text translated by Merle E. Simmons, p. 427.)

5. The Seven Leavenings

Angela Carter notes: 'Fatime again – two tales woven together by the personality of the old woman. The woman moves from father's house to husband's house and at no time has space of her own – but don't dismiss the *power* of the "other" – expressed partly in telling of tales, embroidery, basket-making, pottery, wedding songs, laments.' Then she quotes from *Speak Bird, Speak Easy:* 'for the female, conflict is inherent in the structure of the system'.

A footnote from the editors of that book reads: 'Inability to get pregnant and have children is the most common theme in all the folktales in this collection' (p. 207). Without a doubt this is one of the anxieties expressed by women in tales, particularly since 'a man is more easily forgiven if he hits a wife who doesn't have children' (loc. cit.).

The woman in this story is clearly an old crone with magical instincts, a wily and wise helper of women who speaks in a cryptic language of her own; for example, 'The land is longing for its people, I want to go home.' Perhaps the fact that the bread doesn't leaven means that her work, the deliverance of women from their husbands, is never finished – except of course when it suits the storyteller to bring the tale to its end. Being an old woman, she is particularly suitable as the companion of a younger woman and unlikely to misguide her. This gives her the space to practise the necessary wiles to improve the lot of her protégée. Angela Carter quotes, 'Older women are thought to be asexual; the husband is therefore more ready to believe in his wife's innocence after the old woman confirms her interpretation of "black on white"' (p. 211). The frame/vignette format is standard in the Middle East (cf. the Arabian Nights).

The 'seven' in the title suggests that it is part of a cycle of severn stories narrated in the same formula.

(Muhawi and Kanaana, p. 206.)

6. The Untrue Wife's Song

Another daring woman teaches her husband a lesson in this story collected by Ralph S. Boggs from B.L. Lunsford aged forty-four, of North Carolina. This tale is based on 'Old Hildebrande', a longer tale originating from Europe and with an anti-clerical bias.

(*Journal of American Folklore*, 47, 1934, p. 305.)

7. The Woman Who Married Her Son

This story was told by an eighty-two-year-old woman from the village of Rafidiya, district of Nablus, in Palestine, notes Angela Carter.

The familiar scenario of a wife being replaced by a rival has a twist here, when a mother replaces her daughter-in-law in her son's bed and even becomes pregnant. Muhawi and Kanaana compare her pica (craving) for sour grapes to the western one for pickles. The same theme appears in 'Rom', in Jan Knappert's *Myths and Legends of the Congo* (London, 1979). Rom's mother's action is in part prompted by pity that unknown to him, his sweetheart has abandoned him, so it is the young man himself who commits a grisly suicide, chanting:

> I entered the lap I came out of
> My strength went back where it came from (p. 27).

Here though, the mother is motivated by selfishness and lust. In part her jealousy is triggered by sharing status with another woman. Angela Carter quotes a Palestinian proverb: 'The household of the father is a playground and that of the husband is an education. A woman always belongs in one household or another.' She jots down some phrases: *sexuality* – utterly disruptive of social fabric, especially female sexuality; sexes segregated; 'honour'.

The tale certainly demonstrates the fear of disruption caused by this example of female sexuality gone rampant. The slur to family honour – guarded by men but lodged in women – is punished with death by burning. Interestingly, though the editors Muhawi and Kanaana attribute the teller's omission of the detail of this punishment to her quickening of pace and brevity towards the end of the story, it is really more likely to be her way of reducing the punitive consequences of female transgression. As for the segregation of sexes – perhaps that is what makes it easier to believe that a son could mistake his mother for his wife, however well disguised she may be. Of course, a mother-in-law could be as young as thirty.

The brutality of the wife's action in casually cutting out the innocent servant's tongue is not particularly unusual in fairy tales or for that matter in history.

Here it indicates her commitment to silence. When her time of silence is up she allows the messenger to keep his tongue. The silence of a woman in fairy tales, through either enchantment or commitment, is a standard narrative device to facilitate plot development. This is a legacy from the early Middle Ages, when women in European narratives lost their voices during the period between betrothal and marriage. The silence of heroines appears as a redemption motif in several German fairy tales, where loquacious heroines never became popular. In Europe, the silencing of heroines for fear of evil spells or the threat of ever-lasting condemnation was linked to concepts of power and retribution for the original sin.

(Muhawi and Kanaana, p. 60.)

8. Duang and His Wild Wife

This story was told by Nyanjur Deng, another of Chief Deng Majok's daughters, aged twenty. Angela Carter quotes from *Dinka Folktales:* 'The late Chief of the Nyok extended the practice of diplomatic marriage further than anyone else in the history of the Dinka. He had nearly 200 wives drawn from most of the corners of Dinkaland. The family was closely knit, living in several large villages, and all kinds of dialects were spoken and subcultures represented' (p. 99).

Here Duang considers his wife's pica (craving) to be unreasonable since the Dinka deplore the killing of animals for any reason other than ritual or sacrifice. His deceitful act re-emphasizes that from Amou's point of view Duang has behaved as an 'outsider'. Having gone through the civilizing ritual (see 'Diirawac and Her Incestuous Brother', p. 338 and 'Achol and Her Wild Mother', p. 367) she avenges herself with his death.

(Deng, p. 97.)

9. A Stroke of Luck

One of a body of jocular tales about the inability of women to keep a secret. In some variants the trusting husband gets into trouble; here he turns it to his advantage.

(Degh, p. 147.)

10. The Beans in the Quart Jar

Another cuckolded husband joke, told by Jim Alley to Richard Dorson (see 'Father and Mother Both "Fast"', p. 394, and 'The Untrue Wife's Song', p. 406).

(Dorson, p. 80.)

PART THIRTEEN: USEFUL STORIES

1. A Fable of a Bird and Her Chicks

A stern and darkly humorous fable about preparation for the tough and persecutory side of life, this story is representative of Yiddish humour and aphorisms.

From *Yiddish Folktales*, edited by Beatrice Silverman Weinreich with a foreword by Leonard Woolf.

2. The Three Aunts

'Old Habetrot' is the English variant of the Norse tale in which the helper presents herself to the lazy spinner's husband as an illustration of what might happen to his wife if she is forced to pursue the crafts of spinning and weaving (cf. 'Vasilissa the Fair' p. 314, who actually does spin, weave and stitch the king's shirts to perfection, so is naturally under no pressure to continue). The lazy spinner, though, resists the pressure of her straitened circumstances to tie her to a spinning wheel. Since the only release from her penury lies in marrying an affluent man, guile and sub-terfuge are necessary escape devices. What is most enjoyable is the conspiracy of women, which not only conceals the heroine's trickery but saves her from a future of drudgery and rebuke. Not so the post-1819 editions of the Grimms' story which demands of the reader, 'You must yourself admit that she was a disgusting woman.'

(Darsent, p. 194.)

3. Tale of an Old Woman

'Muriwa' is the Bondes word for sycamore. An almost identical story occurs in the South Pacific. These stories indicate that the conditions imposed by magical helpers are binding. If they are not duly respected, the creatures withdraw (see 'Story of a Bird Woman', p. 391). In both these stories nothing is left behind as a reminder of the days of grace.

(*African Folktales*, edited by Roger Abrahams [New York, Pantheon Folklore Library, 1983), p. 57.)

4. The Height of Purple Passion

An unsolved mystery riddle ending in anti-climax. The author collected it from a nine-year-old American girl in the presence of her stunned parents. The source of the joke is probably a French literary story that still survives under various names including 'The Bordeaux Diligence', which occurs in a Hitchcock anthology of horror stories from the late 1960s.

(*The Rationale of the Dirty Joke*, vol. II, by C. Legman [London, Panther, 1973], p. 121.)

5. Salt, Sauce and Spice, Onion Leaves, Pepper and Drippings

The power of the name is a fundamental premiss of this story. The password – the coveted man's name – is only gained after a specific and vital test has been passed. Unlike the Tom Tit Tot group (stories like 'Rumpelstiltskin') the test is service and generosity of spirit rather than trickery and contest. As in all *Dummling* (simpleton) stories, the most unlikely candidate triumphs.

(Abrahams, p. 299.)

6. Two Sisters and the Boa

A careless joke with a non-human creature results in a scary mistake (see 'The Midwife and the Frog', p. 322). The tale is otherwise of the Beauty and the Beast type. The point that the wicked sister always seems to miss is that the reward lies not in emulating her sister's actions, but in her generosity of spirit. (Source unknown.)

7. Spreading the Fingers

A moral tale from Suriname, reminiscent of an oral Islamic tale in which a pauper shares out the food quota allocated him for his entire life and ensures that he never goes hungry. But his game is with God, who is a willing player in it.

(Heskovits and Heskovits, p. 355.)

ACKNOWLEDGEMENTS FOR PARTS 1–7

Permission to reproduce these fairy tales is gratefully acknowledged to the following: Capra Press, Santa Barbara, CA, USA, for 'Sermessuaq', 'Kakuarshuk', 'Blubber Boy', 'The Woman Who Married Her Son's Wife', 'Tuglik and Her Granddaughter', 'Old Age' and 'The Two Women Who Found Freedom' from *A Kayak Full of Ghosts: Innuit Tales 'Gathered and Retold'* by Lawrence Millman, copyright © 1987; Angela Carter, translator of *The Fairy Tales of Charles Perrault*, for 'Little Red Riding Hood', copyright © 1977, published by Victor Gollancz Ltd.; Columbia University Press for 'Mr Fox', 'Aunt Kate's Goomer-Dust' and 'The Good Girl and the Ornery Girl' from *The Devil's Pretty Daughter and Other Ozark Folk Tales*, collected by Vance Randolph, copyright © 1955; Constable Publishers for 'Mrs Number Three' from *Chinese Ghouls and Goblins* by G. Willoughby-Meade, copyright © 1924; Harvard University Press, Cambridge, MA, for 'Young Man in the Morning', 'The Boy Who Had Never Seen Women' and 'The Cat-Witch' from *Negro Folktales in Michigan*, collected and edited by Richard M. Dorson, copyright © 1956 by the President and Fellows of Harvard College, 1980 by Richard M. Dorson; Indiana University Press for 'The Furburger' from *Jokelore: Humorous Folktales from Indiana*, edited by Ronald L. Baker, copyright © 1986; the International African Institute for 'Keep Your Secrets' and 'The Wicked Stepmother' from *Tales Told in Togoland*, edited by A. W. Cardinall, copyright © 1931, published by Oxford University Press for the International African Institute; Jan Knappert, translator and collector of *Myths and Legends of the Swahili*, for 'The Hare', 'The Pupil' and 'Tongue Meat', copyright © 1970, published by William Heinemann Ltd.; The Mercier Press for 'Feet Water' from *Folktales from the Irish Countryside* by Kevin Danaher, copyright © 1967; Oxford University Press for: 'The Search for Luck' and 'The Three Measures of Salt' from *Modern Greek Folktales*, chosen and translated by R. M. Dawkins, copyright © 1953, 'The Promise' from *Burmese Law Tales* by Maung Htin Aung, copyright © 1962, and 'The Fisher-Girl and the Crab' and 'The Resourceful Wife' from *Folk-Tales of Mahakoshal* by Verrier Elwin, copyright © 1944; Pantheon Books, a division of Random House, Inc., and Penguin Books Ltd. for 'The Little Red Fish and the Clog of Gold' and 'The Woodcutter's Wealthy Sister' from *Arab Folktales*, edited and translated by Inea Bushnaq, copyright © 1986, and Pantheon Books, a division of Random House, Inc., for 'Escaping Slowly' from *Afro-American Folktales: Stories from Black Traditions in the New World*, edited by Roger D. Abrahams, copyright © 1985, and 'The Wise Little Girl', 'Vasilisa the Priest's Daughter', 'The Armless Maiden', and 'How a

ACKNOWLEDGEMENTS FOR PARTS 8–13

Permission to reproduce these fairy tales is gratefully acknowledged to the following: Pantheon Books, a division of Random House, Inc. for 'The Old Woman Against the Stream' from *Norwegian Folktales* by Christen Asbjørnsen and Jørgen Moe and 'A Fable of a Bird and Her Chicks' from *Yiddish Folktales* by Beatrice Silverman Weinreich; Constable Publishers for 'The Werefox' and 'The Mirror' from *Chinese Ghouls and Goblins* by G. Willoughby-Mead, copyright © 1924; The American Folklore Society for 'Old Foster', from *Journal of American Folklore* XXXVIII (1925) and 'The Untrue Wife's Song' from *Journal of American Folklore* XLVII (1934); The University Press of Kentucky for 'The Telltale Lilac Bush' from *The Telltale Lilac Bush and Other West Virginian Ghost Tales* by Ruth Ann Musick, copyright © 1965; University of Chicago Press for 'Pretty Maid Ibronka', 'The Witches' Piper', 'The Midwife and the Frog' and 'A Stroke of Luck' from *Folktales of Hungary* by Linda Degh © 1965 by University of Chicago; 'The Greenish Bird' from *Folktales of Mexico* by Americo Paredes © 1970 by University of Chicago; 'Reason to Beat your Wife' from *Folktales of Egypt* by Hasan M. El-Shamy © 1980 by University of Chicago; 'The Witchball', 'Father and Mother Both "Fast"' and 'The Beans in the Quart Jar' from *Buying the Wind: Regional Folklore in the United States* by Richard M. Dorson © 1964 by University of Chicago; Jonathan Cape and Basic Books for 'The Height of Purple Passion' from *The Rationale of Dirty Jokes*; Stanford University Press for 'The Three Lovers'; Columbia University Press, New York, for 'The Sleeping Prince', 'The Letter Trick' and 'Spreading the Fingers' from *Suriname Folklore*, by Melville J. Herskovits and Frances S. Herskovits, © 1936 and C. W. Daniel Company for 'Vasilissa the Fair', 'Enchanter and Enchantress', 'The Little Old Woman with Five Cows', 'Story of a Bird Woman', 'The Crafty Woman', 'The Dog's Snout People' from *Siberian and Other Folktales: Primitive Literature of the Empire of the Tsars*, collected and translated by C. Fillingham-Coxwell © 1925; University of California Press for 'Šāhīn', 'Tunjur, Tunjur', 'The Woman Who Married Her Son' and 'The Seven Leavenings' from *Speak Bird, Speak Again: Palestinian Arab Folktales*, collected and edited by Ibrahim Muhawi and Sharif Kanaana, copyright © 1988 The Regents of the University of California; Oxford University Press for 'The Frog Maiden' from *Burmese Folktales* by Maung Htin Aung, Calcutta, 1948; Holmes and Meier publishers for 'Diirawic and Her Incestuous Brother', 'Achol and Her Wild Mother', 'Achol and Her Adoptive Lioness-Mother', 'Duang and His Wild Wife' from *Dinka Folktales: African Stories from the Sudan* by Francis Mading Deng (New York, Africana Publishing Company, a division of Holmes & Meier, 1974), copyright © 1974 by Francis Mading Deng;